The CRYSTAL Keeper

Written by
Laurisa White Reyes

Skyrocket Press
SANTA CLARITA, CA

Skyrocket Press
28020 Newbird Drive
Santa Clarita, CA 91350
www.skyrocketpress.com

ISBN: 978-0-9863924-4-3

Publisher's Note: This is a work of fiction. Names, characters, places, and incidents are a product of the author's imagination. Locales and public names are sometimes used for atmospheric purposes. Any resemblance to actual people, living or dead, or to businesses, companies, events, institutions, or locales is completely coincidental.

Ordering Information:
Quantity sales. Special discounts are available on quantity purchases by corporations, associations, and others. For details, contact the "Special Sales Department" at the address above.

Join Our Mailing List at

http://www.SkyrocketPress.com

Book One

EXILE

Book Two

BETRAYAL

Book Three

VENGEANCE

For Jarett

Also by Laurisa White Reyes

The Rock of Ivanore
The Last Enchanter
Contact
In the Eye of the Beholder (a short story)

Table of Contents

❖Book One❖
EXILE

1

I vanore hunched over the parchment, the tip of her quill flicking above her hand like a trapped bird desperate to escape. The tallow candle cast a cramped circle of light across the table, hardly enough to see by. If only the night would last a little longer. Perhaps then she would have enough time to write everything she needed to. But alas, time was one thing she had too little of—that and light.

An older man with long, gray-streaked hair and piercing gray eyes waited beside her. The stone bungalow, their most recent of many hiding places, boasted the barest of furnishings: the table, stool, cot—and a plain wooden chest, its key held tightly in his fist.

A sudden thump sounded at the door, startling them both. A strand of Ivanore's hair, gold as the candlelight, fell across the page. She quickly tucked it back into place and wrote faster.

Zyll laid a hand on Ivanore's shoulder. "They are here," he whispered.

Ivanore finished the document and handed it to Zyll unbound. Turning to the chest, he carefully laid the pages inside.

"Wait," said Ivanore. "Will you keep this as well?" A flat circle of pale green crystal lay in her open palm.

"But you will need it. I mustn't—"

"Please," she insisted, pressing it into his hand. "I can't risk losing this one."

Zyll reluctantly folded his fingers around the cool stone. "Of course, milady," he said. Then, adding the crystal to the parchment, he laid a plate of thin wood atop them both, sealing the chest's false bottom. He closed the lid and locked it.

The pounding at the door grew more insistent. Whoever stood outside was using their full weight against it in an effort to break through.

"We must hurry," said Zyll.

Ivanore allowed herself a quick glance at the chest, offering the briefest of prayers that the gods would keep it safe until her return. Then, taking her by the arm, Zyll led her through the low archway dividing the bungalow's front room from the back.

A loud crash of splintering wood resounded through the bungalow. Their visitors had finally broken in.

"Find her now!" a deep voice bellowed.

Grateful for the trousers she now wore instead of her usual cumbersome skirts, Ivanore clambered onto a stool and through a narrow window, lowering herself as quietly as possible to the ground outside. Once Zyll had done the same, they stole away across the rocky field. Though the sky was black as ink, their path was illuminated by the amber glow of volcanic fissures scoring the area for miles around.

"There she is!" a man's voice shouted behind them. The words sent spasms of fear through Ivanore. She glanced behind her and saw three soldiers emerge from the bungalow, wearing the gold and red cross of her father's crest. They had tracked her even here, to the remotest corner of Imaness. Would Fredric ever let her be?

Ivanore stopped running. She looked at Zyll, her trusted guardian and ally these past months since she had fled Dokur, and knew her time with him had come to an end.

"You'll watch over them until I return?" she asked, out of breath. "Keep them safe. Don't let my father find them."

"You have my vow," Zyll whispered, his voice tight with emotion.

Ivanore's eyes welled with tears as she pressed her lips against the calloused skin of Zyll's hand.

"Go," said Zyll. "Go now before it's too late."

Ivanore released Zyll's hand and sprinted forward alone. As she ran, she cupped her hands around her mouth and let out a loud, sharp call, much like that of a hawk or an eagle. She risked another glance over her shoulder and watched as Zyll turned to face their pursuers. As the soldiers neared, their swords glinting in the fire glow, Zyll held up his hands. A horizontal bolt of cerulean lightning shot out from his palms, striking the oncoming soldiers. The men recoiled, their bodies instantly singed and bloody.

Ivanore ran on. In desperation, she repeated her call, and this time another voice called back. A dark form appeared on the horizon, silhouetted against the light of the volcanic fractures and growing larger as it approached with tremendous speed. As it neared, the creature's massive feathered wings moved the air around Ivanore in warm, powerful gusts. Ivanore saw clearly its eagle's head with a beak large enough to break a man in two, paired with the muscular, furred body of a lion. As she ran toward it, the gryphon lowered its head, waiting.

Behind her, the soldiers reeled in pain, but they did not forget their duty. One man struggled to his knees, grunting from the effort. Reaching over his shoulder, he slid a short bow and arrow from his pack and swiftly took aim.

Ivanore reached the gryphon and in one smooth motion hoisted herself onto its back, twisting her arms deep into the feathers on the creature's neck. In that same moment, a single arrow found its mark in Ivanore's shoulder. She cried out before her body slumped forward and her mind went dark. The gryphon took flight then, and in less time than it took to draw another arrow—or a breath—they had vanished into the night.

2

Twelve months had passed since Jayson had arrived in Hestoria, and for the first time in his nineteen years, he was drunk.

The tavern keeper, a skinny man by the name of Timbrey, had him by the neck. "Cheat me out of two pints, will you?" he said, shoving Jayson out the tavern door. "And keep your silly trinket. I only take real money here! Worthless Agoran scum!"

Jayson stumbled and fell face first onto the wet cobbled road. If he hadn't been so intoxicated, he could have easily fought the man and won. But at the moment, Jayson had neither the strength nor the inclination to do it.

He lay there in the street, cursing the gods and Lord Fredric for sparing his empty, meaningless life. Execution would have been preferable to living as an outcast with only the shadows and his memories to keep him company. Although, that wasn't completely true. He did have Arik, but where the hell was he now?

That's right, Jayson remembered. The boy was still inside the tavern, arranging for a room.

Timbrey's words rang in Jayson's ears. Agoran scum. Was it his fault he was only half-human? That his father had loved an Agoran who had born a child with slitted pupils and claws like a cat? Aside from that and his thick mane of dark hair, Jayson looked like any other man. But no Hestorian would ever let him forget what he really was. A mongrel. A half-breed.

Jayson managed to get up on his feet again. Leaning forward and resting both hands on his knees, he waited for the world to stop spinning. His stomach rebelled against him, and the sickly yellow bile landed between his feet.

If the stench of his own vomit hadn't pervaded his senses, he might have smelled the thief approaching him from behind. Instead, the scrape of a metal blade sliding from its sheath alerted him. Jayson spun round just as the dagger sliced through the edge of his cloak. The dagger came down again, slashing at Jayson's waist, but again the blade had missed its mark.

Or had it?

Jayson slapped his hand against his belt and found the cut end of a thin leather strap. "Gods be damned!" he said.

Though it was the middle of the night, the darkness was no obstacle for his eyes. Even so, his assailant's features were concealed beneath a dirty rag tied at the neck. The thief turned to run, but Jayson lunged forward, catching him around the knees. Both slammed into the cobblestone. Jayson, dizzy from too much ale, tried to hold on, but the thief wriggled free.

As the thief scrambled to his feet, Jayson saw a leather pouch clutched tightly in his fist—the very one he had sliced off Jayson's belt. Jayson lashed out with his claws, but the liquor in his blood slowed his reflexes. He managed only to graze his assailant's arm. The pouch dropped to the ground as the thief's good hand snapped up to clutch his wound. Then he turned and sprinted away into the darkness.

Jayson scooped up the pouch and, deciding to put it out of sight, tucked it into his boot. Once again, he struggled to get on his feet, but the buildings spiraled around him. A gray fog blurred his vision, and it seemed as if a gaping black chasm had opened up in front of him. Jayson staggered forward, wavering at its edge. Then he fell, letting the void swallow him.

3

Jayson awoke on a bed in a sparsely furnished room. His head throbbed and his mouth felt dry as dust, but thankfully the dizziness and nausea from the previous night's drinking binge had diminished somewhat.

Sliding his legs out from under a threadbare quilt, Jayson set his feet on the wood floor. He stood up slowly, testing his equilibrium. Once satisfied he could remain upright, he staggered to the open window, which overlooked the road where he had lain a few hours earlier. The town bustled with people, women, and children dickering with fruit and poultry vendors, and men haggling over livestock. But Jayson's gaze fell on the one who stood out among them all, a large beast of a man with thick, shaggy black hair and a face pocked with scars. Standing a head taller than everyone around him, he was hard to miss. And those that came near him covered their faces with their hands as they passed. Jayson caught the man's scent on a passing breeze—the foul stench of sweat and carrion. It wasn't human at all, he realized, but Mardok.

"So, you've survived after all," said a voice from the doorway.

Jayson closed the window and shutters, and then turned toward the voice. He had to admit that the boy was more a man now, having grown several inches in recent months, but there was still a hint of gawkiness about him. His hair, red as a sunset, was short and well-trimmed, the way royalty would wear it. Indeed, Arik was royalty—a prince. At least he had been a prince until he and Jayson were exiled by Arik's father, Lord Fredric, ruler of Dokur.

"How did you find me?" asked Jayson.

Arik crossed the room and dropped into a chair near the window. "You were hard to miss, sprawled out in the road like you were," he said, leaning the chair back on its hind legs. "Believe it or not, the tavern keeper helped me carry you up here. Apparently, remorse set in once I settled your bill. So, what happened? I left you at our table, and when I'd returned you'd been tossed out into the street."

Jayson returned to the bed and lay down on it, draping an arm across his eyes. "I wanted to die," he said.

"You've been saying that for months now," Arik scoffed.

"I wanted to die more than usual."

"It would take more than a bottle of ale to kill *you*, my friend."

Jayson cringed at the not-so-subtle reminder that he was *different*. Even Arik wouldn't let him forget it.

Jayson curled his claws into his palms, tucking away the evidence of his Agoran blood. "I asked for another drink but didn't have enough money to pay," said Jayson. "I offered the tavern keeper something I thought he couldn't refuse. He threw me out instead."

"Something he couldn't refuse? What do you mean?"

Jayson hesitated. Arik would think him foolish for trying to trade something so valuable for a bottle of liquor. But Arik was his friend, a brother. Surely he would understand the depths to which Jayson had finally sunk.

Jayson shook his head and laughed. It had been a stupid thing to do, the act of a desperate and very intoxicated man. "It was nothing," he said. "Forget it."

Arik's gaze lingered on Jayson. "Well, I know you're too proud for it," he said, "but this should more than cover your expenses, today and for months to come."

Arik dropped a linen sack on the table, reached in, and scooped out a handful of silver coins. Jayson lifted his arm only briefly to look. Then he went back to covering his eyes.

"So that's where you were last night," he said, "off robbing some fool of his money."

"I've robbed no one!" Arik snapped, but then his smile promptly reappeared. "I earned it."

"Doing accounting for Trillium? That's an awful lot of late nights on the table." Jayson listened to the bright *clink* of the coins as Arik dropped them one by one onto the table— more coins, it seemed, than he had seen in his entire life. "How do you always manage to find work in this hell pit of a city? All I ever manage to find is a boot in my backside."

Arik slid the coins back into their sack. "Is it my fault that the Hestorian people despise Agorans?" he asked.

"I'm only half Agoran," answered Jayson bitterly.

"In any case," continued Arik, "there's enough money here for both of us, but it won't last if you throw it all into the bottle."

"You're a little young to be doling out advice, don't you think?"

"I'm only two years younger than you."

"Nearly three." Jayson enjoyed goading Arik, who was as sensitive about his youth as Jayson was about his heritage.

Arik ignored Jayson's comment. "The money isn't from Trillium," he said.

"Oh, you have a new employer?" Jayson asked.

"Not an employer," said Arik. "More like our benefactor."

"*Our* benefactor?" Jayson could not hold back a derisive laugh. "No Hestorian would so much as spit on a half-breed let alone give *me* money."

Jayson groaned as he raised himself to a sitting position and propped his back against the wall. "Give me his name then, this benefactor of yours."

"First, answer a question for me," replied Arik, "and then, if I feel so inclined, I will tell you his name." Jayson thought he noted a flicker of mischief pass behind Arik's eyes. "Last night, what was it that you offered for the ale?"

There it was then. The question laid bare Jayson's very conscience. Perhaps, he thought, if he confessed as if to a priest, his shame would be effaced, his sin absolved.

Arik's eyes widened as Jayson reached into his boot and pulled out the leather pouch. From it, he withdrew a shard of celestine crystal, a flat semicircle of clear crystal tinted with the color of the sea.

Jayson expected any number of reactions from Arik: anger, shock, disappointment, pity, but he revealed none of these. Instead, his gaze fixed upon the object as if it had captured his very mind and soul.

"My sister's stone," whispered Arik.

"Part of it at least," replied Jayson. "She broke it into two halves the night I was arrested. She slipped this piece into my hand when the soldiers weren't looking."

11

"It is safe after all."

Arik's words were spoken as though not meant for Jayson's ears, a sort of muttered private observation.

"You tried to buy ale with that?" Arik laughed, though the laughter sounded forced, unnatural.

"I did, and I'm ashamed of it."

"I'm surprised anyone would pass on such a bargain. That much celestine could pay for the entire tavern!"

"He didn't believe it was real, coming from someone like me," Jayson replied, stashing the crystal back in its pouch. "Now it's your turn. Who gave you the money?"

Arik rose from his chair and went to the window, peering out through a small slit in the shutter. "You've heard of the Vatéz?"

"The League of Magicians From what I know of them, they are an arrogant bunch."

"The Vatéz are a powerful force in Hestoria," explained Arik. "They have significant influence over the government here. Their leader, Emir, has aspirations to secure peace between Hestoria and its neighbors."

"Peace? And you actually believe that?"

"Whether I believe it or not is irrelevant. What I do know is that in time the Vatéz will be the world's ruling class."

"And you want your share of their pie."

"Is that wrong?" answered Arik, turning from the window, his expression resolute. "Surely you wouldn't deprive me of the little power I deserve."

Jayson eyed his young friend with suspicion. "I might be convinced that you'd sell your allegiance for a sack of silver coins," he said, "but I can't believe anyone with as much power as the Vatéz would bother with it—unless you offered something far greater than yourself."

"I *am* the heir to the throne of Dokur!"

"The exiled heir, meaning you are heir to nothing. What did you promise them, Arik? What do you have that they could possibly want so much?"

Something about Arik's behavior was unsettling, to say the least. The boy had never come to terms with his expulsion from Dokur, and at times Jayson was sure Arik regretted his actions which had led to it. As Jayson studied the agitated expression on the boy's face, a thin band of red appeared on his sleeve just above the elbow.

"You're hurt," said Jayson.

Arik glanced down and hastily covered his wound with his hand. The gesture triggered a hazy memory in Jayson's mind of the thief from the night before. It was the crystal he had wanted, Jayson realized, and he had clasped a hand over his arm after Jayson cut him, just as Arik was doing now.

Jayson swiftly got to his feet and strode to the window. Shoving Arik aside, he threw open the shutter, searching for the Mardok in the street, but it was gone.

4

The stench of rotting flesh invaded the room only moments before the Mardok did. The door burst its hinges, the wood frame splintering from the Mardok's blow. In an instant, the creature loomed in the doorway. Jayson had heard tales of the Mardoks' strength and knew fighting this one would be futile.

"What have you done?" Jayson shouted.

Arik pressed himself into a corner of the room, his eyes wild with fear and resolve. "I've done what I must to regain what is rightfully mine," he answered bitterly. "My father is a cruel and ruthless leader who doesn't deserve his throne. You of all people should know that. He tore you from my sister's arms, sent you into exile, and for what? For being nothing more than what you are. For being *half-human*!"

Arik's words struck Jayson to his core. It was the truth, he could not deny it. Perhaps deposing Fredric was warranted, even justified. And even if it wasn't, it meant Jayson could be with Ivanore again. There was nothing Jayson wanted more than to feel her arms around him again, to touch his lips to hers. Until now he had been willing to give anything for it, had pledged to the gods everything he would ever again possess if only they would arrange it for him. But now that the very object he most desired lay before him, Jayson hesitated.

"You speak of treason, Arik, against your own father."

"Fredric is not my father! Not anymore!"

"You've made a pact with the Vatéz for his throne?"

"Yes! With the power of Hestoria behind me, I will not fail."

Jayson hardly knew the boy in front of him now, so motivated by greed. How had the Vatéz taken hold of him? But perhaps he could still be made to see reason.

"You've made a pact with the Devil, Arik," said Jayson. "If the Vatéz want Dokur, they don't need you to do it. You are nothing to them. You *have* nothing."

"I have the crystal!" Arik's eyes were ravenous now, wide and desperate. He stretched out his hands toward Jayson, as if pleading. "Jayson, Emir does not want you. If you give it to me now, no harm will come to you. I swear it."

The crystal. The broken, useless shard of crystal. True, celestine was far more valuable than silver or even gold, and taking Dokur in order to control its mines would be motive enough to invade it. But why Arik? Why *this* insignificant crystal?

"*You* attacked me last night," said Jayson. "You tried to take it from me."

Arik grinned, as though pleased with himself. "I had always wondered what you kept hidden in that pouch. I was returning to our table when I saw you with it and saw you thrown out for it. I nearly had it, but then you cut me, and I dropped it. I searched you while you were unconscious, but I never thought to look in your boot. I thought it was lost for good," Arik said, again holding out his hand. "Give it to me."

A few hours earlier, Jayson would have gladly handed over the crystal for another pint of ale, for a chance to erase Ivanore from his mind. And why shouldn't he give the stone to Arik if he wanted it so badly? But now, some unnamed force inside of him wanted to protect it, though he could not explain why.

"She entrusted it to me," said Jayson.

"Give it to me!" Arik repeated, shouting.

Jayson's friend, his ally, was gone. This boy was a stranger, and the realization both saddened and angered him. "I won't give you the crystal, Arik. I won't give it to anyone."

Arik's empty hands trembled, then clenching them into fists, he roared, "Kill him!"

The Mardok responded by hurling its body across the room like a massive cannonball. Jayson had barely a moment to sidestep the onslaught, slashing at it with his claws. The Mardok bellowed in pain, and then flung its arm back against Jayson's chest. Jayson hit the wall with a force that reverberated through his very bones.

Empty black eyes trained on Jayson, the Mardok pulled back both fists, its large muscles rippling beneath its skin. Even Jayson's above-human strength was no match for this brute. He had only one option.

Jayson threw his full weight against the window shutter. The impact of his body first snapped the wood into several pieces left hanging from their hinges, and then shattered the glass behind them. He glanced up as he fell and saw Arik's face, twisted with rage, at the window.

With the smell of the Mardok still in his senses, Jayson heard Arik's final plea shouted into the streets below him. "I'll have the crystal, Jayson! If I must kill you, I will have it!"

Jayson landed, agile as a leopard, and ran. He wasn't even sure which direction he was heading. He only knew that he must keep on running until the crystal was safe.

5

The waist-high grass of the field was damp with moisture, each drop of dew reflecting the early morning rays of sunlight. The gryphon craned its neck eastward, opened its beak, and tasted the air.

It had stayed with Ivanore through the night, shielding her unconscious body from the cold with its mighty wings. But now the scent of a human approaching released it from its duty. It had carried her safely across the sea to this land, and now it could do nothing more. It sniffed the air once more, and then took flight, disappearing swiftly beyond the horizon.

Only minutes later, a young man strode across the field, whistling a tune he had composed just that morning. At eighteen years, Teak was taller and broader than most boys his age and had no trouble managing the heavy scythe, which he carried across his shoulders. He was to clear this section of the farm prior to tilling it. Uncle had insisted it be ready in time to plant the winter wheat. Teak figured today was as good a day as any to begin.

He first noticed her hair. He had never seen hair that color before, yellow like corn or mustard blossoms. And her skin was pale as milk. He was too surprised at first to react. But then he turned away, embarrassed to have intruded on the girl's privacy. He mumbled an apology, but when no reply came, he cautiously stole another glance. She was lying on her back, the grass around her trampled flat. She appeared to be sleeping.

What was she doing out in the middle of his field? Teak decided to wake her. "P-pardon me, miss," he stammered.

The girl did not stir. Teak wondered if she was dead. He searched for some clue as to how she had come to be there, and more especially who or what had killed her. He took a cautious step forward. The girl's face was clearly visible to him, and he could not help but be taken by her beauty. He saw now that her skin was smooth and tinted with the softest shade of rose, so different than his own earth-colored skin. She looked about his age and was most certainly not from Hestoria.

He wanted to touch her, to feel her hair and skin, but as he lifted his hand, the girl stirred. Teak jumped back, alarmed. The girl moved again, and this time a moan escaped from her lips. He dropped the scythe and dropped to his knees beside her. She was alive, and though her eyes were closed and she was clearly unconscious, she seemed to be in some discomfort.

Teak gently turned the girl onto her side and spotted the source of the trouble. The back of her clothes was red with blood, and a wooden staff several inches long protruded from her right shoulder. An arrow had buried itself deep into the bone and then broken off.

He had no idea how long she had lain there exposed to the elements, nor how much time had passed since she'd been hurt, but from the looks of it, she would not live much longer without help. Careful not to aggravate her injury, Teak slipped his arms beneath the girl's neck and knees and carried her as quickly as he could to his uncle's farmhouse at the edge of the clearing.

"Uncle! Uncle!" shouted Teak as he neared the wooden cottage.

Behind the cottage and off to the right stood a makeshift barn made of hand-hewn planks and, for the roof, an assortment of boughs from the forest bordering the farm. Mikel ducked his head as he stepped out of his barn into the light, an empty milk bucket in his hand.

"What are you bellowing about now, boy?" Mikel hollered. His back was as crooked as some of the tree limbs on the barn roof, and his hands were as brown and calloused as their bark, the consequences of a lifetime of farming. Teak was his sister's son left to him after she was killed in the Sandrian Raids when he was a lad of ten. "What's that you've got there? Have you been out hunting again?"

As Teak neared with the girl in his arms, Mikel raised a bushy, white brow. He shot a worried glance back toward his fields before following his nephew into the cottage. "Put her there on that cot," instructed Mikel, retrieving a fresh rag and a woolen blanket from the linen cupboard. He draped the blanket over the unconscious girl, tucking it in all around her.

"Bring me that bucket," he continued. "She's burning up."

Teak obeyed, setting the bucket on the floor. Mikel dipped the rag into the water and rung it out before using it to clean the dust from the girl's face.

20

"She's hurt," Teak told him, pointing to the injured shoulder.

Mikel examined the injury with skilled hands. "Arrow's gone deep. Infection's setting in. I'll have to take out the arrow. Get a poultice ready."

Teak nodded and hurried away to prepare the poultice, something he'd done countless times for the animals on his farm and once for his aunt when she'd cut her hand during a harvest. He thought of her now, gone two years now, and felt the familiar pang of grief before pushing the feeling aside to attend to the task at hand.

"All right, boy," continued Mikel when Teak returned, "roll her onto her side and hold her there good and tight. Most of the shaft broke off, so there's not much to hold on to. She might squirm a little, but you've got to hold her down. Understand?"

Teak nodded again and did as his uncle instructed, bracing his muscular arms against the girl's back to hold her in place. Mikel grasped the protruding shaft of wood with his fingers and tested it by pulling gently, but the arrow tip was wedged tight into the shoulder blade. When he tried loosening it by rocking the shaft back and forth a little, the girl groaned.

"She's w-waking up," said Teak.

"I'd better get on with it then," replied Mikel. With that, he gripped the shaft firmly in his fist and gave it a fast, hard pull. As the arrow popped out of her shoulder, the girl cried out. Teak held her in place, though she thrashed about like a wounded wild animal. Her screams turned to sobs as Mikel laid the poultice on the wound and bound it in place with strips of linen. Only once he was satisfied with his work did

Exile

he allow Teak to slowly lower the girl back to the cot. Mercifully, she had again fallen unconscious.

Mikel lifted the bucket of water and motioned for his nephew to follow him outside.

"You did good in there, son," he said, dipping his hands in the bucket to wash off the blood.

"W-will she be all right?" asked Teak.

"If she survives the night, she'll have a long road for that wound to heal properly. In the meantime, we will have our hands full looking after her."

Mikel dried his hands on his tunic, and then poured the water into the dirt. The blood tinted the sandy soil red. "Found her in the fields, did you?" he asked, setting the empty bucket on the porch. "Any idea how she got there?"

"N-no," answered Teak. "It's like she c-came from the sky."

"From the sky, eh? Well, then I guess for now where she's from remains a mystery," he added, stealing a glance through the door at his unexpected guest, "at least until she wakes up."

"W-when will that b-be, Uncle?"

"No telling, son," said Mikel. "No telling."

6

How long had it been since Jayson had seen daylight? Felt the warmth of it on his skin, basked in the sun's rays without shame, without fear? He had lost count how many days had come and gone since he had first arrived in Hestoria, and yet he knew them all from the day he arrived to the day he took to the streets, fleeing into the darkness.

He knew them because each one meant he had spent that much longer away from Ivanore. He'd spent countless hours sleeping, or trying to sleep, while the rest of the world bustled about conducting their business, unaware that just an arm span away lay an outcast curled up among the cobwebs and garbage, desperate to remain unnoticed, to be left alone.

Since Arik's betrayal, he had marked the days by scratching lines in the mud. When he moved to another location, he carved them in a stone wall. But he soon abandoned that place as well. Was there nowhere he could be safe? Where the crystal could be safe?

Tonight the moon was full and the streets too light for him to travel freely through them. He stayed in the shadows, keeping his face concealed beneath a black cloak. A cold, brisk wind blew in from the sea, carrying with it the scent of fish and salt and seaweed. The smell was enough to overpower all others, even for Jayson, whose senses were more finely tuned than full-blooded humans.

His Agoran mother had taught him to use his senses well, to stalk and capture prey, to foretell coming changes in the weather, and to protect himself from enemies. Nights like these, when the howling wind and ocean smells overran his senses, Jayson preferred to stay hidden. The risk of an undetected assault was too great, but tonight the moonlight beckoned to him, and he responded.

Perhaps it was the many months that had passed without sunlight that made him hunger so much for the moon. Leaning his back against the rough stone wall of a building, just beyond the moonlight's reach, Jayson gazed up at it. He recalled a moon like this two years earlier, an entire year before coming to Hestoria.

He had held her that night and kissed her, brushing back the hair from her face to see her smile. She had the most beautiful smile, but on this night there was something different behind it, some secret she could hardly restrain herself from telling.

Jayson laughed when she pressed her teeth into her lip, like an eager child.

"Tell me," he coaxed, touching her cheek with the back of his hand.

"Not until you say you love me," she had said, her blue eyes sparkling with the reflection of a thousand stars.

"But I've said it a dozen times today."

"Just once more."

"And then will you tell me your secret?"

"Yes, I'll tell you my secret."

Jayson kissed her cheek, her nose, her forehead, her lips. "I love you," he whispered each time. "Is that enough for you? Will you tell me now?"

She giggled and ran from him into the trees. Jayson chased after her, laughing and calling her name. He nearly caught her once, hiding behind a tree, but she managed to slip through his fingers like a fairy. Finally, he took her arm as she sprung up from behind a fallen log, and they fell together into the soft, yellow leaves of autumn.

He pressed her wrists gently against the warm earth and breathed her in. His face was just inches from hers. Her presence always thrilled him, and he longed to be with her always. From the moment they first met, he knew he could not live without her. It was as if their souls had been searching for each other, like two halves of a single whole.

They were young, just seventeen, but old enough to know what they wanted. The King's punishment for marrying a human was execution. But even the threat of death was not enough to keep Jayson from her. They married in secret and found ways to be together, though for Jayson it was never enough. Even when his time in Dokur was over, he had refused to leave. Over the weeks and months that had passed, he devised a plan to bring Ivanore with him to Taktani, to the land of the Agorans. They had accepted him, a half-breed. Surely they would accept her, too.

He had planned to tell her that night, to ask her to come with him, but the mischievous smile masking some secret of hers had distracted him. He held her now, her breath warm and sweet against his face. The rise and fall of her breasts against him stirred a longing deep inside.

"Tell me your secret," he said, "or I shall hold you here forever."

"Forever?" she replied. She wasn't laughing now, and her expression grew serious. "Is that a promise?"

"You want to stay here in the mud?" Jayson asked, sliding a finger across her brow.

"I'd stay anywhere with you. And now you'll have to stay with me, too."

"Tell me your secret."

Ivanore laid her hands against Jayson's cheeks and gently pulled him closer. "We're going to have a child," she said, and then kissed him.

*   *   *

Jayson blinked against the moonlight and reminded himself that he was alone. He knew now how to track the time away from her—by the moons. There had been twelve so far, twelve full moons. Far too many. Far too long.

A peculiar scent invaded Jayson's nostrils, just a wisp of it masked by the sea air. His muscles grew taut and his senses became more focused. What was it? He could not be certain—some exotic spice or fragrant wood. He turned from the building and ventured across the deserted street, daring to reveal himself by moonlight. Perhaps it would draw out whoever was watching him. He pulled the hood of his cloak down around his face and leaned into the wind, taking his first cautious steps into the light.

He paused. There it was again, stronger this time. It wasn't spice at all, but some kind of incense, rich and pungent. It was a new scent, one he had never smelled before, and it intrigued him. He started forward again, but just as he reached the opposite side of the road, someone grabbed his arm and pulled him roughly back into the shadows.

"Get down," the stranger whispered.

Jayson turned to see who or what had pulled him back, but saw only a dark cloak much like his own. From it protruded a hand, fingers raised, signaling silence.

He looked back to the street and noticed movement beneath the eaves of the building. He peered more closely, narrowing his cat eyes, which drew in far more light than a human's eyes.

It was a small creature, barely as tall as Jayson's knee, and unlike anything he had ever seen before. Its limbs were thin and skeletal, with pale skin pulled taut over the bones. Its head, which was quite large for its small stature, was elongated so that the back of it protruded at an odd angle above its neck. Its tattered clothing was made of coarse fabric, neither the sleeves nor legs of which were long enough, and it had no covering on its feet. This creature crept along with its face low to the ground and seemed to be slowly tracking Jayson's path.

7

"We have to go," said the cloaked stranger.

"Go with you where?" asked Jayson. "I don't even know—"

"If you want to survive this night, you will do what I say."

Snaking through the narrow alleyways, Jayson followed the cloaked guide to the edge of town where a wooden building stood apart from the newer stone ones. Light emanated from a clouded window and from beneath the door. Jayson's guide opened the door and slipped inside.

Jayson questioned his own wisdom in coming even this far without knowing who he was following or why. He knew only that the emaciated creature in the street posed some threat to him, a threat this guide seemed to understand, and for the time being he was safe from it.

The interior of the building was far more substantial than its outer appearance suggested. It seemed to be a meeting hall of some kind. An intricately carved and polished table stood in the center of the room surrounded by twelve matching chairs. A healthy fire burned in a stone fireplace, above which hung a painting of a man in a red robe, a medallion at his chest. There was no one else in the room, though from the bottle of wine and glasses set on the table, it seemed that guests were expected.

"Help yourself," said the guide, peering out the window. "It's not poisoned."

Jayson strode to the table and filled a glass. "Not bad," he said, taking a swallow, "but I prefer hard liquor." He finished off his glass and refilled it.

"The first thing you're going to tell me is who you are," Jayson continued. "The next is what that thing back there was and why it was following me."

The guide pulled back her hood and shook out her hair, which fell in dark ringlets upon her shoulders. Jayson noted the narrowness of her russet-colored face, her delicate cheekbones and nose, her graceful lips.

"My name is Dianis," she said, filling a glass for herself.

"You're a little young for that, don't you think?"

Dianis shot him a sharp glance. "And you're not?" She lifted the glass to her lips and emptied it quickly.

Her fingers, Jayson realized, were longer and thinner than a human's and had in them a distinctive beauty and grace. Most people might not even notice the difference, but being only half-human himself, Jayson paid attention.

"You're not human," he said, "though you might pass for one."

"I am a nymph."

"Really. I've never seen a nymph before."

"At least not that *you'd* have recognized."

Jayson chose to ignore her cynical tone. "And that thing back there," he said, "I'm sure that was no nymph."

"That was a Gorelian tracker sent by the Vatéz to capture you. It's been following your trail for days."

Jayson recalled its unusual scent. "If it was trying to surprise me, it failed."

"Gorelians do not need surprise to subdue their victims. A single bite from a tracker will paralyze the body and bend the mind to its bidding. Should you ever come across one again, I suggest you run."

"I'll do that," replied Jayson. "Now you on the other hand, you did take me by surprise." He leaned forward a little and sniffed the air around her. "Saltwater. You've used a heavy dose of it to mask your scent. Clever."

"I couldn't risk you mistaking me for an enemy."

"Why should I do that? You show up in the middle of the night, insist I follow you with no explanation, bring me to this horrible dungeon, and force this poison down my throat." Jayson rolled his eyes and downed another glass of wine. "You are just the sort of enemy I fear the most."

He filled his glass a third time, then pulled a chair back from the table and sat down on it. Kicking off his boots, he placed his feet on the table, crossing them at the ankles. "Now, would you mind explaining your interest in me?"

Dianis looked at him with unmasked disdain, striding across the room to the opposite end of the table. "We have been searching for you, Jayson."

"Ah, the lady knows my name."

"We hoped to reach you before the Vatéz did."

"You keep saying we. Who is *we*?"

"The Guilde. We are the guardians."

"And you were sent to guard me?"

"No," she answered, her voice thick with cynicism. "I was sent to guard the stone."

Gripping the table with both hands, Dianis jerked it back. Jayson's heels hit the floor like rocks.

"What is your problem?" he shouted, getting to his feet.

"My problem?" she answered, matching his tone of voice. "My problem is that I am wasting my time with a miserable, worthless half-breed! That's right. I've been watching you for a while now, and so far I haven't seen anything worth the Guilde's trouble. So, if you don't mind, just hand over the crystal and you can be on your way. Slink back into the shadows like the good little coward you are. Bye-bye."

Dianis wriggled her fingers, and then held out her hand for the crystal.

For the slightest moment, Jayson considered what the consequences would be should he give it to her. It would be out of his hands then, someone else's responsibility. This Guilde the nymph spoke of sounded all right, certainly a lot better than the power hungry Vatéz. But what did he know of either group? Nothing, he realized. All he knew was that the crystal had been placed in his care by the woman he loved, and therefore it was his burden to bear.

He glared at Dianis, tempted to shove the table back at her. He had managed to get this far on his own, hadn't he? What need did he have of a guardian? Then he thought of the tracker. Perhaps he hadn't been as discreet as he had thought.

"You can't have the crystal," he said.

Clutching her fingers into angry fists, Dianis started to protest, but Jayson held up his hand for her to wait.

"The crystal is mine to carry," he continued, "but if you are to be its guardian then you may come with me."

"What are you talking about?" answered Dianis. "Come with you where?"

31

"To the Guilde. That is where you intend to take the crystal, isn't it?"

"They don't want *you*."

Her words were venomous, yet Jayson sensed a slight softening in her tone. "If they want the crystal, then they will have to take me as well."

Dianis considered this a moment. Then nodded, satisfied. She was about to speak when a loud thump on the door interrupted her, followed by the sound of something clawing at the window.

"Get your boots on!" Dianis ordered in a harsh whisper.

Jayson responded quickly. The clawing turned to rapid banging against the glass and the wooden door. The window was frosted over with dust and grime, so Jayson was fairly certain the tracker had not seen them. He glanced around, searching for another way out, but there was none.

"I need a weapon." Jayson spoke just loud enough for Dianis to hear, but she shook her head.

"If you kill this one, there will just be others," she said. "And it has likely already alerted the Vatéz of our location. They'll send a Mardok."

Jayson cringed. He hated Mardoks. The banging at the door grew more insistent, and the aged wood creaked under the pressure. It would not hold up much longer.

Dianis snatched up the wine bottle and hurled it at the painting. The glass exploded, splattering red liquid across it and most of the wall.

"Here," she said, removing a metal flask from beneath her cloak. "It's seawater. Pour it over yourself. It and the wine will confuse the tracker."

As Jayson obeyed, Dianis hurried to the fireplace, dragging a chair from the table behind her. Standing on it, she pushed against the painting's frame and the whole thing slid to one side, revealing an opening not much wider than Jayson's shoulders.

"Hurry!" she hissed, scrambling from the chair into the opening.

Jayson started after her, but before he could reach the fireplace, the hinges on the door gave way. Through the gap between door and wall, he could see the tracker's pale face, its nostrils flaring with Jayson's scent.

Jayson moved quickly. He ran back to the table and shoved it against the door, closing the gap. The tracker squealed in pain but did not relent its efforts to get inside.

Jayson leapt from the table across the floor to the chair and pulled himself up into the opening. It was a tight fit, far from comfortable, and it was so dark that not even his keen cat eyes could gather enough light to see. Behind him, he heard the window glass shatter.

Reaching down with his leg, Jayson kicked the chair away from the fireplace, and then pulled himself all the way into the opening. The painting slid back into place behind him, forming a tight seal. Ahead of him was nothing but darkness, yet by the smell of seawater and the sound of her breathing, he knew Dianis was there, crawling forward into the darkness. Where she was leading him he did not know, but he followed her anyway, hoping that this one time the gods were on his side.

8

No matter how hard he tried, Arik could not keep his heart from racing. Again and again, he dabbed his forehead with his handkerchief and tried to convince himself that it was the day's heat that affected him. He jumped each time the door to the Minister's chambers opened, and the longer he waited, the more his hands trembled.

He had been summoned to Nauvet-Carum early that morning by an adolescent courier. The scroll the boy carried bore the dragon's seal and was signed by Minister Emir himself. Arik suspected he was less than pleased with his delay in delivering the promised crystal.

Arik had dressed hurriedly in his best clothes and followed the courier to the carriage waiting in the street. Its wooden wheels and the horse's hooves resonated through the deserted cobbled roads. A thin rain had fallen during the night, leaving a trail of muddy puddles for them to follow, each one reflecting the profiles of the shop fronts as they passed. The smell of wet earth combined with the ever-present stench of fish from the docks made Arik's empty stomach churn. He shivered in the damp air and pulled his cloak up around his nose.

The carriage deposited its passenger at the ministry, a structure three stories high with a pair of marble columns out front. Arik ascended the edifice's wide steps and brushed past the two sentries posted at the door. He announced his arrival to the attendant, but was told to wait, and wait he did for three long, insufferable hours.

The morning light that spilled in through narrow gaps in the outer wall displayed a parade of golden bars on the opposite wall. Arik imagined they had once been used to fire arrows during a siege, the last of which had occurred more than a hundred years earlier. He glanced through one to where his carriage still waited below. Carriages, roads, superior architecture. There were no such luxuries in Dokur. His father had seen to that. Despite the wealth the mines had brought them, Fredric insisted his people live simple lives. Most were farmers or herdsman, their towns rural. When he was king, thought Arik, he would end Fredric's trade restrictions. He would use his wealth to carry Dokur and all of Imaness into the new age.

After wasting nearly a year barely surviving on the streets of Nauvet-Carum, Arik had come to this building to pledge his loyalty to the Vatéz. Arik thought Emir unusual even then, his white hair and skin contrasting so intensely with the darker complexions of his countrymen. But Arik's view of the man changed once Emir extended to him an enticing offer: a chance to regain his inheritance in exchange for an insignificant, damaged crystal.

"His Excellency will see you now," said the attendant, bringing Arik back to the present.

35

Exile

The Minister's chambers were deprived of sunlight due to it being situated within the interior of the building, and so relied on an elaborate candelabrum for illumination. The light from it shifted about the room as though it was alive, undulating on the flames' whim.

"You called for me," Arik said, announcing his presence.

Emir sat behind an immense wooden desk whereupon rested a single sheet of parchment, an ink well, and a quill. A small candle burned in a brass holder at the corner, its faint glow throwing odd shadows across the Minister's visage. The rich smell of incense hung heavy in the air. Behind the minister's desk stood a wide bookcase filled with leather-bound volumes the titles of which Arik could not make out in the shifting light. A single chair sat in front.

"How are your new quarters, Arik?" asked Emir, his eyes fixed on his parchment. "Suitable, I hope?"

"More than suitable. Thank you."

Emir dipped his quill into the ink well and wrote upon the parchment, the long white feather trembling with the small, careful movements of his hand.

"And your occupation? How goes it at the depository?"

"Fine, just fine," answered Arik, adding a practiced smile to the lie. "Master Trillium says I make a fine accountant's apprentice."

"And yet you find it unsatisfactory."

"Not at all. It's just that..." Arik hesitated. The Minister had not yet looked up from his parchment, his quill still moving across the page. "Don't misunderstand me. I am grateful, but it's not quite what I had in mind."

"And what did you have in mind, *Prince* Arik?"

The emphasis on *prince* carried just a hint of condescension, and Arik immediately realized how ungrateful he must have sounded. He dared not answer the question for fear of offending his very generous host.

Emir continued writing. "You may sit," he said finally, setting his quill in its holder.

Arik took his seat in the chair. Only then did he notice the cat-sized creature curled up on the floor beside Emir's desk. Iridescent green scales shimmered in the candlelight as its chest swelled and deflated with each breath. Arik scooted his chair back.

"Do not fret," said the Minister. "This is but a hatchling. Its fire glands are not yet developed."

Emir reached down and stroked the small dragon. Its slender, snake-like tail curled contentedly around its body.

"No doubt you've received word," the Minister continued. His eyes, the lightest shade of blue Arik had ever seen, flitted back and forth in their sockets like restless insects.

"What word, your Excellency?"

"About your friend, the half-breed. Seems he's disappeared."

"Yes, well, he ran off weeks ago. I thought you knew."

"We've been tracking him. One of my Gorelians picked up his scent near the docks earlier this evening. Followed him to an abandoned shack, but then the Agoran disappeared."

"Is that why you summoned me? You think I know where's he's gone."

The Minister peered at Arik with an impatient expression that made Arik's spine shudder.

"We know where he's gone. He is on his way to make his alliance with the Guilde."

"The Guilde? But how...?"

"Their leader, Gerard, is a clever one. Oh, he's had his own people tracking Jayson as well. It was simply a matter of time which of us would get him first. But no matter. I am confident Jayson will not give up the shard so easily. No, he will keep it close to him. He will not entrust it to anyone."

"But the Guilde will protect him."

"Of course they will, which will make your task all the more...interesting. You have a connection with him no one else has, Arik. He married your sister. You were exiled along with him for defending him against your father. He feels obligated to you."

"I betrayed him."

"Betrayed him?" Emir leaned back into the shifting shadows, his pallid hands only remaining in the light. "Come now, my boy, you know as well as I that you have always had Jayson's best interests at heart. You care about your homeland as much as he does. You wish him no harm. You must remind him of that. He is alone here in Hestoria. An outcast among strangers. He needs you, Arik. And you will go to him. Then, when you have regained his trust, you will take the crystal and bring it to me."

"He won't give it up."

"He will under the right circumstances."

Arik looked at those hands, a phantom's hands, their long, lean fingers lying upon the desk like those of a skeleton. They had no strength in them, and yet Arik felt their power. It was the sort of power he longed for, that he would kill for.

Emir's voice continued, composed, dispassionate. "I don't need to remind you of our agreement."

"If I fail in what you've asked of me," said Arik, "I'll repay you, every last coin. I swear it."

"Oh, it wasn't a loan, Arik. You cannot repay me. Not with money."

Leaning against the desk, Emir rose to his feet. He carefully rolled his parchment. Then, warming a stick of wax over the candle flame, he let three drops of red fall, sealing it closed. He pressed his ring into the wax, leaving an impression of a dragon behind.

"Here," he said, handing the scroll to Arik. "It is a request for provisions, a horse, and whatever else you require for your journey."

Arik ran a finger over the rough texture of the parchment. "Again, thank you for your generosity, Minister. But I do have one question. As I understand it, the Guilde's location is unknown. They move about like nomads, and their members are bound by vows of secrecy. If Jayson is with them, finding him will be difficult if not impossible."

Emir turned to his bookcase and perused the titles with his fingertips. "At the bottom of the scroll is an added note," he said, "a promise of fifty coins in exchange for the information you seek. Take it to that loose-tongued tavern keeper of yours. If anyone has information worth less to him than gold, it is he."

Selecting a volume from the shelf and brushing off a little dust from its spine, Emir opened its cover and held it close to his face, reading silently. Arik took that as a sign that he was done with him. He nodded his head, gave a brief and polite adieu, and then took his leave, nearly running headlong into another visitor coming in.

The man, his dark hair braided into several thick ropes that hung down his back, stepped aside to let Arik pass. Even so, his large frame nearly filled the doorway, leaving only a narrow gap for Arik to squeeze through. Arik, already agitated from his encounter with Emir, shoved his shoulder into the man's chest and mumbled a curt "pardon me." He was in no mood for etiquette as more urgent matters now weighed heavily on his mind.

*   *   *

"Come in, Brommel. Come in," Emir's voice called from the shadows. Brommel approached the desk and set down a small bundle wrapped in linen. At his approach, the young dragon raised its head and released a guttural snarl.

"Hush, Pip!" scolded Emir as he unwrapped the bundle, revealing several strips of raw meat. Emir lifted one and held it over the dragon. It lifted its head and opened its elongated snout like a baby bird feeding from its mother. A moment later, its jaws snapped shut on the meat, tearing it from Emir's fingers. It fed on its prize with some fervor, causing the intern to step back.

"Any news of Ivanore?" asked the Minister, tossing Pip another piece of meat. He then turned a page of his book with an index finger.

"Little, your Excellency," replied Brommel. "Our source in Dokur reports that Fredric's scouts found her in a remote village, but she escaped."

"Escaped?"

"He assures us that all efforts are being made to locate her."

"An entire year she has eluded that imbecile! And the one chance he has at capturing her, she escapes!" Emir sighed and slapped the book shut. "My patience is wearing thin. You will go to Dokur and recover Ivanore yourself."

Brommel's face revealed none of the surprise and disappointment he felt, and yet he could not hide his true feelings from Emir. It would be pointless to try.

"My wife…" he began, keeping his voice steady. "The baby will come soon."

Emir slid the book back into its place, and then selected another, which he set on his desk without opening it. Emir walked around the desk to gaze up into face of the man he had groomed from childhood to be his successor.

"You will not leave for Dokur until the child arrives," Emir said reassuringly. "Until then, I will personally see to it that Brielle is properly cared for."

Brommel's shoulders relaxed a little. "Thank you, your Excellency," he said.

"In the meantime," continued Emir, "I have a small errand for you."

Brommel should have known there would be a condition to Emir's protection. There always was. He lifted his chin a little and clenched his jaw.

"What would you have me do?"

"I've sent Prince Arik after Jayson, that half-breed I've told you about. He's gone to the Guilde. Arik is to gain back his old friend's trust and obtain the crystal. You will accompany him."

"Certainly, your Excellency. I will prepare for the journey at once."

Emir grinned, approval evident on his aging face.

Brommel turned to leave, but paused at the door. "Do *they* know about her?" he asked.

"Of course not," answered Emir. "If Arik or Jayson suspected Ivanore was in danger, our plans would be jeopardized. Hestoria's future, your future, depends on my getting that crystal."

"Then let us hope Arik succeeds in his task."

Emir returned to his seat behind his desk, his face falling once more into the shadows. Retrieving one last piece of meat from the bundle, he held it high above Pip's head. The little dragon growled and thrashed as it tried to take the morsel from its master's hand. Emir chuckled with delight as Pip grew more agitated. Finally, the dragon leapt into the air, its leathery wings flapping wildly, and clamped its teeth around the meat. It hung there suspended from Emir's hands for a moment before the Minister let it go.

Brommel hated to see the creature taunted so. It aroused a strange fury within him. He felt more anxious than ever to be on his way.

"One last thing before you go, Brommel," said Emir, throwing down the last of the meat scraps. Pip pounced on them in a frenzy, shredding them with its razor-sharp teeth before devouring the lot. "Should Arik fail to retrieve the crystal from Jayson, then the task is yours to carry out. Either way, be sure to dispose of them both before you return. I do so despise leaving loose ends."

9

It was a long ride from Nauvet-Carum to the village of Partha. The sun was high overhead by the time Brommel tied his horse to the evergreen tree in front of the cottage he'd built himself a year earlier. A thin finger of smoke rose from the stone chimney, and the smell of roast chicken and yams filled the air.

Brommel brushed the dust from his trousers and boots before opening the door. As he stepped through the entry, he was greeted by the excited squeals of his young son.

"Papa!" shouted the boy as Brommel swung him high into the air. "Is today my birthday?"

"Your birthday?" laughed Brommel. "You just had a birthday, Rylan. Why would you have another so soon?"

"Because you have come home! It must be my birthday!"

Brommel held him tight and nuzzled Rylan's dark curls. "Then so be it. Let every day be your birthday. How old does my visit make you?"

"I was three yesterday, Papa. So now I am four."

The boy held up four pudgy fingers, and Brommel counted them out loud. Then he planted a kiss on Rylan's cheek. "And where is your mother?" he asked, setting him down again.

A russet-skinned woman with eyes the color of rich honey stepped into the room through another door. A white apron was tied over her very round belly, and she supported her back with both hands. When she saw Brommel, her face broke into a wide smile. Setting Rylan on the floor, Brommel went to her, enveloping her in his broad arms.

"Brielle," he whispered, kissing her hair.

Brielle melted into Brommel's embrace, burying her face in the linen tunic she had sewn for him. As Brommel kissed her again, she noted the hole at his elbow.

"Brom, you haven't been wearing this in the assembly, have you?"

"Aye," he said, pulling the shirt over his head and laying it across her outstretched arm.

She stuck a disapproving finger through the hole. "I shall mend it at once," she said, turning to her sewing basket on the dining table. But Brommel caught her in his arms again and drew her to him. As she laid her cheek against his bare chest, he felt as though the world had vanished. All that existed was right here in this small room.

"The shirt can wait," he said, kissing her once more. "Tell me how you've been this past week?"

Young Rylan eagerly recounted an adventure he and a friend had had in the nearby forest hunting for frogs.

"Did you catch any?" asked Brommel.

"Only one," replied the boy, "but I decided that he ought to have another year to grow, so I let him go free."

Brielle laid the damaged tunic atop her sewing basket, and then went to the bedroom for a fresh one. When she returned, she found her husband and son laughing together.

"Rylan," she called as she pulled the tunic over her husband's head, "set the table for supper. I've got a pot of soup simmering," she added, smoothing the fabric across Brommel's shoulders. "Are you hungry?"

"Famished," he answered, satisfied that their family was whole once again.

Later that night, after Brommel had tucked Rylan into bed, he and Brielle lay beside the warm hearth wrapped together in a goose down quilt. Brommel savored the softness of his wife's neck and bare shoulders against his lips. His large, strong hand rested on Brielle's swollen belly, and he took pleasure in feeling his unborn child moving inside her.

"It won't be long now," said Brielle after a particularly sharp kick from the baby. "Just a few more days and she'll be ready."

"She?" said Brommel, raising a curious brow.

"We'll name her after your mother."

"We will, will we? Are you really so certain it's a girl?"

"Nothing is for certain," said Brielle. "But I've offered prayers every morning for a daughter, and I have felt in my heart that the gods have heard me."

"Brielle," said Brommel tenderly, "you know it does not matter to me if we have a girl or another boy. I would love any child the same."

"I know, Brom," replied Brielle.

"Then why do you desire a girl so much?"

Brielle turned to her side to gaze at her husband. "Because you are a good man, Brom," she said, tracing the line of his jaw with her finger, "a gentle man. I have never known a more loving husband or father. When I married you, I knew nothing of tenderness. My father was a harsh man, and I fully expected that life with a husband would be no better. But you have shown me nothing but kindness these past five years, and I have grown to love you more than I ever knew was possible. Brom, I want to have a daughter so that she can know a father's love the way I never did."

Brielle's words were sincere, and they pricked Brommel's heart. The thought of leaving her, even for a few days, was always more than he could bear. But bear it he did each time he left home to see to his responsibilities at the ministry. The salary was enough to provide for his family, and for that he was grateful. But lately, Emir had been asking more and more of him, placing heavier responsibilities on him, requiring him to spend more time away from home.

He had lost track of just when his duties had shifted to more clandestine activities. As Emir drew him into his confidence, Brommel had been entrusted with important information, information that was to be protected—at any cost. Sometimes that cost seemed to Brommel too high a price to pay, but to keep his family safe, he had pledged his loyalty to Emir. It was not his place to question the Minister's motives, only to fulfill his duty.

It was this duty that weighed on Brommel's mind now as he held his wife and contemplated the arrival of his unborn child. As much as he would like to enjoy the rest of the evening, he could not in good conscience remain silent any longer.

"Brielle," he began, trying not to let the tone of his voice betray his disappointment, "I have been given a new assignment."

Brielle stroked the back of Brommel's hand. "Another assignment," she said, sighing. "How long will you be gone this time? Three days? Four?"

"Longer," he answered. "Much longer. He is sending me to Dokur on the Isle of Imaness."

Brielle's troubled eyes connected with his. "Emir knows the baby is coming. He wouldn't send you away when I need you most?"

"I'm not to leave until after the baby's birth. But until then, he's sending me on a short mission, a few days at most. Emir's given his word to watch over you and Rylan while I'm gone."

"But Brom, I need you here with me."

"I know, Brielle. I will be back in time. You have my word."

Brielle searched Brommel's eyes. Brommel hoped she knew she had no reason to doubt him. He had always been truthful with her in the past. If he said he would do his best to return in time for their child's birth, then he would do it.

"Emir has promised to look after you."

"You said that."

"You don't seem satisfied."

"I don't trust him," said Brielle. "There is something about him that unsettles me, like the chill of the North wind. How I wish you would find someone else to work for."

"No one pays better wages than the ministry."

"I don't care about the wages, Brom, you know that. We've talked about this before. Emir demands too much of you. You say it is for our good, that the money he pays keeps this roof over our heads, but I would rather live in a hovel and have you home with me each night."

"I understand your fears, Brielle," replied Brommel, twisting a lock of her hair around his finger, "and after this assignment, maybe I can speak with Emir about them. But for now, I must fulfill my duties. If it makes you feel better, I will ask Magda to look in on you from time to time."

"Magda the chicken herder?"

Brommel laughed. "I wonder what old Magda would think if she knew we called her that."

"Well, she does own an awful lot of chickens."

"Some of which have found their way into our stew pot. She's always been generous. And she's an excellent midwife. She's birthed most of the babies in this village over the past fifty years."

"Except Rylan."

Brommel squeezed Brielle's shoulders, and then wrapped his arms around her. It was he who had brought their son into the world. The delivery had happened so quickly that there was no time to summon Magda. He had done it himself. Later, Magda had praised him for it. "You'd make a fine midwife," she had said with a mischievous grin. Throughout this second pregnancy, Brielle had insisted that Brommel deliver this child as well, and until this morning he had had every intention of doing so.

"I will do my best to be home in time," he said, trying to console his wife. "But if I am not here when the pains begin, you must promise to send Rylan for Magda."

Brielle scrunched up her nose, and for a moment Brommel was certain she would refuse. But her face softened, and she nodded, though he could tell it was with great reluctance. How he wished he could offer more assurance of his prompt return. In truth, he had no idea how long it would take to locate the Guilde, or how much time he would need to obtain the crystal. What he had decided was that Emir would have to find someone else to search for Ivanore.

"One thing I can promise you," whispered Brommel into Brielle's ear, "on my return, I will see to it that Emir never sends me away from you again. I swear this journey will be the last one I take without you."

10

"Are you all right?"

Dianis's voice cut through the darkness like a beacon. There was not even the faintest sliver of light for Jayson's highly sensitive eyes to draw upon. Normally, he felt as comfortable in the night as in the day because for him there was little difference. No, in truth he preferred the night, for in it he was hidden from those who wished to harm him. But this darkness made him apprehensive. For the first time in his life, he felt as though he were blind.

"How much further?" he asked, trying to mask the anxiety in his voice.

"Not much," Dianis answered back. "This tunnel leads underground and out of the city. But I'm sure you guessed that already."

He had guessed half of it anyway. Concealed behind the portrait in the room they'd left behind, a narrow passageway followed a steep downward path. Once the tunnel leveled out, they had continued crawling for more than an hour, so that Jayson's knees ached. Finally, the tunnel sloped upward, and he and Dianis climbed up a series of carved steps that stopped abruptly at a door.

Dianis pushed open this door, and immediately the tunnel filled with light. The suddenness of it was more than Jayson's eyes could bear, so he shielded them with his hand. As his eyes adjusted, he saw for the first time the passageway he and Dianis had just passed through. It was perfectly round and smooth, hewn from the earth itself and packed hard and lined with smooth stones fitted perfectly together to create a fairly uniform surface.

Together they stepped out of the tunnel. The sun was just making its appearance on the horizon. Jayson stretched out his arms and shook each leg, which had gone numb from having spent so long in an uncomfortable position. As his eyes adjusted to light, he took in their surroundings. They were in a wide, grassy field surrounded on all sides by trees. They had emerged from the side of a small knoll blanketed with yellow wildflowers.

Dianis secured the door behind them, making certain that it was well concealed by earth and moss.

"This isn't our final destination, is it?" asked Jayson.

Dianis brushed a layer of dirt from her cloak. "I've been instructed to take you to Alay-Crevar, a village two days' walk from here. After that, I'll be done with you."

"You know, for having just met me, you seem to dislike me a great deal."

"And for good reason."

"Why? You don't even know me."

"I know you well enough."

"Really?" said Jayson. "Well, I know me, too, and I think I'm a rather decent fellow. So either your source of

51

information about me is inaccurate, or you're a poor judge of character."

Dianis cast him a scorching glance, and then started toward the trees. She didn't even so much as glance back before slipping into the forest shadows.

"Aren't we touchy?" Jayson remarked before following her.

They traveled along a narrow path for most of the day. Dianis spoke little, only to give terse directions such as which plants to avoid or to stop making so much noise. The hours passed slowly, and Jayson took the opportunity to enjoy the daylight, something he had not done in some time.

About noon, they came upon a meandering stream. Dianis announced they would stop to rest. She removed her cloak, spread it over a grassy patch of earth, and laid down on it.

Jayson knelt at the stream and bent forward, submerging his head. The water was colder than he had anticipated, and he flung his head back, gasping for breath.

"If you intend on drowning yourself," said Dianis, "I would appreciate your giving me the crystal first. I detest foraging through the pockets of the dead."

Jayson shook his head, letting the water fly. He hoped some of it landed on his discourteous hostess. "No such luck," he said, squeezing some of the water from his hair. "I plan to go on living, if for no other reason than to provoke you."

When Dianis did not answer, Jayson laughed. "This hasn't quite gone according to your plan, has it? That you failed to convince me, a dirty half-breed, to entrust you with the crystal simply gnaws at you, doesn't it?"

Jayson held out the crystal, taunting her with it. Then he slipped it back into his pouch and laughed again. But Dianis was not amused.

"We know all about you, Jayson," she said somberly. "The Guilde has been gathering information on you for nearly two years."

"I've been in Hestoria for only one."

"But you've been involved for much longer. Two years ago you met someone very important to us. Because of you, she abandoned her calling. For a time, we didn't even know where she was. By the time we finally located her, Fredric had already discovered the truth about the two of you and sent you into exile."

"I assume you're referring to my wife."

Dianis sat up and faced Jayson, her expression more serious than he had yet seen it. Her jaw set with visible irritation. "She belongs to *us*. The crystal belongs to us."

Jayson didn't like the direction this conversation was taking. Whatever authority this girl thought she had was not enough to impress him. He glared at her, letting the weight of his gaze bear down on her. But Dianis only glared back, her eyes unblinking.

She's not worth the effort, he thought.

Letting his expression relax a little, he turned toward the trees and located north. "It's time to move. Which way do we go now?" he asked, trying to sound less angry than he felt. There was no need to pick a fight with the girl. If given the opportunity, she would certainly steal the crystal. Then how would he locate the Guilde? No, for now he needed her and would play along until he got from her what he wanted.

Dianis pointed to a break in the trees. Jayson nodded and started forward. A few moments later, Dianis had joined him.

Exile

They walked in silence for several minutes, passing through a dense forest of thin, white trees. The sun fell on the earth in a mottled pattern, which was in constant motion as the wind moved through the leaves above. After a while, Jayson tired of the silence.

"She doesn't belong to anyone," he said.

"Excuse me?" asked Dianis.

"Ivanore. She belongs to no one but herself. You seem to know all about her so you know she never does anything that she doesn't want to do."

"Yes, even when it puts others in jeopardy."

"You said she abandoned her calling. I can only assume that this *calling* has something to do with your Guilde, and that she didn't fulfill some assignment as expected."

"She ran off with you." Dianis's tone was sharp.

"You say that as if that was a bad thing."

"She acted irresponsibly. We depended on her, and she failed us."

Jayson's steps slowed a little as he considered Dianis's accusation. "Have you ever stopped to think whether falling in love and having a family was more important to her than whatever it was that you exploited her to do?"

"We did not exploit her!" snapped Dianis.

"Really? Then if this calling is so valuable, why did she run and hide? I know her better than anyone," added Jayson. "Ivanore hates the responsibilities of royalty. She hates the control her father has over her. More than anything, she only wants to live a normal life."

"She has told you this?"

"Many times."

"But she never mentioned the Guilde?"

Jayson hesitated. "No."

Dianis smirked. "You are mistaken if you think Ivanore's calling has anything to do with her being Lord Fredric's daughter, or if her calling was *assigned* to her by the Guilde. The fact that you know so little about her proves what I've tried to get the Guilde to understand all along—that you are a nuisance, an obstacle to our purpose, a distraction. In essence," she continued, stopping to glare at him triumphantly, "you are expendable."

Jayson smelled them before he saw them, a dozen men armed with swords and crossbows stepping out from behind the trees. Each wore a dark blue tunic with a yellow triangle stitched on the right shoulder, and each wore an expression that told Jayson they would not hesitate to kill him if ordered to do so.

Dianis held up her hand, and the men focused their aim on Jayson.

"Whoa, whoa!" said Jayson, taking a step back. "If I'd known you were so sensitive, I would have kept the comment about exploiting my wife to myself."

"Hand it over, or they will kill you."

"I'm unarmed. Wouldn't that be a bit, um, unfair?"

"Listen," said Dianis, her frustration growing. "I have wasted enough time with you. If I had had my way, I would have taken the crystal weeks ago. As it is, the Vatéz are already too close to realizing their plans. Now give me the crystal, and you can go on your way."

"*If* you had had your way? You've *tried* convincing the Guilde that I'm an obstacle?" Jayson laughed. "Dianis, this little tea party," he continued, waving his hand toward the men, "does the Guilde know about this? Are they aware that you've taken matters into your own hands?"

He stepped toward her cautiously, still fully aware of the weapons trained on him. He leaned forward and whispered in her ear.

"I think your superiors will be unhappy if you fail to deliver me to Alay-Crevar as they requested."

Dianis's expression grew even harder as she rapidly snapped her fingers into a fist. Jayson readied for a rapid death, but instead, the men all lowered their weapons. Only then did Dianis's face soften a bit, her lips curving into a wry grin.

"Have it your way," she said. "But I assure you, in time you will relinquish the crystal to me. More than that, you will wish that you had died today."

Suddenly, Dianis vanished right before his eyes. Jayson could not tell if she disappeared altogether or if she merely transformed, as Nymphs were known to do, blending instantaneously into her forest surroundings. Either way, Jayson found himself alone and unarmed in the midst of Dianis's men, and it was clear from the expressions on their faces that they meant to take him by force.

As they closed in around him, he flexed his fingers, extending his claws. He loathed killing humans, and considered how he could disarm them with minimal damage. But before he could finish the thought, something solid smashed into the back of his skull and everything went dark.

11

*E*rastus Timbrey slept like the dead. Except for the deep, chesty rumble that escaped from between his lips with every breath, one could easily mistake his pale, scrawny form for a dead man.

Brommel wasted no time. After kicking in the door to the tavern keeper's room, he grabbed fistfuls of Timbrey's nightshirt and hauled the man straight out of bed.

"Get up!" he shouted as he planted the man's bare feet on the floor.

Timbrey's eyes blinked open. When he saw that he was standing, he proclaimed, "By the gods, what has happened here?" Then he took notice of Brommel and Arik standing in front of him. "Is it afternoon already? Am I late for something?"

"Is this Erastus Timbrey?" asked Brommel.

"It is," replied Arik.

Timbrey's watery blue eyes widened with recognition. "You! I provide you with a roof over your head, and this is how I am to be treated? Get out of my room this instant!"

"You have information that is of value to me," said Arik, ignoring Timbrey's demand, "information regarding the Guilde."

"What information?"

"I want to know its current location."

Timbrey regarded the boy with a skeptical eye. "I don't know anything."

"You've heard of the Guilde, no doubt."

"I've heard of them. Aren't they some society whose job it is to guard—what was it now? Oh, that's right. I remember. They guard sheep, don't they? Protecting unsuspecting sheep from the wolves. Now there's a humanitarian cause for you."

Arik bristled with contempt. He drew his sword, cutting a wide arc through the air. But before the blade could meet its mark, Brommel had Arik by the wrist. He had only spent an hour with the lad and was already reaching the limit of his patience.

"Put that away," said Brommel.

"I'll not be ridiculed!" shouted Arik, his face turning red.

"Kill the man if you like, but then don't expect a dead man to talk."

Brommel guided Arik's hand, easing the sword back into its scabbard. It was evident that if left in Arik's hands, their mission would fail before it had even begun.

"Wait outside," Brommel told him.

Arik protested, "I will not!"

Brommel resisted the urge to bend the boy over his knee and spank him, something he doubted Arik had received enough of in his youth.

"The woman we saw downstairs when we came in has likely gone for help," Brommel explained with exaggerated patience. "We don't have much time. Guard the door and inform me if anyone arrives. In the meantime, I will get the information you seek."

"How do you propose to do that?"

Brommel grinned. After working for Emir for so many years, he had his ways. Compliant, but not completely satisfied, Arik left the room. Brommel waited until the door had shut behind him, then he faced Timbrey once again. He was nothing but skin and bones, a waif of a man reduced to a living skeleton by a lifetime of liquor and laziness. The man was visibly trembling now. Where Arik had inspired insolence, Brommel now inspired fear.

Brommel spotted a stout wooden stool beside the window. With a sharp kick, he slid it across the room. It came to rest in front of the door. Brommel strode over to it and sat down. Then he withdrew a rather intimidating dagger from his belt and started cutting his fingernails with it.

"All right then," he began, "let's talk about the Guilde."

12

The first sensation that returned to Jayson was the intense cold seeping into his body. He awoke and shivered. He opened his eyes and found himself lying on a bed of damp stone. The smell of mildew and stagnant water made him want to retch. He was in a stone cell of some kind, barely wide enough for him to extend his legs and arms, and when he attempted to do so, sharp pain in his extremities made him stop.

At first, he thought he had been injured, but then he realized that it was merely the result of having lain so long in one position in the cold. He wriggled his fingers, wrists, feet, and ankles to work out the stiffness. The discomfort soon passed, and he tried to stand, but the ceiling of this little cell was low, Jayson had to stoop. He checked his person for the crystal. As he suspected, it was missing.

"If I ever get my hands on that girl," he grumbled, stepping to the wooden door. Through a narrow opening, Jayson saw a guard standing by.

"You!" Jayson called out. "Where am I? What is this place?"

The guard, who had been leaning lazily against the wall peeling a tangerine, suddenly came to attention. He dropped his fruit to the floor where it rolled several feet before coming to rest in the corner. Then he turned and ran off.

"Wait!" Jayson called after him. "Come back!"

Jayson's cell was much too small and completely bare. There wasn't even a scrap of straw on which to rest. Except for the faint light coming through the door from a lantern in the hall, it was quite dark. So Jayson remained at the door, hoping that eventually the guard might return.

He didn't wait long before someone did come. A man appeared dressed in a simple brown robe, bearing a ring of keys in his hand. He spoke not a word as he unlocked Jayson's door, then stepped back against the wall.

Jayson joined his jailer in the hall. Here the ceiling was high enough to allow him to stand at his full height. Wooden casks were stacked against the walls. This wasn't a prison at all, he realized, but a wine cellar. His jailer handed Jayson a cloth bundle, which contained a clean linen tunic, trousers, and boots. Grateful to be rid of his wet clothing, Jayson quickly changed into the dry garments. Once dressed, he snatched up the stray tangerine and followed his jailer up a stone stairwell to another door. The jailer opened it, and then stepped aside, allowing Jayson to pass through.

Jayson wasn't exactly sure what he had expected, but it certainly wasn't the crowded, smoke-filled saloon that greeted him. The room wasn't much bigger than the basement he had just left; yet every inch of space was occupied by revelers with mugs of ale in their hands and smoking pipes between their lips. A welcoming fire burned in a hearth, and in one corner a group of six or seven men of various ages and sizes leaned heavily on each other while belting out an off-key ballad.

Jayson squeezed his way through the crowd, past the singing drunkards, and took his place on a stool. As soon as he did so, the fellow sitting beside him leaned in close.

"Here," said the old man, setting his nearly empty mug on the table in front of Jayson. "You need this more than I do."

Jayson was about to decline the offer, but from the pain in his stomach, he knew it had been far too long since he'd had a good meal, the tangerine notwithstanding. So he wiped his sleeve across the mug's rim and raised it to his lips. The ale was rich and frothy, the best he'd tasted in a long while. He found the mug empty too soon.

"Mind telling me where I can get a refill?" he asked.

Without hesitation, the old man reached across the table for a half-empty mug whose owner was sprawled out unconscious on the table. "He won't be needing this no more," he said, sliding the mug in front of Jayson.

Near the hearth, the singers ended their song, and the entire room erupted in applause. Some demanded an encore, but the apparent leader of the group waved off the requests. He laughed as he slapped several of the men on their shoulders, and each one returned the gesture by raising his mug in salute.

He wasn't an old man, at least not as old as Jayson's neighbor, but he was old enough. His hair was beginning to thin, and creases decorated the corners of his eyes when he smiled, which he was doing an awful lot of. He wore the clothes of a peasant, but beneath the plain cloth Jayson noticed the defined lines of a strong frame. He was tall, towering over the other men as he crossed the room. Several raised their mugs as he passed.

"That was mighty fine singing," someone said as he neared the bar.

"Aye, it was, wasn't it?" came the reply. The man turned to Jayson then, as though expecting him to comment as well. Instead, Jayson took a long draught of his ale.

The man looked amused. "You won't raise your glass to me?" he asked.

"I don't know you," Jayson answered.

"Reason enough, I suppose. But you might follow the example of the others for the sake of propriety."

"I would raise my glass if I thought it deserved, but as I said," added Jayson, setting the mug purposely on the bar beside him, "I don't know you."

The man glared at Jayson, and a hush fell over the room as all eyes turned to them.

The man stuck his thumbs into his belt and snorted. "You're a fool then," he said. "There are times when a man must behave according to custom whether he wants to or not, such as when going against the grain might endanger his life or the lives of others."

"I don't see how keeping my glass could put anyone in harm's way," replied Jayson, "unless you intend to inflict that harm yourself."

The man considered Jayson a moment, and then broke into a wide grin. "Nay. I've no such intention," said the man. "Just giving a friendly bit of advice, is all."

The tension in the room visibly eased, and the revelers turned back to their drinks.

"In that case," replied Jayson. "I'll raise my glass to you, and to you all."

The man burst into laughter and slapped Jayson on the back. "Daub, my friend," he said to Jayson's neighbor, "why don't you be a good lad and fetch us both a full bottle, eh?"

"Of course," was the old man's answer, and he excused himself from the table. The tall man took his seat then, and cast a disapproving glance at the unconscious man across the table.

"I'll have to carry that one home myself later," he mentioned, smiling. Then he said to Jayson, "I like you. You're a bull-headed fellow, ready for a fight. I can see why Dianis dislikes you so much."

Jayson bristled at the sound of her name. "You know Dianis?"

"Of course I know her! She is my daughter, don't you know!"

"I'd like to speak with her."

"And why is that? So you can tell her how angry you are at having been hit on the head and locked up? My boy, I doubt that would do either of you any good."

Jayson lowered his voice. He didn't like the close proximity the saloon's patrons had to one another. Privacy was obviously a commodity not available here.

"She has something that belongs to me," he said.

"Ah, I see," replied the man, lowering his voice mockingly. "You must be referring then to the crystal."

Jayson was infuriated now. He was being toyed with, and he didn't like it one bit. "Who are you?" he asked with barely restrained anger.

Just then, Daub returned with an open bottle of wine.

"Leave it," said Jayson. Daub glanced at the man for approval. The man nodded, and Daub set down the bottle and left them again.

"I am sorry," said the man. "I failed to introduce myself, didn't I? Must be the ale. I fear I've had a bit too much tonight. But you see, we've cause for celebration," he added, extending his hand. "My name is Gerard. As for the crystal, I assure you, it is safe."

Jayson ignored Gerard's gesture. "I want it back."

"Of course you do. But I'm afraid the crystal doesn't belong to you."

Suddenly, Jayson grabbed the bottle and smashed it against the table. Glass shattered and the wine burst from it, splattering everyone within reach. A moment later, Jayson had the jagged end of it pressed into Gerard's throat. Gerard, however, hardly winced at the danger he was in. Instead he merely grinned, a look of honest compassion in his eyes.

"My boy, I can only imagine the pain you must feel, but there are greater things at work here than your vastly insignificant problems."

Jayson pressed the glass deeper into Gerard's skin. A tiny spot of blood appeared on his skin, but still Gerard showed no fear.

"That crystal is my responsibility," said Jayson. "My wife entrusted it to me and no one else. Whatever you want it for, I don't care. You can use it anyway you see fit. But the crystal stays with me."

"You'd work with us, then?"

"I'll work with you as long as it keeps the crystal out of the hands of the Vatéz."

"All right then. The crystal will be returned to you. I give my word."

Jayson hesitantly lay the broken bottle back down on the bar. "Dianis told me about the protectors of the crystal," he

65

said, finishing off the ale in his mug. "I assume she's given it to them. So, when do we leave for Alay-Crevar?"

Gerard laughed. "But my boy, you're already here." He indicated the crowded room with a sweep of his arm. "Welcome to the secret lair of the Guilde!"

13

It was the order of things that mattered on Mikel's farm, everything from which crop was to be planted in what field, to the schedule of tending the animals, to how the tools were arranged in the shed—it all was set down in a way that gave Mikel a sense of pride and security. When Teak had first arrived, Mikel saw to it that the boy learned what had to be done, and did it in the manner to which Mikel was accustomed. At first, Teak worried that he would not be happy with his uncle, but after losing his mother, Mikel's way of doing things provided the stability he needed to work through his grief. He came to love the rhythm of his life, the repetitive schedule of rising at dawn, tending the animals, eating meals, and farming. His new life was much like the seasons, ever constant in their changing.

Finding the girl was the first disruption to this ordered life that he had faced in the eight years since he'd come here. Suddenly, everything he'd known was displaced. Uncle did not keep the same schedule as before, but spent much of his time checking in on his patient. Meals came at irregular intervals as he spent his time tending to the girl and watching over her. At first, Teak expected to feel angry that a stranger had intruded on their comfortable lives, but he wasn't angry. Instead, the changes in their routine, however insignificant, thrilled him. Even when he was out working the fields, he found himself anticipating what might happen next. Would Uncle send him to milk the cow while he dressed her wounds? Perhaps he would ask him to bring an extra log for the fire to keep her warm.

It was as though the very appearance of this girl had awakened them both to new possibilities, new ways of thinking and of doing things. The order in which things had always been done was unraveling, but neither of them seemed to care. Rather, Teak couldn't help but notice they both liked it very much.

For two days, the girl awoke for only the briefest intervals during which Mikel did his best to get a little broth down her "to get her strength up." Mikel also did what he could to keep the fever under control, mopping the girl's face, arms, and legs with cool water. He sent Teak to the well several times a day to fill the bucket or asked him to manage this errand or that so he could spend a little extra time looking after the patient. Teak did what he could but always felt he should be doing more. When Mikel was busy with chores, he would sometimes ask Teak to watch over the girl and let him know if she stirred.

It was during these times when Teak felt most comfortable sitting on a three-legged stool in the farthest corner of the room where he could watch her sleep.

On the third morning after her arrival, Mikel announced that the fever had broken. "Thanks be to the gods," he said. "She's gotten through the worst of it. Boy," he added, "it's time I fetch a chicken. Then I'll go to the garden to pull some potatoes and carrots, and maybe a leek or two. We'll have a fine stew prepared for her tonight. Look after her, and call for me if she wakes."

Teak took his seat in the corner of the room and leaned his head back against the wall. After two nights of sleeping on the floor, he was feeling a bit stiff in the shoulders. And a little sleepy, too, since his sleep had been restless.

It couldn't hurt much, he thought, if I close my eyes for a while.

He had dozed off for no more than a minute or two when the girl stirred. The soft rustle of her blankets and the sudden shift in the rhythm of her breathing brought him to attention. A moment later, her eyes fluttered open.

From his vantage point in the corner, Teak observed as her curious gaze moved from one object in the room to the next. Finally, her eyes fell on Teak.

"Hello," she said weakly.

Teak fidgeted on his stool. "M-morning," he replied. They considered each other for a moment before Teak remembered Mikel's instructions. He abruptly rose from his stool and started for the door.

"Don't go," said the girl.

Teak paused. "M-my uncle told m-me to call him when you awoke."

The girl tried to lift her head, but she was too weak, and it fell back into her pillow. Teak hurried to her side and adjusted her pillow.

"How's that?" he asked.

"Better, thank you."

Teak turned for the door again, but the girl laid her hand on his arm. "Please don't leave," she whispered, pinching her eyes shut.

"D-does your shoulder hurt b-bad?" Teak asked.

"Yes," she whispered, then cautiously opened her eyes again.

"Uncle p-pulled the arrow out," added Teak. "You've had a fever."

"How long have I been here?"

"This is the third d-day."

"Three days." The girl murmured the words, a strange sadness in her voice, and Teak saw tears in her eyes, but she blinked them away. "So, *you* found me?"

Teak nodded.

"And carried me here?"

He nodded once more.

"It was a brave thing you did. I am indebted to you..." she paused.

"T-teak," said Teak.

"You are a quiet man, aren't you Teak?"

Teak liked hearing her say his name. He wished she'd say it again. "T-talking is hard," he told her. "I d-don't know what to say."

"I see," she said, though her voice was softer now. "Yet here you are talking to me."

Her eyelids looked heavy, and her breath slowed a little. Teak could see she was tired and wanted to sleep. He worried about what his uncle would say once he learned that Teak hadn't called him. But he would go and call him now.

Once more he started for the door. He crept slowly across the floor, trying not to disturb the girl. But before he reached the door, he heard her voice again.

"Teak," she whispered.

Teak turned. "Yes?"

"You may ask me, if you wish."

"Ask you what?"

"My name."

Of course. How rude he had been not to think of it. He had already said more today than he had said in a very long time. He studied the girl for a moment to see if she was merely teasing him. But no, her expression was sincere.

"What is your n-name?" he asked, forming the words carefully.

The girl settled into her pillow and pulled the blanket up to her chin. No angel could have looked more beautiful.

"You can call me Ivy," she said. Then she closed her eyes and fell asleep.

14

Brommel's horse was lagging. Earlier in the day the mare had yearned to gallop ahead, and Brommel was certain that if he had permitted it, he would have arrived at his destination, whatever that might be, far sooner than he would at his present pace. But unfortunately he was bound to travel alongside Arik, and Arik's horse was hellbent on moving as slowly as possible.

Brommel couldn't begin to guess where Arik had found such a sorry beast. Well past its prime, the poor creature stumbled along on wobbly legs, its head sagging from its scrawny neck. Strangely enough, Arik seemed quite pleased with his mount.

"There, there, old boy," Arik said, stroking its mane when it stopped to nibble on some wayside grass. "I guess he's a bit hungry."

"Half-starved is more like it," grumbled Brommel. "Is that the best you could do with Emir's money?"

"I'll have you know I paid a handsome price for this fellow, and the owner wasn't very keen on giving him up.

Only when I mentioned that I was in the minister's employ did the man relent."

"Ah, now I see it. You bragged of your gold, didn't you?"

"I did no such thing," answered Arik, defensively.

"You bragged of it, and the man knew that whatever price you offered he could take you for more, and take you he did. What a fool," Brommel finished with a snort.

They continued on without speaking. Arik brooded while Brommel whistled a tune—just to aggravate his young companion. He had to admit that he enjoyed making the rascal squirm. Serves him right, reasoned Brommel, for thinking himself better for being a royal. The fact that he had been completely cut off from his inheritance and crown didn't seem to weigh on him one bit. Brommel decided that Arik's arrogance was due partly to being so young and partly from being spoiled. That's what he is, Brommel concluded, nothing but a spoiled royal brat.

"Are you ever going to tell me what Timbrey said?" asked Arik presently. "He seemed awfully frightened when you were through with him."

"The man's a coward," said Brommel, "but a shrewd businessman. He offered to sell me the information I wanted for sixty coins."

"Only sixty? I would have demanded twice that if I were him."

"You would have, wouldn't you?"

"The money Emir gave us would cover that ten times over. So?"

"So what?"

"Did you pay him the sixty coins?"

"No."

"How much did you pay him then?"

"Not a penny."

"You paid him nothing, and yet here we are on our way to—well, to somewhere. I assume you got the information we were after?"

"I did."

"Yet you paid nothing for it. How, may I ask, did you extract such valuable information at so low a price? You didn't—"

Arik drew the edge of his hand across his throat.

"There was no need for violence," retorted Brommel impatiently. "In exchange for his assistance, I promised not to turn him over to the tax collector. You see, he's been fixing his books for some time. The ministry has had their eye on him. His tongue flapped well enough after that."

The brow over Arik's left eye rose a little, indicating his approval. Brommel did not care for Arik's approval and wished more than ever that he had pressed Emir into letting him come on this journey alone. He grew increasingly irritated and decided to let his expression show it, but Arik seemed oblivious to the annoyance on his face.

"Where are we heading then?" asked Arik.

"I don't know," grumbled Brommel.

"What do you mean you don't know?" Arik sounded truly shocked. "But you just said Timbrey told you where to find the Guilde."

"I said he gave me the information I wanted."

"We wanted to know the location of the Guilde."

"What good would it do me to learn the current location of their headquarters when it would be moved before we got there?"

Not long after, they arrived at a small pool that had formed between several boulders at the side of a stream. The water was clear and looked appealing. Brommel led his horse into the center of the pool where it reached to just below the horse's knees, just deep enough to drink. Arik did the same.

"You've gone about this thing all wrong," said Arik. "You threatened the man who was our best chance at finding Jayson and the crystal. Whatever he told you, he did so under duress. It is very likely that whatever he told you was a lie. You should have let me speak with him."

"What for?"

"I can be very persuasive."

"You?" Brommel couldn't help but laugh. "I can hardly imagine a scrawny lad like you persuading a sparrow to take flight let alone a man to give up a secret sworn under oath."

For once, Arik grew silent, his face turning nearly purple with indignation. "For all I know Timbrey didn't tell you anything," he said. "How do I know we are going anywhere at all? Maybe you are too much a coward to admit that you don't know what you are doing and that I should have been put in charge of this whole venture!"

Brommel took a moment to judge the distance between the prince and himself, just under an arm's length, and then he quickly threw out his hand and shoved Arik's shoulder. Arik, taken completely by surprise, lost his balance and slid cleanly over the side of his horse into the water below. The shallow splash and high-pitched squeal that followed drew a round of boisterous laughter from Brommel. He laughed so hard he nearly lost balance himself.

Arik flailed his arms about as he struggled to put his legs under him. Once he had, he sloshed through the tepid pool to the shore. Brommel collected the reins of Arik's horse and led it to where its drenched and forlorn master awaited.

Brommel handed the reins to Arik who, for the first time that day, had fallen silent.

"What I learned from Timbrey is far more valuable than all our coins could buy, Prince Arik. For you see, it is not the location of the Guilde I sought, but the secret token one must possess to be given passage to it. However, if you want to make yourself useful," he continued as he reached out his hand and patted Arik on the head, "help me spot the marker. That shouldn't be too difficult, should it?"

Arik scowled. "What marker?"

"A cross of stone."

"That's it? A cross of stone?" asked Arik. "You want me, the prince of Dokur, to play lookout for *you?*"

"If you are unhappy, you are more than welcome to return to Nauvet-Carum and complain to Emir," said Brommel, snapping his reins against his horse's neck. His horse started forward while Arik scrambled onto his, hurrying to keep up. "Or you can keep your tongue and accompany me. Either way," continued Brommel without looking back, "the only thing I want from you is your silence."

15

The sun was high overhead by the time Jayson awoke, the dull ache between his temples a reminder of how much ale he had consumed the night before. Long after most of the taverns' patrons had headed for home, Gerard and Jayson lounged by the fire. Gerard did most of the talking. He seemed to never run low on clever stories to tell, and Jayson found him to be pleasant company. It was only when the fire had burned down to embers that Gerard finally grew silent. Jayson thought at first that his new friend had fallen asleep, but no. Gerard was fully awake and suddenly quite sober as he stared into the orange embers.

"It is no coincidence, your being here tonight," said Gerard finally.

Jayson leaned back in the soft chair. "Of course not," he scoffed. "Your daughter took me hostage."

Gerard's face failed to register that he had even heard Jayson's reply. He continued somberly. "Things are about to change, I'm afraid. The Vatéz grow more powerful every day.

They are fueled by lust and greed. Honor and integrity are not to be found among them."

Jayson studied the half-empty glass in his hand. The golden liquid reflected the dying firelight.

"Dianis told me that they want the crystal," said Jayson. "*My* crystal. But I can't imagine why."

Gerard blinked as if suddenly called back from a dream. He turned his gaze on Jayson.

"The crystal is nothing more than a tool, my boy, but in the wrong hands it would be very dangerous indeed. Without its other half, of course, its powers are weak at best. But should the two halves be reunited, then we would have a serious problem on our hands. Or worse, if it is paired with its brother..."

"There are two crystals?"

"Aye."

"I'm sorry. I know of only the one that belongs to my wife," said Jayson. "The other half is still in her possession."

"All the more reason to keep your half out of Emir's hands."

"Is that why your daughter stole it from me?"

A log broke, and the loud crackle of the embers startled them both. Gerard rose to his feet and rubbed the back of his neck with his hand.

"It will be returned, I assure you. But for now, the hour is late. Come with me. You are my guest for the night."

Gerard led Jayson to a cottage at the heart of the village. Given a warm blanket and a bed stuffed with fresh straw, Jayson fell into a deep sleep in which he dreamed of tender lips on his and of a time that seemed so long ago. The dream made him ache inside, and though he slept, the emptiness engulfed him, dragging him from the embrace for which he yearned. He reached for them and managed one last touch, fingertip to fingertip, before floating away on a black, angry sea. He clenched his fists and shouted with the cry of a man suffering the worst kind of agony. When at last all his tears and energy had been spent, he uncurled his fingers. There lay the crystal in his palm, bloody from clutching its jagged edge.

Jayson awoke with the dream still fresh in his mind. He flexed his empty fingers, then rose from his bed and wrapped the blanket around him for warmth. No fire burned in the hearth, and a thin sheet of ice had formed in the water bucket by the door that had been left for his use. He punched a hole in the ice with his fist and splashed a little of the water on his face, which made him sputter from the cold. On a round table sat a loaf of coarse bread, and beside it a wedge of cheese. These Jayson devoured quickly, and then washed them down with some of the water.

It was then that the cottage door opened and Gerard made his appearance. Smiling broadly, the older gentleman nodded approvingly at his guest's appetite. He carried in his arms several logs of various sizes, which he arranged in the hearth, then set about to light a fire.

"I must apologize," he said, striking the flint. "I normally rise much earlier than this. I'm afraid last night's celebrating was a little more than this old man can handle anymore. I see Dianis brought you some breakfast. She should be in presently."

Jayson noticed the white wisps rising from Gerard's mouth as he spoke and felt a little guilty for allowing his host to tend to him. Even so, Jayson pulled the blanket up around his chin and tried to keep from shivering. A few moments later, however, a small fire blazed in the fireplace, and the cold in the room began to dissipate.

"Thank you for your hospitality," said Jayson.

"You're welcome, my boy. Of course, many of us are merely guests here in Alay-Crevar."

"This isn't your home?"

"I'm afraid not, though my daughter and I do call it home while we occupy it. We tend not to stay in one place for very long."

"Why is that?" asked Jayson.

Gerard pulled up two chairs and invited Jayson to sit on one while he sat on the other. They both warmed their hands by the fire.

"My daughter has warned me not to trust you, but in my heart I sense that you are a good man. I do not believe your wife would have entrusted you with something so valuable if you were not. So I can tell you that none of us is safe while the Vatéz are in power. Emir is relentless in his pursuit of the Guilde. We have managed to elude him thus far by moving about as often as is reasonable."

"So, the Vatéz and the Guilde are enemies," said Jayson.

"It wasn't always so," answered Gerard. "A century ago we were two branches of a single organization. You have heard of the League of Magicians."

"Isn't that another name for the Vatéz?"

"They go by many names: magicians, magi, enchanters, spell casters, sages. They are those who have mastered the art of conjuring magic, something few throughout the ages have been able to do. These enchanters have been endowed with a special gift that allows them to develop their powers. Long ago, such enchanters were feared by those who lacked these powers. They were accused of being witches or devils and were sometimes expelled from their communities or even tortured or killed. But there were others who saw magic as a blessing from the gods and believed those who possessed this power should be revered and protected. So arose the Guilde, a secret association of guardians whose sole purpose was to protect the lives of these magicians at any cost. In order to receive their protection, a magician joined the League of Magicians, or Vatéz, and used secret tokens to make his identity known to them.

"Over time, as magic became more respected, members of the Vatéz became public. Some even held government offices. The Guilde continued to exist, but the Vatéz's need of them diminished.

"Eventually some of these magicians began to misuse their gift, using magic to gain power and wealth. There were still a few enchanters who recognized the great responsibility they had been given by the gods, but they were eventually driven underground by the corrupt Vatéz.

"Then one day the gods decided to bestow on man a new gift, but he gave this gift to only one. This gift was far greater than that which they had been given before. It allowed its bearer to see future events, to translate long forgotten languages, to communicate with others even at great distances. This Seer was given a charge to use his gift to reclaim the first gift of magic, to take back from the Vatéz what rightfully belonged to the gods.

"Well, you can imagine how the Vatéz reacted when they learned of the existence of this Seer. They immediately set out to destroy him. But the gods simply raised another in his place, and another. It was then that the Guilde found a new purpose—as guardians of the Seer. And that is our purpose today."

Jayson sat in silence for a while as he mulled Gerard's story over in his mind. Before today, he had never heard anything of a Seer, though he was familiar enough with magic and enchanters. His own father had been an enchanter, though not affiliated in the least with the Vatéz. As a boy, he remembered watching his father conjure small feats of magic for his entertainment, such as lighting fires without flint or making objects vanish and reappear. But this Seer—he had never heard anything of this before, and it intrigued him.

"Well now, here's Dianis with breakfast," said Gerard, interrupting Jayson's thoughts.

The door opened and Dianis entered carrying a basket in one hand and a wooden bucket in the other. She set both down on the table.

Gerard greeted his daughter with a kiss on her cheek, and then nodded toward the bucket. "Is that from our neighbor?"

Dianis laughed. "I didn't think he'd mind sharing a few eggs and a couple of pints of milk this morning."

"My daughter," Gerard replied, apologetically. "I've tried to teach her right from wrong, but sometimes I wonder how much good it has done."

Jayson glanced into the bucket and found it half full of warm milk. "Neighbor's cow?"

"Aye, and I think we've accepted enough of his hospitality," said Gerard. "No need to be stealing milk for our breakfast."

"No one will know," shrugged Dianis. "The cow won't tell."

"Now, now, Dianis, we don't want to give our guest the wrong impression about us, do we? We're honest folk—for the most part—"

Dianis cut in. "Except when we're hungry, or cold, or broke, or in danger."

She went to a cupboard and retrieved four wooden cups. She dipped one cup into the milk, using it to fill the other three. All the while, Dianis avoided Jayson's gaze. As she handed him one of the cups, however, Jayson grabbed her wrist.

Dianis tugged a little, as though the whole thing was a mistake or a joke, but Jayson's grip tightened. She twisted her arm in an effort to break free, the milk from the cup spilling across the table.

"I'd like my crystal, please," Jayson said with exaggerated civility.

"Let go of me," she growled.

"No," he replied.

For a moment, Dianis relaxed her struggle, but then suddenly her free hand flew up to slap Jayson. Her hand never made contact as Jayson grabbed that wrist as well. Now both her hands were bound. She struggled in vain against Jayson's superior strength.

Exasperated, she turned to Gerard. "Father!"

"Don't look to me for help, Daughter. I'm not the one who knocked him unconscious and locked him up overnight."

Dianis glared at Jayson with a look that could have burned a hole through solid stone. He replied with a comical grin.

"Release me or you will regret it," she threatened.

"Why not just vanish like you did in the forest?" asked Jayson coyly. "Or is that just a little trick you like to play?"

Gerard clucked his tongue disapprovingly. "Dianis, you didn't," he said. "I thought we agreed you wouldn't show off."

"I wasn't showing off, Father. Besides, what else was I to do? He refused to give me the crystal."

"But you told me that he had agreed to come with you."

"We are forbidden to bring strangers into our midst."

"Jayson is no stranger. You know that," Gerard replied casually, refilling his cup with milk. "I'm really ashamed of you, you know. I think you owe this young man an apology."

Dianis's expression changed instantly to one of shock and then disgust.

"I'll do no such thing!"

Jayson tightened his grip on her wrists. Dianis cried out in pain.

"Gerard, is your daughter really so arrogant? I believe this child needs a good spanking."

Gerard laughed. "Be my guest! Just like her mother, she is. Always disappearing and reappearing. They ought to learn to stay put!"

Jayson started to turn Dianis with her back to him when she suddenly relented.

"All right!" she said at last. "All right, I'll return the crystal! It's in a safe place. I'll retrieve it after breakfast."

"And?"

Dianis rolled her eyes and spoke through gritted teeth. "And I apologize—for everything! Now let me go!"

Instead of releasing her, however, Jayson pulled Dianis close enough so that he could feel her breath on his face. He relished the scent of fear on her, and the loathing and alarm in her eyes.

"You're forgiven," he said, then let go.

The moment she was released, Dianis scurried to the farthest corner of the room and slumped into a chair. Gerard was having a difficult time restraining his laughter. Jayson, too, couldn't help but take some pleasure in seeing her so sullen.

Presently, Gerard and Jayson resumed the conversation that had been interrupted on Dianis's entrance.

"Last night in the tavern," began Jayson, "you talked of a need to keep the crystal separated from its missing half."

Gerard emptied his cup, then pulled a cast-iron skillet from a shelf and set it over the fire. He cracked three of the eggs into it. The pan sizzled.

"As I said before, the crystal is nothing more than a tool."

"Then why does Emir want it so badly?"

"Emir is a very powerful enchanter," replied Gerard. "Should the crystal come into his possession, it would not bode very well for any of us."

"I still don't understand," said Jayson. "You keep calling the crystal a tool. A tool for what? How is it used and by whom?"

Gerard removed the pan from the fire and set it aside. The smell of cooking eggs made Jayson's mouth water, but at the moment he wanted information more than he wanted a meal. He glanced at Dianis, still brooding in the corner. But from her expression, he could tell she was listening intently to their conversation.

Gerard leaned forward, placing both elbows on the table and clasping the fingers of his hands together. He spoke deliberately, as though every word he now uttered bore a weighty message.

"The crystal is the tool of the Seer. A Seer is quite powerful in his own right, of course, but with the crystal those powers are fully magnified, completely focused. A Seer without the crystal is like a soldier without his sword. He may possess the skills to fight, but it's the weapon in his hands that will win him the battle."

"So you mean to tell me that my crystal, or at least the crystal before it was broken into pieces, belonged to a Seer?"

Dianis leapt up from her chair and crossed the room in an instant. She dropped an angry fist down on the table between Jayson and Gerard.

"Father," she said, nearly shouting, "you have said enough! If she didn't trust him, why should we?"

Gerard patiently laid his hand over his daughter's, but his eyes never left Jayson's. "She kept it from him not because she didn't trust him," he said, "but to protect him."

Dianis removed her hand, defeated. Gerard continued, speaking directly to Jayson now.

"I know your mind is filled with questions, my boy," he said. "Perhaps you already sense the truth but dare not believe it. To validate your suspicions, I will say it for you. Your wife, the Lady Ivanore of Dokur, is the Seer, and it is her crystal that the Vatéz are so desperate to obtain."

16

The cross of stone.

It was what the tavern keeper had told him. Look for the cross of stone. Brommel had tried to extract more information from Erastus Timbrey, but there was simply nothing more to extract. Brommel knew from vast experience when an informant had been purged of all useful information. He knew as well that when tortured or threatened with imminent death, a man would reveal even his deepest, innermost secrets, but if pushed too far he might also fabricate lies to satisfy his interrogator. Only the most experienced tormentors could discern the difference. That was precisely why, in this case, Brommel had not used death or even pain to coerce Timbrey to talk. Brommel did not want lies. He wanted the truth. And for a man like Timbrey, a man who collected secrets and sold them like the liquor he vended, the Guilde's secrets were nothing more than a commodity waiting to be purchased by the highest bidder.

And how did Brommel know that Timbrey's information was accurate? Because if it turned out to be false, Timbrey could be easily found, and Timbrey was the sort of man who preferred not to have repeat visits from men like Brommel.

The cross of stone.

Not much to go by. According to Timbrey, Brommel and Arik were to follow the road leading west through the forest until they reached the cross of stone.

And what then?

When Brommel asked that question, Timbrey had done something quite unexpected. He had reached out his right hand and clasped Brommel's wrist in an awkward grip. Their connection lasted only a second or two, but it was enough. Brommel knew what must be done.

They traveled for two days, and most of their journey was a silent one. Arik had proven to be a burdensome pest, a child who would have done Emir more good playing jacks in the Ministry lobby than accompanying Brommel on such a critical mission. Brommel felt that he had been hired as a babysitter rather than the job for which he was being paid. And for this he had left his precious Brielle alone to await the birth of their second child. The longer the journey went on, the more Brommel regretted having taken the assignment at all. If only he'd been man enough to tell Emir he could not, would not go, someone else would have certainly been sent in his place.

Arik passed his time swatting at the mosquitoes. Red welts, evidence of the insects' taste for royal blood, were hard to distinguish from Arik's blemishes, making the boy all the more unattractive. From time to time Arik tried to draw Brommel into conversations only to be answered with stubborn silence. Eventually Arik gave up.

Traveling through the forest was pleasant for the most part, though Brommel had seen nothing that could even remotely be identified as a stone cross. All he had seen were miles and miles of trees. Brommel had half a mind to lead Arik off the road deep into the woods and leave him there to find his way home alone. He was imagining the scenario once again when the forest suddenly came to an end, and Brommel's horse stepped out into direct sunlight.

Brommel tugged gently at the reins and shielded his eyes, allowing them to adjust to the brightness. They had come upon a small pasture surrounded on all sides by trees. The road on which they had been traveling continued on the opposite side. There was a second road as well, extending to the south and north of the clearing. Nearby, where the forest and the clearing met, was a house made of rough-hewn logs. The structure appeared sturdy enough, its roof made of a thick bed of pine needles, and the door a panel of flat boards bound together by rope.

Brommel was staring at the odd little house with something akin to wonder when Arik paused beside him.

"A crossroads," remarked Arik. "Let's continue on then."

Brommel did not respond. He was instead considering the pasture more closely. The grass was short and even, cut to that height by someone who took great pains to care for it. Embedded in the ground were dozens of flat stone markers of varying sizes and shapes spaced at regular intervals.

"It's a graveyard," said Brommel. He had seen ones like this before in some of the inland communities. While the custom was not common in the cities of Hestoria where the poor were cremated or buried in mass graves, and the rich were laid to rest in coffers of stone, there was a growing trend among some to bury individuals in the earth and mark their graves with stone.

Arik grunted in disgust and urged his horse forward, tromping across the field and graves as though they were of no consequence. But Brommel remained where he was, his eyes fixed on the pattern of stones in front of him. He did not see it at first, but then the image revealed itself to him— among the stones were twenty or so that were not gray like the others, but black. Whether they were painted black or occurred that way naturally he was not sure, but what he was certain of was that these black stones were intentionally arranged in the shape of a cross.

As Arik's horse neared the opposite side of the pasture, the door to the house swung open and a woman stepped out holding a bow with an arrow pulled taut, ready to fire directly at Arik's chest.

"Get off this land," she said in a voice as steady as her aim.

Arik halted and frowned at the woman. She was thick around the middle and getting on in years, but from her solid stance and resolute glare, it was clear she knew how to handle a weapon. Arik showed no fear, however, possibly the boy's one redeeming quality, thought Brommel.

"Lower your weapon, woman," said Arik, "or I shall march my horse back across this meadow again."

"Then I will kill you and your horse."

"And create unnecessary work for yourself in digging another grave for me? I really doubt it."

The woman's aim remained fixed on Arik. "No, sir, I would instead erect your carcass on a pole as a warning to other trespassers, and let the sun and scavengers devour your remains."

This left Arik too astonished to comply with her request. He remained immobile as if held to the spot by an unseen fetter. The woman pulled the bowstring tighter. Fearing she would let the arrow fly, Brommel made his presence known by calling out to her.

"My lady," he said, dismounting his horse, "please accept my apology for the boy's ignorance. He is from the island and is unaccustomed to the ritual of earth burials."

Brommel led his horse along the edge of the field until he came to the house. The woman lowered the arrow. She was not old, nor was she young, but perhaps a few years older than Brommel. Although her face was plain and her body plump, she carried herself with dignity and confidence. This was not a woman to take lightly.

On seeing Brommel dismount, Arik did the same.

"I am sorry," he said with feigned sincerity. "I was merely trying to determine which road to follow."

The woman glared at Arik. There was no fooling her.

"We get merchants from time to time carrying their wares to the villages around here, and sometimes a wagon with someone to bury," she said. "But rarely do we see travelers such as yourselves. If you tell me where you're heading, I might tell you if you're going in the right direction."

From inside the house, a man's voice called out. "Who's out there with you, Abby?"

"No one in particular, Father," the woman answered back. "Just some strays tearing up the grass."

"We haven't had visitors for a while now," continued Abby's father. "Why don't you bring them in and invite them to supper?"

Abby rolled her eyes. "Well, you heard him," she said. "Hope you're hungry."

Arik and Brommel followed an obviously reluctant Abby into the house. It was surprisingly tidy, as though Abby and her father always expected visitors. The older man sat in a rocking chair in the corner of the room beside a table dressed with a linen cloth and polished silver. His eyes, white and cloudy, stared blankly forward. On a platter were slices of roasted potatoes and squash along with a large wedge of yellow cheese.

The man motioned for them to come closer. "Have you come from the east or west?" he asked.

Brommel answered, "From the capitol."

"Ah," said the man, "then you have been traveling for several days. You must be hungry. Please, help yourselves."

Arik reached for a slice of potato and popped it into his mouth.

"You've met my daughter, Abby," the man continued. "I am Leo, the caretaker here. I couldn't help but overhear that you are not certain of your destination. Is there any way I could be of service to you?"

Leo extended his right hand toward Brommel. Brommel glanced toward Arik who, thankfully, was immersed in his second piece of potato. He had purposely chosen to withhold the details of Timbrey's interrogation from Arik since he was certain the boy could not be trusted. The objective was to find the Guilde and Jayson, win their trust, and obtain the crystal. Brommel very much doubted Arik's ability to manage that without him, and it seemed that Emir felt similarly. The Minister had discreetly placed the responsibility of this assignment squarely on Brommel's shoulders, and he would not take even the slightest risk of failure by entrusting anything of much importance to Arik.

Brommel clasped Leo's wrist with his thumb and little finger and extended the remaining three fingers. Leo's forehead wrinkled in thought. At first, Brommel feared that

Timbrey had led him astray after all, that Leo did not recognize the token. But then Leo nodded and released Brommel's arm.

"Your destination lays to the north half a day's ride from here in the village of Alay-Crevar. Continue on the road to where it turns south, then go the opposite direction through the trees. The village lies just beyond. If you leave now, you should arrive by nightfall."

Brommel thanked Leo and his daughter for their hospitality. Arik accepted a final slice of cheese. As they turned to leave, Leo added one final word.

"When you arrive," he said, "you must greet them the same way you greeted me. No variations. Is that clear?"

"Yes," said Brommel. "Thank you again."

Once Brommel and Arik were outside, they mounted their horses and continued down the road.

"What was that all about," asked Arik, "greetings and destinations and such? Did any of that make sense to you?"

Brommel urged his horse to go a little faster. The sun, it seemed to him, was apt to race him to the finish line.

"Made no sense to me," he said to Arik. "None at all."

17

The afternoon was unusually warm. The moisture from the rich, damp soil collected on Jayson's skin, and the earthy scent of wild mushrooms and tree moss wafted in the air intermittently with the sweet fragrance of jasmine and honeysuckle. The smells were a balm to his heightened senses, which had been overwhelmed the past few months with the smells of the sea. He had had enough of the sea and was glad to be in the forest, his native habitat.

His earliest memories were in a forest much like this one, with tall, thin trees that reached far into the sky. Climbing them was one of his favorite pastimes as a child. Due to his human musculature, he had the physical strength that most of the other pureblood Agoran boys lacked. They were agile and fast, but he was strong. He recalled numerous contests between him and the other boys, most of which he easily won. After a time, however, the contests ended. The other boys eventually lost interest. What fun was there in challenging him when they knew they would lose? So they turned to ridiculing him instead.

It was about that time when Lord Fredric signed the first decree against the Agorans, confiscating their land for human use. The Agorans were reestablished in a vast marshland near the Northern coast of Imaness, a land infested with mosquitoes. Once they had lived among the trees. Now the Agorans lived in the mud and had only small grass huts for shelter.

Food and clean water were scarce while disease was abundant. Jayson's mother took sick and died when he was just eleven years old.

Jayson crouched beside a fallen tree. He ran his fingers over the rotted trunk, its wood breaking off in thin, soft pieces. It had been ravaged by some parasite, a victim of nature. He waited patiently, sniffing the air. Finally, a faint yet unmistakable scent reached him. It was what he had come here to find. Today, thought Jayson, I will be the ravager.

He sniffed the air again and found the scent had come from the north. It could not be far. Jayson rose from his crouching position, but remained hunched over, using the scattered berry bushes and tree trunks for cover. He must stay downwind from it or the element of surprise was lost.

Extending his claws, he started forward, the thrill of the chase already stirring in his blood. He sprinted through the trees with the agility and speed of a leopard, but when the scent of his prey was at its strongest, he slowed his pace. Creeping now through the underbrush, his step light and noiseless, Jayson spotted the deer drinking from a stream. He paused a moment to marvel at the regal manner in which it stood, its sleek, muscular body so much like his own. From the ease of its stance, Jayson knew it sensed no danger. He had tracked it well, but the chase was still ahead. In another moment, Jayson would emerge from his hiding place at top speed. He might get lucky and capture the deer right there at the river's edge, in which case the kill would come easy. But more likely than not, the deer would startle and dart into the safety of the forest. Jayson would pursue it for several minutes before overpowering it and taking it down with his powerful claws. The kill would not be clean then, but it would be satisfying.

Jayson smelled the scent of the beast. It made his mouth water. He smelled something else, too, though what it was did not concern Jayson at this moment. He put it out of his mind and readied himself for the race.

Suddenly, the deer's head shot up, its ears pricked. It wasn't Jayson who had disturbed its peace, but the sound of rustling in the bushes farther upstream. Jayson heard it, too, and it distracted him momentarily. The deer sprinted off through the trees.

Cursing under his breath, Jayson did not follow. To do so would be futile since the beast had several seconds' lead on him. Instead, he turned his attention to the interference. The currents of air shifted course, and the scent that had caught his attention moments earlier was now downwind from him. He would have to go in blind, so to speak. And since the creature, whatever it was, was downwind from him, then it most certainly had already picked up Jayson's scent.

Jayson chose a rapid assault to take the creature by surprise, to prevent it from bolting the way the deer had. Powerful leg muscles pumping, reaching top speed in seconds, Jayson leapt forward, hurtled the stream, and dove into the bush.

A shrill scream shattered the stillness of the forest and nearly burst Jayson's sensitive eardrums. He had landed directly on top of his quarry. Although he could feel it beneath him, he saw nothing. Jayson was so stunned that he staggered back, stumbled, and fell backward into the stream.

The screaming continued.

"Dianis!" shouted Jayson angrily. "Might as well stop screaming. I'm the only one who can hear you."

The shrubs parted and Dianis's pale, frightened face slowly took form. Peering out, she glanced anxiously up river and down.

"It's just me," said Jayson. He sat in the stream letting the cool water flow over his legs.

Dianis emerged from her hiding place, her body now fully visible. Jayson got up, and slogged through the shallow water to the bank where he pulled off his tunic and twisted the water out of it.

"You tried to kill me!" accused Dianis.

"I thought you were lunch."

"Me? Your lunch?!"

"I was hunting, Dianis. You scared off the deer I'd been tracking. I thought you were a boar."

"A boar!" Dianis was indignant.

"Or a rabbit, a fox… What does it matter?"

"That you wanted to eat me matters!"

"I wouldn't have eaten *you*," said Jayson. He was growing more irritable by the moment. "Kill you yes, but," he added, giving her a deliberate once over, "there's not enough of you for a decent meal."

Dianis turned her back to him, obviously perturbed.

"An appetizer, maybe," he continued.

Dianis bent over the stream and, using both hands, flung water into his face. Jayson sputtered. The water was cold.

"I'm already wet, remember? And what were you doing spying on me?"

"I wasn't spying! I was…I was looking for you."

"You were looking for me—in the bushes—while invisible."

Fuming, Dianis held out her hand. Clasped in it was his leather pouch. "My father insisted I return this—immediately."

Jayson took the pouch. He opened it just to make sure the crystal was still inside. "So, waiting five days is immediately?"

"I've been busy."

"That's right. I haven't seen much of you lately. I thought you were avoiding me."

"I was, sort of," Dianis admitted with a haughty flair. "Actually, father sent me to one of the neighboring villages to arrange accommodations."

"Planning to move soon?"

"Not at the moment, but we must always be prepared. Emir's scouts are on the hunt. He would do anything to see the Guilde eliminated once and for all."

"Speaking of the hunt, Dianis," said Jayson abruptly, "might I remind you that you interrupted mine? I would like to get back to it."

Incensed and offended, Dianis turned heel and tromped back through the brush toward Alay-Crevar. Jayson watched her go, the trembling tops of the forest flora marking her path. Despite her talent at disappearing, she was far from discreet. But then again, she had managed to elude his senses before. He laughed to himself imagining her crouching in the bushes watching him. He had embarrassed her, that was clear, and now she was angry—again. He should go after her, try to make amends for Gerard's sake, but the day was quickly coming to an end and he had not yet accomplished what he had come into the forest to do.

His hunger was growing. The animals would be resting, cooling themselves beneath shade trees or at the water's edge. There would be no more tracking, no race through the trees. He would subdue his prey quickly and with precision. For the moment, his interest in the sport of it had waned. He wanted to eat.

He turned his face into the warm breeze, letting it stroke his skin like a woman's sensitive touch. He closed his eyes and let his imagination roam. Ivanore's fingers had tousled his hair with just as gentle a touch. Lying on the ground, his head cradled in her lap, she had explored every inch of his face and head, rubbing his temples in slow, rhythmic circles. He might have fallen asleep there if he had not been so completely seduced by her. Finally, unable to restrain himself any longer, he took hold of her shoulders and pulled her toward him, their lips touching.

A sickening scream erupted from the forest once again, and once again Jayson's thoughts were interrupted.

"What now?" he grumbled, knowing already that his prey, most likely startled at the sudden clamor, had taken flight. No sense in pursuing it now. The source of the scream was some distance off, in the direction of the village. He listened, waiting for it to sound again so he could be certain. Only a moment later, Dianis's shrill cry sent him racing through the forest. His heart pounded and he could hear the rush of blood as loud as her wails in his ears. It was fear that pushed him to run faster than he had ever run before, for he knew that cry. He had heard it many times from the animals he hunted. It was the cry of the wounded and dying. Somewhere ahead of him, Dianis was hurt.

18

Jayson burst through a thick wall of trees into a small grove of saplings. The sunlight filtering through the young, sparsely leafed branches was warm and inviting. He saw Dianis at once lying on her side, her back to him. The screaming had stopped minutes earlier, pushing Jayson faster toward his destination. Her body was still and Jayson spotted a thick trail of blood from the edge of the grove to where she lay. It looked as though she had been injured in the forest, ran here, and collapsed.

Jayson dropped to his knees beside her and touched her cheek. She was warm and breathing—but pale. On her right thigh, just below the hip, blood oozed from a wide, red gash. Jayson examined it and found the cut to be straight and clean, the work of a blade. Someone had deliberately attacked her. Quickly he pulled off his tunic and tied it around the wound to stop the bleeding.

As he knelt there in the dirt, he noted the smells surrounding him: Dianis and her blood, the moist earth covered with decaying leaves, various late-blooming flowers, and one scent in particular that stood out from the rest. The familiarity of it made every inch of Jayson's body bristle with rage.

Jayson sprung from his knees and dove headlong into the forest. Trunks of trees were a blur to him as he raced past, his body hunched forward like a predator on the chase. It took only seconds to overtake his prey. He leapt forward, his claws extended, his sharp canine teeth bared.

The boy barely had time enough to draw his sword, already stained with Dianis's blood. Jayson bit into his arm, and the sword clattered to the ground. The boy shrieked in agony, but Jayson did not care. With his claws, he sliced across the boy's chest, leaving a swath of gaping wounds across it. Jayson was all animal now, grunting and growling in his rage. He had only one desire—to kill. He opened his jaws, the taste of human flesh already in his mouth, and aimed for the throat.

"Stop!" someone shouted.

A man appeared, much bigger than the boy in Jayson's grasp, his sword now poised just above Jayson's neck. Jayson considered finishing off his prey despite the risk to his own life, but should *he* be killed, then Dianis would also die, left alone to bleed to death in the forest.

Jayson released his grip and let the injured boy fall to the ground at his feet, where he lay whimpering and writhing in pain.

The man with the sword motioned for Jayson to step away, which he did.

"You would have killed him," said the man.

"You should not have interfered," Jayson growled.

"Don't you recognize him?"

Jayson's piercing gaze never left the eyes of the sword wielder. He noted the absence of anger in them. This man did not care that his companion was injured.

"Yes," spat Jayson. "We were brothers—once."

By now, Arik had managed to stand. He stumbled toward them, clutching his wounded arm to his bleeding chest. "Jayson!" he cried. "What were you trying to do? Kill me?"

Jayson's eyes remained fixed on the one with the sword. He had no wish to speak to Arik.

The man lowered his weapon and replaced it in its scabbard. Then he gave a cursory inspection of his companion's wounds. "He needs attention," he told Jayson. "Is there a village nearby?"

"He attacked a girl," replied Jayson with a snarl.

Arik cowered. "It was an accident! I heard something in the bushes and thought it was a wild animal. She ran off before we could help her."

Jayson's hands snapped up, a set of claws aimed at each of his unwelcome visitors. "Who are you?"

"My name is Brommel. I am—"

Arik interrupted. "He's my servant. My bodyguard."

Jayson considered the claim. "Bodyguard? Then it seems he has failed in his duties, hasn't he?"

Brommel was large, his dark complexion menacing. Jayson had a hard time believing he was incapable of protecting the boy. Could he have delayed his intervention on purpose? Jayson turned his attention back to Arik, who was trembling now from pain.

"Why are you here?" he asked.

"Searching for you, of course," Arik answered weakly. "I've been searching for you ever since that day you leapt out my window. You're a hard man to follow, you know."

"You still can't have it. I won't give it to you. Not to anyone."

Brommel stepped forward then, ignoring the razor sharp claws at his throat, and placed a hand on Jayson's shoulder.

Jayson flinched, but the touch was surprisingly gentle, and he sensed compassion in it, like the touch of a father. Reluctantly, Jayson retracted his claws and turned his attention back to Dianis, still lying unconscious on the ground.

"Arik needs help," said Brommel. "You've wounded him."

"I meant to kill him."

"But you didn't kill him."

"You've got horses," said Jayson. He could smell the stench of the sweaty animals likely tethered to a nearby tree. "Take him back to the city."

"We've been traveling for days," replied Brommel. "By the time we returned, his wounds will have festered. He could die."

Brommel was right. Arik's wounds were deep and needed immediate attention. Jayson thought of Dianis. If she were conscious, she would likely tell him that he could not bring strangers to Alay-Crevar, to the hive of the Guilde. But he had to consider her needs first, and what she needed was a doctor.

Arik spoke. "Jayson, I came to apologize. You are all the family I have left in this world. I was rash, blinded with greed. Please forgive me, my friend. I didn't come all this way to remain your enemy."

In the time they had stood there among the trees, the shadows had lengthened. The sun had begun its descent and soon daylight would be ebbing. Alone, on foot, it would take an hour to reach the village, maybe two carrying Dianis. Jayson had to hurry.

"Fetch your horses," he said as he lifted Dianis into his arms. "You can follow me if you wish. As for forgiving you," he added, turning a menacing gaze on Arik, "that will depend on whether or not the girl lives."

19

Night had fallen by the time Jayson reached Alay-Crevar, but its narrow streets were well-lit by torches perched on tall, straight poles. A young boy carrying a bucket of water home from the communal well spotted him emerging from the forest, leading a dappled gray horse by its reins. Sitting on the horse, her body slumped forward and secured in place with several strips of torn fabric, was Dianis. The boy, recognizing them both, sped off down the street, calling at the top of his lungs.

"Gerard! Gerard, they're back!" he shouted.

Jayson led his horse to the washing trench where the village women gathered each day to clean their clothes and socialize. While the horse drank its fill, Brommel's horse ambled up beside it.

"Is he still conscious?" asked Jayson, stroking the horse's neck.

Brommel glanced at Arik's limp frame draped over the second horse's back.

"No. Is the physician near?"

Jayson ignored the question. "Secure the horses here," he instructed.

Jayson untied Dianis and let her slip gently into his arms. Brommel was not so gentle with Arik, whom he slumped over his shoulder like a prized boar. Together they headed toward the tavern at the end of the lane.

As they neared, they heard a commotion inside, and a group of a dozen or so men swarmed through the door. Some grasped lanterns in their hands, others their half-empty tankards of ale. Gerard, pushing through the crowd, hurried toward Jayson. He spoke nothing as he quickly examined his daughter, though the expression on his face revealed his concern.

"It's her leg," said Jayson. "This one," he added, indicating Arik, "mistook her for a wild animal."

Gerard examined Arik as well, and then gave Jayson a chastising glance.

"Take them upstairs while I fetch the doctor," he said. "I only hope he's sober enough to stitch them up properly."

While Gerard sent his guests home for the night, Jayson and Brommel carried their charges up a short flight of stairs to the second floor. Jayson entered the first room and laid Dianis on the bed. "Put Arik in the next room," he told Brommel.

Brommel, with Arik still slung over his shoulder, stepped to the next door and shoved it open with his foot. He let Arik's limp body flop across the bed with his legs hanging over the edge. Arik moaned.

"I get the distinct impression you don't like him much," said Jayson from the doorway. Draped over his arm was a folded blanket. He tossed it to Brommel, who covered Arik with it.

"How's the girl?" Brommel asked.

"We'll know soon," answered Jayson. "The doctor's with her now."

Just then Gerard came in. "So, that is my daughter's attacker?" asked Gerard, nodding toward Arik. "He's just a boy."

"A stupid boy," said Jayson.

"And who is this?"

"My name is Brommel," answered Brommel.

"He's the boy's servant," said Jayson.

"Well, Brommel, as long as your master is our guest, I suppose you are as well. This is my room, but you and Arik may use it as long as needed."

Gerard extended his hand to Brommel who took it, wrapping his thumb and little finger around Gerard's wrist, his three remaining fingers extended. Gerard and Brommel considered each other for a moment before releasing their grasp. Jayson noticed the odd handshake and the subtle change in Gerard's expression, but decided to say nothing.

A few minutes later, the village doctor came in to examine Arik. He was a short man with a thin mantle of white hair framing his dark, heavily lined face.

"How is he?" asked Gerard.

"In good condition, actually," replied the doctor. "The mark on the arm is superficial. The chest wounds are a bit deeper, but they'll heal in a few days."

"And Dianis?"

"She lost a lot of blood. It took quite a few stitches to close the wound, but if infection doesn't set in, she will heal in time. I'll be back in the morning. In the meantime, if either has any trouble, Gerard, don't hesitate to call for me."

The doctor excused himself, and Gerard followed him out into the hall. Brommel found a chair in the corner of the room and sat down in it, propping his feet up on a nearby table.

"Wake me when the doctor returns," he told Jayson with a yawn, then closed his eyes to go to sleep.

Jayson left Brommel and Arik, closed their door behind him, and returned to Dianis's room. He closed that door as well. He wanted to be certain he would not be eavesdropped upon.

Gerard stood over his daughter and smoothed out the blanket that covered her. Then he tenderly stroked her hair and face. Jayson located a chair and placed it beside him. Gerard thanked him and sat down while Jayson pulled up a second chair.

"She'll be fine," said Jayson, though his voice lacked the confidence he tried to convey. He looked at Dianis. The paleness in her face troubled him.

"Gerard," he said, wanting a distraction from his concern, "I couldn't help but notice the way Brommel clasped your arm. I've never seen a greeting like that before, but you seemed to recognize it."

"Aye," Gerard replied with as sigh. "It's a token known only to members of the Guilde. I ought not to tell you such things. Dianis would have my hide for it." He glanced up with a weary look. "But I think there are some things you need to know, my boy."

"The token Brommel gave you," continued Jayson, "is he a guardian then?"

"No. No, I am certain he is not, though he wants me to believe he is."

"But if the token is secret, how would he know it?"

"Most likely through bribery or threats. But no guardian ever reveals the true token. You see, when two guardians greet each other they grasp wrists in the manner you saw, and extend *two* fingers, not three. Whoever passed this token onto your friend in there was compelled by force to do so. So he gave it, though with one modification."

"What then, is the meaning of three fingers?" asked Jayson.

Dianis turned a little in her sleep. Gerard rearranged the blanket around her shoulders.

"To extend three fingers is a warning," he continued, his voice low. "It means this man is not to be trusted."

20

"It's a beautiful day. Why don't you set out on the porch a while?"

Mikel's suggestion lifted Ivanore's spirits, which had begun to sag a bit. Though she was grateful for his and Teak's care over the past week since they'd taken her in, she couldn't help but feel restless. She had come to Hestoria for a purpose, had left behind everything she held dear. The details of her escape played over and over in her mind. If only she had fled Imaness sooner, she thought, the soldiers may not have found her at all. She wouldn't have been hurt, and she might have found Jayson by now.

Mikel cleared away the breakfast dishes from the table after first making sure Ivy and Teak had had their fill of fried eggs and sausages. He then announced that he had to tend to some business in town and would be gone until that afternoon. "I expect the dishes to be clean and the animals fed by my return. And keep an eye on Ivy," Mikel added, giving his charges a quick wink. "Make sure she gets plenty of rest."

After Mikel had gone, Teak rinsed off the dirty dishes in a tub of water and dried them with a towel. Ivy watched from the table, wishing she had the strength to help. But it was all she could do to get herself out of the bed and make it to the table, and even then she could only manage with help. Her shoulder was still in a great deal of pain, but if she kept her arm folded across her stomach it was at least bearable.

"Breakfast was delicious," she said. "That's the first solid meal I've had in days."

"Are you still hungry? I c-can throw another egg in the p-pan."

"No, thank you. But I think I will sit outside for bit. I could use a little sunshine."

Ivy pushed her chair back from the table and tried to stand, but her knees went weak and her body trembled from the effort. Teak was beside her in a moment. He put his arms around Ivy and urged her to lean against him.

"Thank you," she said as they made their way through the door to the porch where Teak gently deposited her onto a wooden bench.

Teak disappeared into the house and returned moments later with two blankets. One he wrapped around Ivy's shoulders, and the other he lay over her lap. "You're getting your c-color b-back," he said. "That's a good sign."

Ivy felt the warmth of her own body collecting beneath the blanket. The trembling finally subsided. "I'm sorry I'm such a burden," she began.

"You're no b-burden," answered Teak. "W-we w-weren't sure you'd survive that first n-night, but the gods were looking after you."

"Yes, I suppose they were, though I think I ought to give credit where it's due."

"Oh," Teak said, lowering his head, embarrassed. "No decent person w-would do any different. W-we're just happy to see you on your feet."

A hawk circled overhead, screeching at some unseen prey below. Teak and Ivy watched it dive toward the ground then swoop back to the air, its talons empty. Ivy shifted her gaze to Teak and patted the empty space beside her on the bench.

Teak sat down and tucked the blanket snuggly around his patient. "It w-was strange, how you showed up in those fields, like you just fell from the sky."

"In a way, that's what happened," answered Ivy. "I did come from the sky, from somewhere far away. And as soon as I'm able, I'll leave again."

"Uncle says it'll be w-weeks before you're strong enough."

"I don't have weeks," said Ivy. "I've already wasted too much time as it is."

Ivy felt a familiar burning behind her eyes. She turned her face away to hide the tears. After everything she had endured, everything she had sacrificed, she could not give up now. There was no telling how much time she had left. Months, days, hours. She could never be sure. All she knew was that the longer she waited, the more likely it was that she would be too late.

She felt the gentle touch of Teak's hand on her arm. It felt good to have someone near, someone who cared about her. Ivy turned toward him. Her tears fell freely now, cascading down both cheeks. Her voice choked with sobs, she tried to apologize, but then she buried her face against Teak's chest and cried.

Teak reached up and stroked Ivy's hair. "You're safe here," he told her. "You're safe and n-no one will hurt you again. I w-won't let them."

Ivy's sobs soon faded and the tears stopped falling, but she remained nestled against Teak, feeling safe and secure for the first time in many months. But deep down she knew that this refuge was only temporary, and that soon she and those closest to her would be in more danger than she would have ever anticipated.

21

Jayson spent the next four days at Dianis's bedside. He took his meals there, slept in his chair there, and left only for brief intervals when needed. Gerard spent much of his time with his daughter as well, but with the Guilde's duties pressing on him, he soon left the bulk of her care to Jayson. Brommel couldn't help but admire such dedication in a man who had been scorned for his impure blood and treated no better than a dog on the streets. It took courage, he reasoned, to live as Jayson lived, courage sadly lacking in young Arik.

Brommel had taken the room adjacent to Arik's and made himself comfortable there. On the second day after their arrival, Arik was already awake, eating well, and making continual demands of him. Though Brommel spent a dutiful amount of time watching over his charge, he did manage to slip away from time to time to roam through the streets of Alay-Crevar.

It was a quaint little village, one that had managed to elude the march of progress so prevalent in the coastal cities. He knew there were dozens, perhaps hundreds of towns just like this one scattered all over the countryside, each one isolated and distinct from the next. These towns were usually self-sufficient, dependent on their own small farms and herds for sustenance. Their need of commerce was minimal, generally limited to regular shipments of liquor and those commodities only available via industrial production, things like cookware, farm tools, and cloth. Otherwise, the people who lived here were content to remain secluded in their way of life.

As Brommel strolled past a cluster of cottages one morning, he was struck by the scene before him. A woman, past her prime and grown round with age and motherhood, pinned a pair of boy's trousers to a rope extending from the side of her home to the branch of a tree. Several other items already hung there, flapping in the breeze, and several more lay in a basket at the woman's feet. Nearby, half a dozen children of varying ages shouted and chased each other in play. One little boy paused behind the tree and squatted down as if to hide, but his giggles gave him away. A small girl, Brommel guessed she could not be more than two, toddled up to her brother. She squealed as the boy wrapped his arms around her and swung her around and around. Then, having set her on her feet again, the two ran off hand in hand to join their older siblings in their game.

He glanced back at the woman who was now pinning up a girl's apron. Her face was red and damp with the exertion, but she was smiling. More than that, her eyes watched her children intently, and from her occasional bursts of laughter, he knew she was happy.

Brommel thought of his own cottage back in Partha, a village not much different from Alay-Crevar. He had watched Brielle hang laundry many times, had seen her carry water from the well, sweep the cottage, and perform many other mundane and even arduous tasks. He had even assisted her with them. But had he ever seen that sort of happiness in her face? Brommel let his memory wander through the images strewn through his mind.

Yes, he realized. Yes, he had seen that same smile on her face, but the smile was not always for him. It was for Rylan, their son. And he recalled, with delight, the pleasure that seemed to emanate from her entire being on discovering her current pregnancy. It was a pleasure, a joy, far deeper than Brommel would ever know. Than perhaps any man could know. It was a joy only a mother could know.

Brommel felt a wave of homesickness and the image of the woman and her children grew blurred from the tears welling in his eyes. He quickly pinched them away, then turned back toward the tavern. He had a job to do and the sooner he got it done, the sooner he could go home.

The main room was empty when Brommel arrived. Being late in the morning, Gerard would be out conversing with the other men in the village while they farmed their land or tended their flocks. He still had not figured out just what sort of livelihood was Gerard's. He seemed not to have any job in particular, and yet the townsfolk seemed exceptionally fond of him. Brommel imagined Gerard must have some connection to the Guilde, but as yet neither Gerard nor Jayson nor anyone else had offered so much as a clue about it. It was a curious situation to say the least.

The vacant room felt cold, its thick stone walls shielding it from the sun's warmth outside. Gerard wouldn't light the fire until just before supper.

Brommel headed toward the staircase. Arik was likely up by now waiting for someone to tend to him. They had come here to reestablish Arik's friendship with Jayson, but so far Jayson had managed to avoid Arik completely. It was easy to do since Arik seemed intent on milking his injuries for as long as possible.

A cough from the darkest corner of the room attracted Brommel's attention. He strode across the floor to the spot where Jayson sat at a table, an empty liquor bottle in his hand.

"Boggle," said Jayson in a warbled greeting. "Looking for supper? You're early then. Or if you're looking for breakfast," he continued, indicating the empty room, "you're very, very late."

Brommel did not move, but glared in disgust at the intoxicated half-breed. He thought of the crystal. Surely the Agoran must carry it with him. He probably had it with him at this very moment. Arik had proven ineffective in getting it. He might succeed yet, but it would take days, weeks to win back Jayson's trust let alone to obtain the crystal, and time was not something Brommel wanted to waste.

He glanced over his shoulder to make certain they were alone. His sword, he remembered, was up in his room. He did not carry it with him in the town so as not to arouse suspicion, but he did carry a small dagger concealed in his waistband. He discreetly touched it now with his hand, reassuring himself that it would be there when ready.

Using his bare foot, Jayson shoved a chair in Brommel's direction. "Join me if you like. But if you're looking for a drink, I'm afraid I'm all out."

Brommel hesitated a moment, then sat down. He must be certain Jayson had the crystal before he killed him, or at least learn its location. He would have to be prudent.

"How is the girl?" Brommel asked.

"Alive," replied Jayson, "but I can't say she's well. The fever won't break, though the doctor insists it will in time."

"He seems to know what he's doing."

"But what if he's wrong? What if…"

Jayson's voice trailed off. He raised the empty bottle to his lips and tipped it way back. Then finding it dry, he threw it across the room where it shattered against the far wall.

"I'm sorry," said Brommel. The words seemed hollow, however, and he knew they didn't fool the Agoran. He tried to find something more meaningful to say. "It's clear you care for the girl."

"Dianis?" answered Jayson. "I can't stand her. She's obnoxious and arrogant."

"But, I thought—"

"She's a child, and she could die. And Gerard is my friend. No father should lose a child."

The two of them sat there without speaking for several minutes. Suddenly, without any warning, Jayson let out a horrific, animal-like howl. He clenched his hands into fists and hit the table with them with such force that the table threatened to break beneath them. But then Jayson went silent again and buried his face in his arms.

"This is not about Gerard or Dianis, is it?" said Brommel. "Arik told me about your wife, his sister. He told me how their father separated you. You must miss her."

Jayson raised his eyes to Brommel's. His gaze was severe.

"Miss her? I ache for her. She's always there right in front of me, but when I reach for her, she's gone." Jayson grasped his own arms with his clawed fingers and left marks in his skin. "Do you have a wife?" he asked.

"I do," said Brommel.

"And you love her, like I love mine."

"Yes."

"Do you have children?"

The door to the cottage opened. A wave of warm air blew through the room. Brommel glanced over his shoulder and saw the doctor scurrying toward the stairs. A moment later, he had ascended them and vanished into Dianis's room. In his haste, the doctor had failed to notice their presence.

Brommel turned back to Jayson. "I have a son," he said.

"A son?" Jayson grinned and nodded his head. "I, too, have a son."

"Is that so? Arik didn't mention that."

"Why should he? What affection would Arik have for the heir to the throne of Imaness?"

"I thought Arik was the rightful heir."

"He would have been, I suppose," answered Jayson, "if my son were never born. My wife, you see, is Fredric's eldest child, but as a woman she cannot rule. The next in line would naturally be Arik, her younger brother, and so he was until I came along and spoiled it all. Once my son was born, Arik lost his place in line. Don't you see? But that really doesn't matter anyway. Fredric disowned him. He has lost his inheritance altogether."

"And what if Arik should return to Imaness?"

"Well, I can't let that happen, can I? If Arik is willing to depose his own father and betray me, his friend and brother, to what lengths would he go to lay claim to the throne?"

This was far more information than Brommel had expected or wanted to hear. Was Arik really capable of such cruelty, of killing his own nephew—a child—for the crown? He didn't know him well, but he had a hard time reconciling Arik to Jayson's description of him. Still, what did it matter to him what Arik did once he obtained the crystal? All Brommel wanted was to return home.

"You mentioned your wife," said Brommel. He heard the sound of a door upstairs open and close again. Then the sound of steps on the landing. The doctor was no doubt moving from one patient to the next. Brommel put the trivial disruption out of his mind. "When I left home," Brommel continued, conjuring up some lie that would help him achieve his aim, "my Brielle gave me one of her hair ribbons so that I would think of her often. It isn't much, but it means a great deal to me."

Jayson's eyes lost focus momentarily, as if they were seeing something or someone not immediately in front of him. His wife perhaps. His son. Then his focus returned. He reached into a leather sack tied at his waist and removed an object from it.

"My wife gave me something, too," he said. He laid his hand on the table and opened his fingers revealing a shard of pale green crystal.

There it was! The very object for which Brommel had come—only inches away! He could take it now. In a second or two, Jayson would be dead and the crystal would be in his possession.

Brommel slid his hand forward across the table. He did not reach for his dagger, nor did he take the crystal. Instead, he placed his hand on Jayson's shoulder and felt it trembling. He saw the tears glistening in Jayson's eyes a moment before he brushed them away. Then Jayson seemed to gather his senses. He returned the crystal to its pouch and stood up as if to leave.

The moment Brommel had been hoping for had passed.

Brommel remained in his seat. He would not watch Jayson walk away. It was his way of preserving the man's dignity. Somehow he knew that, if their roles were reversed, Jayson would do the same for him.

But Jayson made no move for the door. The muscles in his jaw clenched, and the claws of both sets of fingers slowly extended.

"Hello Arik," he said.

22

The pants and tunic Arik wore were a little too large for his adolescent frame, a gift from Gerard who claimed they would be more comfortable while his wounds healed. The linen bandage wrapped around his chest was visible through the open collar. If it weren't for the sword gripped tightly in Arik's hand, Brommel might have laughed at him.

"I thought you were resting," said Brommel, rising to his feet.

"I heard voices," replied Arik. "You were so intent on your conversation you didn't notice me. What were you talking about?"

There was something in the tone of Arik's voice that made Brommel feel uneasy. Neither he nor Jayson answered.

"I said what were you talking about?!" shouted Arik. He raised his sword and pointed it directly at Jayson's chest. Brommel stepped forward, positioning himself in front of Jayson.

"There is no need to be angry, Arik. Remember why you're here, to make amends."

But the rage in Arik's eyes told Brommel he was beyond appeasing.

"No," said Arik. "I've come for the crystal. I saw him with it just now, Brommel. You saw it. It is just the three of us down here now, and he's unarmed."

The boy was right. They could kill him now and depart immediately. And if they hurried, they could be home in a few days—home to Brielle and Rylan and the baby.

Brommel took his dagger from its sheath. He weighed it in his palm, just as he weighed the choices in his mind.

"Get out of the way, Brommel," said Arik.

Brommel did not move. Jayson, however, did. Stepping to the side so that Brommel no longer stood between them, Jayson faced Arik.

"You are more like your father than I ever realized," said Jayson. "Like him, you have no honor."

With a wicked screech, Arik lunged forward with his sword, but Jayson easily sidestepped the attack so that the blade bit nothing but air.

Jayson's pupils narrowed into dark slits, focusing on Arik. Brommel noticed that though Jayson was indeed unarmed, his claws were out, ready for the kill.

His pride injured, Arik waited not a second before his second attack. But as he thrust his sword, Brommel slashed his dagger across Arik's forearm. Arik screamed out as the sword clattered to the floor.

"What are you doing?" cried Arik, cradling his arm, the same one Jayson had bitten before. The new wound reopened the old. Blood oozed from it and dripped onto the floor.

"I've saved your life," Brommel answered. "Jayson would carve you to pieces!"

Arik glared at Brommel, his eyes wild with rage. "You're a traitor! You could have taken the crystal, but instead you attack me!"

Jayson bared his teeth, revealing a set of jagged canines. "You are the traitor, Arik," he said, with a forced calm. "You would betray me, your father, and everyone closest to you to obtain Dokur's throne. But you only betray yourself. Stop this madness before it's too late, Arik."

Arik seemed to consider Jayson's words, but only for a moment or two. Then, his decision all too evident in his eyes, Arik scooped up his sword and ran for the door. A second later, he was gone.

Brommel sheathed his dagger and turned to Jayson, whose bowed head and hunched shoulders revealed the depth of his disappointment. Brommel wanted to say something to him to console him, but no words seemed adequate.

The silence between them ended with the sound of a horse galloping past the tavern. They both ran out the door and saw the diminishing image of Arik on horseback. Brommel rushed forward to where the second horse lay dying on the ground. The earth beneath the beast was a pool of red mud. Brommel laid his hand on the creature's neck. The horse's breaths came in short gasps.

"Arik's gone to Nauvet-Carum to tell Emir of my betrayal," Brommel told Jayson, who had followed him outside. "He's taken the faster horse and left me with nothing."

"I'll find Gerard," Jayson said. "He'll get us more horses."

Jayson turned and ran. Brommel did not watch him go. He knew Jayson would keep his word and that they would be on their way as soon as possible. Still, he felt more helpless than he had ever felt before.

Beneath his hand, a tremor went through the horse's body. The animal took one last struggling breath, and then went still.

23

Night had fallen hours ago and only a slim wedge of moonlight illuminated the room in which Ivy slept. Tomorrow would be six days since she had arrived in Hestoria, six days wasted due to her carelessness. Her injury could have been avoided if she had only handled things a little differently, she told herself again. The events leading up to her escape played themselves over and over in her mind, but finally she resigned herself to the fact that she had no power to alter the past. She even began to doubt if she could affect the future.

The vision had first come to her many weeks earlier on a night much like this. The day itself had gone as usual. She had tended to her usual chores around Zyll's cottage, milked the goat, and gathered vegetables in the garden. She kept herself busy to keep distracted.

Nearly a year had passed since her father had exiled Jayson and Arik, since she'd stood on the cliffs overlooking the shore of Dokur to watch their ship vanish in the distance. Not long after, she had taken her infant son and gone in search of Zyll to await her husband's return. It was hard not to worry, not to count the days, the hours, the minutes. Despite reassurances from Zyll and her only friend, Arla, Ivy's hope was fading.

"I saw Jayson come home," she told Arla one day in the fields as they gathered lavender and mustard blossoms. "The night my father sent him away, I had a vision. He had returned to Imaness and was looking for me."

Arla had a child of her own, a little girl she carried in a cloth sling over her back. She spent much of her time with Ivanore, preferring her company to that of her husband who drank too much.

Arla gently cradled several swags of lavender in her hands as Ivy tied them with string. "When will he return?" she asked.

"I couldn't tell," answered Ivy. "The visions show me what is to come, but without both crystals, I have no way of knowing when."

They tied another bundle of the blossoms, and Ivy placed them in a cloth pouch she wore around her shoulder. "I only know he will come," she said, though her voice lacked conviction.

That night, Ivy awoke in a cold sweat. She sat up, her body trembling. She knew that something was different, something had happened. Though an ocean separated them, sometimes when she was completely still, she could feel Jayson as though he were lying beside her. Tonight, as she slept, her pulse raced. She was gripped with fear and confusion.

She checked the cradle to reassure herself, then hurried across the cottage floor to rouse Zyll. The older man did not wake easily, but when he did his eyes flew open, instantly alert.

"What is it?" he asked with sincere concern.

"I don't know." She felt flustered, uncertain. "It's Jayson. He's in danger."

Zyll patted Ivy's trembling hands. "My dear, do not be frightened. You said yourself that you've seen him returning."

"I did. But something is wrong. I feel it."

"But you haven't seen it."

"No."

"Have you tried?"

"It's difficult," said Ivy. "Lately, my visions of him have become unclear."

"You must try."

Zyll rose from his cot and went to the mantel from which he removed a copper bowl. He set the bowl on the table and filled it with water from a pitcher. Ivy stood beside him and both gazed onto the still, clear surface.

To divine the future was no simple task. It took great effort to maintain focus long enough to view a vision in its entirety. Using the crystals made it a little easier, but she had broken one of them into two pieces, one of which she had given to Jayson. Tonight she would have to attempt it with a single crystal, the very one she would later leave in Zyll's care when left Imaness.

The water in the bowl was still, its surface undisturbed. Ivy leaned forward until she could see her own reflection in it. This was how Zyll saw his visions, though his were of the past only. Ivy took several deep breaths trying to calm herself. It wouldn't do if she were anxious. She closed her eyes and let her breathing fall into a slower rhythm, and soon her heart met the pace. Only when she knew she was ready did she open her eyes. When she did, however, it was like coming suddenly upon a shocking scene. She jumped back with a gasp, her arms flailing out and knocking the bowl to the floor.

"No! No!" she cried out. She turned as if to run, her survival instinct setting every nerve on edge, but Zyll caught her, grasping her arms in his hands and holding her firmly in front of him.

"What did you see?" he asked.

She shook her head as if doing so would free her mind from the image burned into it. "I saw him," she said, fighting against her own words. "He was in pain! Horrible, agonizing pain!"

Ivy withered into Zyll's embrace and collapsed into tears.

Even now, lying awake in Mikel's house, she felt that same weight of despair. Not since that moment weeks earlier had she been able to chase the dreadful vision from her mind. It had driven her from Imaness, sacrificing everything she had ever known to come to Hestoria to find Jayson. And yet she had done nothing since arriving that she had originally planned. The vision remained the same. No change had been set into motion, and she feared that the longer she delayed the more certain the future would be.

Ivy sat up on the side of her cot. She listened for Mikel's soft snoring from the other room and the howl of an angry wind blowing outside. The pain in her shoulder was still present, though not as sharp as it had been when she had first awoke from her fever. Mikel said it would be weeks before she was fully healed, but Ivy could wait no longer. If she did, she risked losing Jayson forever.

Teak had placed Ivy's clean and folded clothing on a chair in the corner of the room. Ivy dressed in them now. Careful as she was, as she slipped her arm into the sleeve of her blouse, searing pain pulsed through her shoulder. Ignoring it as best as she could, she went to the kitchen next and tied some cheese and bread into a cloth. She would likely need money, but she would not steal from Mikel after he had been so generous to her. She would find some other way to provide for herself when the need arose.

She regretted not saying goodbye to Teak. Over the past few days, they had become good friends, and she did not doubt that she would miss him. She paused at the door a moment and looked about the room. She hoped they would understand.

Ivy opened the door and stepped out into the bitter cold. As she walked farther into the dark night, she did not look back.

24

The night air was far colder and darker than Ivy had anticipated, but that did not stop her from pressing onward. She would have gone even if she had to travel in the worst storm imaginable. Nothing could have prevented her. She was resolute.

Ivy had not had much opportunity to explore Mikel's farm. What she knew of it, she had seen from the porch or through a window and from her visions.

Ivy walked across the dry, bare fields. The earth was soft beneath her feet. Still, she felt every clod and stone through the soles of the deerskin slippers Mikel had given her. Ivy knew this land, though she had never stepped foot on it before. These fields were not the ones where Teak had found her, which lay on the west side of the house. The ones she now crossed lay to the east, bridging the seemingly endless space between the back of Mikel's barn and the forest. In the darkness, the line of distant trees appeared as a black horizon below the vast canvas of deep blue dotted with millions of glimmering jewels.

She continued heading for the trees, knowing that she would find what she needed just before reaching them. Sure enough, after she had walked for half an hour or so, the soft earth of the field came to an abrupt end and Ivy felt the hard, packed dirt of a well-traveled road. This road ran parallel to the forest and followed the edge of Mikel's field, curving out of sight ahead to the left. Ivy glanced over her shoulder across the barren field she had just crossed. If anyone had been awake in the house, if even a candle had been left burning, she might have seen and taken some comfort in it. But the only light was from the stars and shard of moonlight above.

The road, filled with ruts and stones, was uneven, and Ivy stumbled many times along the way. Six miles north of Mikel's farm was a village, a cluster of stone buildings nestled in a narrow valley. These buildings consisted of a grain mill, dairy house, metalsmith shop, a few dozen cottages, and a tavern. Ivy knew the layout of the village as if she had lived there for years. She knew the faces of those who lived there, though she did not know their names. She saw the whole village so clearly in her mind that when she finally reached the waist-high stone wall that surrounded the entire place, she had to stop and steady herself. A feeling of recognition seized her with such a force that it sent her heart pumping.

Most of the village was dark, as well it should be for in the wee hours of morning when she finally arrived. Light emanated from one building, however, its windows golden with candlelight from within. This was the tavern, she knew, and it was there she knew she had to go.

The lobby of the tavern was quite alive with a dozen or more men sitting at the bar downing tankards of ale. These were the local working class stopping by for a drink before starting their day, rugged men whose faces and hands were far older than their years. There was little noise in the place when Ivy entered. This was not the boisterous days' end gathering. No one had come to get drunk, only to dull the senses enough to manage a long day in the field or at the hammer. They were all quite sober and keenly aware of the woman's presence in this sacred place of theirs.

Several of the men glared at her, standing at the door like a lost lamb. Others ignored her, preferring instead to pay heed to the barkeeper filling their glasses. Only one looked on her with any serious interest.

Ivy was glad for the warmth radiating from a small cast-iron stove in the center of the room. It was a pleasant contrast from the bitter cold she had endured for the past few hours. Though her slippers had provided some protection from the sharp stones in the road, they had not shielded her from the cold.

The barkeeper peered at her and said, while wiping a glass with a rag, "Here now, miss, is there something you want?"

Ivy nodded, her mouth dry. The wind and the walk had taken the moisture right out of her. The barkeeper came round the end of the bar carrying the glass in one hand and a bottle of clear liquid in the other.

"You look worn out, miss," he said. "Want a drink?"

She accepted the glass and held it as he filled it. She had not realized until now, as she struggled to keep the glass steady, how weak she felt. She gripped the glass tighter, and a sharp pain crushed her shoulder. She didn't cry out. Instead, she swallowed the liquor down and returned the glass.

"Thank you," she said.

By now most of the men had lost interest in her and returned to their drinks. The barkeeper, however, took Ivy by

133

the elbow and led her to a chair near the stove. Then he pulled up a second chair and sat down on it.

"It's not common to see a woman in here," he said, filling Ivy's glass a second time. "You must have a good reason."

"I'm looking for someone. My husband."

The barkeeper looked over his shoulder at the men lined up along the bar. "I've known all these boys for more'n ten years, but some days we get travelers, though I doubt I could recall one from another."

"You'd remember him if you'd seen him," said Ivy. She finished her second glass and refused a third. "You see, he's only half-human."

"A half-breed?"

"An Agoran half-breed." She said the words loud enough for all to hear. As she expected, the men at the bar shuffled uneasily on their stools. Some swallowed their drinks with added fervor. One man spat on the floor.

The barkeeper's expression showed his contempt, though his treatment of Ivy did not change.

"No miss, there ain't been no Agorans in here. And I ain't seen none in town neither."

Ivy's head started to swim a little from the effects of the liquor. The pain in her shoulder had increased, and now her entire arm throbbed. She tried to stand, but fell back into her chair. The barkeeper grasped her elbow again to steady her.

Ivy laughed a little, though in truth she felt quite ill. She would ask to rent a room, but then she remembered that she had no money. She would have to either return to the farm or find somewhere else to rest.

"He will be coming here," she said earnestly.

"All right, miss," replied the barkeeper. "When, exactly, should I be expecting him?"

"I don't know. I don't know." It was all too much—the visions, the cold, the pain. If she could just lie down for a moment.

"If you wouldn't mind," she continued, "when you see my husband, please leave word with Mikel at the farm a few miles down the road."

"I know Mikel," replied the barkeeper. "Are you staying with him and the boy?"

Ivy heard the question, but could not answer. The room began to swirl as the pain in her shoulder grew unbearable. Ivy closed her eyes and felt as though she were falling into a deep crevice.

"Miss!"

The barkeeper caught Ivy as she fell forward out of her chair. He saw the crimson circle spreading across her back and called to other men in the room. "Help me get her to a room, and Dagen, go fetch the doctor! This girl's hurt!"

Dagen, a portly man with a thick mane of unkempt hair and a crooked nose from having been broken more than once, rose from his spot in the corner of the room. After taking a particularly attentive look at Ivy, he swept past her and hurried out the door. Outside, he mounted his horse and urged it to a gallop, but he did not stop at the doctor's cottage. Instead, he rode straight out of the village, heading east on the road toward Nauvet-Carum.

25

I t took less than an hour for Gerard to obtain two horses from a local farmer and to send Jayson and Brommel on their way, but Alay-Crevar was a small town, its residents impoverished. Those who had need used a smaller breed of oxen, which were affordable and strong, but slow moving. What horses they did have were used to pull wagons and not bred for speed. Such were the mounts Jayson and Brommel were given.

Even at their fastest pace, it took them two days to reach the forest's eastern border. Along the way they had stopped only for brief periods to water and rest the horses and to get a little sleep, though neither Jayson nor Brommel slept well. On the last night, overcome with exhaustion and having found shelter beside a fallen tree, both drifted off for several hours. Dark clouds had gathered overhead, threatening a storm, and the air was cold. Just before sunrise the first drops of rain awoke them.

"We should reach my village by tonight," said Brommel, stretching.

"Is there somewhere nearby where you'll be able to stay?" asked Jayson. "Somewhere safe?"

"I plan to leave Partha with my family right away. The darkness will shield our escape. We'll travel north and stay with Brielle's brother. We'll be safe there for now."

"You'll need fresh horses and a wagon for provisions."

"I own a wagon and a horse. As for provisions, Brielle always keeps the pantry well-stocked. We'll be ready to go in no time at all."

They ate a little bit of the stale bread Gerard had hastily packed for them. Brommel spoke again. "And you, Jayson? What will you do? Will you come with us north?"

Jayson considered Brommel's question. The invitation was sincere. Of that he was certain, but now that he understood the Guilde's purpose, he felt compelled to remain with them. Thinking of the Guilde reminded him that he carried the crystal with him even now. Gerard had warned him against taking it with him back to the city, but now that Brommel was an enemy of the Vatéz, Jayson could not in good conscience allow him to travel alone, nor could he leave the crystal behind. He vowed, instead, to protect the crystal at all costs and to do everything in his power to keep it and himself out of Emir's hands.

The task should be an easy one. He would accompany Brommel to his home in Partha, help him prepare for his departure, and see him off. Then Jayson would return to the Guilde at his first opportunity.

A few scattered drops of rain began to fall. In the distance, thunder sounded, or at least they thought it was thunder at first. But as the sound began to swell, the earth beneath their feet trembled.

"What is that?" asked Brommel. The horses were agitated. He went to them and stroked their manes in an effort to calm them. Jayson knelt down, pressing an ear to the ground. Then he stood up and listened. Taking the horses' reins, he led the animals behind a thick wall of bushes. Brommel followed.

The tremor grew stronger, the thunder louder. Brommel and Jayson peered through the brush toward the path they had been traveling. A few minutes passed before a contingent of two dozen mounted soldiers galloped past. Behind them marched a unit of at least fifty soldiers wearing the Ministry's royal blue insignia on their uniforms.

"Emir's soldiers," Brommel whispered to Jayson. "On their way to destroy the Guilde. There is no doubt now. Arik arrived well before us and revealed its location."

Jayson felt sickened at the thought of the slaughter that would ensue. The women and children. Dianis.

"I've got to go back and warn Gerard," he said, already mounting his horse.

"There is no need for that," Brommel told him. "The Guilde has likely already gone. These soldiers will find that they have abandoned the village and moved on. Trust me. The guardians are masters at eluding the Vatéz."

Jayson had not counted on the Guilde moving. If Emir's soldiers could not find them, how would he? Then he recalled that he had one thing Emir lacked—the token. Gerard had explained it to him. And yesterday, when he and Brommel passed by a cemetery at the heart of the forest, Brommel told him of Leo and his daughter, Abby, and how they had provided directions to the Guilde.

Brommel and Jayson waited until the soldiers had passed, and then waited a while longer to be certain no additional soldiers were to follow. Once the path was clear, Brommel and Jayson mounted their horses.

They reached the road to Nauvet-Carum by late afternoon. The horses were weary and hungry. Jayson, too, felt the burden of exhaustion weighing on him and imagined Brommel must feel the same. But their objective was now within reach. Soon they would be in Partha and Brommel would be reunited with his family.

The sun was just setting when Jayson and Brommel emerged from the overgrown path and started down the main road leading to Partha. The city was behind them now. Everything glistened with moisture, the tree leaves, the grass, the stones in the road. Soon they neared the outlying farms surrounding Partha. Jayson smelled the cows and sheep and freshly harvested alfalfa. But then another smell came to him, strong enough to overpower all the others. Smoke—or more specifically, the stench of it left behind after a fire.

At the same moment, Jayson and Brommel noticed the brown haze hovering in the air above Partha and urged their horses to a gallop. Brommel was the first to pass through the village gate, and Jayson followed close behind. The village seemed deserted, the doors and windows to every cottage closed tight. In one yard, a few stray chickens pecked at the ground. If it weren't for the occasional face peeking out from a shutter as they passed, Jayson would have believed Partha to be completely abandoned.

Brommel sped on now, pushing ahead of Jayson whose horse simply could not keep up. But not far from the house with the chickens, Brommel brought his horse to an abrupt halt and dismounted. Jayson watched as Brommel ran forward, shouting.

"Brielle! Rylan!"

Jayson's horse came to a stop beside Brommel's. That was the moment he first saw the ruins. Where once must have stood Brommel's cottage, now lay a pile of blackened stones and ashes.

"Brielle!" shouted Brommel as he darted into the charred wreckage that had been his home. "Brielle, where are you?"

Jayson remained fixed in his saddle, compelled to observe the scene that lay before him. The walls of the cottage remained partially erect, though most of the stones had been toppled. The roof was completely gone except for a single wooden beam that had remained intact. Black and disfigured, one end of the beam lay on the ground with the other end resting in the rubble. Among the stones, Jayson spotted the remains of various household items: a table and chairs, candlesticks, a bed, a baby's cradle.

Still calling for his wife, Brommel dug through the debris with his bare hands. He tossed aside small boulders and broken pieces of furniture. He was searching for something—or someone.

The rain fell steadily now, and Jayson sensed someone approaching. A child came to stand beside him. Then suddenly, the boy darted forward. Running as fast as his tiny legs could go, the boy cried out, "Papa! Papa!"

Brommel stood up, his clothes smeared with dust and ashes. On seeing the boy, Brommel threw open his arms, and the child leapt into Brommel's embrace. Father and son were reunited at last.

Jayson was so rapt in watching Brommel's reunion with his son that he failed to notice the woman until she was standing right beside him. At first he thought it must be Brielle, Brommel's wife. But then, as he looked at her more closely, he knew it couldn't be. This woman was old, at least twice Brommel's age. Her gray hair was fastened in a bun at the nape of her neck, and her shoulders were stooped with age. She wore a faded blue shawl over her shoulders, and her calloused feet were bare.

"What happened here?" Jayson asked the woman.

Her voice was hoarse. She could speak only just above a whisper. "Soldiers from the ministry came last night, just after supper. It took only minutes for the house to be consumed."

Brommel held tight to his son. They spoke to each other, though their words were so soft that Jayson could not make them out.

"They accused Brommel of treason," the woman said. "Brommel has served Emir faithfully for years. It doesn't make sense."

Jayson glanced down at the woman, her face marred by deep creases and folds. "The boy's mother, did she—?" His throat constricted. He couldn't bear to complete the question.

"She saved the boy," she said, her voice trembling, "but the baby girl did not survive. And Brielle—I started to treat her burns, but it did no good. It was the smoke. Poison in the lungs."

"Where is she now?"

The woman pointed a gnarled finger toward the cottage with the chickens in the yard.

Brielle had died, not in the fire, but from breathing the poisoned air. Did Brommel know this? Was that the message his son was telling him now?

Jayson looked back toward the destroyed cottage. Brommel and the little boy held each other, their bodies so tightly pressed together that it was hard to discern where one ended and the other began. Together, they wept, and as the last of the daylight ebbed away, their cries were lost in the sound of the rain.

❖ *Book Two* ❖
BETRAYAL

1

The upper corridors of the Ministry were dark and gloomy, and though Erland had walked them hundreds of times, he had never grown accustomed to the ever-shifting shadows cast by the few sconces studding the ancient walls. He tried to make his steps seem confident as he approached Minister Emir's door, knowing the man following behind was likely naïve of the true dangers that lurked here.

He rapped on the solid door. Emir would not be pleased at being disturbed so late at night, but it could not be avoided. He rapped again.

"What is it?" came the reply from within.

Erland hesitated only a moment before turning the handle and pushing open the door. The Minister's bedchamber was as colorless as the corridor, with a wide, black bed at its center and thick curtains drawn over the windows. A single candle burned at Emir's bedside, casting a meager glow across the room. Curled up on the floor at the foot of the bed lay Emir's dragon, Pip. On Erland's entry, the beast jerked awake and gave an irritated snort.

"Oh, it's you. What do you want?" snapped Emir, who was sitting up in his bed, a scowl on his face.

For seven years now Erland had served as Emir's personal aide, recruited from among the many young pages who ran errands for the members of the Assembly. He was just sixteen then, but bright and eager to learn. It was around that time when he had, in his haste to be a good servant, spilled a pan of searing hot cooking oil on himself in the kitchen. The accident left a scar smeared across his chin and down the front of his throat. He had feared that Emir would let him go after that, but instead the Minister paid for his treatments and later his education in the academy. Though Emir was never what Erland could call kind to him, the gratitude he felt for his master was inexpressible.

Erland stepped into the room. "I am sorry to disturb you, but there is someone to see you."

"In the middle of the night?"

"Actually, it is morning, Minister. Shall I pull back your drapes for you?"

Emir huffed, but did not answer.

"He's come from one of the outer villages," continued Erland. "He says it's urgent."

"Of course it's urgent!" barked the Minister. "Those peasants think everything is urgent. Tell him to come back this afternoon during my regular hours."

Erland glanced over his shoulder at the open door. The man stood there, anxiously twisting his wool cap in his hands. Though not very tall, he was thick enough to fill the doorway, and the scraggly scrap of a beard made him look rather pitiable.

"I tried that already, Minister," said Erland, "but he won't go. He said he's here for his reward."

"What reward?"

"For information on the Agoran."

Emir's cloudy blue eyes darted sporadically in their sockets. Their inability to remain stable always unnerved Erland, but it didn't lessen the weight of Emir's glare on him.

"Let him enter," said Emir at last.

Emir slipped from his bed and donned his official robes of the Ministry as the unkempt visitor sidled up beside Erland.

"Who are you?" asked Emir impatiently.

"The name's Dagen," replied the peasant, brushing his fingers quickly through his unruly hair as if doing so might make him appear more presentable. "I come from the village of Ardath, 'bout twenty miles west of here."

"And you've come about the reward?"

"Aye. My brother is in your employ, sir, and told me you was looking for an Agoran. I know you made the offer to your own men, but I thought maybe you'd honor it for me if I gave you what you wanted."

Lifting the candle at his bedside, Emir carried it to the window where another larger candle stood on the table. The wick hissed as he lit it, and the new light consumed the shadows.

"You know where the Agoran is?" asked Emir, returning the first candle to its place beside his bed. "You've seen him?"

"No, sir," answered Dagen.

"Then why do you trouble me with your presence? Don't you know I could have you executed for less?"

Dagen sent a nervous glance to Erland, but Erland could do nothing for this man, even if he had the inclination to do so. Which he didn't.

"Yes, sir. I mean, no sir," stammered the peasant. "I haven't actually seen him, but someone came into our tavern tonight asking about him. This got me thinking, you know? That maybe, if you have her followed, maybe when she finds him—"

Emir paused, his hand hovering near the candle flame. "She?"

"It was a woman, sir."

The Minister turned to meet the peasant's eyes. Dagen shrunk beneath his gaze. Pip snarled.

"A woman, you say," said Emir, laying a gentle hand on the dragon's neck. "And what did this woman look like?"

"Well, I suppose she was like most other women, but young. A girl no more'n eighteen, I suspect. Light hair and skin. An islander."

"I see. Was there anything else extraordinary about this— woman?"

"Aye. She was hurt. The back of her shoulder was bleeding. She collapsed from weakness. I was sent to fetch the doctor, but I came straight here instead."

Emir slid his hand slowly over the little dragon's scales, stroking him as he would a dog. His expression was pensive, though his eyes flitted faster than ever. After a few moments, he turned to Erland.

"You," he said, "listen carefully, for if you do not carry out these instructions to the letter I will personally see you hanged from the gallows. Go to the barracks and gather half a dozen soldiers, but have them wear civilian clothes. No armor, and with their weapons well concealed. You will all accompany this man back to his village."

Erland hesitated. He had often trained alongside the Ministry's soldiers, but had never joined them on any campaign. "Now, Minister?"

"Yes, now! We've lost too much time as it is, with this—" Emir waived a wilted hand at the peasant "—this creature probably dawdling the whole way here."

"Well, now, sir," started Dagen defensively, "I came as quick as I—"

Emir cut him off, ignoring him completely. "It seems a certain missing princess has made a miraculous appearance in Ardath. I want her captured—alive, if you please—and brought to me. Is that clear?"

"Yes, Minister," said Erland, excitement already brewing inside of him.

"And take a Gorelian tracker with you so there is no risk of losing her."

The peasant cleared his throat, and then spoke up. "And *my* reward, sir?"

"Ah, yes," said Emir, turning to Dagen. "When you return with the woman, I will grant you an estate of your own with servants and a year's income to help you begin your new life as a nobleman."

"Thank you, sir!" Dagen slapped his hat onto his head and hurried to the door. He bowed several times, expressing the depth of his gratitude for Emir's generosity.

"Oh, one more thing," added Emir to his departing guest. "Should the woman escape, you will be executed."

2

The gritty, brown soil fell through Teak's fingers, a breeze carrying off a veil of dust. The earth was colder now that winter was coming. Nearly time to plant the winter wheat, which would hibernate underground until spring. Teak glanced toward the sun, which had just made its appearance over the eastern horizon. He had left the house early that morning so as not to wake anyone, and gathered his tools from the barn. Today he planned to harvest the rocks in preparation for tilling. He did this every year, and yet every year a new crop of stones seemed to grow back. He plucked one about the size of his fist from the ground, dropped it into the cloth pouch he wore across his shoulder, and then bent down to pick up another. That's when he noticed the footprints.

The trail of prints led from the direction of the house straight across the field toward the trees. He hadn't more than a minute to consider them before a rider on horseback appeared at the bend in the road bordering their farm. The rider was galloping at full speed and waving one arm above his head. As the horse drew nearer, Teak heard his name being called.

"Teak! Teak, you've got to come quick!" said the man, out of breath.

It was Jon, a friend of Mikel's from the village. A burly-looking man with arms the size of anvils, Jon was the local tanner and had visited their farm on many occasions. He reached the spot where Teak stood and came to an abrupt stop.

"Teak, did you hear me? You've got to get your wagon and follow me to town."

"W-why?" asked Teak. "W-what's happened?"

"There's a woman at the tavern. She came in asking for a half-breed. Said to leave word with Mikel if anyone saw him."

Teak's gut clenched. When he had left the house that morning, he hadn't checked to see if Ivy was in her bed. He had assumed she'd be asleep and didn't want to disturb her.

He looked down at the footprints. She must have left during the night, he realized. But why? Why would she leave like that, without telling Mikel where she was going—without saying goodbye? After everything they had done for her—to abandon them like that...

Teak snatched another stone from the soil and dropped it into his pouch. Jon watched him anxiously.

"Teak, didn't you hear me? You've got to come to town."

Teak didn't look up as he pulled another two stones from the earth. But instead of placing them in his pouch, he pulled back his arm and flung the first stone as hard as he could throw it. He threw the second before the first hit the ground.

"She's hurt," said Jon. "She's hurt bad. Go fetch Mikel's wagon and get to the tavern as quick as you can."

With that, Jon dug his heels into his horse's flanks and sped off across the dry field, leaving a trail of dust behind them. But Teak did not see Jon's departure. He was already running toward the house, his pouch of stones abandoned on the ground.

*   *   *

Several hours later, Teak's wagon came to a stop in front of the home he had shared with Mikel for most of his life. The two of them had been content in their seclusion, and they'd never considered whether they would be happier in some other situation. But now, since Ivy's arrival, they both agreed life was indeed better.

Teak was the first to climb down from the wagon. He hurried around to the other side and helped Mikel down. Then he went to the back of the wagon and lowered the panel. Reaching in, he slipped his arms beneath Ivy's body, now wrapped in a warm blanket, and eased her out of the wagon. He pulled her close to him, making certain that her head was supported against his shoulder. Then he carried her into the house where he laid her back on her bed and arranged the blanket around her.

"W-why did she go?" asked Teak. "She w-wasn't ready."

Mikel stood in the doorway, his hands in his pockets. His face wore a troubled expression. "I don't know," he said. "But I'm sure she must've had a good reason for it. She just wasn't as strong as she thought she was."

"W-will she be all right?"

"She'll be fine, just fine. A few days' rest is all she needs." Mikel tried to sound sure of himself, but Teak could tell his uncle was as worried as he was. "Now, we both have work to do," Mikel continued. "The fields aren't going to plow themselves. There are plenty of hours left in this day. We'll look in on her a little later."

Teak reached out and brushed a strand of hair from Ivy's face. In response, Ivy stirred a little, but did not wake.

Mikel turned and left the house. The door slammed shut behind him, and Teak listened to the heavy clomp of his shoes on the steps outside. He could tell that Mikel was worried—and so was he.

Before he left, Teak took one last look at Ivy. She was sleeping soundly, just as she had been when they found her at the tavern. She had awakened only briefly when Teak put her in the wagon. She had opened her eyes, and on seeing his face, she smiled before falling back asleep. Teak thought of that smile now, but it only troubled him more.

3

Teak worked until after the sun had set, pushing himself harder and farther than he had ever worked before. He managed to clear not only the main field to the east of the house, but the smaller field to the north as well. By the time he was finished, the pile of stones between the two looked more like a monument than a collection of discarded rocks. They would eventually be used to repair the wall around the sheep's enclosure or the well, or to create a decorative border around Mikel's garden. Nothing on Mikel's farm went to waste.

Only when there was not enough daylight left to see by did Teak finally wash himself and come inside. He ate his bowl of stew so quickly he hardly had time to taste it, and didn't even ask for a second.

Just as he took up his vigil beside Ivy's bed, Mikel came in from the kitchen carrying a bowl for Ivy.

"Has she w-woke up at all?" Teak asked.

"She's stirred a few times," replied Mikel, "but she'll have to wake now, though, to eat some supper." He touched the back of his hand to her cheek. "The fever's come back." Then he spoke to Ivy, his voice gentle. "Ivy. Ivy, wake up now."

Ivy moaned a little before opening her eyes. When she did so, she smiled at the two faces looking down at her. But then her smile faded.

"I'm back at the farm," she said, the realization just coming to her. She tried to move, but cried out in pain. "No, no," she repeated over and over. "I can't be here. No, I mustn't be here."

"It's all right," consoled Mikel, holding a spoonful of stew to Ivy's lips. "You have to eat if you want to get your strength back."

"But how?" Ivy's eyes darted back and forth from Mikel to Teak, bewildered.

Teak took the bowl and spoon from Mikel and managed to coax Ivy into taking a bite.

"A friend of mine from town sent for us," Mikel said. "What were you thinking, taking off like that in the middle of the night? It'll be weeks yet before you're well enough to travel by wagon let alone on foot."

Ivy accepted another bite of food. When Teak offered a third, she gently pushed his hand away.

"I didn't want to burden you with my problems," she said weakly, "or put you in any danger."

"Danger?" scoffed Mikel. "What danger is there in caring for a wayward child like you?"

"A great deal of danger, I'm afraid. I had thought to prevent—to protect—but now..."

Ivy's voice faltered. Her face wore the expression of someone who carried a terrible sorrow. "You deserve to know the truth about me," she said.

155

Mikel pulled up his stool to sit beside them. He took Ivy's hand in his, patting it gently. "Go on," he told her.

Ivy looked from Mikel to Teak. There was a look of deep concern in her eyes, as if what she wanted to say were a heavy burden she could no longer bear. Teak set down the bowl and leaned closer to listen.

"Nearly two years ago," Ivy began, "I defied my father's will by secretly marrying the man I loved. When my father found out, he exiled my husband, and I ran away. I saw—I *believed* that my husband would come back for me, but as time went on, I feared that something had happened to him. In fact, I am certain of it. So I decided to search for him. But in the meantime my father's soldiers found me. I barely escaped with my life. I might have died, Teak, if you hadn't found me that night in your field."

Ivy is married, thought Teak. The realization struck him like a blow. She has a husband.

"Your father," asked Mikel, "who is he?"

Ivy's gaze clung to Teak's for a moment, before she turned her eyes away. "Lord Fredric, ruler of Dokur."

Mikel released Ivy's hand and gasped. "Not Ivy then," he said, haltingly. "Lady Ivanore."

Lady Ivanore. Teak blinked hard. Could it be? Was she telling the truth? But of course she was. There was no reason to lie. But she had hidden the truth from them—from him. Teak felt the muscles in his jaw clench.

After several awkward silent moments, Mikel spoke again. "You're a princess," he said, his words humming with awe and disbelief. "And you escaped from your father and came here, to Hestoria, in search of your husband?"

"Yes," said Ivy. "That's why I had to leave last night. I've already wasted so much time. I have to find him."

"I understand, but you won't do your husband or yourself a bit of good if you kill yourself trying," said Mikel.

Teak clasped his hands together, squeezing until his knuckles went white. Something about Ivy's story didn't make sense to him. "In the field that d-day, there w-were no footprints."

Teak thought back to that night when he first saw her lying in the grass. He had been so intent on her that he hadn't paid much attention to anything else. He had seen no footprints, no sign of her having walked there on her own. But thinking back, he did recall one thing out of the ordinary, something that at the time he had dismissed.

"There w-was a mark right beside you," he said. "A large d-depression in the soil, like something w-was there with you."

"A large animal in my field?" asked Mikel, concerned.

"Yes," said Ivy. "That animal brought me here and left me in your care."

"What animal leaves only two tracks in the earth without any path behind it?"

Ivy hesitated. "It was a gryphon," she said, finally.

"A gryphon, you say?" said Mikel, running his arthritic fingers through his thinning hair.

Teak abruptly stood and went to the window. This was more than he had ever imagined, more than either he or Mikel would ever dare to take upon themselves. They were farmers. They weren't ready for this.

"But that could only mean," continued Mikel, his words a sharp whisper. "But that's impossible!"

"It's not impossible," said Ivy. "I'm afraid it is true."

"Then you are the Seer!"

Teak's stomach twisted inside of him. He felt betrayed, but by whom? Ivy never made any promises to him, never expressed any feeling for him other than gratitude. It was he that had imagined there was more, had assumed... And now—of course she wouldn't have thought more of him. How could she? A princess—and the Seer.

He turned from the window and found Ivy watching him intently. Her blue eyes were moist with tears. Teak did his best to ignore how seeing her like this made him feel.

"You talked of d-danger," he said.

"I am being tracked," Ivy explained, "by whom I'm not sure. I've seen his face, but I don't know him. My being here has put you in danger. That's why I must leave before he finds me here."

Mikel stood up and began to pace the room. "What utter nonsense!" he said. "You'll stay right here until you are fully recovered. And as far as danger goes—well, I may be old," he continued, smiling, "but I do know a thing or two about fighting an enemy. No, you'll stay right here with us." He bent over Ivy and planted a kiss on her forehead. "You go on and rest. We'll talk more of this in the morning. Come," he said to Teak. "Let the poor girl get some sleep."

After patting Ivy reassuringly on the arm, Mikel stepped out of the room.

Teak watched his uncle leave. Didn't he understand what Ivy was telling them? Ivy was the Seer! She had likely seen this danger already in a vision. Mikel must know that, and yet he didn't seem concerned at all. Or maybe he was concerned, Teak thought, but what good would it do to show it? Ivy was in no condition to leave the farm. They had no choice but to watch over her. But he had a choice, didn't he?

"You're angry," said Ivy, shifting her position on the bed so she could see him better.

Teak shook his head. "N-not angry."

"Disappointed then."

"N-no."

"I know how you care for me, Teak. I've seen it in your eyes. Another reason why I had to leave."

"You d-didn't have to leave."

"Yes I did." Ivy's voice was insistent. "I should have told you why I came, right from the start."

"W-why didn't you?"

"I was trying to protect you. Once I arrived here, things changed. My visions changed." Ivy leaned closer to Teak, urgency in her voice. "I've seen things, Teak. I don't want any harm to come to you. The best thing for everyone is for me to get as far away from here as possible."

"You heard my uncle. You're n-not going anywhere."

"No. I couldn't leave again even if I tried. I'm too weak. But you could take me, Teak."

Teak stiffened. "Take you w-where?"

"Anywhere. Just take me in the wagon and leave me somewhere—the village, the forest—"

"Uncle w-would kill me if I did that."

"He'd understand."

Teak turned back to the window. Night was coming on now, and a sliver of moon was rising. He loved the land at this time of day, when the colors began to bleed into one another and things were not so distinct as they normally were, when the world was a single, unified whole.

Maybe Ivy was right, Teak reasoned. Maybe the best thing would be to take her away from here. He could wait until his uncle was asleep and then take Ivy in the wagon back to the village. He could rent a room for her at the tavern. Or they could go farther, someplace where Mikel wouldn't find her and bring her back.

Outside, a slight breeze stirred the tops of the distant line of trees. He wondered what lay beyond them. Since he was a boy he had been forbidden to go into the forest. His uncle never gave a reason, and Teak never questioned him. He had had no reason to disobey. But tonight something about them drew his attention.

Teak leaned forward and blew out the candle, and then he stepped back from the window into the shadows of the room.

"What is it?" asked Ivy.

Teak kept a steady eye on the fields. "Someone's out there," he said.

4

"What's going on, Teak?" asked Mikel, coming back into the room. Teak motioned for him to stay away from the window. Though the strangers were still far off, he didn't want to take the chance that they could see into the house.

"Out there, n-near the road," said Teak.

Mikel cautiously stole a brief glance outside. "I count seven men," he said.

"Seven?" asked Ivy, suddenly alert.

"Aye," answered Mikel, "and a smaller creature." He looked out once more. "It's a tracker, the filthy beast."

Ivy reached across the bed and grabbed Teak's arm. Even though the room was dark, with only the moonlight coming in through the window, Teak could see the fear in her face.

"They've come for me," she said urgently. "I saw them in my vision. I didn't expect them so soon. I've endangered you both and must leave at once."

"Yes," said Mikel, thoughtfully. "Yes, I think that is best."

"W-what?" Before Teak could protest further, Mikel had hurried out of the room again. He returned moments later with a curved dagger in his hand, the kind he used when harvesting corn, and a cloth bundle tied at the corners.

"You're in no condition to be going anywhere—at least not by yourself. Take this," he told Teak, handing him the bundle. "Some clothes for you and Ivy, and enough bread for two or three days at least. There are some herbs as well. Brew them into a tea for the fever. Mash the roots to apply on her shoulder."

Teak continued looking out the window. The men were closer now, though not close enough to make out their faces. The tracker walked several paces ahead of them, its face low, sniffing at the ground.

"Take Ivy out the back door," Mikel told him.

"W-what about you?" asked Teak, lifting Ivy into his arms.

"Someone has to stay behind and lead these scoundrels off Ivy's trail."

Ivy rested her head against Teak's shoulder. He could feel the fevered heat of her trembling body against him. She must be in pain, he thought. And yet she managed to speak with more force than he thought her capable.

"Mikel, you've done enough. You can't stay."

But Mikel ignored her, instead hastily tucking her blanket more securely around her. Ivy reached over the blanket and gripped Mikel's arm. "I beg of you," she pleaded, tears spilling onto her cheeks. "Come with us. If you don't, they will kill you."

Mikel pried Ivy's fingers from his sleeve and kissed her hand. "To give my life for the Seer is the greatest honor I have ever been given."

Ivy nodded through a fresh wave of tears. Then she withdrew her hand and tucked it beneath her blanket.

Teak wanted to compel his uncle to come with them, but he knew it would be futile.

Mikel turned to Teak and laid his palm against his face. The look in Mikel's eyes expressed years of affection and pride that until now had gone unsaid.

"Go to the river and follow it north," Mikel instructed firmly. "There is a cabin deep in the woods. Take Ivy there. When she is well, you must find the Guilde. They will protect her. Until then, she is your responsibility, Teak. Now hurry. There isn't much time."

Mikel slid his hand from Teak's face, and then turned away. Without looking back, he opened the front door to the cottage and stepped resolutely outside. From the window, Teak watched as he stepped down from the porch and approached the strangers. As Mikel passed the tower of stones Teak had created earlier that day, he grabbed a large one and held it behind his back. From where Teak stood, he could see the stone in his uncle's hand but knew the strangers could not.

What was Mikel doing? Teak knew he needed to leave with Ivy, but he felt compelled to watch.

One of the men stepped forward. He was quite heavy and seemed to be the one in charge. Teak thought he looked familiar, that he had seen him in the village. The small, white-skinned tracker stood at his feet. As Mikel and the other man spoke, the tracker began sniffing the area around Mikel's legs. In a blurred moment of time, Mikel lifted his arm and smashed the stone into the tracker's skull. The creature fell to the ground, shuddered, and went limp.

In the very next second, the fat man with whom Mikel had been conversing drew a sword from a hidden scabbard and ran Mikel through with it.

Teak nearly screamed, but the sound died in his throat. Mikel remained tall and rigid, and for a moment, Teak thought maybe his eyes had fooled him. But then slowly, like a leaf's leisurely descent, Mikel's body relaxed and collapsed to the ground.

Teak spun around and dashed out the back door with Ivy in his arms. She was surprisingly light, and he was able to run at almost full speed. The men had come from the road that ran between the edge of Mikel's fields and the forest. They were, as far as Teak knew, still out front of the house, so there was no way he could reach the road without being seen. Extending beyond the back of the house was another field, though this one had fallen into disuse. As Mikel aged, his ability to manage multiple fields lessened. This one had gone to weeds. It, too, extended toward the road. To cross it would be treacherous because of stones, tangled growth, and uneven ground. As long as Mikel's murderers were in front of the house or inside it, they would have no clear view of Teak's escape. Once he reached the road, Teak reasoned, he could head to the village to find help.

Holding Ivy tightly against him, Teak ran with all his might toward the abandoned field. The sight of Mikel's death played over and over in his mind, like a cadence, pushing him onward. Night had finally fallen, and a thick layer of clouds had gathered to hide the moonlight. This was to Teak's advantage since it would make it more difficult to be spotted, but it also made it hard to see where he was going. He knew the moment his feet crossed onto the field from the sudden softness of the once-tilled soil. Though now studded with stones, dirt clods, and plant roots, the dirt gave way beneath his feet. The soft earth slowed him down. It was almost like trying to run in snow. With each step, his feet literally sank into the soil, and his ankles became entangled in the weeds, their stubborn stems and leaves slicing into his skin. Soon his legs itched and bled from the assault.

He dared not look behind him. He feared he might find himself face to face with a sword. Instead, he hurried on as fast as his legs would carry him.

About halfway across the field, Teak's right foot came down on a sharp stone. His ankle twisted, and he cried out in pain. Thrown off balance, he stumbled. Ivy flew out of his arms and hit the ground. Ivy clutched her shoulder, groaning in pain.

Teak knelt beside her, his knees pressing into the dirt. His injured leg throbbed, but he was more concerned about Ivy than himself. Her groaning stopped. Ivy lay motionless on the ground. The memory of the first time he had seen her, lying in the field as though she was dead, came back to him along with a sudden wave of fear.

When Teak stood up, a spike of pain shot up his leg. Flinching from the pain but doing his best to ignore it, he carefully scooped Ivy back into his arms. Cradling her like a father cradles his child, he continued on toward the distant trees. There was no fear now that the men would see them. The clouds had completely covered the moon; the sky and the air all around were as dark as the sea.

Teak's steps now came slowly, each one sending stabbing pains through his leg. Each minute seemed endless, and Teak wondered if he would ever reach the road. But in time, his feet stepped onto hard, level ground.

Teak paused. He had planned to carry Ivy into the village and seek help there. Ivy certainly needed medical attention. There was no doubt of that. But now it occurred to him that these men—these intruders—had most likely come from Ardath. Perhaps they had spoken with someone who had seen her there. How else would they have known where to find her?

No, he could not go to the village. He remembered what Mikel had said about hiding in the woods. But how could he prevent being followed? That's why Mikel killed the tracker, he realized. Without a tracker, following their trail would be impossible. But once morning dawned, his footprints through the field would be visible.

Teak looked at the dark line of trees. As a child, his uncle had told him tales of the terrible creatures that lived in the forest. Of course, Teak now told himself, those must have been stories meant to frighten him so that he would not go into the forest and get lost. But even now, as a man, the memories of those stories sent a chill through him.

He started walking down the road away from the village. Should he follow the road long enough in this direction it would take him to the sea. There was no hiding there, however. The shore was flat and wide with nothing but low grassy plains between the forest and the sand. He might be able to procure a boat, but then where would he sail? He had never piloted a boat before and might very likely drown them both if he tried.

He continued walking, though not far. If he walked too far it would bring him to the edge of Mikel's good field, and he just might come upon the strangers face to face. The ground beneath his feet was rutted and dry. He knew no footprints would be left here. And if it rained, as he supposed from the darkening clouds that it might, there would be no trail left at all by morning. Should the strangers return the next day, they would not be able to determine which direction he had traveled, or if he had been on the road at all. Of course, they could bring another Gorelian tracker, but that was unlikely as the only ones he knew to live in this province were in the service of the Ministry.

The realization struck him as though it were lightning. The Ministry. The Ministry had sent these men. And that very well meant the Vatéz had sent them, since the Vatéz and the Ministry were one and the same. The Vatéz knew the Seer was here on Imaness—and they wanted her.

But they will not have her, Teak told himself. I must get Ivy to the Guilde.

Teak stepped off the road at a particularly rocky spot and headed deep into the forest.

5

"Where *is* she?"

Emir's fingers tightened into a fist as he slammed his hand against his desk. The candlestick wobbled, then found its balance and went still. The dim light danced with the shadows, the two moving in strange lifelike patterns across Emir's tight-lipped expression. The image seemed a vision of hell to Erland, the young assistant who had accompanied the peasant Dagen to capture Ivanore. He could almost feel the fear radiating off the corpulent man who stood trembling beside him.

"She escaped," said Dagen, timidly.

"Escaped?" replied Emir.

"Yes, your Excellency, through the fields. We found some footprints in back of the house where she'd been hiding."

"And her scent led where?"

Dagen shook, and his words cowered in his throat. Erland might have answered when Dagen could not, but he chose to remain silent.

"We couldn't track her," said Dagen, after composing himself enough to speak again.

Emir's face hardened like stone. "The Gorelian could not track her?"

"The farmer killed it. Smashed its skull with a rock. So I ran him through with my sword."

Emir ground his teeth together so loudly that Erland could hear it even above the low growls of the infant dragon held back by a heavy iron chain. The thing glared at Erland with unblinking red eyes. He tried to ignore it.

"Was there no one else in the house?" Emir asked.

"No one, my Lord," answered Dagen, his voice tremulous and desperate. A thin sheen of perspiration gathered on his brow. "The woman—she may have escaped into the forest."

"*May have* escaped into the forest?" repeated Emir, his flitting eyes fixed on the reward-driven peasant. The little dragon's slitted eyes, too, were trained on the terrified man.

Dagen wavered. "Or she might have gone west to the shore, or to the village. Someone there might be harboring her even now."

"This farmer you killed, I suppose he could have told you where she'd gone."

Erland understood the severity of Emir's accusation. Dagen had acted too hastily.

"I-I am sorry," Dagen stammered. "I'll return at once. Give me another tracker, and I'll find her."

"The scent has grown cold by now," said Emir, shortly. "Last night's storm has washed most of her trail away. It would take days, weeks, to pick up a fresh trail, if at all. You have failed me."

Emir moved to the front of his desk. Leaning over, he stroked the dragon's neck, his fingers pale against the iridescent scales. The creature hummed softly but did not take its gaze from the peasant's face. Erland took a discreet step back into the shadows of the room.

"Do you know anything about dragons, Dagen?" asked Emir. "They are extremely loyal creatures. Like many animals, imprinting takes place within moments of hatching, usually with its mother or, as in this one's case, with its caretaker. That is why there are so few of them in captivity, you see. Unless raised by humans from that very first moment, they are impossible to tame. Even then, they are loyal only to the one who raises them. All others are considered enemies."

Emir's hand paused at the iron manacle around the dragon's neck. The dragon strained against it, its small but powerful muscles rippling beneath its skin. It opened its mouth revealing two rows of jagged, needle-sharp teeth.

Dagen backed away, his hands held protectively out in front of him. "No. Please, your Excellency—"

The clunk of the manacle dropping to the floor resonated throughout the room. Try as he may, Erland could not avert his eyes as the peasant turned and darted for the door. Grasping the handle with both hands, he pulled it open, but it was too late. There was time enough only for a brief cry of alarm before the little dragon tore out his throat.

6

The fire, though small, was sufficiently warm and cast a ring of light just wide enough for Teak to work by. He had managed to gather enough wood to both feed the flames and erect a crude shelter. Branches broken off nearby trees and covered with a blanket had provided some protection from the rain that first night, and once the weather had cleared a bit, he had started the fire.

During that entire first day, Ivy neither opened her eyes nor stirred, but remained still as death. On several occasions, Teak actually feared she had died and checked for her breath and a pulse. Each time, however, his fears were unjustified. Then late on the second night, Ivy began to moan in her sleep.

Teak, who had dozed off, awoke. Ivy's lips parted, and from them came a haggard moan that could only mean she was in pain. The sound almost formed a word, but Teak could not make out what it was. As the night wore on, Ivy grew more restless, her muscles tensing and easing, fists clenching and unclenching.

Teak tried everything to calm her. He stroked her hair, rubbed her arms, spoke soothingly to her, but nothing worked. He could not reach her. She was, it seemed, in another place entirely. Teak watched her with ever growing concern.

Shortly before sunrise, Ivy's agitation peaked. Still with her eyes closed, Ivy struck out both hands, the muscles in her arms flexed and taut, her fingers grasping for some invisible object just out of her reach. She cried out one single word— *Jayson!*—And then her body went limp.

For a few moments, Teak remained paralyzed where he laid, his heart and lungs racing. But then he was up on his knees bending over Ivy. He laid his ear to her chest, his cheek to her lips. This time, however, there was no breath. No heartbeat.

"N-no," he whispered. And then louder, "No!"

He did not pause to consider his options. He had none. Grasping Ivy by the shoulders, Teak shook her gently at first, and then harder.

"Ivy, w-wake up!" he shouted, wrestling with each word. "W-wake up! It w-was only a dream, Ivy! It w-wasn't real!"

He shook her again, but her head hung back, her hair falling to the ground like a curtain of gold.

Teak laid Ivy's head and shoulders back down, but he was not ready to give up. Balling the fingers of his right hand into a fist, he pounded on Ivy's chest.

"Ivy!" he screamed, his voice choked with tears now. "Ivy, come b-back!"

He let his fist fall again and again and again until finally he collapsed, weeping, beside her.

Perhaps only seconds had passed, though to Teak it felt like an eternity, but Ivy took a breath. And then she took another.

Ivy tried to speak but was too weak to form words. Teak leaned closer so that his ear was near her lips. She tried again, but managed only a faint, indiscernible whisper.

"I almost lost you," Teak said, brushing his fingers against her face. "You w-want to tell me something?"

Ivy nodded, but even that trivial movement seemed to drain her of energy. Teak noticed how her body shivered from the fever.

Ivy opened her eyes and looked at Teak with an intensity beyond her strength.

"Jayson," she said. "I must—find him." Then she lost consciousness once again.

7

Was it day or night? It was difficult to tell as Jayson stood in the open field, the waist-high grass swaying in the warm breeze. Jayson held his hands above the grass, letting the tips brush against his palms. The sky was the color of wet stone; and in the distance, the trees of the forest were muted gray and nearly indistinguishable from the sky. Jayson tuned his senses to his surroundings, yet no sounds or smells came to him. Everything around him, except the grass, was motionless and silent.

He wasn't exactly sure when he sensed her presence, but in time he raised his face, looked across the field, and saw Ivanore standing afar off with her back to him. He started to run toward her, but the thick, tall grass hindered his progress. The faster he ran, the father away the grass carried him.

He called to her, and she turned, her blue eyes searching for him. But at that moment, the field transformed into a wide, black sea. Jayson was in the water. Ivanore stood high above him on a cliff of dark gray rocks, her eyes wet with tears. He called to her again, but the sound of the waves crashing against the cliff drowned out his voice. Then he was sinking, and as the icy saltwater filled his lungs he reached out for her, grasping nothing.

Jayson sat up and gasped. The blanket that Magda had draped over him during the night slipped silently to the floor. His hands trembled, and his skin was damp with perspiration.

"That must have been some dream," whispered a voice from the shadows of the room. Magda rocked slowly in her chair, working a web of red string through her fingers.

Jayson set his feet on the wood floor and wiped the sweat from his forehead with the back of his hand. "It was too real to be a dream," he answered.

Magda continued rocking, her eyes fixed on his. "You know what they say about dreams?" she said. "They are messages to the soul."

"What message could such a nightmare possibly bear?"

"One of great importance."

Jayson watched as Magda wove the strands between her fingers, forming a pattern that grew with each new connection. He marveled at how something so seemingly simple could result in something so complex.

"If my dreams are so important," he said, "then why can't I understand them?"

Magda ceased her weaving. "Often dreams are delivered as ciphers," she said, slipping the string from her fingers one by one and laying the small, square mat of it on her lap. "We will only come to understand them when we are ready. But you ask the wrong question, my friend. The better question is this: If dreams are messages to the soul, then *who* is the messenger?"

Jayson peered across the room through the darkness that was no barrier to his eyes. Brommel lay asleep on a cot, his arms wrapped protectively around young Rylan. Jayson envied them. Though Brommel had lost his wife and daughter, at least he still had his son.

Jayson had no one.

8

rielle's casket was hastily constructed of rough-hewn planks. When it was finished, Brommel laid Brielle inside with their little baby wrapped in her arms. It was almost more than Brommel could bear. He might have buried himself along with his wife and daughter, but, as Jayson reminded him, he had his son to live for now.

The next morning, he and Jayson loaded the casket onto a wagon. Brommel thanked Magda for allowing them to stay with her. Then Jayson took the reins and pointed the wagon toward Nauvet-Carum.

Brommel sat beside Jayson on the wagon seat, the boy in his lap. "You'll see that they are buried?" asked Brommel, stroking Rylan's hair.

"I give you my word," replied Jayson. Watching Brommel and his son together made him ache inside. He preferred to keep his eye on the horse instead. "I'll head to the crossroads as soon as I've seen you off."

"The caretaker's name is Leo. He and his daughter, Abby, are guardians and will help you find your friends."

177

The road was still muddy from the previous day's storm. The wagon wheels slogged laboriously on. Though the sun was now partially visible through the clouds, the air was chill. Brommel removed a blanket from the bag he had packed and covered Rylan with it. They had nothing left after the fire, but several families from the village had provided them with clothing, blankets, and a few other items they would need on their journey. Brommel thought of that journey now and wondered what the future held for him and his son.

"What is it like, the island?" Brommel asked Jayson.

"Imaness?" Jayson considered the question before answering further. It had been well over a year since he'd seen it last, and yet every detail remained clear in his mind, though he had tried hard to forget it. He wanted to tell of the island's beauty, of the Jeweled Mountains and the Black Forest. But these were not part of his childhood. His memories were of infested swamps and a life of hardship. "There is only one port," he began matter-of-factly, "as the remainder of the coast is too treacherous to approach by ship. The port city of Dokur is where I lived before being sent here."

"Are you from Dokur originally?"

"No, I'm from a place called Taktani in the North."

"Is that where your family is?"

"I have no family," answered Jayson. "My mother died when I was a boy. My father, my human father, abandoned us years earlier. He lives in Quendel. If you ever end up there, you can tell him I'm alive, in case he's wondering."

"And your wife?"

Jayson glanced at Brommel, then back to the road. "I left her in Dokur along with our son. He's a bit younger than Rylan. About a year and half old by now."

"I'll find her," said Brommel, "and I'll tell her you're all right."

Jayson forced a half-hearted smile. "Yes," he said. "Tell her I love her."

The day wore on, but by mid-morning they reached the city. Despite the inclement weather, the streets were alive with merchants and customers bartering for wares. Horses and wagons crowded the cobbled roads, and the noise of it all was almost tangible. The chaos of the city would provide the cover Brommel and his son needed to get safely to port without being noticed by the Ministry. To ensure their remaining unseen, the three of them wore long, dark cloaks obtained by Magda for the dual purpose of veiling their identities and providing Brommel and Rylan warmth during their sea voyage.

On the docks, workers were busy loading and unloading cargo from a large merchant vessel, a sleek black ship with an impressive mast and blood-red sail. Jayson stopped the wagon near a man barking out orders.

"Pardon me," Jayson said to him. "Could you tell me how to obtain passage to Dokur?"

"Aye," said the man, scratching at his sparse gray whiskers. "The Silver Mist leaves within the hour. You've asked the right man, as I'm the first mate," said the man. "Is it for yourself?"

"No. My brother and young nephew," answered Jayson, having already worked out his story.

"Two then? You're in luck today," he said, rubbing his palms together. "Captain Dawes has got room on board—if your brother can pay the going rate."

Jayson hesitated. He had no money and knew that the small amount Brommel carried with him would be needed to pay for food and shelter once they reached the island.

"I had hoped to find them free passage," he said.

"Free passage?" the ship's mate laughed as if it was a joke. "No one gets free passage on Dawes's ship."

Jayson looked back toward the wagon where Brommel cradled the still sleeping Rylan in his arms. Brommel had his lips against the boy's cheek. Jayson turned back to the man.

"Sir, if you could please entreat the captain on my brother's behalf. Yesterday his house burned to the ground. His wife and daughter were lost. Their casket sits on the back of my wagon. It is my sad task to bury them."

The man's expression grew solemn. "I am sorry for your brother's terrible loss," he said, "but I know Captain Dawes. He's a hard man. Has seen far worse tragedies in his life and hasn't shed a tear for a one of them. He will only agree to their passage in exchange for some sort of payment."

"I will be his payment."

"Pardon?

"I have no money, but I am strong. Though I can't fulfill the terms of our agreement until I've buried my brother's family, if Captain Dawes will deliver my brother to Dokur, I will consign myself to his service for as long as it takes to pay the debt. Please, give my proposal to the captain."

The ship's mate contemplated Jayson's request, then said, "All right. I'll tell him everything you said. Wait here."

He walked away toward a group of sailors dressed in white tunics and blue sashes at the waist standing near the gangplank of the ship. He spoke briefly to another man, whom Jayson assumed must be the captain. He was a broad man, and taller than the others. The collar of his gray woolen cloak stood stiff around his neck obscuring his face from Jayson's view.

Once the ship's mate stopped speaking, the captain raised his eyes, the only part of his face visible above his high collar. The dark orbs scrutinized the coffin on the back of the wagon. He shifted his gaze to Jayson, nodded once, and turned back toward his ship.

Jayson returned to the wagon.

"It's done," he told Brommel. "Bring the boy. You'll be traveling on the Silver Mist. The captain's name is Dawes. When you arrive in Dokur, go to the Seafarer Tavern. The keeper there is a man named Peagry. Tell him who you are and how you know me. He can be trusted. Now hurry."

Brommel gathered up his son and wrapped the boy's cloak around him like a blanket. Jayson accompanied Brommel onto the ship and saw to it that they were given a comfortable berth. The trip would take several days if the weather held. If they stayed to themselves and kept clear of the captain and his men, they would be just fine.

Once satisfied that he could do no more, Jayson turned to leave, but Brommel stopped him, enfolding him in his brawny arms. The embrace was brief, but heartfelt, and Jayson understood it was Brommel's way of thanking him.

"Don't forget what I told you," Jayson said.

"I won't," replied Brommel. "But Jayson, I have one last favor to ask of you. If you do this for me, I will leave this place and not look back."

"Anything."

"Swear to me you will make Arik and Emir pay for what they have done."

Jayson answered, "I had already planned to do it."

Betrayal

The ship's ropes were already unfastened from the pier when Jayson stepped off the gangplank. The ship's mate was waiting there for him. He handed Jayson a sheet of parchment folded in half. "From Captain Dawes," he explained. "The terms of your agreement."

Jayson opened the document, read it, and then slipped it into the pouch at his waist. As the Silver Mist pulled away from the dock, Jayson looked for Brommel's face, but saw only the captain watching him from the bow. The captain touched two of his fingers to his brow, and Jayson returned the gesture. The pact between them was sealed.

9

Teak studied the darkening sky, which threatened another storm. He doubted the makeshift shelter he had built would hold up against another onslaught. With Ivy's fever worsening, it would be best to reach the cabin as soon as possible.

After covering the hot coals with dirt and tying what few items he had in their only blanket, Teak gathered Ivy into his arms and left the shelter behind. The sun set too quickly as Teak made his way through the trees. He reached the river within the hour and then turned north, as his uncle had instructed, pausing only long enough to pour a little river water into Ivy's mouth with his hands.

He marched on for what seemed an eternity. He was not sure exactly how long he walked, but it was longer and farther than he had ever traveled before. To pass the time, he played memories of his life over in his mind. He recalled once, when he was a small boy, when Mikel ended the workday early. Loading him into the wagon, they had traveled down the dirt road until they reached the sea. Until that time, Teak had never seen the sea. He and his parents had lived inland, near the mountains, and in the year or so he had spent with his uncle, his time had been preoccupied with farming.

Mikel had stopped the wagon just at the shoreline so that it faced directly west. The two of them had sat staring without a word between them. The scene was the most glorious Teak had ever witnessed in his young life. The deep hues of orange, gold, and violet were more beautiful than words could express. He had watched in awe as the red orb of the sun descended through the layers of color until it just touched the horizon, spilling a sparkling trail of diamonds across the water. The sun had continued its descent until it vanished from sight, and the diamonds and the brilliant colors faded into a soft deep blue.

He and Mikel had remained there until the blue turned to black, and night had fallen completely. Only then did his uncle turn the wagon around and head for home.

The experience was as fresh in Teak's memory today as it was back then, and thinking of it still filled him with the same awe. He had seen many sunsets since then, but none had moved him so deeply as that first time so long ago. He was thinking of it when he saw the silhouette of the cabin against the moonlight. Though he knew he would eventually stumble upon it, somehow seeing it right in front of him, within reach, took him by surprise.

"Ivy! Ivy, w-we're here," he said, though he knew she couldn't hear him. She had lain limp in his arms since leaving the shelter many hours earlier. He could feel the heat from her body against his skin.

The cabin stood on the banks of the river, sheltered between moss-covered tree branches that twisted at odd angles, as though someone had purposely guided them to grow that way. Constructed of logs with a simple wooden door, warped from rain and time, it wasn't very large and looked to be in a state of disrepair as if it had been abandoned long ago.

The sound of the river running gently nearby soothed Teak's apprehension. He paused at the door a moment before pushing it inward with his foot. At first, he could see nothing of the interior, but his eyes soon adjusted to the moonlight streaming in from a window.

The cabin was even smaller on the inside, about the size of a single room in Mikel's house, and furnished with a wooden bed frame, an iron cookstove, and a table and chairs. In one corner sat a wooden bucket partly filled with stagnant water. Teak looked up and saw patches of silver moonlight through the roof. The room stank of mildew and damp wood. The roof definitely needed repair, but the structure itself seemed sound enough.

Teak lay Ivy down on the driest section of the floor. Then working as quickly as he could, he untied the blanket and spread it over the bed frame. He arranged the items he'd brought on the table, then lifted Ivy from the floor and put her on the bed. He found several more dusty blankets folded in a cabinet and covered her with one. Finally, he fetched the bucket and went down to the river.

After he rinsed and filled the bucket, he carried it back inside. On the way, he noticed a pile of wood situated between the river and cabin. Though much of it was still wet from the previous night's storm, he managed to find several logs near the bottom that were relatively dry. Back inside the cabin, he lit a fire in the cookstove and prepared the tea as Mikel had instructed him. He poured a small amount into one of the cups he had packed for him. Then he cradled Ivy's head in the crook of his left elbow while using his right hand to spoon the tea into her mouth drop by drop. Once the cup was empty, Teak tore a square from one of the blankets, dipped it into the bucket of water, and wiped down Ivy's face and arms with it. The water helped to cool her fever for a short time.

The sun was just beginning to rise when Teak finally spread out a blanket on the floor and lay down. He was exhausted from the long night of walking and the hours spent caring for Ivy. He wanted desperately to remain vigilant beside her, to watch over her every moment until she recovered, but his eyes grew heavy. Soon he drifted off to sleep.

It was late in the day when Teak awoke. Stiff and achy from lying on the cold, damp floor, he stretched every limb. He then warmed the rest of the tea from the previous night and served it to Ivy as before. She was still feverish and still unconscious. Teak's stomach grumbled.

Daylight spilled in through the windows and the holes in the roof. He took his first good look at the inside of the cabin. The furniture was as he had seen it last night, but in daylight everything took on a different appearance. The room, though dusty and obviously neglected, was still very tidy. On the walls hung several framed sketches of flowers and other plant life. A set of carved wooden bowls and cups was displayed neatly on a shelf. A brightly colored woven rug lay on the floor beneath the table. He stomped his foot on it, and a cloud of dust billowed into the air.

Again his stomach rumbled. He searched a row of cabinets for anything edible and found three round winter squashes. He also found two loaves of bread so stale that Teak considered using them to prop the door open when airing out the cabin. He did find a length of good rope and a bag of walnuts.

He decided that he would ration the bread and cheese Mikel had given him to make it last three days. He would have to rely on his wits and his knife to catch some small game. After a small but satisfying meal, he took the rope, the walnuts, and the water pail outside. He explored the area around the house and stumbled upon an overgrown vegetable garden. Most of the plants were dried up, but a thorough examination resulted in half a dozen brown onions, a few misshapen potatoes, and two wrinkled turnips.

He noted that much of the vegetation appeared as though it had been devoured by an animal of some kind, most likely a rabbit or squirrel. Teak chose a good spot, tied the rope to the bucket handle, and propped the bucket up so that it would fall at the slightest tug. He then broke open several of the nuts and scattered them about, placing a nice, tempting pile of them beneath the bucket. Finally, Teak settled himself behind a nearby tree, the end of the rope in his hand.

Fortunately, he didn't have to wait long. He had captured many small animals this way on the farm, critters determined to devour Mikel's vegetables. The secret, Teak had learned, was patience.

He waited calmly for the rabbit to discover the small treasure of nuts and soon found itself imprisoned in Teak's bucket. After that, its end came swiftly.

Later that day, Teak stirred the simmering stew with a ladle he found in the cabinet. The iron kettle he found with it proved just the right size to hold the entire rabbit and most of the vegetables. He raised the ladle to his lips, blew, and then tasted. Though a little bland, it would do to fill his stomach.

Pouring some of the soup into Ivy's cup, he carried it to her bedside. Earlier in the day, he had prepared and applied the poultice. Ivy moaned a bit from the pain, but still she did not fully wake. Teak worried that her fever might never break. What if he did something wrong? What if he couldn't make her better?

Again cradling her head in his arm, Teak spooned a little of the broth into her mouth. When he was finished, he stayed with her, gently stroking her hair.

"C-can you hear m-me?" he asked. "I got rid of the dust and cobw-webs. I'll go out tomorrow into the forest to find w-wood to fix the roof. Another storm is c-coming. I c-can smell it in the air."

Teak went on like this for some time, talking to Ivy as though she might actually respond. Eventually the sun went down. Teak dragged the carpet closer to Ivy's bed, then lay down and fell asleep.

The following morning, Teak rose again. A little less stiff and sore than he was the previous morning, he lit a fire in the stove and set the stew on to warm. It would make as good a breakfast as it would supper. He then warmed some tea for Ivy.

Setting her cup on the floor, Teak arranged Ivy's head in his arm. That was when he realized something had changed from the night before. Her clothes were damp with perspiration and the hair around her face was wet and stuck to her skin. But what was most important, and which filled him with relief, was how she felt when he touched her. She felt cool. The fever had broken.

10

J ayson stood before the mound of fresh, damp earth—the final resting place of Brommel's wife and child. A chill wind blew, carrying with it the smell of an impending storm. A chill ran up his spine, and his nerves responded with a shiver.

"It's a sad, sad end," said the old man standing beside him. Leo leaned on the handle of his spade, his clouded eyes staring past Jayson. "I remember the man that sent you here, though I met with him only briefly. He gave me the sign of caution. Normally, I would have given false directions in such a case, but there was something about him, something good. I knew Gerard would know what to do with him. I hope I was correct."

"You were," answered Jayson. He gently pressed his foot against the grave, leveling out an uneven patch of soil. "Brommel defied the Vatéz and has paid dearly for it."

"Is he bitter?" asked Leo. "Does he blame the Guilde?"

"No," replied Jayson. "He places the blame squarely where it belongs, as do I. You remember the boy that accompanied him?"

"I do."

"He betrayed us both." It was impossible to conceal the pain in his voice. He did not try.

"Careful, my new young friend," answered Leo. "Vengeance is a terrible thing. Those who seek it above all else find, when all is said and done, that they have lost more than what was taken from them."

Jayson contemplated Leo's admonition in silence, but it did nothing to alleviate his anger. His fingers grasped the leather pouch at his waist and felt the outline of the crystal within. Had he given it to Arik to begin with, this woman and child would still be alive. He blamed Arik for their deaths. He blamed Emir. But deep down he knew where the blame truly lay.

"I'll leave the wagon," said Jayson. "I won't need it now. Perhaps you could sell it."

"Perhaps," answered Leo. "Abby will give you some cheese and bread, though it is poor compensation. Is there anything else I can give you for it?"

"I need to find Gerard. I know he's moved from Alay-Crevar."

Leo turned his cloudy eyes toward the sky, squinting at the vast blue expanse. "The Guilde has relocated to a small village at the heart of Mount Naresh. I only received word this morning. From here, you continue on the road through Alay-Crevar. Cross over the bridge and follow the river upstream two days."

"And what then?"

"I don't know. It's all the instruction I was given."

Leo placed a feeble hand on Jayson's shoulder, offering what comfort he could. Then using the spade like a walking stick, the old caretaker made his way across the cemetery toward his cabin where his daughter stood waiting for him.

Jayson knelt beside the new grave. In Nauvet-Carum, prior to his departure, he had stopped at a merchant's tent and purchased a small box carved from a single block of pale wood. On the fitted lid was a simple design of a tree. Jayson filled the box with a handful of soil from Brielle's grave and replaced the lid. He would send it to Brommel when he could. He had also purchased a dagger. It wasn't new, but the blade was sharp, its hilt heavy in his hand. The yellow boar hide sheath and belt were soft and supple to the touch, like a woman's lips.

Jayson drew the dagger, and with its tip scratched the names of the grave's inhabitants onto the limestone marker he had chosen from the quarry behind Leo's cabin. After replacing the dagger, he removed the pouch from his waist. Weighing the crystal in his palm, he hesitated a moment before laying it in the depression left from the handful of soil he had taken, and placed the stone marker over it. He stood and brushed the dirt from his trousers. He then tucked the wooden box into a sack he carried with him, and followed after Leo.

11

Jayson rode his horse steadily through the night. Although the thick canopy of trees blocked out much of the moonlight, the road was relatively easy to follow, his eyes accommodating the dim light. As the hours passed, his mind drifted from thought to thought. He stopped briefly at Alay-Crevar to water his horse. It was a pleasant little village with several good wells, plenty of livestock and crops, and amiable residents. Gerard and his companions were practically spoiled by the locals. In the short time that Jayson had lived among them, he hadn't seen a single weapon or witnessed a dispute or outburst of any kind. That was probably the reason Gerard chose it for the Guilde's lair. It seemed a shame that they were compelled to leave it, though Jayson understood that the Guilde never stayed in one place for long. Arik had certainly revealed its location to Emir at his first opportunity. So the decision to move was the only reasonable option. He only hoped Leo's directions were accurate, and that he would not have too much difficulty in finding their new location.

Jayson's thoughts strayed from Gerard and the Guilde to Imaness. Brommel would soon reach the harbor at Dokur and be settled at the Seafarer Tavern shortly after that. How Jayson yearned to be in his place. He wished more than anything that it were him riding on the Silver Mist rather than Brommel—that it were him stepping off the gangplank into the arms of his beloved. Jayson closed his eyes, allowing the steady sway of the horse's back and the rhythm of its hooves clopping against the ground lull him into a waking dream.

Ivanore would be waiting for him on the cliff just above the shore. He would see her silhouetted against the evening sky, her hand raised to her brow searching the horizon. Their young son would be waving his arms beside her, his sweet voice calling out to him. His ship would drop anchor in the harbor and lower the gangplank, and Ivanore would run from the cliffs, her golden hair billowing behind her in the cool, salty breeze. And as she came nearer, Jayson would open his arms for her, waiting to fill them with the only thing in this life worth living for.

The horse staggered, its hoof catching on a stone. It righted itself immediately, but the rhythm was broken, the vision dispersed.

Jayson followed Leo's directions precisely, veering off the main road just far enough away from the village to keep the river in sight. He followed this path for a day, a night, and a day, stopping occasionally to rest his horse.

On the second day with the sun high overhead, Jayson reached the base of a tall mountain. Leo had called it Mount Naresh. The river he had been following led to a wide, green pool fed from an impressive fall that sprang from a cleft in the rock a hundred feet above. The mountain itself was nearly vertical, its face a shield of jagged rock with random greenery sprouting from it like tufts of hair on a giant's body.

Jayson examined the wall before him. He could climb it with ease, his claws and inhuman strength being assets in such a situation, but he doubted that would be necessary since such a climb would be nearly impossible for mere humans, especially humans carrying an injured girl with them. Jayson saw no evidence of anyone having climbed—no fallen rocks on the ground, no broken plant life. No, Gerard and the others had gone in some other direction. Unfortunately, Jayson had no more information than this. He rode his horse slowly around the circumference of the pool, searching for any clues as to which direction they had gone, but found none. The earth was smooth, undisturbed. He wondered if Leo had been correct after all. It was very likely that he could have given him false information to mislead him, or Gerard had given him instructions to do so. They did not like outsiders. They might very well have decided to prevent Jayson's return.

He nudged his heels into the horse's flanks and tugged the reins to the right. He followed the perimeter of the lake until he again reached the granite wall. The base of the steep and treacherous cliff extended for several miles in either direction, though Jayson was certain that if he followed it long enough eventually he would either reach a pass or the mountain would yield a slope hospitable enough for humans to climb. Either possibility still seemed unrealistic to him. *I've been deceived,* he finally admitted to himself. *Led to a dead end.*

He was about to turn his horse back toward Alay-Crevar when he noticed a man watching him from the opposite side of the lake. The man stood on the shore beside the cliff with the waterfall between them. A gossamer mist rose from the water. Jayson urged his horse to a gentle trot and rode back around the perimeter of the lake. When he reached the stranger, he dismounted. The man wore a blue tunic with a yellow triangle on the shoulder—the Guilde's symbol. He did not speak, but held out his hand. Jayson took it, pressing two of his fingers against the man's wrist—the token Gerard had showed him. Satisfied, the man released Jayson's hand and then walked toward the water. A moment later, he disappeared behind the waterfall.

Jayson hesitated. His horse whinnied and shook its mane. It wanted to follow. Jayson relented. Nearing the water, he noticed a ridge cut deep into the rock. It was wide enough for a horse, but just barely. The rock wall directly behind the waterfall had been carved away. The space between it and the back of the falls was sufficient to pass through without getting too wet, though a fine mist filled the space and settled on every inch of Jayson and his horse. He saw, too, that the flat shelf on which he traveled ended abruptly several feet ahead. Beyond that was the granite cliff on the opposite side of the falls where he had been when he first saw the man— who now had mysteriously disappeared from view altogether. There was no way he could have continued across to the other side of the falls. At the end of the shelf was nothing but solid rock, the falls themselves, and the depth of the lake. Jayson urged his horse on despite his own urge to turn around. He could not help but think he was being deceived once again, that someone was playing him for a fool.

As he approached the end of the shelf, however, he found a narrow cleft in the vertical rock, again just wide enough for his horse to pass through. He led his horse through the opening. The fissure was oddly shaped and almost too narrow in places. But soon it widened and finally came to an end.

Jayson stepped out of the cave into bright sunlight. He found himself in a small valley nestled between two mountain ranges, the first of which he had just passed through. The entire valley was barely large enough to accommodate the village that occupied it. Here stood no more than twenty small cottages constructed of stone surrounding a single larger structure. The plain on which they stood was flat and grassy, and several dozen thickly fleeced sheep grazed nearby. Eight tents had been erected in whatever empty space remained. It was into one of these tents that Jayson saw his guide disappear.

Jayson led his horse to the nearest patch of grass and released his reins. The valley was completely surrounded by menacing cliffs, and he doubted his horse had the courage to traverse the narrow fissure without him. So, leaving him to graze along with the sheep, Jayson headed for the tents. Before he could reach them, however, a familiar face emerged from one. The moment he saw Jayson, Gerard sprung from the tent, a wide grin on his face, both arms extended.

12

"Jayson, my boy," said Gerard, wrapping his arms around Jayson. "You've finally returned. I was beginning to think you might have taken a wrong turn—or worse. Your friend, Brom, is settled then? All is well?"

"No," replied Jayson. "All is not well I'm afraid."

Gerard's countenance fell as he listened to Jayson tell of finding Brommel's home and family destroyed, and how he had sent Brommel and Rylan to Imaness by ship for their own safety.

When he was finished, Gerard patted Jayson's shoulder. "I never expected Emir to go to such lengths. He's finally gone mad."

"Not mad," answered Jayson. "Emir knows exactly what he is doing. Word of Brommel's fate will soon spread. Others will be too afraid to protect you. The Guilde will have nowhere to go, nowhere to hide."

"Which is why we have come here," said Gerard, indicating the space around him. "This is not the first time

197

Naresh has concealed us. We don't come here often for fear that too frequent use of it might eventually lead to its discovery. But when we really need protection, we are welcome here."

Jayson turned his eyes toward the circle of sky above. Naresh reminded him of the Isle of Imaness. Like Imaness, Naresh was, in a sense, an island, though surrounded on all sides by mountains rather than water. He felt a familiar sense of calm here, reminding him of the serenity he used to feel when standing on the cliffs of Dokur looking out over the sea. It was the feeling that here he was safe—something he had not felt in a long time.

Not far off, a young boy led a goat toward a bit of grass between the tents. The goat bleated as the boy tugged at its lead.

"How is Dianis?" Jayson asked.

"Doing well," replied Gerard. "Had a dickens of a time keeping her in the wagon during the journey here. She would have got out and led the whole caravan if I'd let her. But her leg isn't up to it—not yet. The doctor said to give it another month. You can imagine how irate Dianis was at the news."

"Oh, I can imagine."

"Would you like to see her? I'm sure she'd welcome the company."

Jayson followed Gerard down the row of tents to the farthest from the cottages. A woman carrying a platter of cheese and fruit passed as they approached. The woman extended the platter. Gerard took a wedge of cheese and handed it to Jayson. He took another for himself.

"Thank you," Gerard said, and the woman continued on into the neighboring tent. "She is one of about fifty locals who live in Naresh. They are descendants of the earliest guardians. Their fathers were given the express responsibility of protecting this sacred valley, and so they still do today."

Gerard opened the tent flap. "You go on," he said. "I, uh, have some other things to attend to." Then he hurried off after the woman with the tray.

Jayson ducked inside the tent. His cat eyes adjusted immediately to the dim interior and found Dianis lying on a cot in the back of the spacious tent. A woven mat of dried grass completely covered the dirt floor and gave off a pleasant hay-like smell. There were two cots in addition to Dianis's, both empty. Several large overstuffed pillows were piled in the corner.

Dianis lay on her back, her hands held upright above her, string wound through the outstretched fingers of her left hand. She held the end of the string in her right hand and was winding it around her thumb as Jayson came in. From the look on her face, Jayson surmised that whatever she was doing was more aggravating to her than enjoyable. She glanced in his direction, and on seeing him gave a loud, indignant huff.

Jayson grinned at the unenthusiastic greeting. "At least you acknowledge me," he said, stifling a laugh.

Dianis twisted the string through her fingers, pulling so tightly that her fingers turned white. Jayson watched, amused. She hastily unwound the entire length of string and pitched it to the floor, then crossed her arms over her chest.

"You're angry with me," said Jayson. "I don't blame you."

"Angry with you? Why should I be angry with you?" Dianis replied with feigned indifference. "I'm not your keeper. You have as much right as any man to come and go as you please."

"I had hoped your father explained my hasty departure."

"He did."

"Then you understand. I had to go."

"I understand nothing." The anger in Dianis' voice was unmistakable. But there was something else there, more than anger. It was distress.

"You were worried about me?" asked Jayson.

Dianis uncrossed her arms and abruptly sat up. Her injured leg, bound in a wooden brace and bandages, lay stretched out on the cot. Dianis winced in pain as she propped herself up on her arms.

"Worried? Never!" She was nearly shouting. "I was glad you'd gone, if you want the truth. You nearly got me killed that day in the woods, you know."

"Actually, I saved your life. You would have bled to death if I hadn't brought you home."

"I would never have been in the woods at all if I hadn't followed you there."

"Ha!" Jayson pointed at her. "You admit it then, it was your fault!"

Dianis bit her lip in defeat. A moment later, she pointed her angry glare at him. "I would have been safe had your brother-in-law not mistaken me for you. It was you he was after, so it should have been you bleeding to death in the woods."

Jayson fell silent. Her words stung. They burned his conscience like a snake's venom. Without another word, he turned and left the tent. Suddenly, he wished he'd never come to Naresh, or to Alay-Crevar. He thought again of Brommel's family, and of Dianis lying unconscious with her leg splayed open like a butchered animal. Finally, he thought of Ivanore and of their fatherless son. Dianis was right, of course. It should have been him. They should have all been him.

13

The recent rains had transformed the streets of Nauvet-Carum into a muddy red slick that sucked at Arik's boots threatening to remove them from his feet altogether. He imagined that hands of the dead reached up through the muck grasping at him in an attempt to drag him down to hell. The image made his feet and heart move faster.

Once he had reached the stone steps of the Ministry, he did his best to scrape the brown glop from his feet, but the stubborn stuff clung to him. Finally, he gave up and went inside.

"Take these," he told the first attendant to approach him. He removed his boots and handed them to the astonished boy. "Rinse them off, dry them, and return them to me in Minister Emir's private chambers."

The boy, who was too thin and couldn't be more than ten, nodded and quickly departed.

Arik strode, in stockinged feet, down the main corridor to the reception desk. "I request an audience with his Excellency," he said.

The man responded with a derisive glance at Arik's feet. Arik considered explaining himself, but then decided against it.

"He is expecting you," replied the man. "Shall I escort you?"

"No," said Arik, surprised. "That won't be necessary. I know the way."

He continued down the hall with a brisk stride until he reached the foot of a narrow staircase spiraling upward into the darkness above. This was not a part of the Ministry that was commonly visited by outsiders; Arik had discovered that since his first visit months earlier. There were other chambers, brighter chambers, where the public was welcomed to address the governing body of Hestoria. He had learned, as well, that only a select few were allowed admittance to Emir's personal chambers, and only then by invitation. While Arik was surprised to hear that Emir expected his arrival (he had not sent word), he would have demanded an audience even if it had not been so.

Arik was out of breath by the time he reached the top of the staircase. He paused at the landing, waiting for his pulse to slow. When he was once again composed, he continued down the corridor. Unlike the passageways below, which were marked with white and gray marble and suffused with natural light, the upper passages were made of darker stone. Bronze sconces hung on the wall at regular intervals, limp flames burning in glass lamps.

Arik came to a wooden door with wide strips of metal bolted across it. The crest of the Ministry appeared in relief. He rapped heavily on the door.

"Come in," a voice called from within.

Arik grasped the ornate iron handle and shoved the door inward, just wide enough to slip into the room. He found Emir at his desk, crouching beside his little dragon.

"Emir, I need to speak with you immediately," Arik said, his courage already failing him.

Emir stood. He was not a tall man, nor a large one, but there was an air of authority about him that made Arik tremble.

"What is it?" asked Emir.

"I disapprove of how you're handling the problem with the Guilde."

"I see," said Emir. A low chortle vibrated in his throat.

"Do you mock me, sir?" said Arik.

"Of course not. I just find your sudden emergence of conscience amusing."

"I assure you, I have always had a conscience."

"Really? Is that why you were so willing to betray your brother-in-law? And I saw no evidence of conscience when you revealed Brommel's treachery."

Arik smoldered with suppressed anger. "You burned his wife and child alive! If I'd known what you were you capable of—"

"What did you expect I would do, Prince Arik? You yourself called him a traitor, and I do not respond lightly to treason."

Emir stepped closer so that Arik could see the red veins woven through his ever-shifting eyes. "Would you have been satisfied if I had merely punished Brommel?"

"Y-yes," answered Arik uncertainly.

"You see," continued Emir, "that is where your weakness lies. You think that disciplining the criminal will put an end to his crime. But that is not the case at all. Others will always rise up to take a martyr's place. No, Arik, to truly put an end to the offense you must punish not the offender, but those who love and support him. Leave him alive to carry the burden of regret. Let him shrivel with guilt and shame at the suffering he has created. Only by doing so will his cause die with him, and those who remain will see his cowardice and denounce him. If there are any who still believe in his cause, fear will prevent them from ever stepping forward to take his place. I ask you, Arik, where is Brommel now? Have you not heard? Why, he has fled Hestoria by ship. And those who once called him friend huddle like frightened children in their pitiful little huts."

Emir stepped behind his desk and sat down in his chair. He leaned back a little, a satisfied grin on his face. Arik could not look away from his gaunt features, unnaturally pale in the shifting candlelight.

"It seems you have a choice to make, Arik," continued Emir, pressing the fingertips of both hands together. "If my methods displease you, then you may take your leave. I will not stop you. I have no need of you. However, I suspect that your desire for your father's throne surpasses whatever meager scrap of conscience you have within you."

A timid knock at Emir's open door interrupted them.

"Sir, forgive me," said the attendant. "I've come with the gentleman's boots as he instructed."

Arik hastily snatched the boots from the boy, feeling suddenly embarrassed, yet grateful for the disruption. "I'll be going then," he said, nodding toward Emir.

The minister made no move to stop him. He spoke instead to the attendant.   "You there," he said, waving the boy into the office. "Come in and close the door."

The attendant did as he was told.

"Come closer," instructed Emir.

Again the attendant obeyed, though his expression revealed a growing agitation within him. "Yes, my Lord? How might I be of service?"

Emir held out a reassuring hand to the lad. The attendant hesitantly lay his own hand on Emir's, like a son with his father. The boy's dark skin clashed against Emir's white palm. The Minister grasped the boy's hand, turning it until the underside of his wrist was exposed.

"My servants are all devoted to me," said Emir. "None are ignorant of the consequences should they betray me."

Emir lifted a penknife from his desk and slowly, deliberately drew it across the boy's wrist. A line of blood bubbled up on his brown skin. To Arik's astonishment, the boy did not resist. Though his face revealed the fear that gripped him, he made no move to escape. Emir moved the boy's arm away from the desk and held it over his little dragon. The creature's nostrils flared as it snapped its jaws at the air. All that prevented it from attacking was the iron manacle and chain about its neck. Several drops of blood fell from the boy's wound, the dragon lapping them from the air before they hit the ground.

Arik turned away in disgust. "You are the Devil!" he hissed.

Emir raised his eyebrows in an amused expression. "Am I?" he said.

Emir released the attendant's arm. Immediately the boy clasped his good hand over the wound. Emir dismissed him and the boy promptly left.

"Perhaps you will think differently when I tell you how we have been failed."

"We? I don't understand."

"Several days ago, I sent one of my men to fetch a certain important visitor to our shores, someone quite close to you— your sister."

Arik's eyes grew wide. "Ivanore? Here in Hestoria?"

"Fredric's soldiers located her on Imaness, but she escaped. She's been hiding on a farm outside a village west of here. I sent some of my men to bring her to me. I'm sure even you can see the wisdom in that. But she escaped once again. I had no choice but to discipline the man responsible. Would you not have done the same?"

Arik's mind was suddenly a jumble. He thought of Jayson and the crystal. The crystal alone was powerful, but in the hands of the Seer...

"You understand the value of my quest," continued Emir. "With Ivanore and the crystal, obtaining Fredric's throne is almost certain. Am I still the Devil, Prince Arik?"

Emir's words faded in Arik's ears. His thoughts were beyond this place. They were far away on the island of his birth. He saw not Emir sitting in front of him, nor the charred remains of Brommel's home. He saw himself seated on his father's throne with a crown of gold on his brow.

"What about Jayson?" asked Arik. "Has there been any word on his whereabouts?"

Emir laid his pale hands atop his desk. "I sent out a small band of soldiers to scout the area you visited with Brommel," he said. "The villagers were questioned, but all claimed to know nothing of Jayson or of the Guilde."

"They're protecting them, of course."

"I would send my men out again, but with winter coming, their efforts would likely be in vain. Gerard is most certainly well concealed in his current location, wherever that might be."

"I will find them," said Arik.

"You?" asked Emir with feigned astonishment. "You are just a boy, young Arik."

"Nevertheless, I have been to Alay-Crevar and have been among the Guilde, even if for a brief time."

"I've already told you, my men have been to that village."

"I'll go back to Timbrey—"

"The tavern keeper has been dealt with." A faint grin played at the corners of Emir's lips.

Arik shuddered to think how the man might have met his end. "Then give me your best men and trackers. Let me scout the surrounding villages, the forest, the mountains. They are hiding somewhere."

"And what of your sister?"

"Ivanore came to Hestoria to find Jayson. Once we have him, it is only a matter of time before she comes to us."

Emir reached down and stroked Pip's back. A content hum resonated from its throat. "Do remember, Arik," he said, "I don't take kindly to failure."

"Nor do I," said Arik, a new resolve building within him. He clenched his fists to hide their trembling. "I will find Jayson and the crystal, no matter the cost. I swear it."

14

The first sensation Ivy felt was warmth, as though her body was securely wrapped in something soft, like a cocoon, and she felt safe and nurtured in it. She also sensed that this warmth emanated from some source nearby, but since her eyes were closed, she could not be sure. She felt her head being lifted and cradled as a bitter liquid was dribbled into her mouth. She swallowed, which took great effort. Her head spun before sinking again into blackness.

The next time she awoke, her shoulder burned. She was on her side, and the wound, which had festered, throbbed so painfully that she wanted to scream. In her mind she *was* screaming, but she couldn't be sure her throat and mouth obeyed. But the pain was brief as she again succumbed to the void of unconsciousness.

Ivy had no concept of time. She didn't know if it was day or night, or how many of them had passed. At times she wondered if she had died. At other times she prayed to the gods that she *would* die. Somehow, just when hunger began to awaken within her, her stomach was filled. When she felt cold, she was warmed. When she was in pain, she was comforted.

Incoherent images assailed her mind: vast fields of swaying grass, a room, a marble column, a dark door, a man's pale face.

And Jayson.

Jayson, she would say to him in her dreams, I have come for you. I am searching for you. And there he would be, standing just out of reach—just far enough so that he could not hear her. And every dream ended the same.

The sky was gray with an approaching storm. A cold wind whipped through Ivy's hair and stung her cheeks and eyes. She stood on a high cliff overlooking the sea, which was as dark and gray as the sky. Above her loomed a tower of stone, part of a much larger structure—some sort of castle or cathedral. Below her, the waves assaulted the rocks with a fury she had never before seen. And something was in the water.

She peered closer, struggling to make it out in the hastening darkness. Then she knew—though she could not say how she knew. It was Jayson floundering in the waves. She screamed his name over and over, but her voice was no match for the storm. Panic seizing her, she stepped to the edge of the cliff and prepared to dive in after him. She searched the water once more to discover his location so she could go to him. But he was no longer visible. The waves had claimed him. Dropping to her knees, Ivy felt her very soul rent in two, and the sound that exploded out of her was not of this world.

"JAYSON!"

Ivy's eyes flew open. She frantically gasped for air as if she were drowning. But a moment later, she knew it had been a dream, the same dream she had dreamed a dozen times before. As her eyes focused to the faint light, she realized she was lying on a bed in an unfamiliar room. Slowly, she sat up. Her shoulder ached, but the discomfort was tolerable. The room was small yet welcoming. In the center was an iron stove from which radiated a great deal of heat. A pot of something simmered on top of it. There was a rug beside the bed, a table, some chairs. Ivy's mouth watered from the smell of freshly baked bread. She saw a crudely shaped loaf of dark bread on a nearby shelf and craved a slice.

On the floor beside her bed were her slippers. She pulled them on and then set her feet on the floor. She tried to stand, but she was too weak, and her first attempt resulted in failure. She sat on the side of the bed for a while longer, and then tried again. She stood on feeble legs and reached for a chair, resting against it. When she felt strong enough, she managed to cross the room to the shelves. She lifted the loaf and broke it in half. Steam rose from the soft, warm center, and its sweet fragrance was more than she could resist. Setting one half back on the shelf, she took the other half and ate it with ravenous delight.

With the bread devoured, Ivy felt her strength returning. Stepping to the window, she pressed her face to the glass. The glass was cold, and her breath fogged the area around her mouth and nose.

How long had she lain unconscious? Hours? Days? Her memories of the night Teak carried her away from Mikel's farm were sketchy at best, but she was beginning to understand, at least in part, what had happened in the time since then.

Ivy turned from the window. Keeping a hand against the wall to steady herself, she reached the door and opened it. A gust of cold air blew into the room. It felt crisp and invigorating in her lungs. For the first time since before leaving Imaness, she felt truly alive.

The air was silent except for the gentle babble of running water nearby. Ivy took a few halting steps outside of the cabin. The banks of the nearby river were crusted with ice, and a steady stream of crystal-clear water flowed between them. The trees growing near the river glistened, their branches studded with frozen drops of dew, and the ground was dusted with morning frost. Ivy spotted a trail of footprints in it. She decided to follow. It would be fun to surprise Teak. He would be pleased to see how much better she was.

The prints led Ivy around the far side of the cabin toward a dense cluster of trees. Teak must be out hunting, she thought. The cold penetrated the thin fabric of her clothing, which she realized with appreciation—and some uneasiness—that they were clean, which meant they had been removed from her and washed, perhaps several times. In any case, they provided little in the way of protection from the chill, so Ivy decided it would be best to wait for Teak inside the cabin.

As she turned back, however, she caught a glimpse of something moving out of the corner of her eye—not in the forest, but behind the cabin. She was shivering now, but she could bear a few minutes more. She headed toward the back of the cabin and saw the remains of what, at one time, must have been a garden. Straggly dead sticks stuck out of humped rows of earth like frozen fingers forever pointing toward the sky.

Another flash of movement, this time near the river.

"Teak?" Ivy called out. Her voice was raspy and hoarse from disuse. Her teeth chattered now, and her body trembled from the cold. Exhaustion quickly consumed her. Still she went on, following a new set of tracks in the frost.

This time the tracks led her between the river and the cabin, back to where she began. Ivy caught her breath. The prints led to the door, parallel to her own prints leading away.

"Teak, is that you?" she whispered. A shadow passed across the open doorway. Ivy stepped forward, eager to return to the warmth of the cabin. But just as she reached the threshold, a figure stepped into the light. Ivy gasped—then she collapsed from fright. The person standing before her wasn't Teak at all.

15

"There now, you're coming 'round."

The voice sounded distant and muddled, as if from a dream. Indeed, when Ivy opened her eyes, she thought the woman leaning over her was another one of her visions. The woman nodded approvingly as she rubbed Ivy's hands. Since she was nothing more than a dream, Ivy didn't think the woman would mind her staring at her, for the woman was a sight to behold. Long, gray tendrils of hair framed an equally gray and wrinkled face from which protruded a prominent bulbous nose. Below that were two pale, thin lips etched with creases. Her shoulders were stooped, and her ragged shawl hung limply from them. She wore a silver pendant on a leather cord around her neck. Ivy's eyes rested on the pendant. On it was the image of a gryphon, its wings spread wide as if in flight.

"All right then," the woman said. "Had a good scare is all. I tend to do that to some people. But you're fine now, dear, aren't you?"

Ivy lay on the same bed she had found herself in earlier. For a moment, she wondered if she had ever left it and if all this was part of her dream. She glanced around the room. It was just as she had seen it before, but there was the half-eaten loaf of bread on the shelf. It hadn't been a dream.

Ivy was about to tell the woman so, when Teak appeared in the doorway carrying a load of cut wood in his arms. When he saw the old woman hovering over Ivy, the wood fell to floor in a terrible clatter.

"Stop!" he shouted. "Get aw-way from her!"

Teak darted forward, a fiercely protective expression on his face. Ivy was certain he meant to pull the woman away, but just as Teak reached them, the woman raised her hands and jutted her fingers outward into a stiff, spider-like pose. Teak's advance came to an abrupt halt as he flew backward to the floor. But he was not to be so easily stopped. He leapt to his feet and once more ran forward. The woman repeated her gesture and held it this time. Teak froze, his arms and legs held in an awkward position.

"You'll not be harming me," said the woman in a crackly voice. "And I'll not be harming the girl. Now, you can stay that way all day if you like, or I can release you and have your word that you'll behave yourself in my house."

"Your house?" Teak sputtered, struggling against his invisible bonds.

"That's correct, young man. *My* house."

The woman lowered her hand, and Teak's body relaxed, freed from the power that held him.

"Take a chair," the woman commanded.

Teak hesitated, and then cautiously obeyed.

Ivy didn't like the tone the woman used with Teak. With some effort, she sat up on the side of the bed. "There's no need to be unkind to him," she said. "He's done no harm to you or your cabin."

The woman scrutinized Ivy with a skeptical glare. "I should hope not! Gone for a few weeks on business, and I come back to find squatters eating my food and sleeping in my bed! And why is it so cold in here?"

The woman snapped her fingers and a flame burst alive in the fireplace. "That's better," she said.

Teak's eyes widened. "Are you a w-w-w-"

"Speak up, boy! I haven't got much patience!"

"A w-witch."

"Me? A witch?" The woman guffawed. "Heaven's no. That sort of mischief is better left to the Vatéz. No, I am an enchantress."

Ivy gripped the bedpost as a wave of dizziness passed through her. "The Vatéz are enchanters as well, are they not?" she asked.

"They are magic gone bad. I won't cast myself among the lot of them." The woman spoke with such contempt that Ivy was certain she spoke the truth. "Now," continued the woman before Teak or Ivy could ask any more questions, "I think I deserve some explanation as to why you are *in—my— house*."

"W-we were sent here," answered Teak.

"Sent here by whom?" she scoffed. "No one knows I'm here. I've lived alone for nearly ten years!"

Teak seemed to shrivel under the woman's glare. Ivy knew how confrontation was not something with which he had had much experience.

"It was my fault," said Ivy. "I became ill while traveling and needed shelter."

"Well," continued the woman sarcastically, "that would explain why you were wandering about outside without a shawl."

Teak shot a critical glance at Ivy.

The woman went on. "So you stumbled onto my cabin, found no one home, ate my food, burned my wood, slept in my bed, and now I am supposed to just accept you as part of my family?"

"N-no," said Teak.

"Then you'll leave."

"N-no," Teak repeated. "We c-can't. *She* c-can't."

The woman glanced at Ivy and back at Teak. "Why the devil not?"

Teak fell silent, uncertainty in his face. Ivy wished she were near enough to place a reassuring hand on his arm. He had obviously gone through great pains to care for her; it wasn't fair for him to be treated this way.

"If you want us to leave," said Ivy, "we will leave. Just tell us which direction we should go to find the nearest town."

Ivy tried to stand, but the dizziness threatened to topple her back into the bed. A moment later, however, Teak was beside her. He gently pressed his hands against her shoulders, urging her to lie back down. Ivy obliged, letting her head fall back against the pillow.

To Ivy's surprise, Teak turned to the woman and spoke with more firmness than she thought him capable.

"W-w'ere not leaving," he said, pulling himself up to his full height. His jaw tightened as he spoke. "N-not until Ivy recovers. If you let us stay, I'll w-work for you. I've already fixed the roof, but the w-windows are w-warped, your garden is overgrown, and the path to the river is rotted. I can hunt and fish and carry w-water. I'll do anything you ask, but w-we are staying."

Teak towered over the old woman, but she was not intimidated. She narrowed her eyes at him and twisted one of her tendrils between her fingers as if considering his proposition. The moments that passed were agonizing. Ivy could see it on Teak's face, but he remained resolute. He would not take Ivy away.

After a while, the old woman turned from Teak and hobbled to the cookstove where the kettle of tea was still warming. She bent over it and breathed in the steam.

"Get me a cup," she demanded. Teak hesitated only a moment before hurrying to the cupboard. She took the cup from his outstretched hand, poured the tea, and took a sip.

"You made this tea?" she asked. "Can you cook?"

Teak nodded.

"All right," the woman said, as though she had come to an important decision. "You can stay until spring. But first, you will build another bed. It will be a bit snug in here, but I'll not sleep on the floor. You found my tools?"

Again Teak nodded.

"Then stop dawdling! Get to it! I've been traveling for days, and my bones are weary. I would like a place to lay myself down tonight."

Teak's face transformed into the happy, boyish expression Ivy knew so well. He did not hesitate, but ran out the door, ready to work.

The two women, left alone, considered each other. The woman fetched another cup, filled it, and offered it to Ivy. They finished their tea in silence, and then the woman collected the cups and set them on the table.

Ivy wondered if the woman would speak again. She had been so forthright before, her present silence seemed odd.

"Thank you," said Ivy, more to end the silence than for anything else. "I'll try not to be a burden."

"You're already a burden," replied the woman, "but then again, it will be nice to have some company to help me pass the winter."

At first glance, the woman seemed severe, but her eyes twinkled in a way that set Ivy instantly at ease.

"The name's Agnora," said the woman. "And you're Ivy. Is that right?"

"Yes."

"I know I'm a little rough around the edges, but I have to be cautious. There are those who would love to see me dead. I had to make sure the two of you were sincere. The Vatéz don't much like apostates."

"You were in the Vatéz?"

"Yes. That's why I shun unexpected visitors. But you seem harmless enough." Agnora swiped a fingertip across a shelf and scowled. "I don't like strangers nosing around my things."

"We're sorry. In all honesty, today is the first I've been well enough to be aware of my surroundings, let alone nose around in your things."

"Then why are *you* apologizing?"

"Teak was only trying to help me. He's done the best he could."

Agnora's expression changed suddenly. Her face went pale, and her lips trembled. "What did you say?"

"I said Teak was doing his best to care for me under the most difficult circumstances."

"Teak…" Agnora repeated the name, curiosity in her eyes. Then just as suddenly as her expression had changed, her brusqueness returned.

"You said you were sent here," said Agnora, "but you didn't say by whom."

"We were told to come by Teak's uncle, Mikel."

"And where is he? Why hasn't he come?"

Ivy looked down, trying not to let the memory of what had happened to Mikel overwhelm her. "He's dead," she said simply.

Another strange look passed over Agnora's face, one of disbelief and of anguish, but the expression was nothing more than a flicker and then it was gone.

Agnora smiled, but Ivy sensed that sorrow lurked behind that smile. To further mask it, Agnora turned the conversation to something trifling.

"If you are to be my guests, I shall have to teach you both to make decent tea. This stuff tastes like weeds," she said, carrying the whole kettle to the window and pouring it out. "I'll fix us up an indoor garden of lemongrass and mint. Then we shall have a fine cup of tea indeed."

16

Arik, mounted on a glossy brown stallion, lifted his hand into the air to signal his men to come to a halt. The two dozen horses in the company pawed the ground. They had been traveling for two days through dense forest to reach this place. Now, seeing open space and sunlight made both the horses and the soldiers who rode them eager to move on.

Beside him, on a white mount, Erland waited for his orders.

"Keep to the trees," Arik told him. "I don't want to alert the old man to our presence."

Should a full company of armed soldiers suddenly march up to his front door, Leo would surely flee—or worse, give false information. No, this was a visit Arik had to make alone.

"Take the men through the forest around the perimeter of this field," Arik continued. "Stay well away from the clearing. Do not let yourselves be seen. The road continues on the opposite side. Follow it a mile or so, and wait for me there."

Arik urged his horse forward. He had scarcely passed halfway across the stones when the door to the cabin opened. The man was just as Arik remembered, thin and frail looking, a blank stare in his eyes. He stopped in front of Leo, who reached up to stroke the horse's nose.

"We don't get many visitors here," Leo said. "Can I help you?"

"Just passing through," replied Arik, "but I could use some refreshment for my horse."

Leo jutted a chin toward the side of the house. "There's water in the trough and fresh hay beside it."

"Thank you." Arik dismounted and led his horse to the water, wrapping its reins around a post. He looked around for signs of the daughter.

"Abby," he said in as casual a tone as possible, "is she inside?"

Leo's face revealed no surprise at the question. He held onto the porch rail as he rested one foot on the bottom step. "Afraid not," he said. "Gone hunting, but she'll be back soon, I imagine. You're welcome to wait for her if you like. Are you a friend?"

Arik stepped closer to Leo. "Don't you remember me?" he asked.

Leo paused thoughtfully. "Your voice sounds familiar, yet your name escapes me."

"My name is Arik. I was companion to a man named Brommel who visited you not long ago. You directed him to the village of Alay-Crevar."

Leo's expression stiffened, his jaw set. It was as though the old man sensed Arik's intent. "Yes," he said. "I remember Brommel. And I do recall you helped yourself to several slices of my cheese. I make it myself, you know. Have you come for more?"

There was only the slightest hint of sarcasm in the man's voice, enough to grate on Arik's nerves.

"I've come for directions, same as you gave Brommel."

"Why do you need them? You already know the way to Alay-Crevar."

Arik's patience wore thin, and he restrained his contempt no longer. "You know as well as I that Gerard and his followers abandoned that place and are hiding somewhere else. What I want is the current location of the Guilde."

Leo's empty gaze slowly came to rest on Arik's face, giving the illusion that he was looking right through him. Arik shuddered at the thought that maybe he could.

He drew his sword and placed its tip at Leo's throat. "Tell me where to find Gerard," he hissed, "or there will be no one left here to guide the way."

Leo remained stubbornly silent, and his silence incensed Arik. Of course, Leo would not betray the Guilde so easily. If the daughter had been present, he might have used her against him. Threatening her would surely have given him the result he wanted. He might wait for her return, but patience was not one of Arik's strongest virtues.

Arik pressed the point of his blade into Leo's skin. A thin line of blood trickled down his throat, staining the collar of his tunic red.

"You'll die, old man. Is that what you want? Is the secret of the Guilde really worth such a sacrifice?"

Arik waited for some protest, but none came. Arik growled angrily. He was glad he had sent his men ahead and that they were not witnesses to Leo's insolence.

Arik twisted Leo's shirt in his fist, pulling him close. "Tell me where to find the Guilde. There is a man, a half-breed, among them who has something that belongs to me. It is him I am after. The others will not be harmed."

Leo narrowed his eyes. Though empty and lifeless, Arik felt as if they peered into his very soul.

"I know you, Prince Arik," said Leo, his voice as hard as stone. "And I know what you seek—but the crystal will never be yours."

Rage erupted from Arik in an uncontrolled, bestial scream as he plunged his sword through Leo's throat and out the back of his neck. Blood gushed down Leo's chest and back in two thick, red streams. As Arik jerked his blade out again, Leo's body collapsed at his feet.

Arik loomed over the old man, his lungs gasping as his fury subsided. He had never killed before. A heaviness swelled in his gut, churning his stomach. He raised the back of his hand to his mouth, which felt suddenly dry. His sword, which he held so tightly his knuckles had blanched, dripped with blood. Arik noticed that both his hands were trembling. He felt lightheaded, as if he might faint or vomit, neither of which would become a man of his station. Ashamed of his own weakness, he drew in several deep, sharp breaths to clear his head.

"The crystal *will* be mine," Arik said. "How will you defend it now that you are dead, old man?"

Arik wiped his sword clean on Leo's tunic. There was no time to waste. His men were waiting for him. He would lead them to Alay-Crevar, and he would find the crystal if he had to kill a hundred men to do it.

Betrayal

Arik mounted his horse and departed at a full gallop, but he left with such haste that he failed to see the pair of dark eyes watching him from the nearby woods.

17

Jayson didn't think he'd be missed at Naresh. Though he'd spent the past two weeks in the secluded village, he hadn't garnered much attention. The natives busied themselves with their herds while the members of the Guilde made preparations for winter. Tents were secured and covered with skins, firewood collected and stacked neatly beneath makeshift shelters, clothing and boots sewn and distributed, game hunted and cured.

Jayson had helped with the hunting. He and several younger men had made three trips to the outside so far, but upon each return he was forgotten. The only one who seemed to notice his presence at all was Gerard. Jayson had managed to avoid Dianis, since she was still cloistered in her tent, but he supposed she would be on her feet soon enough. He just wasn't sure if he wanted to be around when she was.

He found himself spending more and more time beyond the falls—always with hunting as his pretext. Today he tracked his prey alone.

The drab gray sky foretold the coming change in the weather. The first snow of winter would come soon, but for now the air still clung to the last remnants of autumn.

Jayson sniffed at the air, but his heart was not in the hunt. He considered turning back when another scent arrived on a thin breeze. He brought his horse to a halt and listened.

Footsteps—running—nearing the lake!

Jayson urged his horse to a gallop. He reached Naresh's falls just as Leo's daughter, Abby, dropped to her knees at the water's edge. Gulping down handfuls of water, Abby cast Jayson a sideways glance as he approached. He waited as she splashed a little of the water on her face, which was red with exertion.

"I've been mostly running for two days to get here," she said, still gasping for breath.

She paused, bracing her arms against her knees. Her body trembled, and she swayed unsteadily. Jayson quickly dismounted and hurried to her side just as Gerard and several other guardians emerged from behind the falls.

"My father's dead," said Abby. Jayson now saw that her eyes were swollen and red from crying. "I was just returning from the woods when I saw—I saw my father slain. I ran to him, but it was too late. He was already gone, his killer fled."

Her voice broke, but she clenched her jaw against the sorrow that so obviously consumed her. She went on.

"I recognized him, the boy with red hair. He'd come before with the man whose wife you buried. I wanted my revenge, so I took my bow and followed him. But he wasn't alone."

Abby's eyes swam with tears. She choked on her words.

"Soldiers—the Ministry—I followed them to Alay-Crevar—the entire village—"

Abby collapsed against Jayson's chest, weeping.

Gerard had reached them by now and gently took Abby into his arms. "Go," he told Jayson. "Go, and tell me what you find."

Jayson rode his horse to near exhaustion. During the journey his mind reeled with fragmented thoughts: Brielle and her baby lying in their coffin, the blackened ruins of Brommel's home, Ivanore watching from the cliffs of Dokur, Leo lying dead among the black slabs of stone. Was he to blame for it all? Could he be?

As he neared Alay-Crevar, Jayson was taken aback by a foul odor in the air. The offensive smell was strong enough for him to cover his nose and mouth with the edge of his cloak. An image from his childhood reluctantly brought itself to his memory. He had smelled something like this once before as a boy hunting in the marshlands near his home. The putrid scent had aroused his curiosity, and so he followed it to where the carcass of a full-grown warboar lay decaying in the hot afternoon sun.

Jayson forced the picture from his mind. He knew what the smell must be, and was drawn to it—not from curiosity, but from a desperate hope that he was wrong.

Up ahead, the first glimpses of Alay-Crevar were visible through tree branches. The road whereon Jayson traveled led directly through its center, passing by all the shops and inns, over a small bridge, and through the fields and settlements beyond. Jayson's horse slowed its pace without any prompting from its master. When they reached the border between the forest and the village, the horse snorted and tossed its head, reluctant to continue. Jayson rubbed its neck and spoke soothingly to it. Finally, he managed to coax it forward.

The stench had grown so strong now as to make Jayson want to vomit, but still he pressed on. The town was completely still. Not a sound reached Jayson's ears except for the *clop clop* of his horse's hooves against the cobbled road and an incessant hum in the air. As he passed by the familiar structures, he half-expected someone to come bounding out one of the doors to greet him. But no one came. There was not even a face at any of the windows. It was as though the entire village had been abandoned.

Jayson reached the bridge that spanned the small stream that served as a natural boundary between the town and the farmlands. He stopped his horse and dismounted. The hum was louder now, like the sound of a thousand whispered voices. The stench, too, hung so heavy in the air that he could feel it on his skin.

Wrapping his horse's reins loosely around the trunk of a tree, Jayson started across the bridge. He had advanced only a few steps when the scene that suddenly unveiled itself turned his heart to stone.

Off to one side of the bridge in the midst of the river lay a large, black heap the surface of which moved and undulated in chaotic patterns. At first glance, one might have thought it was a living creature, but Jayson realized at once what it was.

He spun to the opposite side of the bridge and retched over the side. The grotesque image of flies feasting on the massive mound of bodies was more than he could bear to witness. He thought of what Abby had told him about the boy with red hair. He closed his eyes and let the scents come to him.

Yes. Yes, there it was. Though it had grown weak with time and smothered by the overwhelming stench of death, the evidence of Arik's presence here—at this slaughter—was

228

unmistakable. The realization sent a tremor through Jayson's body. He gritted his teeth against it and fought the urge to cry out. Arik, who had fought beside him against his own father's soldiers and had willingly been exiled along with Jayson. Arik, who had been his friend and brother until greed overtook him—he had led Emir's soldiers here. He was responsible for all these deaths.

It crushed Jayson to know how changed Arik had become, how unlike the boy he once knew and loved. But this was not the time to mourn for him. Arik would have to account for his actions later. For now, Jayson had to report what he'd found to Gerard and the Guilde. Though his legs trembled weakly beneath him, he hurried back to his horse and, urging her to a gallop, rode swiftly away from Alay-Crevar.

He did not stop until he arrived at his destination, with both he and his horse nearing collapse. He wasted not a moment in telling Gerard all he had witnessed. Gerard immediately called a council of the Guilde, which meant Jayson was no longer needed for the time being. And for that, he was glad.

Jayson wanted to run, but the valley was too small. There was nowhere to go. He stepped out of Gerard's tent and headed for the cave behind the waterfall. There, concealed by the darkness, he dropped to his knees and pressed his fists against his eyes. Like the cleft in the mountain, something inside of him rent in two, leaving a fissure wide enough to swallow his very soul. The pain inside of him was real, and greater than any he had ever before known.

In agony, he released an excruciating cry—a cry that, were it not for the incessant roar of the waterfall crashing against the lake and rocks outside, might have shattered the very mountain and sent it collapsing down around him.

18

The waterfall of Naresh was a window to the outside world, one through which Jayson could see yet not be seen. He sat in the darkness of the cave staring out through the ever-moving curtain of water. He felt at home secluded here amid the shadows within the mountain.

The air in the cave was particularly cold today and the shadows were deeper and darker than usual. The clouds had turned black, and the Naresh valley fell into a perpetual twilight. Winter had arrived.

"It isn't your fault, you know."

Jayson did not turn to look behind him. He had heard Dianis—smelled her—moments before she spoke.

"Leo and the village," Dianis continued, "Emir is to blame. Not you. Anyway, Abby's all right now. She's sleeping."

Jayson remained silent, his eyes fixed on the blurred image beyond the veil of water. He should at least look at her, he thought. But he couldn't. He did not want the burden of one more image to carry.

"I shouldn't be here," he said.

Dianis hesitated. When she did speak, her tone was sharp. "Fine. If you want to go, then go."

"I do want to go," he replied. He could almost feel Dianis bristling behind him. "But I also want to stay."

Dianis approached him, supported by a makeshift crutch fashioned from a tree branch. Jayson could tell from the heaviness in her breathing that using it took a great deal of effort. This was her first venture outside her tent in weeks. He was touched that she had come to him.

He slid over a little to make room for her on the stone ledge on which he sat. She lowered herself down beside him and stretched out her injured leg.

"If I have to spend one more day in that tent, I'll just scream," she said, laughing a little. "Papa about had a fit when I insisted on venturing out on my own. Can you believe he actually wanted to follow me around?"

"He's just trying to help, Dianis."

"I'm not a child! Or an invalid. I can get around just fine on my own."

"Your father will be cross when he finds out you've come here."

"Let him be cross then. I've had enough confinement. I need sunlight and fresh air or I'll go mad!"

Jayson chuckled. Dianis was determined, and he was certain even Gerard was no match for her once she set her mind to something.

"Well, if you're looking for sunlight, I'm afraid you'll be disappointed," he told her, nodding toward the cave opening where the world seemed oddly muted. Dianis considered this a moment before replying. When she did, the edge was gone from her voice.

"Do you really want to leave?" she asked.

Jayson did not know what to say. He slipped the folded piece of parchment from his pocket and ran his finger over its edge. Then he handed it to Dianis.

"What is this?" she asked as she read it.

"A contract," answered Jayson, "between myself and Orrin Dawes, captain of the Silver Mist."

Dianis's eyes flickered up from the parchment, then down again, an expression of disbelief on her face. "It's for indentured servitude," she said.

"That's right. In exchange for passage on his ship to Imaness, I have agreed to spend six months in his employ."

"Passage to Imaness? For whom?"

"A friend," answered Jayson with a shrug. "That doesn't matter anyhow. Captain Dawes, it turns out, owns a rather large plantation in the midlands, just beyond Hestoria's northern border. He's at sea most of the time, but he returns home during the winter."

"It says here that you are not expected until spring."

"To help plant the next crop and stay through harvest."

"Then you'll stay with us through the winter?"

"What for, Dianis?" replied Jayson. "The people of Naresh are shepherds. They are a peaceful people who rarely have contact with the outside world. I've seen the way they look at me."

"Have they been unkind to you?"

"Unkind, no—but they're wary of me. I am strange to them. I don't belong here. I don't belong anywhere."

"That's not true!" Dianis's voice was urgent. "You're right about the Naresh, but what does that matter? The guardians think nothing of your mixed blood. My father is very fond of you. He'd be heartbroken if you left. I'd—"

Her voice broke off. She held her bottom lip between her teeth, fighting back tears. He quickly returned to her side and wrapped his arms around her.

A few tears fell, but Dianis wiped them away. She looked up at Jayson. In her face he saw a fierce determination to hold back the emotion that threatened to overcome her, but a moment later her façade crumbled, and tears streamed down her cheeks.

"It's more than that," Jayson told her. "I'm haunted by so many things. I've caused so much pain."

"I told you before that it's not your fault!"

"They—the soldiers—the Vatéz—they want *me*. They slaughtered all those people because of me."

"No," said Dianis, shaking her head. "They want the crystal."

Jayson brushed Dianis's tears away with his fingertips. He had never seen her so vulnerable. Perhaps coming so close to death and spending so much time inside the confines of a tent had taken its toll. He was about to embrace her, to tell her he would stay if she promised not to cry anymore, when Dianis did something that took him completely by surprise. She closed her eyes and lightly pursed her lips, tilting her face toward his.

As Dianis leaned forward, however, Jayson leaned away. Without thinking, he scooted back on the ledge until he was up against the wall of the cave. A few moments passed, and then Dianis blinked open her eyes. She stared at Jayson, horror-struck.

"I-I'm sorry," she stammered.

Jayson relaxed a little when he saw how embarrassed Dianis was. Then he laughed. Dianis's expression immediately turned hard.

"What are you laughing at?" she shouted.

"You tried to kiss me!" Jayson said.

"I did not!"

"You did!"

Dianis responded by folding her arms and pouting. Angry and defeated, she said nothing more. Jayson was amused to see Dianis's all too familiar stubbornness showing. It meant she was feeling herself again.

"Well, your leg may be healed," said Jayson, "but now I've injured your pride."

Dianis shifted her body so that she faced away from him.

"Dianis," Jayson said, his voice tender. "I am flattered, really, and if circumstances were different I might have responded the way you wanted me to, but..." Here he chose his words carefully. "You are very young, Dianis. It would be wrong to take advantage of your affection for me. And I do have a wife."

"Whom you haven't seen in more than a year," snapped Dianis.

"Whom I still love—and will forever."

They remained silent for a while, the thunder of the waterfall the only sound between them. Jayson waited for some sign from Dianis that he was forgiven, but she remained rigid. Finally, he stood and walked toward the fading light of the valley. He paused at the cave opening, but did not want to turn around.

From where he stood, he could see the entire Naresh valley. In a few days, it would be covered with snow. Soon the falls would freeze, and from what Gerard had told him, there would be no way in or out of the valley until spring. The villagers and the guardians alike were well prepared for their winter siege. Jayson had no reason to worry. He had access to ample supplies himself, enough for two journeys north if need be. His horse was strong, having grazed on the valley's rich grasses and eaten the abundant treats of carrots and apples supplied to him by the children here.

Jayson would not say goodbye.

"I'm going north to Dawes's plantation," he said. "I'll be gone before morning."

As he stepped forward, resolute on his decision, Dianis sprung from her spot on the ledge, hobbled forward on her still bandaged leg, and flung her arms around him from behind. The fierce embrace was brief. She said nothing as she retrieved her crutch and limped past Jayson out of the cave. He watched her as she crossed the distance to her tent. She paused uncertainly. Then she looked back, lifted her hand, and gave a short wave. Then she disappeared into her tent. Only once she had gone did Jayson think to wave back.

19

The journey to Dawes's plantation took Jayson through sweeping valleys and across towering mountains. The road on which he traveled strung together a dozen different villages and towns, each one nearly identical to the next. Even the wary glances from the townsfolk were the same. These were humble farm folk who had spent generations within their own little spheres. Most had never seen an Agoran before, let alone one who bore an uncanny resemblance to themselves. Jayson passed through each town as quickly as possible, stopping only occasionally to verify that he was heading in the right direction.

On the fourth day, the weather turned bitterly cold. The dark clouds that had been threatening snow made good on their threat, and the first flurries began to fall. By noon, the ground was lightly dusted in white, and by nightfall all evidence of earth had entirely vanished from view. The horse kicked up billowy clouds of snow with its hooves, the wind swirling them into miniature cyclones. As the day wore on and the wind grew stronger, Jayson could no longer distinguish the snow that was falling from the snow blowing up from the ground. The trees and stones and even the sky above were all a single landscape of endless white.

The wind slashed through Jayson's clothes and bit at his skin. His fingers burned from the cold. He knew he should find shelter, but locating anything in this blizzard would be impossible. He managed to stay on the road by watching the faint outline of it below him. He had traveled through a very small village called Ashlin that morning. From Dawes's instructions, he knew that his plantation was within a day's ride from there. He pressed on, hoping he might reach it before dark settled in.

As Jayson pondered the inevitability of night and the unbearable cold it was certain to bring, he came upon a post at the side of the road. Stopping his horse, he climbed down to have a better look. There was a sign attached, covered in ice and snow. Jayson wiped it away with his nearly frozen hand and read: DASTENE AL ASHLIN.

Jayson peered through the haze of white and spotted a yellow glow not far ahead. Leading his horse by the reins, he approached what appeared to be a large structure of some kind. A house.

The light grew brighter as he neared. Its front window was aglow with several lanterns. Drawn toward the light and the inviting warmth they promised, Jayson was tempted to go directly to the door and let himself in. But first he located the barn, which thankfully was nearby, and secured his horse inside where it would be protected from the storm along with the six other horses there. Only then did Jayson venture to the front door of the house, which was the largest he had ever seen. His fingers were far too numb now to knock. So he kicked at the door instead.

By now, the cold had seeped deep into his bones. He no longer felt his fingers or hands for that matter, and his lips and cheeks and nose burned. As he waited and hoped for someone to admit him into the welcoming amber glow, he imagined he was standing on the cliffs overlooking the harbor at Dokur, watching the yellow orb of the sun creep across the darkening sky.

The door opened a crack, and a stout, plump woman with a severe expression stood silhouetted against the light. Jayson shivered violently. He tried to control it enough to speak, but his words came in erratic jerky syllables.

"P-pardon me," he said, forcing the sounds from between chattering teeth. "I've c-come by invitation from Captain Dawes." He held out the contract. The woman snatched it from his trembling hands and read it silently.

"Your contract doesn't begin until planting season starts in the spring," said the woman sharply.

"I know, and I have no argument with that. I came because I had nowhere else to go, and I hoped Captain Dawes wouldn't mind my waiting out the winter here."

"We don't generally admit your kind," she replied, her lips drawn into a perpetual frown.

"And what kind is that?" answered Jayson.

A moment of silence passed awkwardly between them.

"Captain Dawes isn't expected home for another week," she said finally. "Laborers sleep in the bunkhouse out back. You can stay there until he returns. Hold on," she added, disappearing into the house. Jayson felt the warm air seeping out of the open door and longed to go inside, but a moment later the woman returned carrying two folded blankets, a lit lantern, and a clean tunic. He accepted them all gratefully.

"Breakfast is at dawn," she told him. "You may join the house staff in the kitchen for the time being. Come spring, however, laborers eat outside. If you require anything else, you will ask for me. My name is Nira."

Her tone was dispassionate, though the disdain in her expression was unmistakable. Jayson turned back to the storm. The wind felt like a hundred daggers stabbing at his skin. He didn't have time to even thank Nira before she closed the door loudly behind him.

The snow had let up enough so that he could see the general layout of the property, which was flat and sprawled for miles in every direction. The house sat near the road whence he came, but the plantation itself seemed endless. In the distance, Jayson could just make out the dim outline of a mountain range.

A sudden shiver took hold of him, reminding him of his need for shelter. He hurried around to the back of the house and immediately spotted the bunkhouse, a long narrow structure made of odd-sized wooden planks. The door to it opened easily and Jayson stepped inside, grateful to be out of the cold once and for all.

Once inside, he turned up the flame in his lantern, and the room came into view, though much of it remained in shadow as the lantern's feeble flame was unable to fully light so vast a room. Animal pelts and heads adorned the walls, and a rug of thick fur lay on the floor.

In the center of the room stood a long wooden table, a bench running along each side of it. A third bench stood in front of a cold fireplace. A dozen empty cots lined the walls. Jayson set the lantern on the table. He unfolded the blankets and arranged them on the nearest cot. He then pulled off his wet clothes and dressed in the dry tunic, which was made of a rough material most likely provided to the laborers. He was grateful for it just the same. He noted the woodpile near the fireplace and set about arranging some of the smaller logs in the fireplace. Lighting a strip of kindling with the lantern's flame, he used it to ignite the logs. Finally, feeling more exhausted than he'd ever been in his life, he collapsed onto one of the cots and slept.

20

By the time winter had settled on the forest of Hestoria, Ivy had learned to call Agnora's little cabin home. Though still too weak to walk far from it without help, she did manage to get around inside without much trouble. Sometimes, on better days, she would venture the short walk to the river to fetch a bucket of water or to the garden to watch Teak work on repairing the fence. She grew accustomed to Agnora's brashness and learned to appreciate her company. Though often abrupt in her manner, Agnora was a generous hostess. Ivy especially enjoyed watching Agnora perform small feats of magic, such as starting the cook fire with a mere snap of her fingers, or melting the snow from the garden so that Teak could clear it of stones. The magic came so easily to her, yet she used it sparingly. She accomplished most tasks the same way Ivy or Teak would, by the work of her own hands. But once in a while, when a task was too menial or too tedious, Agnora would flick her wrist and it would be done.

It was just that sort of thing that finally got the better of Ivy's curiosity. It was a particularly crisp morning, and the night had left a fresh layer of white on the ground. Ivy and Agnora had gone together to the river to get water for the tea and found a new sheet of ice extending well out from the bank.

Ivy knelt on the frozen earth and hit the bucket against the ice hoping to smash it, but the ice was too thick. Agnora stood above her grumbling.

"Hit it harder."

Ivy tried again and again to no avail. "I just don't have enough strength," she said.

"Then move aside. It's too damn cold out here to waste another second."

Agnora lifted her hand and twisted her wrist quickly. A light blanket of steam began to rise from the ice. As it thinned, Ivy saw the fish swimming against the current below it. A moment later, the ice had melted.

Agnora grunted, and then turned back toward the cabin. Ivy dipped the bucket into the icy water, filling it a little more than halfway.

"Let m-me take that." Teak had approached without her notice. He took the bucket from her and frowned. "It's half-empty," he said.

"If I fill it any more than that I'd have to leave it here by the river," answered Ivy, laughing. "I'm afraid I can't carry more than that just yet."

Teak squatted and dunked the bucket deep into the current, and then hauled it up without so much as a hint of strain on his face. Water sloshed out of one side of the bucket as he switched the handle from his right hand to his left, and then he offered Ivy his free hand. It took some effort for Ivy to move from her knees to her feet, and she was grateful for Teak's steady hand to help her. She realized that without him she might not have been able to manage it at all. The thought of being stuck kneeling at the edge of the river for the rest of the morning struck her as funny, and she laughed.

"W-what is it?" asked Teak.

"Nothing, really," she replied, "just thinking how silly I'd look trying to stand up on my own just now."

"You shouldn't be out here alone."

"Oh, I wasn't."

"Agnora left you here?" asked Teak disapprovingly. The two walked at a leisurely pace up the pathway toward the cabin.

"It's not like she abandoned me," Ivy said. "I'm sure she thought I'd be strong enough by now."

"But you're n-not."

"I'm getting stronger every day."

"You should be resting."

"I've been resting for weeks. Teak," said Ivy, pausing at the cabin door, "I know you don't care for Agnora. She is a bit coarse but she means well, and I am grateful for her kindness to me—to both of us. I should be completely well soon, and we'll move on. Until then, please try to be gracious for my sake."

Teak did not reply, but Ivy saw in his eyes a reluctant agreement to her request. He released her hand and pushed open the cabin door.

"Ah, there you are," said Agnora. She was busy chopping herbs at the table. She did not look up as Teak set the bucket of water on the floor beside her. "I was taking inventory of my farming tools yesterday," she continued. "The spade handle is quite weathered. It's sure to give me a fistful of splinters come planting season. It needs a new one. Teak, go out into the forest and fetch me the straightest branch you can find. Clean it, shape it, and have it ready by week's end. You'll find everything you need out back."

Agnora filled her kettle from the bucket, dropped in a handful of the herbs, and set it on the stove. Only then did she finally glance up.

"Go on now," she said in a shrill, impatient tone. "We've got women's work to do."

As Teak turned to leave, he rolled his eyes for Ivy's benefit. Ivy stifled a chuckle.

Once Teak had gone, Ivy sat down at the table beside a bowl full of dried corn and began to crush it with a pestle. "Thank you for helping at the river," she said. "How you managed to melt the ice that way is simply amazing."

Agnora shrugged.

"I hope you don't mind my asking," Ivy ventured, cautiously, "but I've been wondering about your magic."

"What about it?" replied Agnora.

"You're obviously very adept at it. I was wondering why you don't use it more often, or for more important things."

"What's more important than fetching water?"

"Well, repairing the roof for one thing," said Ivy. "It took Teak days to do it. You could have done it in moments."

"That wouldn't have done Teak any good then, would it? How else would he have passed the time?"

"I hadn't thought of it that way," answered Ivy. "I suppose you're right. It did keep him occupied. But then what about the garden? We could use fresh vegetables, but the soil is frozen. Couldn't you warm the earth enough to plant some seeds early?"

"I could. But what is the sense in that? Everything in its season, I always say, and a nice harvest of spring vegetables is a pleasant thing to look forward to." Agnora poured the ground corn from Ivy's bowl into a bag already half full of it. Then she replaced it with another handful of kernels. "Why so interested in magic?" she asked. "It's a nuisance really."

"How can such a gift be a nuisance?"

"Do you see these hands?" asked Agnora, holding hers up for Ivy to see. The skin was papery thin and marred by dark spots. "These are the hands of an old woman. And my face…" She touched the tips of her fingers to her cheeks. "I am not as old as I look. The magic ages me."

"How is that possible?" asked Ivy.

"Each feat of magic, no matter how small, requires some part of me in return. I try to use it as little as possible. I've tried to avoid it altogether, but the temptation is too great. Once you learn the magic, you cannot abandon it. It is a privilege—and a curse. But this is something *you* will never understand."

"But I do," answered Ivy, eagerly. "Perhaps not fully, but I do understand. I have a gift as well, though I did not learn it. I was born with it, and sometimes I wish I hadn't been. I was told from the time I was small that I was special, that I had a great responsibility. But all I wanted was to live like any other girl. I have since learned that that is impossible. One cannot hide from such a gift."

A column of white steam rose from the kettle, twisting its way upward until it dissipated in the cooler air. Agnora poured a cup and offered it. Ivy accepted, and then held it close to her face. The minty fragrance had a way of soothing Ivy's mind and body even before the tea reached her lips. Agnora made many kinds of tea from the dried herbs and spices she kept in her cupboard, but mint was one of Ivy's favorites. She sipped the hot liquid as Agnora spoke.

"Most gifts are pleasant ones, but yours has brought you sorrow," Agnora said, removing the kettle from the stove and setting it on the table. "It might be that you have not learned to use your gift correctly."

Ivy considered this a moment, but dismissed the suggestion. "Who is there to teach me? I know of no one else with such a gift."

"Perhaps I do. Tell me about your gift, and I will tell you if there are any others who possess it."

Ivy wanted to share her gift with Agnora, to explain her visions to her. She had told Mikel and Teak, but only to protect them. But in the end she had not been able to protect them at all. In fact, she had endangered them more by revealing her true identity. She thought of Agnora and the kindness she had shown her and Teak. She could not in good conscience endanger her. No, her gift must remain a secret.

Ivy decided to change the subject.

"I am more interested in learning your gift, Agnora," she said, setting her cup on the table. "I've always been interested in magic. One of my dearest friends is an enchanter."

"Then why don't you have him teach you?"

"He lives far from here and it may be a long time before I see him again. Couldn't you teach me? It will help pass the time."

Through the window Ivy saw Teak heading off into the forest, a saw and long knife across his back. Agnora saw him, too, and wrinkled her nose critically at him.

"He's forgotten the axe," she griped. "Doesn't he know he'll need an axe?"

"Agnora," repeated Ivy, bringing the woman's attention back, "teach me magic."

The old woman continued staring out the window long after Teak had disappeared through the trees. She tugged absentmindedly at a tendril of hair.

"I cannot teach you," she said finally.

Agnora's words took Ivy by surprise. They were not what she had expected to hear. She had expected the woman to complain or object, but not to reject her altogether.

"But I want you to teach me," protested Ivy.

"No," said Agnora firmly. She turned from the window and looked at Ivy with a strange, melancholy expression on her aged face.

Agnora turned back to the window and sighed. "It would be a waste to lose your youth and your beauty. No," she continued. "I will not teach you. It is too high a price for you to pay."

21

Winter clutched at time like a cat hanging from a tree branch. It refused to let go. The days were indistinguishable from one another, a smear of gray and white on an endless canvas. Jayson passed his time helping with the animals. Dawes had half a dozen prize horses bred from the finest stock. He also slaughtered chickens, geese, and pigs as per the cook's commands. Eggs were gathered, cows milked, animals fed and groomed, stalls cleaned. Nira gave him enough work to keep four men busy. Jayson wondered how she had managed without him.

Each night, following supper, Jayson returned to the bunkhouse where he'd collapse on his cot and fall into a restless sleep tormented by dreams of Ivanore.

He had lost count how many days he'd been at the plantation when one night he was summoned to the main house. Once there, Nira gave him some clean clothes and instructed him to change and then wait in the sitting room. He had never been admitted farther than the kitchen, so he obeyed Nira's command out of curiosity. The spacious sitting room was decorated with ample furnishings made of light-colored wood and animal skins. Like the bunkhouse, a large skin served as a rug on the floor. Most of the chairs in the room were arranged around an elaborate marble fireplace wherein burned a generous fire. Displayed over the fireplace was a crossbow of the finest craftsmanship.

"Do you hunt?" asked a deep, bellowing voice that rolled. From one of the chairs, a man slowly leaned forward until his face was lit by the fire's glow. It was a menacing face, though it bore only the most tranquil of expressions. There was something in his eyes and the determined lines of his jaw and nose that gave him an intimidating air. Seeing it this close for the first time, Jayson could understand why so many people respected and feared Orrin Dawes.

"You weren't to come until spring," said Dawes, raising a steaming mug to his lips.

Jayson approached the fireplace and stood before the captain. He was broadly built, much like his ship, the Silver Mist, with wide shoulders atop a thick, barreled chest. Though he was getting on in years and his skin bore the evidence of his age, there was no weakness in him. Rather, Jayson thought he had not seen any man in as good condition as Orrin Dawes.

His countenance was stern, just as a man who commanded a ship's crew should be, but his words were marked with just a hint of humor. Jayson felt immediately at ease in his presence.

"I hope I'm not imposing," said Jayson.

"Of course not," Dawes replied. "It's your own choice if you want to freeze to death working out there. That's no imposition to me, except if I have to bury you. As long as you show up to plow my fields once the frost passes, I don't care what you do in the meantime."

"So, I can stay in the bunkhouse?"

Dawes sipped his tea and grunted. "If you can bear it."

"I have for two weeks already."

"Well, good for you then."

Dawes emptied his mug and set it on the table beside him. Nira arrived to offer Jayson some tea. He accepted and tried to ignore her contemptuous glare. Jayson waited until Nira left the room and then asked about her.

"She detests inhumans of any kind," replied Dawes. "I've brought a few here from time to time, though I've never had an Agoran, let alone a mongrel like yourself. Those I have brought tend to bring trouble with them. You see, human dents don't like them taking their work, as if there isn't enough to go around."

"Dents?"

"The indentured. The inhumans get bullied by them so much I end up having to let them go early just to get them off my land. The dents resent that, too. There's no pleasing dents, and who can blame them? Most have given up everything they ever cared about— home, family, their reputations, their futures—just to pay off a debt most of them didn't need to begin with. It's a sad state of affairs."

"Why do you exploit them, then?"

"Exploit them? Bah! They've exploited themselves. I simply buy and resell their contracts. And I'm far more evenhanded than some masters. I bring those with the best hope at emancipation here. The others I sell off to masters I know to be just men. And I make a profit in the bargain."

"Is that what you plan to do with me?"

"You?" Dawes chuckled. "No. You're a different case entirely. Buying passage for a stranger with your own life."

"He is my brother."

"You and I both know that's a lie, and a bad one at that. When I questioned him about you, he knew next to nothing. I am no fool, Jayson. I heard about what happened in Partha, how Emir's men set that cottage aflame with a woman and child trapped inside. Makes a man want to tear the Ministry to shreds with his own bare hands. I may be a shrewd businessman, but I am no devil."

Dawes rose from his chair and stood before the fire.

"What has become of Brommel?" Jayson asked him.

Dawes held his hands out toward the flames to warm them. "I spent a good part of the voyage getting to know him and his young son," he said. "He's a good man, Brommel, but his heart is broken. He is in despair, and there is no telling what a desperate man might do. Fearing for the boy, I went ashore with them and helped them get settled at the Seafarer, per your instructions. Then I presented him with a business proposition and some money to get him started. I doubt he'll get on it right away. He still has some mourning to do. But I suspect come spring, he'll mull over my offer. By then, he'll have gotten his remorse under control and will be ready to provide for himself and his son. Yes, I think he'll do very well, very well indeed."

Dawes briskly rubbed his hands together. "Well, I've had plenty of nights sleeping in the snow beside my horse to get here. I think I've earned a bath and a good night's rest. So, if you'll excuse me."

The captain hefted himself out of the chair with a grunt. Jayson watched him as he ambled across the room for the door. This man had a generous heart, even if it was not apparent from looking at him.

"Thank you," said Jayson, "for everything."

Dawes waved off the comment. "I don't mind helping someone who thinks more of others than of himself. But then again," he added with a grin, "come spring when the real work begins, you may wish to retract your thanks."

22

The river water was nearly as cold as the slowly melting crust of ice along its edges, so cold that Ivy's hands stung painfully from it. She dipped each item of clothing into the water, taking care not to prolong her skin's exposure. But try as she might, after wringing out the excess water, her hands burned with cold.

Though the air had warmed a bit now that the heart of winter had passed, the ice and snow were taking their time to depart. Ivy anxiously waited for winter to recede enough for her to venture farther away from the cabin than the river or the edge of the garden. But until she had fully recovered from her illness, she dared not take such risks. It would do no one any good should she fall ill again. She had already been too much of a burden.

Ivy dropped the wet clothes into her empty bucket and hauled them up the bank to where Agnora's line was drawn between the tree and one of the wooden posts supporting the roof. She spread out each item along the line. The sky was clear today and the sun warm. She anticipated that all would be dry by that afternoon.

As she hung the last item, one of Agnora's yellow aprons, she heard a familiar voice behind her.

"I'll be needing that," said Agnora.

Ivy replied apologetically, "I just washed it, Agnora. I'm sorry, but couldn't you use your blue one today?"

"The blue one's for gardening. Yellow's for baking. I'm baking six loaves of honey bread today, and I've got to have it."

"But you told me to have it washed, and it's got to dry."

Agnora contemplated the dripping apron for a time, a dour expression on her face. Ivy did not know what to say. Agnora was particular in her ways, and since coming here, Ivy had been keenly aware of how her presence had disturbed the woman's normal routine. Though Ivy would have preferred to be anywhere else, there simply was nowhere else to go. She tried to be as useful as possible, but even her best efforts often resulted in Agnora's disapproval.

"Why don't you let me help you with the bread?" asked Ivy, seeking some compromise in the situation. "I'm quite good at baking, and you wouldn't get your dress soiled."

"I like making bread," snapped Agnora. "No, this simply won't do. I've got to have my yellow apron, and I've got to have it now."

Ivy hesitated, and then removed the wet item from the line. She held it out to Agnora, but the woman stuck her fists into her hips.

"I suppose I might as well teach you something. Hold it in your left hand."

Ivy, confused, did as she was told and grasped the fabric as instructed. "Like this?" she asked.

"It doesn't matter *how* you hold it—just hold it! Now, visualize all the warmth that exists around and inside of you. You'll need plenty of it, so focus."

"I don't understand," Ivy started to protest, but Agnora shushed her.

"This is one of the simplest tasks to master. Now, do as you're told. Visualize the energy around you. Feel it radiating from the sun, from the tree, from me, from you. Gather it together now, and focus it onto my apron. Stay focused now."

Ivy kept her eye on the apron, a damp clump of fabric in her hand. She wasn't exactly sure what Agnora wanted her to do with it, but she gathered her thoughts together as told. In her mind, an image of pale golden light materialized in the air around her. The light seemed strongest around the tree, Agnora, and herself, as if it actually emanated from them. Ivy realized that the light was energy or heat. Ivy concentrated on this energy and tried to collect it into a single point. Then she directed the energy onto the apron.

The task was not a difficult one. She was used to concentrating on mental images in the form of her visions, which often took a great deal of concentration to hold onto in order to see them in their entirety. She thought of Agnora's instruction as almost a game, until she realized that the fabric in her hand had changed somehow.

Ivy blinked in disbelief. The apron, which was practically drenched with water a moment earlier, was now dry.

"How did you do that?" asked Ivy.

Agnora shrugged as if the act were a trifle, though Ivy thought she caught a fleeting glimmer of astonishment in Agnora's expression.

"I did nothing," said Agnora. "You did it, though I must say getting it on the first try is a bit out of the ordinary."

"On the first try? What do you mean?"

"What I mean is that most enchanters begin their training at a young age. It takes years to accomplish what you just learned in minutes."

Ivy took the apron in both hands and held it out in front of her, examining every bit of it. Not an inch of it was even damp. The energy she thought was merely a mental image had been real, and it had evaporated the water in an instant.

Agnora snatched the apron from Ivy. She put it on and tied it around the back. "No sense gawking. What you did was nothing more than a simple trick. Any child could have done that."

"But you just said it took years—"

"I know what I said," snapped Agnora, "and don't let it get to your head, young lady! If you think drying your laundry or starting a cook fire or anything mundane is the object of magic, then you're a fool and I'll waste no time on you."

The woman fluttered her hands in the air, then turned abruptly and stomped into the cabin. Ivy hesitated a moment, then followed. She found Agnora hastily grabbing ingredients out of her cupboard. She scooped out a cupful of flour from a grain sack and dumped it into a large wooden bowl. Her movements were tense and abrupt, as if done in anger.

"I've offended you," said Ivy, standing behind her. "I would apologize, but I'm not certain what I've done."

Agnora snatched a mixing paddle from the shelf. "I'm not offended," she answered brusquely. She added salt and yeast to the flour, and poured in some water. She stirred the mixture vigorously as if taking vengeance on it. After she had sufficiently beaten it, Agnora set down the paddle, grabbed the edge of the table with both hands and sighed in defeat.

"All right, all right," she said, tossing a handful of flour onto the table and turning the dough onto it. "I haven't had an apprentice in thirty years at least, so don't expect me to be patient with your mistakes. Before I teach you anything, let me see what you are capable of. I've got several loaves of bread to bake, and the oven hasn't been lit yet."

Ivy noted the stack of kindling in the stove. "What do I do?" she asked.

Agnora shrugged. "You need heat. It's no different than drying the wash, you just need more of it—concentrated to a single point."

Ivy closed her eyes. She tried to visualize the warmth emanating from her own body, but felt it instead. The more she concentrated on it, the more tangible her energy became. She lifted her hand and imagined the energy flowing down her arm through the air to the wood.

When she opened her eyes, she was startled to see the wood in flames. Agnora stared in astonished disbelief, but the expression was fleeting. The enchantress shut the door to the stove with a bang. Then she pounded a fist into the bread dough.

"I'm not much of an enchantress," she said. "I use my magic sparingly and for good reason. I'll teach you what I know, though what you need is control. Your magic is sloppy, weak."

Ivy nodded that she understood, though inside she felt ready to burst with excitement. Agnora must have noticed her enthusiasm, because Ivy caught a glimpse of a smile beneath her stern face.

"Maybe," added Agnora, "this will help us both wait out the rest of winter."

Ivy was so full of excitement she wanted to kiss the old woman's cheek, but she restrained herself to a simple, soft-spoken thank you, after which Agnora demanded she be left alone to her baking. They would begin their lessons later that day.

23

The season was beginning to change. Teak felt it in the warming of the soil and air. Small pockets of green emerged from receding husks of snow. The forest itself seemed to be basking in the ever-lengthening hours of day.

Teak knelt in the center of Agnora's garden, a broad beam of sunlight striking him from above. He turned his face up toward it and listened to the gentle rustling of leaves. The smell of earth and pine revitalized him, as if waking him from winter hibernation. He thought of the grains of wheat that lay dormant in Mikel's fields. Soon they would grow and blossom, and would be ready for spring harvest. Suddenly, Teak's stomach tightened into a solid mass. He had not been there to plant the wheat. Mikel was dead, and there was no one to tend the farm. The thought of spring with no wheat to harvest filled him with anguish.

Teak was so immersed in his own thoughts that he failed to notice Ivy's approach until she had knelt beside him. When she touched his arm, he drew back, startled.

"I'm sorry," Ivy said. "I didn't mean to startle you."

Her hair and skin shimmered in the sunlight, and as he watched her slender fingers burrow into the soil, the solemn images of Mikel's farm vanished.

Ivy raised a handful of dirt, letting it cascade from her palm back to earth. "What are you going to plant?" she asked.

"M-melons," Teak said. "And m-maybe onions and parsnips. Lots of things."

Ivy drew her fingers across the surface of the earth, leaving four miniature furrows behind. "What will you do once spring has come, Teak? Will you go back to your uncle's farm?"

Teak considered her question. It was one he regularly asked himself. He shook his head. "N-no," he replied.

Ivy studied his face for a moment before her gaze shifted to the ground beside him. "What's this?" she asked, picking up the curved stick of wood.

Teak felt his face turn red. He hadn't planned to show it to her yet, not until he'd proved its usefulness. "It's a b-bow for hunting," he said. "See?"

He picked up the loose end of a thin strip of dried animal gut and strung the bow. "It w-will be easier to hunt with this. It's n-not very good, though."

"No, it's wonderful," said Ivy, plucking the taut string. Suddenly, Ivy was on her feet. "Stand up," she said, taking his hands. "I want to show you something, too."

She glanced around the garden, and then led Teak to the far corner where the snow had been desecrated by a substantial pile of discarded soot from Agnora's stove. Deep gray ash and scraps of wood, blackened and crumbling, formed a wide wet circle.

"W-what do you w-want to show me?" asked Teak.

Ivy did not answer. Instead, she held out her right hand and, one by one, folded her fingertips into her palm.

That was all.

A moment passed, and then Teak saw it—a quivering strand of pale gray smoke rising from the ash. Another moment, and a gentle amber flame grew from the spot, like a brilliant orange blossom.

Teak could hardly believe what he was seeing. His eyes skipped from Ivy's face to the fire and back again. He tried to speak, his enthusiasm wanted to burst from him, but somehow the sounds stumbled over each other on his tongue.

"F-f-f—"

"Fire?" Ivy suggested.

Teak nodded. "It's w-w-wonderful."

Ivy looked at Teak. She seemed pleased with his compliment. But there was something more in her eyes—concern—for him.

Ivy raised her hand and placed a palm on each side of Teak's face. Being this close to her, Teak could see the cobalt specks in her azure blue eyes. The warmth of her hands spread through him, dissolving all his fears, all his worries. He closed his eyes as her fingers caressed his lips, and then gradually slid over his chin and down his throat. Teak's body relaxed beneath Ivy's touch. It was the touch of an angel—not a mere human. And then it was over.

"What did you—?" Teak started to ask, but the clarity of his own voice surprised him. He said nothing more. His eyes remained closed long after the sensation of Ivy's touch had ended. When he opened them, she was gone.

Teak placed his fingers, calloused and caked with earth, against his lips. He could not explain what had just happened.

He only knew that he had been changed. He was different now—complete—and Ivy had done it.

24

The sun had only just begun to rise. Dewdrops glistened like jewels from the tips of every pine needle and every leaf. Like tiny pearls threaded into a tapestry, they adorned each spider's web. Ivy paused beside one, admiring its intricate beauty, its dark eight-legged host staring intently back. Ivy had left the cabin before dawn, just as she had been doing for the past few weeks. Each morning, she slipped away before Agnora or Teak awoke, taking a basket with her to collect herbs or flowers or birds' eggs. She would return in time to help Agnora prepare breakfast.

Ivy enjoyed her newfound independence. After spending so many weeks in bed and being hovered over by her two watchful companions, she had nearly forgotten what it was like to be completely alone. Those first few days that she had slipped away in the darkness of early morning had sent Teak into a panic. He had taken out after her only to find her turning the soil in the garden or gathering moss near the river. After a while, both Teak and Agnora grew accustomed to her little ventures and no longer seemed concerned. Ivy had recovered from her illness, and her wound had completely healed. She was strong and full of energy, and was anxious to use it.

Once she was certain that no one would follow, Ivy began venturing deeper into the woods, a little farther each day. She explored every hill and glade within reasonable distance, returning each morning once the sun had risen. These hours alone gave her time to think, to sort out the events that had led her to this time and place, and to consider her options for the foreseeable future.

On Imaness, she had spent nearly a year in seclusion, hiding from her father's spies and soldiers. She had believed that Jayson would return for her, but as time passed without word, she worried about what had become of him. And then the visions began. Jayson was in trouble, or at least he would be. She could no longer wait idly for the months and years to pass. He needed her, and she would go to him.

She had left the most vital parts of herself behind on Imaness, perhaps the only things that might have stopped her from going, but her heart yearned for her husband even more than it yearned for home. She thought now of Zyll and the oath he had made to protect and care for that which she loved so very dearly. If it weren't for him, she could never have left at all.

Ivy strolled among the moss-covered trees, letting her fingers brush each one as she passed. She had never intended to stay away so long. Her plan had been to come to Hestoria, find Jayson, and return with him to Imaness as quickly as possible. It was true that Jayson could still return on his own before she found him. In case of that event, she had written him a letter explaining her plans in detail and left it with Zyll. Her plans were thwarted, however, when her father's soldiers located her latest safe house. In her hasty escape, she had been injured, and that injury had cost her dearly.

The sun ascended higher, spilling its brilliant gold across the lush canopy overhead. Ivy continued on, pausing now and then to pry a spray of moss from a tree trunk and place it in her basket. Moss made excellent kindling for the cook stove and gave off a pleasant aroma as it dried. She was lost in thought as she went along, allowing her mind to roam through her memories. Sometimes, in her solitary treks through the forest, the grief of being so far from everyone she loved overwhelmed her. She played her memories over and over in her mind, clinging to every minute detail as though grasping for something to keep from drowning.

Ivy felt the all too familiar melancholy envelope her. She continued on, though the sun was now well above the trees. She would normally be back at the cabin by now, but she could not go back, not just yet. She needed to compose herself first.

She glanced around and realized that she was in an unfamiliar area. She had wandered farther than she ever had before. She was not lost. She could easily find her way back, of that she was certain. She merely felt surprised at how far she had gone, and she also felt glad. She wanted to be alone, and now she was.

Ivy let her sorrow come to the surface now. The tears began to flow, and her breaths came in ragged sobs. She did not hold anything back. There was no one to impress out here, no one for whom to present the mask of serenity she normally wore. She cried aloud and didn't mind that her voice resonated through the trees.

She pressed onward, heading farther away from the cabin. She had been gone an hour at least. She would soon be missed, but she didn't care. The basket on her arm was full and was heavy to carry. She set it down and walked on. Ahead, from between several trees, Ivy noticed that the sunlight grew brighter. Thin bars of light shone through like individual rays. They drew her toward them, and when she had reached their source she stopped.

She stood on the crest of a steep hill overlooking a glade. The hill itself was rough and rocky, but farther down it sloped gently until it leveled out into a small grassy knoll dotted with tiny yellow and purple flowers. Across this clearing the woods continued on.

Ivy stood transfixed by the tranquil scene before her. Her tears ceased, and the melancholy that had gripped her moments before vanished. She considered the hill a moment and wondered if she should undertake it now or return some other day. If she were gone too long, Teak and Agnora might come looking for her. It would be better to hurry back to the cabin with her basket full of moss and make some excuse for her tardiness. Tomorrow she would come straight here to explore this little haven further.

She had just turned away to go in search of her mislaid basket when she spotted movement out of the corner of her eye. Ivy glanced back toward the clearing, but decided that what she had seen had been a shadow flitting across the knoll from a cloud passing overhead, nothing more. Ivy turned once more to go when her breath caught sharply in her throat and her heart raced. What she had seen hadn't been a cloud at all.

* * *

"Where are we going?"

Ivy suppressed a giggle as she took Teak by the hand and led him through the maze of trees. Each time he asked her where she was taking him, she merely held a finger to her lips. The branches overhead, heavy with new spring leaves, formed a tangled canopy that undulated in the wind. The snow had left behind only occasional patches of white in the trees' shadows, places where the sun had not yet had a chance to warm the earth.

Teak had never seen Ivy this excited. Since she had first appeared in Mikel's field, she had been recovering from injury and illness. She had been weak and pale, but during these past few weeks a change had taken place. Her wound had healed, and her illness had vanished. Slowly, her strength returned. She began smiling, and her face flushed with color. Her eyes were vibrant, her laugh enchanting. So when she had drawn him away from the woodpile this morning, coaxing him to leave his axe behind, he had followed her much like a child would follow a fairy if he came upon one.

"How much farther?" he asked, stumbling over a fallen tree branch. Ivy held his hand tighter, urging him onward.

"Not far," she said. "Just ahead through that clearing."

Teak saw a break in the trees where the sunlight wove itself among the shadows. A few seconds later, they ducked beneath a thick archway of branches. The sudden brightness hurt Teak's eyes, and he squeezed them shut. After a moment or two, he opened them. As they adjusted, he saw that they stood atop a hill overlooking a very small clearing, not much larger than Agnora's cottage, completely surrounded by a dense tangle of trees.

He looked at Ivy. A look of absolute contentment adorned her face. Sunlight cast a halo of gold around her, and for a moment, Teak was taken aback by her beauty. Since that moment in the garden when she had touched his lips and healed his speech, he had thought of nothing but how much he wanted to kiss her, to pull her close and feel her against him. He looked away, distracting himself with the landscape.

"So, this is what you dragged me out here to see?" he asked.

Ivy shook her head. She released Teak's hand and sprinted, laughing, down the hill.

"Wait up!" Teak called after her, but she continued on. Teak took a cautious step forward. The hill was quite steep. He could easily fall if he wasn't careful. Watching Ivy plunge exuberantly ahead, however, he found his courage and took off after her. By the time he reached level ground again, he was laughing, too.

The field, while small, brimmed with life. Dozens of golden butterflies the size of his thumbnail flitted about. Several heavy black bumblebees buzzed about searching for clover blossoms. A family of quail darted across the open land.

It was a beautiful place, and Teak could see why Ivy wanted to bring him here. Still, he wondered, could this be the only reason for her enthusiasm? As the question rested on his mind, Ivy cupped her hands around her mouth and let out a loud, shrill cry.

The sound startled Teak. Ivy waited a moment and then did it again. This time, a reply came from somewhere beyond the trees. Suddenly, the clearing fell into shadow as a large, dark figure loomed overhead, blocking out the sun with its massive wings. The creature alighted on the ground. The sun returned when it folded its wings against its body.

Teak was too much in shock to run or cry out. He stood as still as a stone, gaping at the giant bird-like creature. A quick glance at its powerful beak and lion's paws and tail verified Teak's suspicion. This was the legendary gryphon, guardian of the Seer.

Ivy approached the gryphon with her arms outstretched and embraced it, burying her face in the feathers of its neck. Then she planted a kiss between its eyes. The creature squawked gently in reply, ruffling its feathers and blinking its eyes.

"Where have you been?" Ivy asked the creature as she caressed its neck. "I've missed you, you know? Have you missed me, too?"

Ivy turned to Teak. "Don't be afraid," she told him. "She trusts you. She left me in your care, remember?"

Teak took a hesitant step forward. The gryphon's large dark eyes remained fixed on him.

"What if it bites me?"

Ivy laughed as though the suggestion was absurd. "Go ahead," she coaxed, "touch her."

Teak reached out his hand and took another cautious step. Then he let just the tips of his fingers brush against its wing.

"She's beautiful, isn't she?" asked Ivy.

"Magnificent," replied Teak. "Where *has* she been all winter?"

"Hard to say, though I doubt she's been far. She must have found a good place to conceal herself these past months."

"Why would she need to hide?"

"If anyone were to find the gryphon, they would know the Seer is not far off."

Ivy opened the bundle she had been carrying and withdrew two round winter squashes. She held the first one out to the gryphon who gobbled it greedily.

"I came across this place this morning," continued Ivy. "I found her waiting for me, as though she knew I was ready."

"Ready for what?" asked Teak, stroking the gryphon's feathers more confidently now.

"To go," replied Ivy matter-of-factly. "Winter's over, Teak, and I'm well enough to be moving on."

"Moving on? What do you mean?"

She looked at him then with an almost apologetic expression on her face. She took both his hands in hers and spoke gently to him.

"I came to Hestoria for a purpose that I have not yet been able to accomplish. I must get on with it now."

Teak couldn't help it. He felt a sense of panic rising within him. Why did it seem as though she were trying to say goodbye?

"I'll take you to the Guilde," he said. "We can leave tomorrow morning."

Ivy dropped Teak's hands. "We don't even know where the Guilde is," she said, exasperated.

"We'll find them," answered Teak.

"It could takes weeks, months—"

"We'll search everywhere. We'll ask everyone."

"I've already wasted too much time as it is!" Ivy turned away from Teak. Teak felt his heart racing inside his chest as though it might explode through his rib cage at any moment. She wanted to leave, she'd made that much clear, but what he was even more certain of was that she wanted to leave *without* him. She hadn't said so, but he sensed it, felt it as though the words had been spoken.

Maybe it would be best to separate, thought Teak. He could return to the farm and continue with the planting. If

Ivy did not want to go to the Guilde, he was not obligated to take her there.

Somehow he knew Mikel would be displeased with this line of thinking. He would be disappointed in him. Teak knew that he had to keep his promise to take her to the Guilde. He was about to tell Ivy so, when the gryphon jerked its head up. Its black pupils constricted as it nervously sniffed the air.

"What is it, girl?" asked Ivy. "What's wrong?"

Without warning, the gryphon threw out its wings, nearly knocking Teak to the ground. The animal lifted quickly and noiselessly into the air and within moments had disappeared beyond the treetops.

Teak and Ivy watched the now empty sky, perplexed by her sudden departure. That was when Teak saw it, a flash of yellow through the trees at the top of the hill. Teak touched Ivy's arm to draw her attention.

"What is it?" Ivy asked.

Teak pointed up the hill. "We're not alone," he whispered.

25

"Ivy! Come on!"

Teak's words sounded hollow as though coming from a distant place. The knowledge that someone other than Teak had seen the gryphon left Ivy feeling sick. She stood, fixed to the spot in the clearing, staring toward the hilltop where a moment earlier she had caught a glimpse of someone escaping through the trees. It was as though her feet were suddenly made of stone. They refused to move even though she willed them to. Finally, it was Teak who, by taking her hand, pulled her along behind him. Together they climbed up the steep hillside that had seemed so innocuous coming down. The loose soil gave way beneath their feet, making the ascent slow going and precarious.

"Who do you think it was?" Ivy asked, though there could be only one answer.

"You know as well as I do who it was," answered Teak.

"She wouldn't tell anyone."

"We can't be sure. We know little about her except that she likes to garden and keeps to herself."

Ivy's foot slipped on a loose stone. Teak grasped her wrist and hoisted her up closer to him.

"We've got to catch up to her," he said. "We have to know what she'll do."

They reached the top of the hill and did not bother brushing the dirt off their clothes. Up ahead, Ivy caught a glimpse of Agnora disappearing behind a cluster of white tree trunks. They followed, hurrying to catch her, but no matter where they turned or how fast they ran, she remained out of reach. How Agnora moved so quickly at her age seemed a mystery to Ivy. But Ivy reminded herself that the woman was not as old as she appeared and had likely traveled through these woods a hundred times before. They were second nature to her, while to Ivy and Teak they were a labyrinth.

Just as Ivy feared she could go no further, for she was out of breath and out of energy, she and Teak burst through the last barrier of trees into the familiar garden behind the cabin. Teak leaned over grasping his knees with his hands, heaving great gasps of air. Ivy steadied herself against a tree trunk. Her legs threatened to give way. She saw a flash of yellow through the cabin window. Agnora's apron. The woman had, of course, reached home ahead of them and had already lit the fire. A plume of smoke puffed out of the little stone chimney.

Ivy tested her legs. Though wobbly, they held her well enough. She made her way through the garden and around to the front door. Teak followed. Neither of them spoke as they entered.

Agnora was busy at the stove slicing potatoes and dropping them into a pot of water. She did not look up when they entered, nor did she acknowledge them in any way. She finished the potato and hurriedly began another. Teak took a seat at the table where he anxiously clasped and unclasped his hands. Ivy remained in the doorway not exactly sure what to say. She decided it would be best to be forthright. No sense in pretending.

"I should explain what you saw in the clearing just now," she began, but Agnora shook her head furiously and cut into the potato more feverishly than ever.

"I saw nothing," she exclaimed.

Ivy was perplexed. Agnora had been at the top of that hill. She and Teak had seen her. Surely she had seen the gryphon.

"There's no need to be frightened," said Ivy.

Agnora laughed nervously. "Frightened? Frightened of what? A potato? Surely not!"

"The gryphon—"

"Sh! Sh! Sh!" Agnora turned abruptly and threw a finger to her lips. Her eyes were wide with fear. "Do not speak of it here!" she hissed. "Do not bring the name of it into this house!"

"You did see it," continued Ivy, cautiously. "You were there and then ran off. But there was no need to fear. The gry… the creature you saw would never harm me."

Agnora turned back to her pot. She finished slicing the potato and wiped the blade of her knife against her apron.

"I know that," she said. "I'm not a fool. But allowing yourself to be seen with it is foolish—and dangerous." Agnora nodded toward Teak who sat in silence, his eyes watching the women. "Does he know who you are?"

Ivy nodded, but still she was unsure how to proceed. Again she wanted to speak plainly. She had had enough of hiding, enough of lies.

"Do *you* know who I am?" Ivy asked.

Agnora scrutinized Ivy much like the first time they had met. Agnora set down the knife and took Ivy's hands in hers. Ivy felt the woman's fingers trembling.

"You are the Seer," whispered Agnora.

Ivy drew back her hands. There was something in the way Agnora looked at her that seemed wrong. Gone was the critical glare, the perpetual scowl. Agnora now looked at her with what could only be described as awe. Though Ivy understood the inviolability of her calling, she had always been surrounded by those who were not impressed by such things. Later, she had fled her father and was in hiding, and she had managed to keep her identity a secret. Until Teak's family, no one but Zyll had known the truth. Now, with Agnora, the secret was in jeopardy.

"Please don't tell anyone," pleaded Ivy. "If you do, my life will be in danger, as would be anyone who is with me."

Agnora's low chuckle took Ivy by surprise. "I won't tell a soul," she said, her gray eyes sparkling with mischievous humor. "Except I should perhaps tell Gerard."

Ivy cast Teak a wary glance. "Who is Gerard?"

"Who is Gerard?" repeated Agnora, with feigned offense. "Who is Gerard? Why, he's only the leader of the Guilde, the very society sworn to protect you! I should think he has a right to know you're here in Hestoria."

Agnora retrieved three bowls from her shelf and ladled a little broth into each. Then she set them on the table along with half a loaf of warm bread. She sat in a chair across from Teak and pulled another chair to the table for Ivy.

"You know where the Guilde is?" asked Teak, tearing off a chunk from the loaf and dipping it into his broth.

"Of course I do!" Agnora retorted. "I'm one of Gerard's most loyal guardians, though I've spent these many years in hiding myself and haven't been of much use, I'm afraid. Got myself into a bit of trouble with the Ministry, and so I try my best to stay out of their way. So," she continued, motioning to Ivy to sit down, "why don't you tell me how it is you came to be here. Last I heard, the great Seer had gone missing. Run off with some good-for-nothing half-breed, or so I was told."

Ivy took a sharp intake of breath. Hearing Jayson referred to in that way was no less offensive to her now than it had been before her father exiled him.

"That isn't true," she said. "My husband is a good man, and I believe he's in trouble."

"Is that so?" answered Agnora. "Well, then, why not come and tell me about him. Perhaps there might be something I can do to help."

Ivy reluctantly joined Teak and Agnora at the table, and while they ate their stew, she recounted how she had managed to escape her father's soldiers and how the gryphon had brought her to Mikel's farm. Then Teak described the terrible night when Mikel had killed the tracker only to be killed himself. They went on to explain how Mikel had told Teak to deliver Ivy to the Guilde and how they ended up in Agnora's cabin. Through all this, Agnora listened intently, nodding occasionally to show that she understood. When Teak and Ivy had finally finished, Agnora placed her elbows on the table and cradled her chin in her hands.

"You say you've see him in a vision?" she asked Ivy.

"Since even before I arrived in Hestoria, I've been having the same one over and over. I see a grand fortress, white walls and six tall turrets with narrow openings. I see my husband in the street and I follow him up the wide steps through the door, down darkened corridors and into vast, empty chambers. In one room, a room eerily lit by candlelight, I find him standing, waiting for me. I go to him and rest my hand against his shoulder. But when he turns around it is someone else's face I see, a man I do not know. And though I have never seen him, I know he means to harm me."

"A fortress you say?" remarked Agnora. "With turrets and white walls?"

"Do you know the place?"

"Aye. You speak of the Ministry in Nauvet-Carum."

"Nauvet-Carum?"

"The capitol. About half a day's walk east of here along the coast. It's the largest city in Hestoria, too much hustle and bustle for my taste."

"That's where I have to go then. That's where I will find Jayson."

"You can't go there," said Agnora.

"But I must. Jayson needs me. In my vision, he is suffering. I can see the agony in his face. You see, my vision abruptly changes. We're in another place, or maybe it's the same place but another time, I can't be sure. I stand at a window, my hands and face pressed against the glass. I see him below me in the courtyard. I call to him and pound my fists against the glass, but it's dark, and he cannot see or hear me. And then the vision changes once more. He is falling. There is blood on his hands, and he falls away from me, plunging into the sea. That is where the vision ends."

Agnora considered this a moment. Then she stood abruptly, clearing the bowls from the table.

"You cannot go there," she repeated more resolutely than before. "It isn't safe. The Ministry is crawling with Vatéz. If anyone means to harm you, they do. No, it is best you let Teak keep his promise and take you to the Guilde."

"I must first find my husband," replied Ivy, her voice edged with anger. Teak tried to calm Ivy by placing his hand on her arm, but Ivy ignored him. "That is what I came here to do."

To her surprise, Agnora turned on her, her expression twisted with rage. "You are in danger! Can't you see that?" she shouted. "As the Seer you have an obligation far greater than to your husband. You must be protected at all costs." Agnora's voice calmed a little, but her expression remained rigid. "Tomorrow Teak and I will take you to the Guilde. That is the end of it."

Ivy pushed her chair away from the table and stormed out of the cabin. The sun was beginning its descent, and remnants of the day lay scattered across the river, sparkling like tiny stars. She stood on its bank, regretting all the time she had wasted. Nearly half a year had passed since she fled Imaness. If only she had been more careful. If only she had not allowed herself to be injured.

She heard Teak approach from behind, but she did not turn around.

"I am worried about you." His voice was calm and soothing. "I want you to be safe."

Ivy, still angry at Agnora, pinched at her eyes trying to prevent the tears that gathered there from falling.

"I will go to the Guilde," she said, "but not until I find my husband."

The soft murmur of the water making its way over and around boulders and bulrushes did nothing to calm Ivy's unease. Instead, it reminded her how quickly time was passing.

"I know this must be difficult for you," said Teak. "I can't imagine how hard it was for you, waiting so long for him to return."

Teak stepped closer to her until she could feel the warmth of his breath on the back of her neck. He placed his large yet gentle hands on her shoulders. "You waited and waited," he continued, "but he never came."

Ivy tried to hold back the tide of emotion brewing within her, but she could not. Her throat constricted and she choked on her words. "He would have come if he could."

Teak's lips were near her ear now, his words sensitive yet certain. "What if he chose not to come, Ivy? What if he did not want to return?"

Like a dam giving way to the pressure pushing against it, Ivy's tears could no longer be stayed. They fell, and she broke into sobs.

"I have sacrificed everything to find him," she said. "Everything!"

Teak turned Ivy's trembling shoulders so that she was facing him. He gazed down at her, his eyes filled with a tenderness Ivy had not known in a long time. Teak wrapped his arms around her, drawing her close.

"I am here, Ivy," he whispered. "I am here. I won't let anything harm you."

He placed a finger beneath Ivy's chin and lifted it. Ivy's eyes spilled over with tears. Teak was perhaps the kindest man she had ever known, and she believed that he could protect her, would protect her with his own life if necessary.

Teak leaned in close and pressed his lips to hers. Ivy felt his heart beating and wondered if he felt hers as well. She let him press her body tightly against his, let him hold her to him and kiss her long and sweetly. She felt safe with him. She trusted him like she had not trusted anyone in a long time, but she could not kiss him back. Teak loved her, and knowing that he loved her broke her heart into a thousand tiny pieces.

When their lips parted, Ivy withdrew from Teak's embrace. The confusion on his face pained her. He clearly had expected her to return his affection, but that was something she simply could not do.

"Teak, I—" Ivy began, but the words stuck in her throat. She swallowed hard and tried to regain control of her emotions. "Teak, I'm so sorry. I never meant to mislead you."

Teak raised his hand to stop her from speaking. He tried to smile, but his eyes betrayed his disappointment. "No. *I'm* sorry. I shouldn't have done that," he said. He cleared his throat and turned his eyes toward the river. "I care about you, that's all. So, if you care for me at all, please let me take you to the Guilde."

He glanced at her for only a moment, but in that brief sliver of time, Ivy knew she had hurt him more deeply than she had ever thought possible. The tears stopped, and she felt composed enough now to think clearly, though Teak's kiss had left her feeling a little shaken.

"All right, Teak," she said, "I'll go with you, tomorrow at first light."

*   *   *

Later that night, long after Teak and Agnora had fallen asleep, Ivy crept out of the cabin into the dim moonlit night. She took with her two loaves of Agnora's bread, which she had baked for tomorrow's journey to the Guilde, and a goat's bladder filled with water. Around her shoulders was the wool cloak she had been wearing the night she and Teak escaped from Mikel's farm.

281

Betrayal

The moon was no more than a sliver, but it was enough to light her way through the woods back to the hill and to the small clearing. She wasted no time summoning the gryphon. It took only minutes for the creature to appear. Ivy quickly mounted its back, and a moment later they were aloft.

As they headed east over the forest, Ivy stole a glance over her shoulder. She could just make out the silver curves of the river where it meandered gently past Agnora's cabin. But a moment's glance was all she could spare. She would not be distracted from her aim. She could not concern herself with the consequences of her decision. Soon she would reach Nauvet-Carum. Soon she would be within Jayson's reach.

❖*Book Three* ❖
VENGEANCE

1

At the heart of the city of Dokur on the Isle of Imaness stood a square, wooden building with two amenable front windows and a sign above it that read THE SEAFARER TAVERN. The proprietor had been a sailor for a good many years, working on various merchant ships. Only when he had found himself a wife on one of his visits to the port city of Dokur did the idea of settling down ever occur to him. He never left Dokur after that, but invested his wages into an abandoned baker's shop that had some promise in it. His wife had a knack for decorating and cooking, so in time they transformed it into the town's most prominent tavern and lodge.

All went well for the Peagrys for several years. Though there was some competition, the Seafarer had a better location and more prominent customers. Business was prosperous. The only complaint they had was that the gods had failed to send them any children. Mr. Peagry never minded so much, his tavern kept him busy enough. But being childless weighed heavily on Mrs. Peagry and made her bitter.

Then one day the gods saw fit to bless them with a child, though not one of their own making. Mr. Peagry found the poor waif sitting atop a cliff overlooking the sea. It was sunset, and her tiny frame stood out like a scrawny shadow against the brilliant gold backdrop. He had asked the child for her name, but she said nothing. He asked many more questions, but again came no reply. He dared not leave the child there. Night was coming on, and by the looks of it the dirty little girl hadn't eaten in a good long while. So he took her by the hand and led her home.

On seeing the child, Mrs. Peagry exclaimed, "Goodness, Mr. Peagry, what have you managed to dig up?"

"Found her abandoned on the cliffs," he said. "Little thing hasn't eaten in days."

"Why, she can't be more'n four or five!" Mrs. Peagry squatted down until her face was level with the child's. "How old are you?" she asked. "Where are your parents? Do you have parents?"

The little girl said nothing, though she did finally respond with a slow shake of her head. Mrs. Peagry stood up and wiped her hands on her apron, a habit she had picked up while preparing meals in the tavern's kitchen. She often wiped her hands on her apron to soothe her nerves even when they were clean and dry. She placed her hand atop the child's head and turned her about, examining her from top to bottom.

"All right then," she told her husband. "I've got a fresh pot of dumplings simmering. Fill a bowl with it, and let it cool while I bathe her."

Mr. Peagry obeyed, ignoring the evening's customers still waiting to be served. Several called after him as he scurried between the tables toward the kitchen, and he politely assured each one that he'd be with them shortly. Mrs. Peagry led the child around the back of the tavern to the well, drew up a bucket of water, and washed her down with it. The girl's clothes, though soiled, were of surprisingly fine quality, not like most children in the city. Mrs. Peagry rinsed the dress and hung it out to dry. Then, bundling the little girl up in a blanket, Mrs. Peagry carried the child upstairs where she was fed and put to bed in a spare room.

Over the almost two years that followed, Mr. Peagry hoped that his wife would take to the girl, and that her bitterness at not having children of her own would be soothed; and perhaps it might have been had the child ever uttered a word. But the continued silence served only to fuel Mrs. Peagry's resentment. The tavern keeper's wife was not unkind to her, but instead of becoming part of their family as Mr. Peagry had originally hoped, the child was nothing more than a servant girl, wiping tables and fetching wood for the fire.

Despite her youth, she was strong and a willing worker. The Peagrys never abused her nor took advantage of her, but expected her to work alongside them to earn her keep—and that she did. However, she had the most unusual habit of disappearing each night just at sunset and returning again at bedtime. No matter how firmly the Peagrys forbade her from leaving, nor how carefully they plotted to prevent her escape, the child always managed to elude them, finding the most clever ways to vanish and reappear. Finally, the Peagrys ceased trying to control the child at all. Instead, Mr. Peagry marveled at the child's resourcefulness. Between that and her silence, and since she had given no other, she earned herself a name.

"Mouse!" shouted Mrs. Peagry from the kitchen. "Come in here and fetch these tarts!"

Vengeance

The little girl, now nearly seven years old, wound her way quickly through the tables and chairs to the door of the kitchen where Mrs. Peagry waited with a tray of six willenberry tarts in her hands. The woman's face was flushed and damp with perspiration from working over the hot oven all day, and her hair stuck up all over her head like red weeds. The sight of her mistress in such disarray brought a good-humored smile to the little girl's lips. Mrs. Peagry scowled as Mouse took the tray from her.

"See that table with the four men—that one where Mr. Peagry's refilling their tankards? Set a tart down before each one. And the other two go there," she added, pointing a plump finger toward the far corner of the room where a man and a young boy were finishing off their bowls of stew.

She had come to know their faces well in the weeks since they'd settled into their rooms at the Seafarer. A ship's captain had brought them from Hestoria, paid for their accommodations, and then left again. She had heard Master Peagry refer to the man as Brommel, but she did not know the boy's name. Since their arrival, she had seen very little of either one. Except for coming down for their meals twice a day, they spent most of the time in their room. They spoke little, even to each other, and from the way Brommel leaned heavily on the table and drank more ale than other men she'd seen, Mouse imagined he was a very sad sort of man. She felt sorry for the little boy. Though he was younger than she, no boy would want to spend his days hidden away in a dark room. Certainly he would prefer to be out of doors, running and playing like other children. When she wasn't helping in the tavern, even Mouse enjoyed romping about from time to time.

Mouse set the tarts on the table, one in front of Brommel, the other in front of the boy. The boy's eyes lit up the moment he saw it, and he licked his lips. Taking it up in both hands, he was about to take a bite when he paused.

"Thank you," he said, smiling widely, then proceeded to devour the tart.

Mouse took pride in the boy's delight. She had picked the willenberries herself that morning and helped roll out the dough. The boy's father watched him with a sullen expression on his face. The man made no move toward his own tart. When the boy had finished, Brommel slid it across the table.

"Here," he said, his speech slightly slurred from too much drink, "eat this one as well, if you like."

The boy nodded and picked it up. Mouse nearly laughed at the blue smear across the boy's eager face. The boy turned and looked directly at her, his deep brown eyes gleaming with pleasure. He held out the tart to her.

"Papa, can I give it to her?" he asked. "I'm full."

For the first time, Brommel seemed to notice her presence. He gave her a brief sidelong glance and nodded his consent. Mouse did not know what to do. Since coming to the Seafarer, no one had ever offered her anything before, nothing she hadn't had to earn. She hesitated, but then accepted the tart gratefully. She might have gotten one later from Mrs. Peagry if any remained once the kitchen closed for the night, but this small offering from the little boy was far better.

The boy waited in anticipation. He wanted to watch her eat it, and Mouse realized that he wanted to see how much she liked his gift. Mouse glanced over her shoulder to be certain the Peagrys were not watching her, and then she took her first bite of the tart.

The sweet and tangy flavor of the berries startled her taste buds. Her mouth watered for more. She took a second bite, letting the thick, honey-like sauce swim around her tongue. It was delicious. She looked at the boy and nodded, making sure that her face expressed all the gratitude and pleasure she felt at that moment. The boy seemed pleased as he puffed up his little chest proudly.

"Papa," he said, tapping his father on the hand, "can I go play with her?"

Brommel again glanced at Mouse as she finished the last of the tart.

"She's busy," he started to say, but his expression softened. "Let me look into it."

Master Peagry was taking an order from another table when Brommel called him over. Mouse shrunk back a little. What if he told about the tart? She might get a scolding for it. But Brommel said nothing about the tart.

"My boy's in need of a friend," he said to Peagry, "and it seems these two have hit it off. Would you mind if the girl took a break with him for a while?"

Peagry scratched at his chin and glanced warily toward the kitchen. "Well, I don't know. We're pretty busy this hour, and Mouse here has her duties to attend to."

"She'd be doing me a favor," said Brommel. "She could watch over him a while so I can rest."

Peagry's eyes never left the kitchen door. It was as if he was waiting for Mrs. Peagry to come out and scold him as well. Finally, when she did not appear, he gave Mouse a quick pat on the head.

"All right, go on. Hurry up, though," he told her, "before the missus comes out with more of those dreadful tarts."

In a flash, the little boy had Mouse by the hand, pulling her across the tavern and out the front door. They were outside now, beside the main thoroughfare of the city. Not far off stood the fountain, a lofty stone monument encircled by a shallow channel of crystal clear water, which served as the heart of Dokur. The thoroughfare itself was alive with people, hurrying past in every direction, some toting fussing children behind them, others carrying baskets of food or other wares, and still others pushing or pulling empty carts that had earlier born bushels of winter wheat or other late-season harvests and which had either been sold or delivered to the mill to be ground into flour.

The scene before them was typical for that time of day, and Mouse was quite accustomed to the noise and chaos of it. But from the look on her young companion's face and the firm grip he had on her hand, she could tell it was more than he could tolerate. She squeezed his hand gently to reassure him, and motioned for him to follow her. She led him off the main road down a quieter alley between two rows of shops. At the end of the alley, they stepped out into a rocky outcrop overlooking the sandy beach below. From there, the entire harbor lay in clear view. Mouse loved the way the land reached out and around the bay like two arms encircling the water, leaving an opening wide enough for three or four ships to pass through. Beyond that gap was the sea itself, mysterious and infinite.

To their left, situated on a grassy hill on the far side of Dokur, stood the Fortress, a menacing stone edifice that gazed down on the city like an oppressive sentinel. This was the home of Lord Fredric, ruler of Dokur. Most people in the city had never seen him, and yet they feared him. Known for his merciless and often cruel judgments, his notice was to be avoided at all costs. To be noticed was to risk being summoned, and to be summoned was to risk being never heard from again.

Remaining unseen was improbable, however, as none could escape the view of the watchtower, which overlooked the city and the bay. This tower was known as the Eye of Dokur, and while its main function was to watch the sea for signs of enemy ships, the people of Dokur believed its true purpose was to watch them.

Mouse, however, did not care about the tower. She did not care about the Fortress or about Lord Fredric. She knew them better than most and might have reason to fear, but she was not intimidated in the least. Each night she stood out in full view of them both as if daring them to notice her. Should she be summoned, it would all be in vain, for they would never get her to speak. She would never betray the one who had entrusted her with the truth.

"Is this your place?" asked the boy. He let go of her hand and took a few steps forward. Then he sat down with his feet dangling over the cliff. Mouse sat down beside him.

The boy pointed across the bay to the east. "The sun's going down. Where I live, the sun goes down behind the fields. The sea is not too far away, but not close enough for me to see."

They sat in silence for a few minutes, watching the sun's descent. Suddenly, the boy bumped against her with his shoulder.

"My name is Rylan," he said, smiling broadly. "I heard that man call you Mouse. Is that your name?"

Mouse shook her head.

"Then why does he call you that?"

She bit her lip and shrugged her shoulders.

"You don't talk? That's all right. You don't have to if you don't want to. Maybe he calls you Mouse because he doesn't know your real name."

Mouse smiled back at Rylan. She couldn't help herself. He was a nice little boy and she found she liked him very much.

The sun completed its setting, and the sky turned a deep violet. The bay was a dark circle now. Night had come, and Mouse knew that Mrs. Peagry would soon be looking for her. But for the first time since the Peagrys took her in, she was not alone. It was nice not being alone, and she didn't want it to end just yet. So she remained there with Rylan, sitting on the cliff and listening to the tide colliding against the rocks below.

Rylan reached for her hand. "Maybe someday you'll tell me your name," he said.

Mouse gave his little fingers a squeeze. Maybe someday, she thought, I will.

2

As the gryphon closed the distance between Agnora's cabin and the outlying villages surrounding Nauvet-Carum, Ivanore could see the layout of the land for many miles in all directions. The forest itself appeared as an ocean of deep green, and soaring above it gave Ivanore the sensation that she was sailing on a calm sea. North of the forest were the jagged peaks of the mainland's longest mountain range. She could not see what lay beyond them, but caught glimpses from time to time of wide expanses of what appeared to be farmland. The land south of the forest, where Teak lived, was also patchworked with farms and small villages. But Ivanore and the gryphon flew southeast toward the sprawling seaboard city of Nauvet-Carum.

Though Ivanore had never been there, she knew it from her visions and recognized the towering Ministry as soon as it loomed on the horizon. If her visions were accurate, she would find Jayson there. And if fortune were on her side, she might reach him in time to protect him from the awful suffering she had witnessed in her worst nightmares. She was certain Arik would be there, too. He and Jayson were like brothers and had been exiled together. Ivanore was sure that where she found one, she would find the other.

She had to be cautious, of course. Agnora had told her about the Vatéz and their relentless pursuit of power. The image of the pale-faced man and his unquenchable lust for it still plagued her visions. She would have to watch herself and do her best to avoid notice. As soon as she found her husband and brother, they would all find some way back to Imaness. They would be a family again, her father be damned.

Ivanore eased the gryphon down in a small clearing just inside the border of the forest, a few miles outside of the city.

"It will be best if I walk from here," she said, stroking its neck. "I will call for you in a few days. But if I fail to return…"

Her voice broke. She smiled, though, trying not to show her fear.

"Should I be delayed, you must return to Imaness without me. I need you to watch over those I left behind. I won't worry so much knowing you'll protect them as you have protected me." Despite her best efforts, tears trailed down her cheeks. Ivanore pressed her damp face against the great beast's warm body. She could hear the gentle hum inside its throat, its way of soothing her. They had been companions her entire life. It had been her guardian and friend. And now she feared this might be their final moment together.

"I must go now." She placed a kiss on the gryphon's beak. It blinked its eyes and fluttered its wings. Then, pulling her cloak tightly around her, she headed off toward the city.

The day had passed by the time Ivy entered the gate of Nauvet-Carum. The sun had already set, and the streets were nearly deserted. A damp fog had settled along the ground, blown in from the sea. Ivy shivered and pulled her cloak up around her neck. The cobblestones were slick with moisture, and she slipped several times. At one point, she fell against an abandoned cart. She held on to the edge of it and scolded herself for not having borrowed better shoes from Agnora. She still had only the slippers she had brought with her from the farm, and by now they were worn thin and provided little protection for her feet.

She scanned the storefronts lining the narrow street and saw that one of them was a shoemaker, another was a dress shop.

"I will have to get myself some decent shoes and clothes in the morning," she told herself. But with what? She had no money. In fact, now that she thought of it, she was quite hungry as well. She noticed a bakery not far down the road, its door locked for the night. Ivy made her way to the shop and looked in through the window. Her mouth watered at the sight of the pastries displayed there. She considered taking a moment to eat some of the bread she had brought with her from Agnora's, but despite her hunger, she was too anxious to waste anymore time.

The fog turned into a fine mist that seeped into her clothes and skin as Ivanore continued through the streets of Nauvet-Carum. After a while, she stopped in front of a stone pillar reaching upward through the mist and disappearing from view. It stood before her like a sentry, its white marble surface glistening with moisture. There was something familiar about this. Yes, she had seen it before. She had reached the destination of her visions.

Ivy forced herself to take a breath, for breathing had suddenly ceased to be natural. Beneath her cloak, Ivy trembled. She reached out and let her fingertips glide over the column's surface. Could she really be so close, she wondered? After so much time, would her visions prove correct?

She willed herself to ascend the first step. The second step came easier. As she proceeded higher, she left the column behind trusting the clear image in her mind to lead her onward. On the top step she paused, and then reached for the door.

Ivy was mildly surprised to find the entrance to the Ministry unlocked. The narrow corridor was paved in marble to match the column outside, and the scuffle of hurried footsteps filled the air. Several clusters of men wearing robes of various colors moved throughout the hall, most too absorbed in their heated discussions to notice the presence of the damp, cloaked stranger. Some men hurried past her to the door through which she had just come.

"Thought winter was behind us," remarked one.

"I'll be drenched before my carriage arrives," said another.

One of them managed a brief, disinterested glance in Ivy's direction. She hurried down the hall in the opposite direction and soon found herself standing before a door made of a very dark wood. The pillar. The men in the hall. This very door. It was the right place, she was certain of that, but it was all wrong. In the vision that had led her here, this hall had been bathed in sunlight, streams of light filtering through the tall windows along the outer wall.

A sick feeling filled her gut. Why hadn't she thought of it before? It was nighttime now, but even it weren't, the mist outside was so thick and gray, it would certainly block out the sun.

This *was* the right place, she realized, but the wrong time.

Ivy turned and made a hasty retreat toward the outer door. She would prefer to brave the wet, cold night than to face the unknown. The trembling returned as she now tried to avoid the glances of the men who remained in the room. She had lingered too long. They had noticed her.

Stay calm, she told herself. Do not draw attention to yourself.

Keeping her face low, she glanced up only to see how close she was to the door—to freedom. What was she thinking? Did Agnora's warnings mean nothing to her?

The door was almost within arm's reach now, and she quickened her pace. She wanted—needed to get out before she was discovered. As she neared the exit, relief washed over her. But then, as if from the shadows, someone stepped in front of her, blocking her path.

3

At times it seemed winter would go on forever, and that the plantation was damned to an eternal state of hibernation. Jayson hated the long, dark nights and the days where the sky was an interminable shade of gray. He spent most days trying to stay warm inside the bunkhouse. Other days he'd go hunting, either alone or with Captain Dawes. Orrin Dawes, as it turned out, was an adept hunter. Proficient with an array weapons, he was as skilled at felling a deer with an arrow as he was tracking and killing a warboar with nothing but a knife. Jayson found that the hours passed quickly when in Dawes's company. He respected the man, and Dawes respected Jayson as well.

By early spring, Jayson was a frequent guest in the big house, taking his meals with Dawes as they made plans for the next hunt and entertained the servants with tales from the last one. By the time the snows began to melt and the first hints of blue appeared in the sky, Jayson had grown accustomed to life on the plantation. He had even come to like it.

Over a cup of tea, Jayson suggested another hunt. "Warboar are in abundance," he said, letting the tea's woody aroma soothe his senses.

Dawes shook his head. "We've cured three already and several deer," he replied. "That will get us through until summer. I'm expecting two dozen men by month's end. After the first frost, they'll be plowing the land and planting seed."

"And until then?"

"I'll be leaving soon, returning to sea on The Silver Mist."

Though Jayson had expected this, he felt disappointed.

"Have you ever thought about going to sea?" asked Dawes.

"Many times," answered Jayson. "But I've only taken to it once, and that was enough for me." His thoughts momentarily turned to his exile from Dokur, how he'd been shackled to a ship's mast and forced to watch the diminishing figure of his Ivanore as he sailed away.

"In that case," said Dawes, "I'll be needing a foreman. Are you up to the task?"

The invitation took Jayson by surprise. He wasn't sure how to respond. Before he could, Dawes grasped his cup in both hands and finished off his tea in a single swallow. Then he sighed heavily as though disappointed it was tea instead of liquor.

"You know, one last hunt is not such a bad idea after all," he said, rising from the table. "Jayson, fetch my knife. There's a warboar out there just waiting to be killed."

*   *   *

The hunt went well. Jayson used his keen senses to track a large male warboar through dense underbrush. He could have taken the animal himself, but Dawes reveled in the hunt as much as he did. So they took the beast together, Jayson with his hands and Dawes with his knife. Once the animal was dead, they cleaned and dressed it on the spot, burning the entrails while packing the meat and skin for the journey back home. Both Dawes and Jayson were covered in blood by the time they were through, so they washed in a nearby stream.

Jayson jumped into the water and splashed about. The water was cold as ice. Snow still clung to the banks in crystalline clumps of white and gray. The water invigorated him, made him feel as though life were worth living again. Over the past several months of winter, a weight had fallen on him pushing him down as if into a deep well from which he could not climb out. Perhaps it was the many hours he passed in darkness that increased his feeling of isolation, but remorse for having failed so many, for being the cause of so much suffering, weighed on him incessantly. He thought daily of Dianis and wondered if she had fully recovered from her injured leg—and broken heart. He thought of Brommel and Rylan who no doubt would never recover from Brielle's death and of Alay-Crevar. But he thought mostly of Ivanore, left alone to raise their son in a land so far distant that it seemed a mere memory. Only while hunting did these thoughts cease their endless pursuit.

Dawes rolled up the legs of his trousers and stepped into the shallow water at the bank. "I'm an old man," he shouted, laughing at Jayson's antics in the deeper part of the stream. "If I flailed about like that, my heart might very well fail me!"

"Nonsense!" answered Jayson. He lay flat in the water, letting its gentle currents roll over him. Though the temperature of the water numbed him, for the present, he was content.

Later they sat on the rocks at the stream's edge and let the sun dry them. It was then, when there was nothing but silence between them that Jayson's bitter memories returned. Yearning to put them off a little longer, he foraged for a topic of conversation.

"You mentioned earlier that you'll need a foreman while you're away," he said.

"That I did," replied Dawes. "Are you interested?"

"I am, but how would that affect my indentured contract with you?"

Dawes stretched his legs out in front of him. "Well, the contract is for one season's employment, which would more than cover the cost of Brommel's passage to Dokur. If you act as foreman, the contract is still binding for that period of time, but I will see to it that you receive reasonable compensation for the added responsibility."

The heat of the sun had warmed Jayson through to his bones, soothing his aching muscles and calming his mind. He laid his palms against the rough stone on which he sat, splaying out his fingers. "And what do you consider to be reasonable compensation?" he asked.

The captain peered at Jayson, raising his hand to shield his eyes from the sun. "How would the entire plantation do?"

Jayson's claws slipped, grazing the rock. "Pardon?"

Dawes sighed, but his eyes remained serious. "The fact is," he said, "I'd like to name you as my heir."

4

"If you're trying not to get noticed, I'm afraid it's too late for that."

The voice was deeper than Ivanore remembered but unmistakable. Ivy glanced up into her younger brother's face. He looked a little older, as he naturally would after a year and a half, but his hair was as red as ever and his complexion just as ruddy as when he was a boy. Seeing him instantly set her at ease and put a smile on Ivy's face.

"Arik," she began, but Arik quickly grasped her by the arm and roughly ushered her through the doors and down the steps of the Ministry.

"What were you thinking, going in there?" he snapped once they'd reached the street. He kept his grip tight on her arm. "If you'd been recognized—"

He cursed between clenched teeth.

"You're hurting me," Ivy whispered, fighting back the tears that suddenly stung behind her eyes. "This wasn't quite the greeting I expected."

303

Arik released her but his expression remained hard. "Did you expect me to embrace and kiss you? You're the reason I was exiled, remember? So, forgive my lack of enthusiasm."

"You're not surprised to see me."

"Surprised?" Arik glanced nervously around him, and dropped his voice even lower. "The entire Hestorian army has been searching for you for months. The last place anyone expects you to be is *here*."

"Then I suppose here is the best place I could possibly be."

"Sarcasm won't protect you, Ivanore."

"And *you* will?"

She realized that Arik was a good four inches taller than her. When she had last seen him she could look him directly in the eye. And there was something else about him that had changed, something in his eyes.

Arik's expression softened. "It's not safe for you here," he said. "Let's go somewhere where we can talk in private. Are you staying anywhere?"

Ivy shook her head.

"All right then, you'll stay with me for now."

They walked briskly along the cobbled road, and Ivy was actually grateful for his steadying hand. Her slippers were soaked through, and her feet were so numb with cold that they refused to function properly.

The air had grown completely dark by the time Arik led her into a tavern and up a narrow flight of wooden stairs. They passed through a door at the top into a room lit by a single candle cradled in an iron sconce.

Arik took the candle and used it to light a lantern. The room's shadows fled, and Ivy found herself in as nice a room as she had ever known. Though small, it housed a collection of fine furnishings: a bed, velvet padded chairs, a wide desk, a table. An iron stove stood in the corner with a pile of split wood ready to go. A plush carpet covered the floor.

"You've done well for yourself," Ivy commented.

Arik hung the lantern on a hook near the bed. "I have as of late," he replied. "I've acquired these things little by little. Though it hasn't been easy."

Ivy walked to the bed and patted the quilt with her hand.

"Does Jayson live here, too?"

Arik selected two logs from the woodpile and placed them in the stove. He fetched the candle and held it to the end of a piece of tinder. Using the tinder, he lit the stove and shut the door.

"Jayson's been on his own for a while now," he said.

"Where is he?" asked Ivanore.

"I don't know. The Ministry's looking for him, too."

"Why?"

"You know why, Ivy." Arik gave her a reproachful look. "The leader of the Vatéz wants the crystal. You should have considered the consequences before giving it to Jayson."

Ivy thought again of her vision. Jayson would eventually be in the hands of the Vatéz, imprisoned in the Ministry. But they hadn't found him—not yet. Maybe there was still hope that she could keep him and the crystal safe.

"Arik, you've every right to hate me. It's my fault father disowned you. I will make it up to you one day if I can. In the meantime, I've got to find Jayson," she said. "Oh, Arik, I've had the most terrible visions. I've got to find him before it's too late. Will you help me?"

Ivy thought she saw a flicker of emotion behind Arik's eyes. But then it was gone.

Arik went to a wooden cabinet and removed a bottle from it. He poured the amber liquid into a cup and swallowed it down. She had never seen her brother like this before, so angry and anxious, nor had she anticipated any such anger to be directed toward her. And there was something else about him as well, the edge in his voice, the critical glare. If she didn't know him better, she would say he was jealous. But jealous of what?

Arik filled his cup a second time. "How long have you been in Hestoria now?" he asked, keeping his back to her.

"Nearly half a year," she answered.

"And Jayson and I arrived here a year before that."

"Yes."

"So the boy, the *new* heir to Dokur's throne, is about two years old then."

It was the way he said it, so flippantly, as if he were purposely concealing an intense interest. And yet he spoke of his own nephew. Why not show interest? Why not express concern that the child had gone so long without his mother?

Arik turned to face her, and there it was—an unmistakable loathing. Though he tried to mask it, the evidence was in his eyes. Ivy wrestled against her doubts, but something inside of her felt wary of him, as though he could not be fully trusted. Even so, she balked at the thought that Arik would ever betray her. He was her brother, and yet…

"My son is dead." The lie tasted like bile on Ivy's tongue. She looked away as she said it, afraid Arik would see the deception in her eyes.

Moments passed in silence. Arik set down his glass. He walked to Ivy and took both her hands in his. Arik's expression, which had been cold and angry until now, softened. But was it empathy Ivy saw now—or relief?

"I'm sorry," Arik said. "I've been so callous. You came so far to find Jayson, but found me instead. You must be disappointed."

"No," Ivy protested. "I knew you'd be here. That's why I went to the Ministry. I saw Jayson there and I assumed you'd be with him. He's in danger, Arik."

"Yes, I know," said Arik.

Despite her best efforts to prevent it, the tears came, though they fell as much for Arik as for herself. "Please, Arik," she said. "Please help me find him."

Arik's lips played at a smile. An attempt to be reassuring? This wasn't the same boy Ivy had known in Dokur, the boy who had raised a sword against their father in defense of Jayson. The fire was still there; she could see it burning in his eyes, but now it seemed tinged with something less noble, something ominous. And yet what choice did she have but to appeal to him, to trust him?

"I'll find him," Arik said with a conviction that sent chills through Ivy's bones. "I swear to you, I will find him no matter the cost."

5

"You want *me* as your heir?"

Orrin Dawes's words had been spoken with such indifference that Jayson thought he must be joking. Jayson laughed until he saw the solemn expression on Dawes's face.

"You're serious, aren't you?"

"I have no son," Dawes went on. "I am gone at sea for long stretches at a time. And one day I will simply not return. The sea will eventually claim me, which is what I'd wish anyhow. As it stands, when I die, the plantation will be left to whoever can lay claim to her. I'd prefer to have some say in the matter. So, should I die or fail to return to my property within a certain number of years, the land will be yours."

"You're serious," said Jayson, hardly believing what he'd just been told. Dawes fixed a solemn gaze on him and replied in as serious a tone as Jayson had ever heard from him.

"I most certainly am."

A warm breeze began to blow, and the trees neighboring the stream swayed gently. Soft, yellow fluff, the seeds of a new year, drifted along invisible currents of air. Jayson lay back on a patch of fresh grass. It felt cool against the skin of his arms and neck, and the smell of it reminded him of the marshlands of Imaness. Dawes's offer was a generous one— more than generous. Jayson couldn't think of anything he had done to deserve it. But that was the point, he supposed. Dawes needed someone to pass his land on to. Might as well be him. Still, accepting such a gift seemed almost selfish, and he couldn't quite ignore the twinge of guilt he felt, as though he had manipulated the old man somehow, even if only subconsciously. But no. Taking a careful inventory of his behavior over the past few months, Jayson could find nothing artificial in his motives. Dawes liked him, trusted him. It was as simple as that.

Jayson closed his eyes and envisioned the wide expanse of earth he currently called home. *Home.* The word sent a strange sensation through his body. Not since he was a child had he ever called any place home—not really. Though the Agorans had lived in the marshlands of Imaness for most of Jayson's life, they always thought of it as a temporary residence and that one day they would be allowed to return to their original homelands in the forested heart of the island. And since coming to Hestoria, Jayson had wandered like a nomad from place to place. There was one time, however, when he felt at home, though the feeling had less to do with where he was than with whom. Even now, just thinking of Ivanore made him tranquil, though the feeling was only fleeting.

He opened his eyes and took several slow, deep breaths in an effort to untie the knot that had formed in his stomach. "Are you sure about this?" he asked.

Dawes pulled his boots onto his feet one at a time. Then he paused, wrapping his thick arms around his knees.

"Jayson, you're young, but there will come a time when you will awake one morning and find that life has ebbed. Of course I would like to live another fifty years, and perhaps I shall. But lately I've been troubled by a sense that I've reached the end of my journey, so it is time to finish my business and pass the relics of my life on to someone else."

"There must be someone besides me you can give your land to," he said, "a distant relative or friend."

"I have no friends," Dawes replied casually, "and whatever relatives I may possess are of no concern to me nor I to them."

His voice trailed off, and for several minutes he stared up at the sky, his face void of expression. After a while he blinked, as though suddenly returning from some faraway place. He scratched at his temple and cleared his throat.

"I've learned a great deal about you these past months, Jayson," he said. "Not by way of details perhaps, but I've learned about your character. You're a determined man, a hard worker. You've got brains, which is more than I can say for most men I've come across in my lifetime. My land is yours, if you'll have it."

Jayson stood up and brushed off the back of his trousers. His clothes were mostly dry now and smelled of sunlight and fresh earth. He hoisted the pack bearing the warboar's carcass onto his shoulders and helped Dawes don the pack with the hide.

"I accept your offer," Jayson told him, and once the words were said they filled him with a fervor he had not felt in a long time.

Dawes laughed heartily and slapped Jayson on the back. "Good!" he bellowed. "The deal's done, then!"

The two men strode resolutely toward home, Dawes recounting stories from his adventures at sea and Jayson responding with appropriate enthusiasm. By the time they reached the plantation, the sun had just set behind the distant mountains. Their steps slowed on reaching the gate, though the fire glow visible from the big house's windows invited them to hasten. It was the silhouette that stood before the window, waiting on the porch that caused them to measure their pace. There two men stood side by side. Jayson recognized the first at once, and though he took pleasure in seeing him, Gerard's presence could only mean bad news.

The second man was taller and much younger than Gerard. He was a stranger to Jayson, and yet the man held in his eyes a look of definite loathing. He might not know the man, but there was no doubt this man knew him and felt disdain for him. As he followed Dawes up to the porch, Jayson wondered how he could possibly have offended this young stranger.

6

"What shall I do with her?" asked Arik, beads of sweat forming on his brow. He had just explained to Emir, to the very head of the Vatéz himself, how he had stumbled upon Ivanore right in the Ministry's own entrance hall.

Emir stood at the window of his private chambers and stared down at the darkened city below. "Where is she now?" he asked.

"In my room," replied Arik.

"And she believes you are going to help her find Jayson?"

"Yes. I've told her as much." Arik paced the floor, his hands clenched behind his back. "I've done it wrong, haven't I? I should have brought her to you immediately. It's just that I was so surprised to see her—I wasn't thinking."

Emir turned from the window and motioned for Arik to sit in an embroidered chair. "You've done just as I would have asked," said Emir.

"I have?"

"Quite so. You are her brother, and she knows only of your loyalty to her and to Jayson. Of course she trusts you."

"But I've promised to help her find Jayson."

"Is that a problem?"

"Is that a problem? I've spent months scouring the entire country for him. He, like the guardians, has simply vanished! How am I to find him now?"

"Oh, you won't find him," said Emir. "*She* will."

7

Arik's room was comfortable enough, but after spending five days inside with only the window to connect her to the outside world, Ivanore grew anxious. She shared her breakfast with Arik each morning before he hurried off "to take care of business." Apparently, he was quite needed at the Ministry, which had found some use for him in the area of political management. Each day as he left, he reminded her of the dangers that lurked about the city and pleaded with her to stay inside where she would not be seen. She obeyed, naturally, not because she felt obligated to obey her younger brother, but because he was most likely correct. It would do no one any good should she be taken captive.

After each long and lonesome day Arik would return sullen-faced and ill-spirited. Only once he had dressed in his night clothes and eaten a good meal did she venture to press him about his promise.

"Have you any news of Jayson?" she would ask, probing.

And each day would come the disappointing reply. "Nothing yet," followed by an encouraging, "but don't give up. I'll find him."

By the sixth day Ivanore had gone nearly mad staring at the same four walls day in and day out. She was determined to convince Arik to take her out that evening. The fog had long since dissipated and the evenings were warm and clear. She made sure to dress in the nicest smock of all those that her brother had bought for her and laced up her new calfskin boots, such a nice change from the worn slippers. The day crawled by, and it was late in the evening when Arik finally returned home. His countenance was hard, like that first night he had found her in the Ministry.

Ivy greeted him at the door and took his coat. "You're later tonight than usual. Are you well, Arik?"

"As well as can be expected," he muttered, pushing past her to the bed. He sat down and pulled off his boots, tossing them roughly aside.

Ivy picked them up and set them beside the wall. She laid his coat over the back of a chair, which she turned toward him. She sat down on it and studied Arik's rigid expression.

"What is it?" she asked. "Is something wrong?"

He raised his eyes to hers. In them she saw both grief and confusion.

"Is it Jayson?" She could hardly form the words for fear of what Arik's answer might be. To her surprise, Arik's expression twisted in anger. He threw himself to his feet and paced the floor like a caged beast.

"Why must you always ask about him?" he said, nearly shouting. "Don't you know I've tried everything? Yet he continues to elude me!"

"I am sorry, Arik. I don't doubt you've tried."

315

But Arik did not look at Ivanore when he spoke. Instead he ranted at some unseen being.

"How many innocent people must die before he surrenders? And why must I always be the one with blood on my hands? Why?"

His voice had risen to a frantic pitch. Ivy quickly rose from her chair and took Arik's shoulders in her hands. His eyes found hers, but they seemed lost somehow. The expression in them frightened her.

"Arik, you're talking like a mad man."

"I am mad, Ivanore. How could I not be? No sane man would do what I have done and allow himself to go on living."

"What have you done, Arik? Tell me. I'm sure everything will be all right."

"I can't tell you. I can't utter a word of it for fear that the faces that hound me in my dreams will take on flesh and come for me."

Ivy wanted to comfort Arik as she often had when they were children. Though only two years Arik's elder, she still considered herself his guardian, and he would come to her with his troubles and fears to be soothed by her. But they were children no longer. She was a woman—a wife and mother—and Arik was on the verge of manhood.

"I understand a little of dreams," Ivy said, "and of nightmares."

Arik bobbed his head. "Yes, you do, don't you? Perhaps both our nightmares can finally come to an end once we find Jayson."

Ivy noticed for the first time that his speech was slightly slurred. "Have you been drinking, Arik?" she asked.

"Your visions," he said, ignoring her question. "I know you see him in your visions. Tell me what you see so that I can find him."

"But I've already told you. I see him here, in the Ministry."

"Well, he isn't here in the Ministry, is he? At least not yet. There must be something more!"

Arik slammed his fist against the cabinet. Ivy jumped at the sound.

"What else have you seen?" he asked, his anger restrained.

Ivy hesitated, but this made Arik angrier still.

"Tell me what you've seen!" he shouted. He turned away from the cabinet as he spoke and faced her. His eyes were red and dilated. There was such loathing in them that she felt she was in the presence of a stranger. It was all Ivy could do to not let her fear catch in her throat.

"I see a man," she began haltingly, "a white-skinned man who wants to destroy me. He sent someone after me, but I hid in the woods and they never found me. I think he's the cause of Jayson's pain in my visions."

"Who hid you? The Guilde?" Arik demanded, the muscles in his neck and shoulders growing taut.

"No. I was told I should go to them, of course."

"But you didn't."

"For several months I couldn't. I was too sick. And as soon as I was able, I came here."

"You said you were told to go to the Guilde. Who told you to go there?" Arik's expression grew frenzied. It was all Ivy could do to restrain herself from fleeing.

"I don't—" she stammered. "I can't—"

Suddenly Arik crossed the room, grabbed Ivy by the shoulders and shook her. "Who sent you to the Guilde? What directions did they give you?"

"Does it really matter who sent me?" Ivy choked on the tears that had finally won out.

Arik stared at her as though calculating his next move, his fury suddenly abated. It was this rapid shift between emotions that frightened Ivy more than the anger itself. Arik released Ivy and returned to the cabinet. Taking a bottle from a shelf, he filled a glass with a red liquid.

Ivy, trembling, lowered herself into a chair. What had possessed her brother to behave in such a manner? How long would she have to depend on him to help her? The longer she stayed with him, the more she feared for not only Jayson's safety—but also her own.

Arik downed the wine. "No. No, of course it doesn't matter," he mumbled, his anger held in check. "It's just that if Jayson has the crystal, then it would only make sense that he'd be with the Guilde. They are its guardians, are they not?"

He strode back to Ivy and dropped to his knees before her so that his face was level with hers, his eyes now full of desperation.

"If we could track down the Guilde, then we might very likely find Jayson as well. You said you were told to go to them. Please, Ivy, tell me what directions you were given to find them.?"

"I wasn't given any directions, but—"

The word came too late.

"But?" coaxed Arik.

It would do no good now to hide the truth from him, nor did she wish to. This boy in front of her now reminded her of the frightened little boy she had once known. She reached out her hand and smoothed back his hair the way she had when they were young. He was desperate to help her, she told herself. He wanted to find Jayson, for her, but had thus far failed in his attempts. How much he must love her to want so badly what she wanted.

"I once had a vision," she told him, "during my fever. I saw Jayson near a small lake. He stood beside a waterfall. And then there was fire, and then water again, only this time a vast sea. He was in the sea drifting far off from me. I called to him, but to no avail. The waves carried him farther and farther away."

Ivy shuddered at the memory. She was surprised how well she recalled it. The vision had not repeated itself, and she hoped it never would.

A look of recognition flitted across Arik's face. "A waterfall, did you say?"

"It was only the briefest of images. I doubt it meant anything. It was so long ago, and I haven't seen it since. If Jayson was at such a place, I'm certain he is not there now."

She again smoothed back Arik's hair. He closed his eyes, his expression tranquil. He laid his head in her lap.

"That's all right," he told her. "I will try to locate this place. There may be someone there who can tell us where he is now. In time, he will be found."

Arik's breath slowed, his muscles relaxed. The tension in Ivy's own body left as well, but deep inside her fear remained.

8

"Gerard!" said Jayson, stepping up onto the porch.

Gerard embraced Jayson as though he were a long lost son, then held him out and looked him over. "No worse for wear," he concluded. "You've been eating well, I see. I suppose my concern for your well-being was unfounded."

"Is that why you've come, to see that I'm eating enough?" asked Jayson with a laugh. He turned to Dawes, who now stood beside him.

"Gerard, this is Orrin Dawes, captain of the good ship The Silver Mist. This is his plantation."

"It's a pleasure to have you here," said Dawes, extending his hand.

Gerard took it and gave it a vigorous shake. "Thank you, sir," he replied. "We've traveled a good long way, and we apologize for not sending word of our arrival."

The young man with Gerard stood aloof during the greeting. He shifted uncomfortably, and Gerard finally took notice of him.

reunited with her was enough to make him want to weep. But she had been injured, ill, had been cared for by strangers when it should have been him beside her. The thought enraged him.

"Where is she now?" he demanded.

"I told you, she's run off," answered Gerard.

"Run off? What do you mean? Where has she gone?"

Gerard stammered, obviously wanting to give Jayson the answers he so desired, and yet having none to give. Jayson turned to Teak, who through all this had remained composed and silent.

"*You* must have some idea," Jayson said, not even attempting to control his anger.

Teak nodded, but said nothing, which infuriated Jayson even more. Suddenly Jayson rose from his seat, crossed the floor in two quick strides and grasped Teak by the front of his shirt.

"I do not know you," he said in a low growl. "I only keep my temper out of courtesy for Gerard who seems to trust you, and for my host who prefers to keep his home unsoiled from human blood. But I assure you, Teak, that if you do not speak now I will extract the information I desire even if I must tear it out of you." Jayson held up his free hand, extending his claws.

If Teak felt any fear, he did not show it. When he spoke it was with an unruffled calm.

"She's been plagued by visions of you," he began. "She came to Hestoria to find you, but during her escape from Imaness, she received an arrow to her shoulder. My uncle and I watched over her until someone from the Ministry came in search of her. How they knew she was with us, I do not know. My uncle was killed protecting Ivy, while she and I fled into the forest.

"We were taken in by Agnora, a friend of the Guilde and an enchantress. It took all winter for Ivy to regain her health, and as soon as she was strong enough I was to take her to Gerard. However, six days ago I awoke to find her gone."

Jayson was growing more impatient with each word Teak spoke. He held him tighter, closer.

"Where did she go?"

"To the place in her vision where she believes you will come, a great stone edifice near the sea."

Gerard interrupted. "It can only be Nauvet-Carum. Dianis left for the city days ago to search for her while we came here to find you."

Jayson released Teak and turned to the fire. Six days had passed. If the gryphon had carried her, then she would have arrived in little time. It would take another two days before he could reach the city himself, and what would he do then? How would he find her?

"If Ivanore is in Nauvet-Carum, or worse, at the Ministry itself," said Gerard, "then Emir may have already found her. He has spies everywhere. The chance that she would have escaped his notice is slim. Hopefully, Dianis will have information for us when we arrive."

"Then I must leave immediately," said Jayson.

The door to the kitchen opened and in strode Dawes, his sleeves rolled up to his elbows and wiping his hands on a cloth.

"Leaving?" he said, tossing the damp cloth over a hook beside the fire. "Forgive me for intruding, but are your circumstances really so dire?"

"I'm afraid they are," answered Jayson. "I am sorry, but I must reach Nauvet-Carum as quickly as possible."

There was an uncomfortable silence as Jayson waited for Dawes's reaction. This man had generously offered him everything he owned in exchange for managing the plantation in his absence. Jayson would not hold it against him if he were angry with him. But to his astonishment, Dawes clapped his hands together, summoning Nira from the kitchen.

"Provisions for four, Nira, enough to get us to the city. And be sure to have some horses prepared before first light. Now then," he said, turning to Jayson, "we'll eat a hearty supper, get a good night's rest, and set out at dawn. In two days' time we will be in the capitol."

9

While Arik slept, Ivy listened to his rhythmic breathing from the corner of the room where he lay on the makeshift bed he had made for himself out of a pile of blankets. Ivy lay in Arik's bed, grateful once again for her brother's generosity. But was it generosity that motivated him to keep her hidden here in his room and to search so desperately for Jayson and the crystal, or something else entirely?

She chastised herself for doubting her brother. He loved her as surely as she loved him, and he must realize that their father was as enraged at her as he was with Arik. No, he had not exiled her, but he had threatened her child, had sworn he'd never let a mongrel sit on his throne. She had taken her son then and fled, seeking shelter with the enchanter Zyll. Ivy thought of them now. They would be sleeping, the child most likely curled up in the crook of the enchanter's elbow, his face resting against Zyll's soft gray beard. Did he dream of her, she wondered, the way she dreamed of him? Or had he already forgotten her, her memory having faded from the young boy's mind?

A tear fell from the corner of each eye. Ivy did not wipe them away. She lingered on the faces of the boy and Zyll, but then another face came into view, one so painful to recall she could not bear it. Ivy squeezed her eyes shut and pushed them all from her mind.

Rolling to her side, she focused again on Arik's breathing, trying to match her own with his. Doing so relaxed her, numbed her mind and eased her memories. In time, her mind finally slipped into darkness, and she slept.

The hall in her dreams was as familiar to her now as if she had walked along it a hundred times, and indeed she had, though only in her mind. Full of shadows, lit only by a faint candle set in a tarnished brass sconce, the corridor stretched before her like a tunnel, drawing her ever farther in.

She came to a door, dark and heavy. The sharp smell of blood emanated from it, the stench of death. Resisting the urge to flee, she pushed the door open with a strained creak.

He was straddling a chair in the center of the room, his back to her. His shoulders were hunched forward, his head down. Deep red gashes crisscrossed the skin on his back, and blood dripped from them onto the floor. The coppery smell of it filled her senses, shooting stabs of fear through her brain.

"Jayson?"

At the sound of her voice, his head jerked up. Ivy stepped hesitantly toward him. He turned suddenly and the terrorized, desperate expression on his bruised and battered face made her blood freeze in her veins.

"Ivy, run!" he hissed. And then louder. "RUN!"

Ivy spun, ready to sprint through the door. Her heart hammered against her rib cage, her blood throbbing in her veins. She grabbed for the door handle, but as her fingers made contact, it was not cold metal she felt, but the rough, damp bark of a tree.

She stepped back, surprised, and saw before her not the door, but a wooded glen. The corridor had vanished. She knew this place. She stood at the edge of the pasture where she had taken Teak to see the gryphon. Relief washed over her. Not far from here was Agnora's cabin. Surely she and Teak would be there still, waiting for her. Perhaps she had never left at all.

She started forward at a run, wanting to reach the cabin quickly. She called their names and listened for their replies. She continued on, but the air grew dark around her. Night had come, but instead of slowing, she ran faster, desperate to reach the cabin.

Suddenly, not far ahead, someone stepped out from behind a tree. Ivy halted, her chest burning from breathing so fast. It was too dark to see who it was, but it must be Teak. Who else would know she was here? She called his name, but he did not reply. The figure stepped forward, and as he did he passed through a pale beam of moonlight filtered through the trees.

She had seen his face before, his gaunt skin like faded parchment, his eyes pale and menacing. It was he who had sent the tracker, who had captured Jayson and caused his suffering. And now he wanted her.

Ivy turned and ran, back through the woods, back toward the pasture. She did not know if the man followed, but she ran on. Tree branches slapped against her face, thorny twigs snagged her cloak and skin, but still she ran. Blood trickled from her wounds, but the pain was nothing compared to her fear. Ahead she saw the spot where her journey had begun, the edge of the wood and the top of the hill that descended into the pasture below. She bolted forward, but just as she reached the edge, she threw her arms around a tree and came to an abrupt stop.

Ivy's eyes widened as she peered down not into a grassy field, but into a storm-tossed sea. She stood at the edge of a rocky cliff and clung tightly to a wet, slippery outcropping of stone. Sheets of rain sliced through the air like millions of icy daggers. Like the corridor of her dream, she had seen this before as well. *Not this*, she cried, *anywhere but this!*

Knowing already what was to come, Ivy narrowed her eyes, peered up through the storm. Above her loomed a solitary tower made of dark gray stone. In its window was a figure—a man. Ivy's stomach twisted when the man leapt, though she had witnessed this over and over again. And he fell—silent and still—into the sea.

Ivy desperately searched the blackened water. Yes! There he was among the waves!

"Jayson! Jayson!"

She screamed his name until she was certain her lungs would burst, until her voice went hoarse. He would not hear her over the storm. And as he drifted farther and farther out to sea, Ivy reached out toward him, straining her arms, hers hands and fingers out as if, by sheer force of will, she could snatch him from the depths and draw him to her.

The rain fell harder, splashing off the slick surface of the stone. Her hand that gripped it slipped. Ivy tumbled forward off the cliff, the dark turbulent waters rising up to meet her.

Ivy's eyes sprang open. She gasped for breath expecting her lungs to fill with ice-cold seawater. Instead her chest expanded, drawing only warm air into them. She reached out into the dark and found not stone nor water, but the soft bed on which she lay.

A dim light still burned on the sconce, illuminating the room with a gentle light. Arik lay curled up in the corner, just as he had been before Ivy had drifted off to sleep. She rolled out of bed and slipped out of her nightdress and into her clothes, careful not to make any unnecessary noise that might wake her brother, though she imagined nothing would wake him after the amount of liquor she was sure he had consumed. Still, if he knew what she intended to do, he would surely reprimand her. She smiled at the thought of her younger brother chastising her for doing something dangerous.

Using extreme caution, she slipped her brother's dagger from its sheath. The blade was heavy in her hand and she curled her fingers around the leather-bound grip. Arik would never know about this, she told herself. She would go quickly and return before he awoke, though doing so would probably prove futile. Last night's vision was just one of many she had had over the past two years. She was beginning to think that maybe they were not visions at all, but merely nightmares. All this talk of being the Seer, of knowing the future, seemed so absurd. Ivy didn't feel special, nor did she want to be. She did not ask for this calling and would gladly give it up if she could. Still, in the deepest recesses of her heart and mind she knew it was true, every bit of it. Jayson would come to the Ministry, if not now, then soon. He was in danger, and she was the only one who could save him.

10

By the time Ivy reached the steps to the Ministry, the sun had just begun to peak above the horizon. She didn't have much time. Nauvet-Carum would soon awake, and so would Arik. She would slip in, have a look around, and get back to Arik's room. She just had to be sure.

The great hall was just as it was when she had first stepped into it a week earlier, only without a soul in sight. She headed left toward the door at the end of the hall, and a moment later she was through it, looking up a flight of winding wooden stairs. She hardly paused before ascending them at half a run, past the second floor to the third where she stopped on the landing. It was just as she had seen dozens of times in her mind: dark shadows on the walls, the smell of stale dust in the air. And down at the end of it all a door, a wide, dark door with a round iron handle.

For a moment, her feet remained frozen to the floor, unwilling to move forward. She closed her eyes and forced herself to breathe, and her feet followed. The air was so still, so silent that she could hear the breath going in and out of her lungs. Then she heard a creak from the wooden stairs below. She hesitated and held her breath, waiting for the sound to repeat. Of course, there would be others roaming about the building now. That's what she had heard. Soon the building would be full of people milling about. She had to hurry. She had to be sure.

Quickly now, to the door. She wrapped her fingers around the handle and pushed it slowly, gently open. Oddly, the air that wafted out of the room smelled of candle wax and incense, not the overpowering stench of blood from her dreams, though there was a trace of something, gone before she could be certain what it was.

She stepped through the doorway and found herself in a spacious office with candles burning from several multi-tiered sconces. The walls were adorned with elaborate tapestries and a thick rug covered much of the floor. Near the far wall was a large desk and behind it a bookshelf that reached clear to the ceiling.

She had expected a bare cell, not the luxury of this room. The hall and door were the same, but not this—this was all wrong. She took several steps forward and laid her hand against the smooth wood of the desk. What was it about this place? It had never made an appearance in her visions, and yet there was something oddly familiar about it. It wasn't the room she recognized but the person who belonged in it.

"No," she whispered. "No, it can't be."

Ivy turned back for the door, but it was too late. Someone stood in her way, a lean man with white skin and tremulous blue eyes. Ivy gasped at the sight of him.

"Well, well," said the man, "how fortunate. After scouring the entire country for the great and mysterious Seer, here she is at my very own doorstep."

It was the man from her vision, the one hellbent on destroying her. The one destined to make Jayson suffer.

Ivy held Arik's dagger out in front of her, its tip pointed at the pale man. "Where is he?" she demanded.

The man was unperturbed, his expression indifferent. "He?"

"My husband!" Ivy shouted. "Where is my husband?!"

"My dear, I'm afraid the half-breed is not here. Oh, I have tried to find him. But I am sorry to say I have been unsuccessful thus far."

His erratic gaze was unsettling. Ivy struggled to suppress the fear that mushroomed inside of her.

"Who are you?"

"But I thought you knew, my dear," said the man. He took a step toward her, but stopped when she jutted her dagger squarely at his chest. "My name's Emir, Minister of Hestoria and leader of the Vatéz."

The Vatéz! The League of Magicians! Panic clutched at Ivy's heart and her hand began to tremble.

"Let me go," she said, though she already knew the request was a futile one.

"Let you go?" said Emir with an amused chuckle. "You are witty, aren't you? Of course I won't let you go. You are *the Seer*."

His voice was so light, amiable, and distracting. He gazed down at her with an almost fatherly expression, the way her own father had looked at her when she was very young. Emir took another step forward, his palms turned out to her. But she held the dagger tightly in her fist, keeping her eyes intent on his.

"You are much too valuable to me," Emir continued, "but I promise you will not be harmed—as long as you cooperate."

"You want to destroy me!"

"Not at all, my dear. Nothing could be further from my mind. I want to—oh, how do I put it—*utilize* your talents. Hmmm?"

And then she understood. Emir had sent the tracker after her because he wanted to use her powers alongside his own. He needed her. Exactly how or why she wasn't sure, but the idea of assisting him with anything left a vile taste in her mouth.

"Never!"

Ivy had one chance to push past Emir and escape through the door. She lunged forward and threw her full weight against him, knocking Emir off balance. As he fell, he clutched her tunic, nearly pulling her down with him.

Desperate, Ivy slashed her dagger across the pallid hand that held onto her. A streak of red appeared, and Emir cried out, releasing her. Ivy sprung for the door. But just as she reached for it, the door swung shut with a terrible crash, and the iron bolt slid into place of its own accord. Ivy grabbed the iron ring and pulled on it with all her might, but to no avail.

Trapped!

Ivy spun back to face Emir, who stood clutching his wounded hand, the amused grin on his face gone. His eyes burned with rage, and the corners of his lips twitched.

"That was a very unwise thing to do," he hissed. He raised his good hand and brandished his fingers through the air. As he did so, a solid mass of air suddenly struck Ivy with such force that it knocked the wind out of her lungs.

She sucked in a deep breath, but before she could recover, a second wall of air slammed into her, crushing her against the door. She struggled to free herself from the increasing pressure of the invisible force.

"Why…" she wheezed. "Why do you want to kill me?"

"Kill you?" answered Emir. "I have no intention of killing you. *Use* you, yes. Imagine what I will accomplish with the Seer at my command! The possibilities are truly endless."

The wall of air dispersed. Ivy fell forward, landing on her hands and knees, struggling for breath. "I'd rather—die than help you."

Ivy grasped the dagger tightly in her fist, and then half a second later, she let it fly. As it left her fingers, she turned back for the door, not waiting to see if the weapon had found its mark. She reached for the bolt, preparing to slide it back, when a powerful cyclone of air encircled her, lifting her off the floor. Like a snake squeezing its prey, the air constricted around her, compressing her body so tightly that she feared her very bones would break. Ivy cried out in pain as her body slowly rotated until she again faced the Minister. The dagger, she realized with horror, hung suspended in the air above Emir's outstretched palm, twirling on its tip as delicately as a dancer performing a pirouette.

"You are making this difficult, Seer," said Emir. "I said I would not kill you. But if you resist me, I *will* make you suffer."

Emir twisted his wrist only slightly, and Ivy was catapulted across the room, crashing into the wall. Searing pain radiated across her shoulders and down one arm as she crumpled to the floor. For a moment, she thought she would black out. Nothing was broken, she was certain of that, but damage had been done. She bit down on her lip to keep from crying out again. She glanced up at Emir, defiance in her eyes, but he was unmoved.

The hand beneath the dagger flipped suddenly, and the dagger shot through the air like an arrow. Ivy screamed as its point embedded itself deeply in her thigh. Shaking now, her fingers slid around its handle. She pulled, screaming again as it came free. A thick line of blood oozed over her leg onto the floor. She had to get out, for she would never cooperate with Emir, and once he realized that, he would certainly destroy her.

She thought of Agnora. Her lessons in magic had been only simple ones, but the old enchantress had been astonished at Ivy's abilities. Ivy glanced around the room and knew what she had to do. She focused all her energy into a single thought, a single image: Fire!

The flames of the candles on the iron sconce erupted in a wild blaze that expanded into a massive ball of fire. The heat of it drew beads of sweat from Ivy's skin. It took tremendous focus to make the fire reach out and engulf Emir. Ivy recoiled as Emir's robes ignited and the flames curled up around him. She wanted to avert her eyes, to somehow escape having to witness Emir's demise, but she could not look away.

The fire grew hotter, more than Ivy could bear. She crawled with great difficulty across the floor and again tried to unbolt the door, but she lacked the strength to pull it back. She shrank into a corner of the room, trying to escape the inferno. Would it consume the entire room? Would it consume her? She raised both her hands and reached out toward the flames. There was little energy left in her now. It took all she had to think of the cool, damp air, and to gather enough of it to put out the fire.

As she struggled against the blazing heat, she felt herself go limp. She was simply empty. She was too inexperienced, too feeble to wield enough magic to save herself.

Ivy fought to remain conscious. Her head was spinning, and a wave of nausea hit her. But just as she resigned herself to failure, the flames retreated. Ivy lifted her eyes to see the inferno collapse in on itself, shrinking until all that remained were the small, flickering flames on the candles. The room itself was unscorched, as though nothing out of the ordinary had happened at all. And in the center of it stood Emir, not a thread of his robes or a hair on his head even slightly singed.

"Bravo," he said, clapping his hands together three times. "A Seer and an enchantress. My, my. You are talented."

Though she had not a drop of strength left in her, Ivy managed to stand. She wanted to scream, wanted to pound her fists against the wall and shout until her lungs burst. Instead she gazed at her captor with expressionless eyes.

"You win," she said, "I won't—I can't fight you anymore."

"Very good," said Emir with a satisfied sigh. "Now all I need is Jayson."

Hearing his name sent a new wave of fear through her. "You have me," she said. "You don't need him now."

"Need *him*? No, I don't need *him*. I have the Seer, but I still need the Seer's crystal."

The image of Jayson beaten and bloody returned to Ivy's mind as vivid as ever. The realization struck her like a stone. Not only had she failed to alter the events that would bring him here, she had set them into motion. Jayson would come to the Ministry—*for her*.

Ivy's stomach clenched, and she stifled the cry that rose up into her throat. Her knees buckled, and she collapsed onto

337

the floor. Deep sobs erupted from her with the comprehension that her presence in Nauvet-Carum and the Ministry would lead to the very suffering she had wanted so desperately to prevent. Knowing that Jayson would suffer because of her was more than she could bear.

The room spun, and Ivy clutched at the floor. As consciousness slipped from her, the iron bolt across the door slid back with a heavy, grating sound. The door swung open, and she caught a glimpse of another figure in the doorway, his red hair bright against the shadows of the hall beyond.

Arik!

Relief washed over her. Maybe she'd been wrong about him after all. He had come for her. She would escape this place and all would be well in the end. She tried to call out to him, tried to reach for him, but darkness consumed her, and Arik was gone.

11

I vy blinked open her eyes, but the room spun around her, so she shut them tight again. How long had she been asleep? Not asleep, unconscious.

The memories came to her in fragmented images, visions and reality colliding against each other like clashing weapons, sending stabs of pain through her skull. She tried to lift her head but dropped it back against the soft pillow and moaned. The memories continued to assault her. She heard the sound of water trickling softly, like in a gentle stream. She saw the river by Agnora's cabin, and a wide lake with a waterfall. And then she felt something cool and damp against her face. She remembered that feeling, remembered Teak's hand stroking her hair when she was sick.

The coolness went away, and Ivy heard the water again. Then the coolness returned. She slowly opened her eyes, just a little.

"You're finally awake," said Arik, gently wiping Ivy's face with a wet cloth. He dipped the cloth into a bucket beside him on the floor, wrung it out, and laid it across Ivy's forehead.

"Where am I?" Ivy asked. She tried to look around, but she was too dizzy to keep her eyes open for long. "Are we back in your room?"

"I'm afraid not," replied Arik. "You're in the Ministry."

The jumbled images began to right themselves in her mind. She saw a desk, fire, a man's face. Ivy jerked back in sudden fear.

"Emir! The fire!"

"Relax, Ivanore," Arik soothed. "You're all right. Your leg is wounded and you hit your head when you fainted, but you'll be just fine. I promise."

Ivy opened her eyes again. At least the room had stopped spinning, though she felt weak and lightheaded. The room she was in was not much larger than the bed on which she lay. Beside her was a simple wooden table on which stood a candle in a brass holder. Aside from that, there was only the stool on which Arik sat.

"It's not much, I know," said Arik, anticipating her reaction. "It's not generally used for visitors."

Ivy glanced behind Arik at the door which stood slightly ajar.

"Am I being held captive?" she asked.

"Captive? What makes you think that?"

"The door has no handle on the inside, and there are no windows."

"Well, yes, this is one of the many cells in this place, but it was the only room where we could accommodate you. You were unconscious and needed care. This happens to be above the rooms where I found you."

As the realization of danger came over her, she sat up in a panic. "He's here, Arik, in those rooms!"

"Who, Ivy?"

"The man with the white face! He tried to kill me!"

The room spun once around. She squeezed her eyes shut as Arik took her by the shoulders and laid her back down.

"Nonsense," he told her.

"But it's true, Arik. We have to get out. You told me not to come back here. I should have listened."

Arik smoothed back the hair from her face and laid the cloth back in its place.

"He didn't try to kill you," he said. "He needs you alive."

Ivy opened her eyes. The room had steadied itself, but she took care not to move too quickly to keep the dizziness at bay. She looked up at her brother. Again she was struck by how much he had changed since she had last seen him in Dokur. He was older, that much was evident, but there was something more—or was it that something was missing?

"I saw you," Ivy said. "I thought you had come for me, but…"

"I did come for you, Ivy."

"No, not to *help* me. You came to help *him*."

Arik held her gaze for a moment, but then turned away. He stood up and crossed the small space to the door. There he hesitated.

"You promised me, Arik," said Ivy. "You promised to help me find Jayson!"

Arik's jaw tightened. "And I will keep that promise. Emir says Jayson is sure to come here now."

"Of course he will come now that I am here. But don't you see, Arik? Emir only wants the crystal. He'll do anything

341

to get it. I've seen it in my visions. He'll destroy Jayson. He'll destroy me!"

Arik said nothing, but stood still as stone. Ivy waited for some response, but as the moments passed in silence, a horrible realization struck her.

"You already know that, don't you?" she said, clenching her teeth to fight back tears. "You know what Emir will do, and you've agreed to help him do it."

Arik closed his eyes, squeezing them shut. When he opened them again, he spoke earnestly, as if trying to gain Ivanore's approval. "Yes, I am helping him, but only because he's promised to help me in return. That's fair, isn't it? Our father stripped me of my inheritance to Dokur's throne, and Emir will get it back for me."

"You're talking treason against your own father, Arik. It was wrong of him to banish you, but in time he'll see the error of it. He'll forgive you—"

"Forgive me? Forgive *me*?!" shouted Arik, suddenly enraged. "It's not forgiveness I desire nor deserve. I want what is rightfully mine, what has always been and will always be mine. You cry for your beloved Jayson, but have you cried for me, Ivanore? I hid you both from our father's wrath, defended your honor and sacrificed my own. And what did I get in return?" He stabbed his finger toward her, trembling with fury. "My inheritance was stripped from me and given to your mongrel son! Thank the gods he is dead."

The moment the words left his lips, Arik's expression twisted in vehement agony. He covered his face with both his hands. When he finally lowered them, the pain and the anger were gone. In their place was a look of bitter resignation.

"I am sorry, Ivanore," Arik said, his voice now steady. "I never wished to hurt you, but I will not be cast aside, do you hear me? Emir will have his crystal, and I will have Dokur's throne."

The tears did not come until Arik had left the room, until the door had been shut tight behind him and the key turned in its lock. Only then, when she was alone in the dimly lit room, did Ivanore allow despair to triumph. Rolling onto her side, she brought her knees to her chest and folded her arms around them. And then she cried with more misery than she had ever known.

Outside, unseen in her present state, Dianis pressed her ear to the door and listened to Ivy's tortured weeping.

12

The day had grown unusually warm by the time Jayson and his companions reached Nauvet-Carum, evidence that winter had at last departed and spring had taken hold. The hardest part of the journey was passing by the village of Partha and seeing the empty plot of land where Brommel's cottage had once stood. Now cleared of the blackened ruins, all that remained of the place were the images etched forever in Jayson's mind.

The four men rode into the city sitting high upon their horses. They had discussed the fact that both Gerard and Jayson were wanted men with a price on their heads, but it was agreed that even the Vatéz would never suspect them to so boldly march into the capitol. As long as they did not make spectacles of themselves and kept their faces somewhat covered, their presence would most likely go unnoticed.

The first place they visited was a small inn set back off the main thoroughfare, a quaint little place run by an elderly widow. "The beds are clean and the food is hot," said Dawes, who had stayed there a number of times. "And best of all, the widow has a particular distaste for the Ministry and their ever-increasing tax rates."

Dawes introduced his friends by names other than their own and laid two silver coins in the widow's palm.

"For your discretion," he told her. The woman closed her spotted fist around the coins and dropped them into a pocket in her apron. She led them to two bare but spacious rooms at the rear of the inn and then went back to her business.

Gerard and Teak took the first room, while Dawes and Jayson took the one adjoining it.

"By the gods, what a long journey," said Dawes, testing the straw-stuffed mattress with both hands. "I propose we eat a good meal, settle in, and maybe take a look around town. I know some people who might be of use to us. After that a good long nap, eh?"

Gerard stood in the doorway to his room and tossed his knapsack inside. Teak, however, held tight to his. "We're here," he said. "Why waste time?"

"Waste time?" answered Dawes. "My boy, from what you've told us, Ivanore's been here a week, possibly longer."

"All the more reason for haste."

Teak's determination stirred mixed emotions in Jayson. In the course of their journey, not a word had passed between them. Jayson's imagination ran wild, wondering what must have transpired to arouse such fierce loyalty to Ivanore. No, it was more than loyalty. His passion for her was as evident as the sun in the sky. And did she share that passion? The possibility drove Jayson mad.

Gerard took a gentle hold on Teak's pack and coaxed it from him, then laid it on the floor beside his own. "The day is growing late," he said. "Captain Dawes and I are old men, and two days and nights on horseback have taken their toll.

Surely you wouldn't begrudge us a few hours' rest, would you? Ivanore's here...somewhere. She won't be suddenly vanishing now that we've arrived."

Dawes laid back on his bed and spread out his arms. Closing his eyes he added, "We'll set out again tonight."

Jayson watched Teak surrender to Dawes and Gerard, reluctantly retiring to his room. The door to Gerard and Teak's room slowly swung shut. Jayson stood just outside the room he was to share with Dawes, debating on what to do next.

Dawes opened one eye and peered at him. "Well?" he said. "The boy's been detained for the afternoon. It's what you wanted, isn't it? Now, get on with it, man."

Jayson slipped out of the inn as quietly as a field mouse. The streets of Nauvet-Carum were even more congested than they had been the previous autumn. With the arrival of spring, the entire city had emerged from hibernation, swarming like ants in the narrow passages between the rows of storefronts. Farmers bartered for sacks of seed and new tools for preparing their fields. Auctioneers called out the prices of wagon teams and slaves, and whores beckoned to any man who looked wealthy enough to afford them. Children adeptly wove their way through the crowds, now and then snatching an apple or pear from an inattentive vendor. Jayson couldn't help but pause a moment to take in the scenes that played out before him, the sort of scenes from which he had always been exempt.

As a youth, he and his people had struggled for survival in the marshlands on the remote northern shores of Imaness. Forced from their homelands, the Agorans had lived in isolation and squalor. The first time Jayson had seen a city like Nauvet-Carum was when he had arrived at Dokur as an

346

emissary of his people. He had been selected by his tribe's chief because of his being half-human. They believed, naïvely, that Lord Fredric would be more likely to hear his message. As it turned out, Fredric had little interest in the Agorans' plight. Jayson had come to Dokur for nothing, or so he thought, until he saw Ivanore.

The sound of a wagon's wheel cracking and its cargo toppling to the ground drew Jayson back to the present. He turned from the busy street and gazed across the square to the Ministry's headquarters, its turrets reaching skyward like fingers pointing toward heaven. According to Teak, this is where she saw him. This is where she had come to find him. Dianis was here as well, and he hoped he would find them both safe.

Jayson considered walking up the front steps and in through the main doors, right into the enemy's lair. The last place Emir and Arik would expect him to be was within their stronghold itself. And could he pass for an average human, blend in with the dozens of people passing in and out of those doors at any given moment, he might have tried it. But a single glance from an alert guard would put a hasty end to his plan. His fingers were tipped not with flat human nails, but with sharp dagger-like claws. And his eyes, slitted pupils rather than round, were impossible to conceal. Emir would be alerted to his presence before he'd taken two steps into the Ministry. No, he would need to find a more stealthy approach.

He stood across the road from the Ministry for several hours, the hood of his cloak pulled low enough over his eyes so that he could still observe his surroundings and yet avert making direct eye contact with anyone. The street was crowded enough so that he felt confident his presence would not arouse suspicion. There he stood throughout the afternoon watching—and waiting.

As the sun descended and the shadows grew long, the crowds on the street began to thin. Fewer, too, were the numbers of people visiting the Ministry. By sundown, no one was going in at all, only leaving. Soon the doors would be bolted for the night. High above, in the upper levels of the building, several windows glowed yellow from torch or candlelight.

Jayson stepped forward. Making his way up the steps, he paused only a moment at the massive entryway door before pulling it open and slipping inside.

The long, narrow entry hall was all but dark except for the pale moonlight filtering in through the windows which gave it all a silvery finish. Jayson moved into the shadows and crept forward hugging the outer wall. There were certainly still people milling about who would soon be leaving for the night, and then someone would come to secure the door. He had to get out of the lobby as quickly as possible. As he moved, he tuned his senses to his surroundings. The dull odor of humans filled this place, each distinct scent creating an invisible trail through the building. Jayson took his time sorting through them in his mind, but none were familiar to him. Though he was certain Arik had walked these halls, it had not been recently, not within the past day or two when his scent would still have remained. Nor had Ivanore been in this corridor in that time.

He fought an overwhelming sense of despair. He had allowed himself to entertain the hope that finding her here would be simple. That she would appear as though she had been waiting for him. Jayson resisted the urge to call out for her. Of course her scent would not be here. Had she been taken captive by force, she might have been brought in through another entrance. Or if she had gone this route, she might have done so many days earlier and her scent would have dissipated by now.

Jayson hurried toward a large wooden door at one end of the corridor. At the opposite end stood a matching door, but the density of smells was greatest there, suggesting that it was where most visitors and members of the Ministry traversed. Most likely the public meeting halls and offices were located there. Since the scents were sparse on this other end, Jayson could only assume this door led to private chambers.

Behind the door was a staircase which spiraled upward against rough stone walls. Glancing upward, Jayson could see four landings, four levels. He reached the first and found himself standing at the end of another corridor much like the one below, but darker, lit only by a few sconces along the wall. Several doors lined the corridor from one end to the other with one door at the opposite end. These were most certainly the private offices and chambers of the Ministry themselves. Jayson smelled nothing of interest to him, so he continued ascending to the next level.

Here, the scents were even sparer than before. One scent in particular stood out from the others, one heavily tainted with candle smoke and incense. Jayson started down the dark, musty corridor. Here the smell of dust and old wood nearly overwhelmed his senses. The air here was thick and stagnant. He followed the unusual scent to the door at the end of the hall. It was wide and dark, made of heavy wood, and had a round metal handle attached to it. The scent was strongest here, but there was another scent as well. Jayson paused and closed his eyes. The distinct smells here were far older than those below, but with so few other scents to mask them they were impossible to miss. Here he smelled Arik. In fact, there were several layers of him here, both old and recent. And there was a lighter fragrance, one that instantly filled him with relief. Ivanore had been in this corridor, at this door, perhaps as recently as a day or two earlier. But there was yet another smell, quite faint yet undeniable.

Blood.

Not Arik's blood, of that he was sure. But the evidence that someone had died here once was unmistakable. Jayson's stomach tightened at the thought of it. He had seen more death than he hoped to ever encounter again. Then he caught a trace of someone else's blood in the air. Fresh. Recent.

Fury seethed inside of him. Jayson reached for the metal handle.

Just then his senses were overwhelmed with the smell of seawater rushing toward him from the darkness. And then there was pressure against his mouth, holding his lips tightly closed.

"Shhh!" a voice whispered in his ear. "You have to get out of here. Now!"

13

Jayson wrapped his fingers around something solid. The arm in his grip materialized. Where there was only air moments before, now stood Dianis.

"I won't leave," he told her. "Not until I find Ivanore."

"What are you doing here? Are you crazy?"

Jayson had to restrain himself from laughing at Dianis's reaction. "You're not happy to see me?" he asked with mock disappointment.

Dianis narrowed her eyes and landed a punch on his arm. "You could have killed us both if you'd gone in there," she said angrily.

"Why?" asked Jayson. "What's in there?"

He saw at once that his humor was out of place here. Dianis motioned for Jayson to follow her. Together they hurried back down the corridor to the stairwell. When they were safely hidden in the shadows, Dianis sat down on a step and pulled Jayson down beside her. She glanced both below and above them and kept up her vigil as she spoke.

"Is my father here?"

"He's at an inn," answered Jayson, "with some boy who supposedly knows more about my wife than I do."

"His name is Teak," said Dianis defensively. "We all owe him our gratitude."

"I don't owe him anything."

Dianis shot him a critical look. "Really? Well, apparently Ivy was found with an arrow in her shoulder, a parting gift from Lord Fredric's soldiers. If it weren't for Teak, you're wife would have been dead months ago, and we would have never known she'd come here in the first place."

Jayson scratched at his chin and decided it was best to change the subject. "So, you've been playing spotter here in the Ministry. What have you discovered so far?"

"More than I ever intended, actually. That door down the hall, the one you were so carelessly about to open, happens to be the office of Emir, Minister of the Vatéz. His private rooms are across the hall."

"Ivanore's been here. I smelled her blood."

"She's fine. I promise," Dianis said. "I'll take you to her, but not now. We have to wait until it's safe."

Jayson wanted to tear the place apart to find his wife, but he trusted Dianis. He would wait.

The wooden floor above them creaked. Jayson and Dianis listened to the slow, grating steps. Finally, a door opened and shut.

"That's the jailer," said Dianis. "We need to move. The guard posted to these floors will be here soon. Come with me."

Dianis stood and took Jayson's hand. "Down here," she said and led him to the level directly below. Jayson followed her through a narrow door, which she closed behind them. The room lacked even a trace of light for his sensitive eyes to detect. But then he heard a quick scratch of metal against flint, and a thin orange flame bloomed in the darkness. With the flame, Dianis lit two candles, and the small, bare room was bathed in pale light.

"What is this place?" asked Jayson, noting the folded blanket and knapsack on the floor. Dianis let one of the candles drip onto a wooden crate in the corner, then set the candle into the soft wax. She did the same with the second candle.

"I think it must have been used for storage at one time, but there are so many others just like it in this building that this one seems to have been overlooked. Not many people come to this part of the Ministry. There were a few things in here, a couple of empty crates and cleaning rags, but everything was covered in dust. Hadn't been touched in years, I suspect, so I figured it was a safe place to stay."

Dianis reached into another crate and removed a small bundle of cloth. She pulled back the corner and revealed a wedge of cheese.

"They've got a wonderful kitchen at the other end of the building where chefs prepare elaborate meals for members of the Ministry and their guests. I help myself to whatever I want."

"That's one benefit of being invisible."

She offered him the cheese, but he shook his head. Dianis broke off a small piece and popped it into her mouth.

"Another benefit is my being able to listen to even the most secret of conversations. In fact, shortly before I found you, I had been eavesdropping on one of the senators dictating orders to his page. Apparently, he is plotting some sort of coup against Emir. Says he's gone mad with blood, and several other senators agree with him. What he doesn't know, however, is that his own page reports everything directly to Emir, at least I assume that's why the page visits Emir's chambers so often."

"You don't know?"

"I don't go into Emir's office."

"Why not?"

"He's got a dragon in there, that's why not! It would give me away the moment I stepped through the door. Dragons have the most sensitive sense of smell. Not even seawater would hide me from it."

"Well, I'm not here for any senator or Emir. Dianis, tell me about Ivanore. Have you seen her?"

"No," Dianis answered quietly. She looked at Jayson, a hesitant expression in her face. "I haven't *seen* her," she said again, "but I know where they're keeping her. And I'll take you as soon as it is safe. I promise."

Jayson nodded, reluctantly agreeing to wait. He'd been so long without his Ivanore, waiting even another hour felt like the worst kind of torture. He leaned back against the wall and slid down to the floor, resting his arms on his knees. Dianis did the same, and they faced each other in the quiet gloom.

"She calls for you, you know," Dianis said between bites of food. "In her sleep. She dreams of you."

"And I of her," replied Jayson. "But our dreams are not happy ones, but full of anguish and longing. I thought I'd never see her again, Dianis, and now being so close to her—it is almost more than I can bear."

On the other side of the door, the wood flooring creaked under the slow and steady steps of a guard. Jayson held his breath as the sound traveled away from them and finally vanished altogether. Then both he and Dianis nervously released the air from their lungs.

Dianis folded her arms around herself as if trying to keep out the cold. "Tell me about her," she whispered. "Tell me about Ivanore."

Jayson leaned his head back against the wall and closed his eyes. The memories, which he had struggled so hard to keep at bay until now, swirled around his brain, washing it in a euphoria of emotion.

"It was the first time I'd ever been to Dokur," he began. "Having been raised in a small village, I knew nothing of cities or ships or castles. I was awestruck. I'd been sent to meet with Lord Fredric as an emissary of my people on account of my having human blood. Fredric was no friend of the Agorans. He had forced us off our lands, and the swamps where we had settled were infested with insects. Many of our people, my mother among them, died of disease. So I was sent to appeal to Fredric to allow us to return home, or at least to find a more suitable location for our tribe.

"My trip was a waste. He refused to even see me. I was angry, frustrated. How could I return to Taktani empty-handed? I was contemplating how I might take revenge on Fredric when I saw her. She passed by me in the courtyard of Fredric's Fortress, escorted by half a dozen armed guards, but she glanced up at me and smiled.

"She was the most beautiful creature I'd ever laid eyes on—hair gold as sunlight, eyes blue as the sea. I'd found my reason to delay returning home."

That first image of Ivanore had seared itself into Jayson's mind like a brand, and it warmed him now as though it were made of flames. He ran his fingers through his hair, trying to keep it from consuming him.

Dianis laid a gentle hand on his arm, and feeling her touch soothed him. "What happened?" she asked.

355

Jayson opened his eyes, but he didn't look at Dianis. He couldn't. "What began as a passing glance between us resulted in a clandestine courtship. We met when we could, where we could. I wanted to marry her, but her father's law forbade any union of humans and non-humans. Should our relationship be discovered it would mean death for us both. But we didn't care. So we wed in secret.

"When Ivanore became pregnant, I came to realize that I had jeopardized not only myself and Ivanore, but I had also endangered his people. Once Fredric learned of his daughter's condition, he would declare war on the Agorans. The only option was to hide. And that is what we did.

"For a time, we lived in the forest, oblivious to the outside world. The only person we trusted was Ivanore's brother, Arik, who would, from time to time, bring us news and supplies. After the birth of our son, we made plans to escape Imaness altogether, to sail across the sea to the mainland where we would be free to live as we pleased. But soon after that, Fredric's soldiers discovered our hiding place and I was arrested. Rather than face the humiliation of publicly revealing that his own daughter had married an Agoran, Fredric exiled me and Arik to Hestoria."

Jayson could never erase from his memory the image of his beloved Ivanore standing on the cliffs of Dokur, her delicate hands pressed against her lips as she wept and cried out for him. But he was far out of reach, his hands and feet shackled to the mast of a ship carrying him farther and farther away. Until Gerard had arrived at Dawes's plantation with the news of Ivanore's arrival in Hestoria, he had believed that sight of her on the cliffs would be his last. Now the prospect of seeing her again filled him with almost unbearable anticipation.

When Jayson had finished talking, he pinched the moisture from his eyes before raising them to look at Dianis. When he did, he saw the pale glimmer of candlelight reflected in Dianis's tears.

Fearful that she was perhaps hurt in some way, he took her shoulders in his hands. "Dianis, what is it?" he asked gently. "Are you all right?"

She wiped away the tears with the heel of her hand. "It's nothing really, just a girl's silly fantasy is all."

"What do you mean?"

Dianis shrugged and tried to smile. "All this time I had hoped that you might come to forget Ivanore. But now I see that would be like forgetting to breathe, wouldn't it?" She gave a nervous little laugh, embarrassed by her own emotions. "I told you it was silly."

Jayson leaned forward and placed a kiss on Dianis's forehead.

"It's not silly at all, Dianis. And I promise one day someone will love you the way I love Ivanore."

Dianis nodded, wiping away another tear. "Well, I think the guard has finally finished his rounds. It is deathly quiet out there." She peered into Jayson's eyes, her gaze uncertain. "Are you sure about this?" she asked.

Jayson got to his feet. Then he took Dianis by the hand and helped her up as well. "I can't bear to wait another moment," he said. "Please, take me to her now."

14

The uppermost level of the Ministry was swathed in darkness. The only light existed in the form of thin lines of weak yellow beneath the doors that lined the hall. The air here stank of urine and rotting wood, and rats scurried underfoot. Jayson's stomach churned at the thought that somewhere up here, in this neglected corner of the world, his beloved Ivanore was being held hostage.

Jayson and Dianis crept through the shadows, pausing before each door. Dianis seemed to be listening for something in particular, but Jayson dared not speak, fearing his voice would shatter the fragile silence that cloaked their presence here.

Dianis held her ear close to one particular door. Jayson's keener sense of hearing did not need such close proximity to detect the sounds within: the scuffing of boots against the wooden floor, a chesty cough, a man's incoherent grumblings.

"This is the jailer's room," Dianis explained in a whisper. "He drinks at night, but we have to be very quiet so as not to alert him."

"Which door is hers?" Jayson asked.

Dianis did not answer but pointed to a door at the end of the hall. As he watched, a slight shadow passed through the light emanating from below the door. Someone inside that cell had just crossed the room. Knowing that Ivanore stood nearly within arm's reach, with only a few inches of wood between them, was almost unbearable. Jayson made his way to the end of the hall and pressed his body against the door, breathing in the scent of her. He laid both his palms against the wood as if trying to feel Ivanore through it. The wood felt rough and damp against his cheek and hands. He wanted to call her name, to somehow alert her to his presence. But doing so would also alert the jailer. He had to be patient.

A moment later, Dianis was beside him, whispering in his ear.

"I have to get the key," she said. "He's been talking in his sleep. I'm going to slip inside. I'll be right back."

The next few minutes seemed the longest of his life, but then suddenly there was a click and the metal lock gave way. Jayson glanced down and saw a rusty key extending from the door. The hand that had inserted it was unseen, and yet Dianis's voice was beside him, urging him forward.

"Go on," she told him. "I'll keep watch out here."

The door swung slowly open, propelled by Dianis's invisible hand. The room was dim, lit by a single candle on a wooden stand near the door. Jayson's eyes detected a figure in the far corner of the room, her arms clenched tightly about herself, a mixture of alarm and curiosity on her face. Her voice, however, was calm as she spoke.

"Who's there?"

Jayson stood frozen at the door, his frame and features still hidden in the darkness. He felt a gentle nudge from behind. He took a step into the room, and then another. The door closed quietly behind him.

He stood now within the circle of candlelight. Surely she saw him, recognized him. He should speak, he realized, reassure her that he was no vision, but his throat constricted. He watched her as she relaxed her hold on herself. She seemed bewildered, perplexed. There passed a momentary look of doubt across her face, but then...

"Jayson!"

Ivanore sprang forward, her voice breaking into sobs. She crossed the small cell and flung herself into his arms. Only then, feeling her arms tight around him and her body pressing against his was he able to regain his full capacities. He spoke her name over and over, and kissed her face, her hair, her lips.

They cried together, and then they laughed together. They clasped each other so tightly that Jayson felt as though their separate bodies should meld into one. Finally, Jayson raised both his hands, cradling Ivanore's face. He stared into her eyes and saw his own reflection in them.

"Ivanore? My Ivanore," he said, then pressed his lips against her forehead. She laid her head against his chest. He held her there, savoring the explosion in his senses—the sight, sound, and touch of her were more than he had ever hoped to experience again.

"Is this a dream?" asked Ivy. "Another vision? Because if it is, I cannot bear to wake from it."

"This is no dream," Jayson answered. "I am really here."

Jayson combed his fingers through her hair. She had changed little since he had last seen her. But then he remembered what Dianis had said about the arrow. He ran his fingers along the collar of her dress and gently pulled it down over her shoulder. He brushed his fingers across the jagged red scar at her shoulder blade. A new round of tears spilled from his eyes as he thought of how much she had suffered without him.

"I'm so sorry I wasn't there to protect you," he said.

"Shh." She placed her fingers against his lips, and he kissed them. "We have found each other at last. That is all that matters now. But you shouldn't be here. You're in danger."

"We're both in danger. I have to get you out of here. You were safe in Imaness. Why did you come here?"

"But we weren't safe. My father…"

Her voice broke, and a tear fell down her cheek.

"The boy?" asked Jayson, his concern growing. "Is he all right?"

Ivy nodded, swiping a tear from her cheek. "Yes, yes, he's fine," she assured him. "He is safe, and he misses his papa. But I had to tell Arik that he was dead."

"You've seen Arik?"

"He betrayed me, Jayson."

The pain in Ivanore's eyes was enough to break Jayson's heart all over again.

Ivanore could no longer contain her emotion. Bursting into tears, she buried her face against Jayson's shoulder.

"What is it?" he asked. "What is wrong?"

She lifted her head, and Jayson saw that through her tears she was smiling. Raising her hands to his face, she gently stroked the line of his chin.

"Nothing is wrong now that you're here," she said. "There is something I must tell you—something wonderful—and I've waited so long to tell it."

Suddenly, the door to the cell opened, and the smell of seawater filled the room as Dianis materialized before them. Jayson saw the look of confusion on Ivanore's face, but knew there was no time to explain.

"The guard is awake. He'll be coming soon," said Dianis in a harsh whisper.

Jayson turned to Ivy. "We have to go."

They said nothing as they followed Dianis out of the cell and down the shadowy corridor. As they reached the stairwell, Jayson heard the creak of the jailer's door open and the weight of his footsteps as he made his way toward Ivanore's room. And then there was shouting.

"She's gone!" screamed the jailer. "The Seer's gone!"

Above and below them, the Ministry came alive with people running and shouting orders. Dianis, Jayson, and Ivy flew down the stairs. But as they reached the next landing they met a Ministry guard, his sword already drawn. Jayson didn't waste a moment. Drawing his dagger, he slashed it at the man, who tumbled backward down the steps, his sword clattering noisily as he went.

The jailer and two more guards descended on them from behind.

"There they are!" shouted the jailer, pointing his finger.

But this time Ivy responded. As she jutted her hands toward the attackers, some invisible force knocked them back. They fell in a jumble against the stairs.

Dianis darted a derisive glance back at Ivy. "You're going to have to do better than that if we're going to get out of here alive."

They continued on at a run and soon reached the bottom of the stairs where they were met by another pair of guards.

"Duck!" shouted Jayson. Dianis did more than duck. She disappeared as Jayson's claws and blade cut an arc through the air. The first guard cried out as a gash opened wide across his chest, but the second dove forward, the point of his blade hurtling toward Jayson's heart. An orb of white-hot flame ruptured between them, setting the guard's uniform on fire. He screamed and dropped his weapon, flailing his burning arms in the air.

Ivy sent a second orb, this one of icy air, to put out the flame. The force, however, knocked the wind from the guard's lungs, and he fell to the floor unconscious.

Dianis reappeared. "Better," she said snidely, "though I would have let him burn."

Jayson paused at the door before opening it a crack and peering through it. "It's clear out there," he said. "Not far to the outer door."

Dianis grabbed Jayson's hand, pulling. "Let's go then. We need to get out of here before more guards show up."

"Something isn't right about this," he said. "It's too easy."

"Too easy?" said Dianis. "We just fought off a bunch of guards."

"No, he's right," said Ivy. "I've seen this before."

"Then let me go ahead to check," said Dianis. "I'll be back soon."

Dianis disappeared, the only evidence of her being the door as it opened wide enough to let her through.

Jayson took Ivy's hand in his as they pressed themselves into the shadows and waited for Dianis's return. The minutes felt like years, but Jayson could wait a millennium with Ivanore if he had to. He wanted to speak with her, to ask her

363

the hundreds of questions spinning in his mind, but they would have to wait until they were far from the Ministry and the Vatéz.

Soon, the door opened again and Dianis stood before them, gasping for breath.

"What is it?" asked Jayson, noticing the tears streaking down Dianis's cheeks. "Are you all right?"

"I'm so sorry," she said. The expression on her face was one of absolute anguish. "I'll do whatever I can to help you both. I swear it!"

A moment later, Dianis had vanished again.

15

The door to the stairwell was flung open. The dark space was suddenly flooded with torchlight.

"Well, well," said a voice from the midst of guards, their swords raised. "Fate is certainly with us, isn't it? First, after a long and fruitless search, the Seer appears as if by magic at my very doorstep. And now *you* have done the same."

Two guards came forward, one leveled his blade at Ivanore's chest while the other snatched away Jayson's dagger. A third man, clad in a blue and gold robe and with hair and skin as white as winter frost, stepped through the door. Jayson thought he looked like a spirit, translucent and ephemeral.

"If I had known that all I had to do was wait for my prey to trap itself within my web," continued the ghostly man, "I would not have wasted so much effort pursuing you."

"Who are you?" asked Jayson.

The man's ice-colored eyes flitted nervously from side to side. "I think you know who I am. I'm sure Arik has told you all about me."

Emir.

Jayson extended his claws threateningly. "How did you know I was here?"

Emir shrugged. "I've been watching you since you first stepped foot inside the Ministry. My trackers and guards have been on alert since the Seer arrived. It was only a matter of time before you came for her."

One of the guards reached for Jayson's arm, but Jayson lashed out with his claws and sliced into the man's shoulder.

"No!" shouted Ivanore. "Jayson, don't!"

Emir raised one of his emaciated hands, his bony fingers jutting out like gnarled and brittle vines. As he rotated them slowly in the air, Jayson felt a jagged tearing within his rib cage. He cried out in pain and clutched his chest.

"You should listen to your wife, Jayson," said Emir. "Did you really believe I would let you take my most prized possession? Even if you did escape, could you live with the consequences?"

Emir's tone was condescending, as though he were toying with Jayson the way a child might dangle a mouse in front of a cat only to snatch it away.

Jayson struggled against the mounting pain inside him. It felt as though something within him was clawing its way out. "What consequences?" he managed to say through clenched teeth.

"Your friends' lives, of course. You did arrive in Nauvet-Carum with three companions, did you not? My informant tells me they are staying at a local inn. Or perhaps the nymph? It has been a bit tiresome having her sneaking

366

around. Yes, Jayson. I know about Gerard and his daughter. And should I wish it, they would both be dead by sunrise. Gerard is far more valuable to me alive. But the girl…"

"Leave her out of this!" Jayson felt as though his very bones would rupture. "You've already murdered Brommel's family, slaughtered dozens of innocent people at Alay-Crevar. Isn't that enough blood for you?"

"Compassion is not one of my strengths. Although, I cannot take full credit for Alay-Crevar." Emir briefly glanced at Ivanore. "That was your brother's doing, I'm afraid. The young can be so—impulsive."

Ivanore, who had until now managed to maintain her composure, lunged toward Emir. Before he could react, she swiped her curved fingers across his face and left a deep gash on his cheek. The attack broke Emir's concentration on Jayson. Suddenly released from the Minister's power, Jayson dropped to his knees, doubled over, and gasped for breath.

One guard drew his sword and held it to Ivanore's throat. The other guard grabbed her arms, pulling them roughly behind her back. She clenched her teeth from the pain, but did not cry out.

Emir touched his cheek, and then looked at his bloodstained fingertips. An amused expression appeared on his face. "You are a feisty one, aren't you? Not at all like that pitiful little flower of Brommel's. I understand she begged for mercy as the flames crawled up around her."

Jayson lifted his head, hatred burning in his blood. But his strength had left him. "What do you want with us, Emir?"

"What do I want with you?" repeated Emir. "What an odd question. I would think you'd know what I want from you, Jayson. It's nothing really, just an insignificant, broken piece of crystal."

Ivanore's eyes widened. Panic flew into her face. "You have me," she said. "Isn't that enough?"

Emir took Ivanore's chin in his hand. "Is it enough, my dear?"

Jayson wanted to leap up and rip the man to shreds with his claws. He wanted to hold his still beating heart in his hands and then crush it. But Emir's magic had weakened him. Even breathing took effort. His eyesight began to blur.

"I don't have the crystal," Jayson managed to say.

Emir nodded to one of the guards, who slammed his fist into Jayson's chin. The sickening crack that resounded through the room mingled with Ivanore's cry. The guard then patted Jayson's clothing. He glanced at Emir and shook his head.

"I don't have it," Jayson repeated, blood dripping from his jaw.

"I see," replied Emir. "Well, that does pose a problem, doesn't it?"

The guard took hold of Jayson's wrists and bound them with a strip of leather. Jayson squeezed his eyes shut and opened them again. The room was nothing but a smear of color now. But he could hear Ivanore's muffled cries. She was trying to be strong.

Jayson's resolve to remain silent under Emir's invisible lash broke once the first agonizing stroke tore into his body. Even he could never have anticipated how severe the pain would be and how quickly it would reduce him to a quivering heap. When the assault finally ended, the guard tried to pull him to his feet, but his body would not obey. Jayson saw nothing. The room was going dark. But he heard Ivanore's voice reaching through the void.

"Where are you taking him?" she cried out.

"Do not fret," said Emir. "I will not kill him...yet."

Jayson heard Ivanore's heart-wrenching sobs. More than anything Jayson wanted to hold her, to console her, to take her away to some deserted place where they could finally live in peace together. She screamed his name, her voice shattering the air like glass. Jayson heard the sound of a lock clicking into place and felt the rough floor planks scraping against his feet and knees as he was dragged away. Ivanore continued screaming his name. Even when the air had grown still and silent, and as he slipped from consciousness, Jayson still heard her in his head, and he knew that he would never cease hearing her for as long as he lived.

16

How long Jayson had been unconscious, he didn't know. When he finally awoke, he was no longer in the cell but in a spacious room, lying on a thick, soft bed. He was first aware of the smell of incense, the spices warm and soothing to his senses, and then of the sound of water. He noticed a figurine of a tree beside him on a table fashioned from thin sheets of metal. Water trickled from its leaves into a miniature pool at the base of its trunk. The sound reminded him of rainfall in the forest.

The room itself could only be described as luxurious: silk sheets on the bed, velvet drapes, ornately carved furniture, and complex woven tapestries on the walls. Jayson noticed, too, that the pain that had so completely overwhelmed him during Emir's attack had diminished to a dull throb. He felt a little lightheaded and pleasantly relaxed.

He wore a clean tunic. He had been bathed and his hair combed. Even his mouth felt surprisingly clean. Someone had gone to great pains to care for him, and he supposed that without this care he might have died.

As his senses slowly recovered, his mind struggled to grasp the events that had brought him here. However, he found that his mental capacities were somewhat dull, still affected from whatever had been administered to ease his pain. But no drug was strong enough to dull the pain of losing Ivanore a second time. This pain inflicted a wound deeper and more permanent than any lash or blade ever could.

Jayson sat up and set his feet on the floor. The room spun for a moment and then settled into a somewhat stable view. He tried to stand but found that his legs lacked sufficient strength to hold him, so he remained sitting on the side of the bed.

It was at this point that he noticed someone sitting in the shadowy corner of the room, the figure so still that Jayson nearly mistook him for a statue. He might have noticed his presence before if his scent had not been so completely masked by the heavy incense. Now aware of him, Jayson picked out the thin strain of his smell and recoiled from it.

"Are you all right?" asked Arik, remaining partially veiled in the shadows.

Jayson snarled and flexed his claws. If only he had the strength, he would carve his old friend into shreds and not care about the consequences.

"You're improving," Arik continued. "I did have my doubts for a while. No mere human could have survived losing so much blood, but then again you are no mere human."

An image of Ivanore filled Jayson's mind. Her scent, though faint, mingled with Arik's. He had been with her recently, which meant she was still here within the Ministry.

371

"How long have I been here?" asked Jayson reluctantly, his instinct to kill nearly overwhelming him.

"Well, you laid in your cell all night before we realized you weren't going to die. So then we brought you here and had you cleaned up a bit. You've been here, in Emir's chambers, for two days. You must be hungry. A plate will be brought in shortly. In the meantime, there is a glass of wine beside you. Help yourself."

Jayson saw the goblet on the nightstand, but hesitated to take it.

"It's all right," coaxed Arik. "There's nothing in it. I did keep you sedated for a while to give you a chance to heal a bit. Had you been conscious, the pain would have been unbearable. You're on the mend now, though. You'll be all right in a week or two, though I'm afraid your scars will never heal completely."

Jayson wanted to leap up from the bed and tear him to pieces. He could smell the guards on the other side of the door. So he resisted the urge and drank the wine. When he had emptied the goblet, he set it back down on the table.

"Now then," said Arik, "I've been sent to discuss the terms of your – hmm, shall we say, your release?"

"My what?"

"Your freedom. Emir is holding you captive, you know. But he's willing to negotiate."

"I won't leave without Ivanore," Jayson said, his voice hard.

"I'm afraid that's out of the question. You see, she is too valuable to us. She is the Seer. By now you've probably realized how vital she is in our campaign against my father and the siege of Dokur. Of course, that is only one small part of our plan. With Ivanore's gift at our disposal, Emir and I can foresee any failure and correct it prior to an attack, whereby guaranteeing the victory. Oh, we intend to conquer not only Dokur, but the regions north and east of here as well. And to keep peace, the residents of those regions will pay a handsome tribute. So, as you can see, Ivanore is simply too great an asset to just let go."

This was too much. Somehow, Jayson found enough strength to dive across the room and wrap his hands around Arik's throat. His claws dug into the base of Arik's neck, and the heels of his hands pressed against his throat. A sick gurgle bubbled out of Arik's mouth, and his eyes opened wide with fear. Jayson knew that once the guards came in, there would be no mercy for him, but he didn't care. Not anymore. He only wanted to see Arik dead.

"Wait—" the sounds coming from Arik's mouth were mangled. Jayson eased the pressure just enough to let Arik speak. "Emir—wants to trade!"

"Trade what?!" hissed Jayson.

"Ivanore for the crystal!"

"I already told Emir that I don't have it."

"But you know where it is," said Arik, gasping. "And Emir will do anything to get it. Anything!"

Jayson released his grip and stepped back. Arik slumped forward, gulping air and rubbing his now bruised throat with his hands.

"The crystal is broken," Jayson said skeptically. "You know I only have half of it. It's useless."

Arik sat upright and glared at Jayson. "Yes," he answered, "we would prefer the entire crystal, and finding the missing piece will be a priority. But for now, Emir will settle for your half."

"It's a trick, isn't it? Emir would never let Ivanore go. What good would the crystal be to him without her?"

Arik got to his feet, but kept a safe distance from Jayson. "He's not without certain abilities. He's quite adept in magic and divination. Of course, without the crystal he can only see the past and present, no better than the most common of enchanters. But once he has the crystal..."

"So, once he has it, he'll let me take Ivanore?"

"Not exactly," said Arik. He held up a defensive hand, fearful of a second attack. "You're forgetting that you are in exile, Jayson, and for what? For marrying a human. True, there is no actual law against it here on the mainland, but that is because social mores prevent things like that from occurring often. You know very well that should the two of you try to live together anywhere, you will be shunned. Is that really the sort of life you want for Ivanore? It is what *she'd* want?"

Jayson hated the smug expression on Arik's face, but he was right. On Imaness, the only time they could be together was when they were in hiding, and even then it hadn't lasted long enough. Could he ask her to live like that, in isolation, for the rest of her life? Did he have the right to ask it of her? No, he realized. To do so would be an act of supreme selfishness. From the moment he had first told her he loved her, he had endangered them both. And from what Gerard and Dianis had told him, she had even shirked her responsibilities as Seer to love him. So many people had been adversely affected because of him. Because of him too many people had suffered, too many had died.

No more, he thought. I will be the cause of no more suffering.

Jayson hesitated, but the time had come to face the truth. "No," he said. "This isn't the life either of us ever wanted."

Arik nodded, his mouth curving into a satisfied grin. "That is why Emir has offered an alternative. You deliver the crystal, and he will send Ivanore back to Imaness."

Ivanore return to Imaness, to their son. That was where she belonged, whether Jayson was with her or not. Jayson again thought of the crystal shard buried alongside Brielle's grave. Ivanore must have left the other half back home. Yes, Jayson realized, sending Ivanore home was the only option.

"And what about me?" he asked, pushing down the sadness now welling up inside of him.

"Maybe someday you can return to Dokur as well, once Fredric is dead. In the meantime, you'll be free to go. You do have somewhere to go, do you not?"

"Yes," said Jayson, thinking of Dawes's plantation.

"Very well, then. Do we have an agreement, Jayson? You bring me the crystal, and I will personally see to it that Ivanore is on the next ship bound for Imaness."

Jayson gathered what little strength he had remaining. His attack on Arik, though brief, had left him feeling weaker than before, and yet the journey to the stone cross would take a great deal more effort than that. He placed his hand on the bed to steady himself. Then he looked at Arik, who had once been his friend, his brother, but was now an enemy. He thought of the promise he had made to Brommel to exact revenge on him. I will do it, he thought, but first I must get Ivanore home.

"I'll get you the crystal," he said finally. "But on one condition."

"And what is that?"

"I go alone."

17

"I'm coming with you!"

Dianis's body materialized the moment Jayson stepped through the doors of the Ministry. The few people passing nearby jumped back in surprise, and then hurried on their ways. Jayson glowered at her.

"You couldn't wait until we were in private to do that?" he said gruffly, not breaking stride. Dianis had to nearly run to keep up with him.

"Hold up!" she told him. "Jayson, wait!"

Jayson stopped abruptly in front of the bakery. The wounds decorating his back ached horribly. The fabric of his tunic brushing against his skin sent fresh spikes of pain through him.

"Why?" he snapped. "Why now? You've been slinking around in there for days, and what good has it done anyone? Do you think you're some hero, running off against your father's wishes? Putting yourself in danger?"

"But I led you to Ivanore—"

"I would have found her on my own anyway. Emir knows all about you. He knows everything. He could very well have spies lurking around this very moment, following me, reporting every word we say to him. The only reason why he hasn't killed you is because he sees no use for you. He knows that even if he held you ransom, Gerard, your own father, wouldn't sacrifice the Guilde for you. So what value are you to him, hmm? I'll tell you, Dianis. You're only as good as the trail you leave behind. Go back to the Guilde, and he's sure to have you followed. Do you understand me?"

Jayson's voice was loud enough for anyone who might be watching them to hear.

Dianis's eyes filled with tears. She blinked them away, but others appeared in their place. "I hadn't realized..." she said. "I never meant to endanger anyone."

Jayson sighed in exasperation. "Whether you meant to or not, you've made yourself a target. If you return to the Guilde now, you'll lead them right to it."

"But they already know where the Guilde is hiding, don't you see?"

"What are you talking about?"

"I overheard Emir giving orders to one of his captains—someone named Erland. He told him about the waterfall."

"How would he know about that?"

"Ivanore's visions. She must have told Arik about them. Erland and his men left yesterday to search for the Guilde. They don't know the exact location yet, but they'll eventually find it."

Jayson stared at Dianis, his eyes penetrating deeply. His mind was reeling with this new information. Without realizing it, Ivanore had given Arik and Emir exactly what they wanted.

How long would it take them to find the Guilde? A week? Two? Jayson's expression turned hard.

"The Guilde is on its own then," he said angrily.

"What?"

"I have more important matters to worry about now. Emir has sent me on an errand. But I promise I'll send word to your father the first moment I can. In the meantime, the best thing you can do now is to get as far away from the Guilde as possible."

"But where will I go?"

"It doesn't really matter, does it?" Jayson glanced around to be sure they were alone, then added in a whisper, "Take the north road, two days' ride from here, to the plantation just beyond the village of Ashlin. I'll be heading there myself eventually. You'll be out of trouble there."

Dianis burst into tears. Jayson glanced around, embarrassed by her sudden show of emotion.

"That's enough now," he said, trying to sound sympathetic. "Here, take this. Buy enough supplies to get wherever you plan to go."

He lifted Dianis's hand and placed several coins in her palm, then curled her fingers tightly over them. Then he turned away from her and strode briskly down the street, his heart hurting as much as the stripes on his back.

18

ianis kept her fist clamped tightly shut until she was as far from the Ministry as she could get and still be within the gates of the city. Jayson was right, of course. She had caught glimpses of a spotter with a Gorelian tracker at his heel. Maybe they thought she would lead them to the Guilde, but the pair had turned their interest to Jayson once he'd told her to go toward Ashlin instead.

Dianis stalked the streets and alleys of Nauvet-Carum for over an hour after that just to be sure they were no longer following her. Finally, she slipped into a shadowed alleyway. She uncurled her fingers revealing Jayson's coins—and a small slip of parchment. There were only three words on the parchment, but Jayson's message was clear. The spotter would follow him, leaving her free to do as he asked. She would be careful and would take the longer route that he advised just in case, but he would ensure she had sufficient time to carry out his instructions.

There was no time to lose. She would buy her supplies and leave immediately. Dianis slipped back out into the street,

Vengeance

the tiny note lay on the floor, the now fading sunlight barely illuminating its succinct message:

WARN THE GUILDE.

19

J ayson wove his way through the crowded streets of Nauvet-Carum walking only as fast as was necessary to give the appearance of haste. He kept the scent of Emir's spotter in reach, occasionally slowing his pace or pausing to glance in a shop window to ensure that the spotter stayed close. When he reached the inn, he made the pretense of casting furtive glances through the crowd before entering. The spotter would remain hidden somewhere with the entrance in full view. He knew his time was short. He must act quickly.

He found Gerard and Dawes in their room, engaged in a heated discussion, which came to an abrupt end on his entry. On seeing him, Gerard wilted in relief.

"By the gods," he said, "where have you been? We heard you'd been apprehended by the Ministry."

"I was," answered Jayson. He moved quickly to the window and pulled the shutters closed.

"How did you escape?" asked Dawes.

"Emir let me go. He's sent a contingent of soldiers out to Naresh."

"The Guilde's been discovered?"

"Not yet, but it's only a matter of time before it is. I've sent Dianis to warn them. I can only hope she arrives in time."

Gerard scratched at the white stubble on his chin. He looked troubled.

"You've been inside the Ministry then?" he asked cautiously. "Did you find the Seer there? Is she all right?"

"She's safe," Jayson lied.

"And the crystal?"

Jayson hesitated. As the leader of the Guilde, Gerard's sworn duty was to protect the Seer and the crystal even at the peril of his own life. What would he do if he knew Ivanore had been captured by Emir and would be freed only in exchange for the crystal? Gerard would do anything he could to stop Jayson from retrieving the crystal.

He gave Gerard a confident smile. "The crystal is hidden far away from here," he said. "I am the only one who knows where."

This was the truth, and it satisfied Gerard.

As Gerard scurried about the room collecting the few items he'd brought with him, Jayson spoke with Dawes in hushed tones.

"The Ministry will soon be needing a ship. I don't have time to explain, but I'd be indebted to you if it happened to be The Silver Mist."

"Indebted to me even more than you are now?" Dawes said with a laugh.

"Can you arrange it?"

"I'll need time to gather my crew."

"I'll be back in Nauvet-Carum in four days."

"All right then," answered Dawes. "I'd better get on with it."

He started for the door, but stopped. He gave Jayson a firm handshake and a slap on the shoulder, and then he left.

Gerard joined Jayson at the door just as Teak came storming in. He carried several parcels of cheese and bread. He'd been buying provisions.

"So the prodigal returns," he said coldly. "Since you are alone, I can only assume your valiant attempt to find Ivy was a failure. Maybe now, Gerard, you'll let me go after her."

"Calm down, my boy," said Gerard. "He's just come from the Ministry."

"Really? Is that how you spent the past two days? Negotiating with that fiend, Emir? Or maybe you weren't at the Ministry at all, but at a tavern drinking yourself into a stupor."

Jayson ground his teeth. It took great effort to restrain himself from slashing Teak's face with his claws. Instead, he kept his peace. How could Teak possibly understand what he had been through?

"Get your things and come with me," he said.

Jayson lead Teak and Gerard out of the room and toward the back of the inn. They found the small kitchen area where a round, red-faced woman muttered to herself over a cauldron of steaming soup. Jayson opened the door leading to the alley behind the inn. He stepped aside, letting Gerard and Teak pass through.

"Dianis is heading up the north road," he told them. "It's a longer route, but there's less risk of detection. If you hurry, you should make good time."

"You're not going with us?" asked Gerard.

Vengeance

"I'm being followed by a tracker. I'll leave the way I came in and make certain he stays with me. He expects me to lead him to the Guilde, but of course, I have other plans."

20

Jayson set out on the west road out of Nauvet-Carum. Despite the fierce drive he felt to get the crystal and return as quickly as possible, he kept his horse at a steady trot. It would not do to lose his tracker and have him head back and pick up Dianis's trail instead. He stayed just far enough ahead to keep the faint scent of the spotter and his Gorelian in his senses. From time to time he even dismounted just to stretch. He was careful to never turn his eyes in the direction of his spies. As long as they believed him to be unaware of their presence, they would continue to follow him.

It took two days to reach the stone cross. Jayson rode around the perimeter of the cemetery to the cabin where Leo and Abby had lived. It stood abandoned, ransacked by random travelers. Piles of rotted leaves had collected on the roof and against the foundation. After the slaughter at Alay-Crevar and the murder of her father, it was understandable that Abby would not have returned. She had found a new home with the Guilde. Again, Jayson thought of Dianis and hoped she would arrive at Naresh soon. Somewhere in these

385

forests, Emir's soldiers were already searching for the waterfall.

Jayson dismounted, tying his horse to one of the wood pillars that held up the porch roof. A warm breeze had picked up, blowing leaves and dust into tiny whirlwinds. The Gorelian's and spotter's scents told him they were close at hand, probably watching him from the edge of the forest. He ambled across the cemetery, careful not to disturb the markers, until he came to Brielle's. He knelt on one knee and brushed the dirt from her name with his hand. The earth surrounding it was no longer soft, but had become packed from the winter rains and snow. Using his claws, Jayson pried up the marker, leaving an indentation in its place. The earth here was still damp and soft. He scraped away a layer of soil until the leather pouch came up in his hand. He shook off the bits of soil that clung to it and loosened the strings.

The breeze blew harder now, and the smell of tree blossoms and ground daisies calmed Jayson's senses. Spring had brought new life to Hestoria, but not for Brielle or her child. Anger bubbled up inside of Jayson once again as he thought of the charred remains of Brommel's home. Brommel had made him swear revenge, but now kneeling at Brielle's grave, Jayson no longer had a taste for blood. So many had died. Did he really want to add to those numbers? Could one death justify another?

Jayson tipped the pouch, and the shard of celestine tumbled out onto his palm. It felt cold from having been underground for so long. It was hard to believe that this broken scrap of crystal had been the cause of so much trouble. He would be glad to be finally rid of it.

Jayson dropped the crystal back into the pouch and tightened the strings, then slipped the pouch through his belt beside his knife. The wind whipped his hair across his face. He smelled the dust and pollen in the air. And then he realized that was all he smelled. Jayson darted his eyes along the edge of the forest, scanning for glimpses of the tracker. Wherever it had been a few minutes before, it had now shifted downwind of him, leaving Jayson blind, in a sense, to his location.

Staying where he was, Jayson tuned his hearing toward the rustling tree branches. The sound of footsteps in the undergrowth, or even the steady rhythm of breathing, would alert him to the tracker's whereabouts. But he heard nothing.

He reached for his knife, but it was too late. The Gorelian, smeared in mud, rose up from the ground directly behind Jayson. Its mouth was open wide, baring needle-sharp fangs, which it used to clamp onto the back of Jayson's neck. He slashed at the creature with his claws, but the Gorelian released his bite and leapt free of him. An intense burning spread through Jayson's neck and across his arms and his back. His arms fell limp to his sides. A moment later, he dropped forward onto Brielle's grave, his face lying atop her marker.

Stepping out from his hiding place in the forest, the spotter approached with his sword at the ready. He was not much older than Jayson, his youthful face adorned with a sparse, brown beard. He approached cautiously, nudging Jayson with his toe. When Jayson did not move, the spotter laughed. "Gorelian venom works fast, doesn't it?" he said, snickering. "I know you can hear me. It's just your body that's gone numb. It's only given you enough for a few minutes, but it can kill you, you know. I have to make sure you've got what we've come for first, though."

He squatted down beside Jayson and patted around his waist until he found the pouch. He tore it from Jayson's belt, opened it, and looked inside.

"This it? This is what Emir wants so badly?"

Jayson felt a strange warmth throbbing in his fingertips. He moved them just enough to insure that he could. Thanks to his Agoran blood, the numbness was already beginning to wear off.

The spotter stood up and tossed the pouch into the air, catching it several times in succession. "Emir thanks you," he said smugly. "And I thank you. I'll be getting extra pay for this."

He whistled, and the Gorelian jerked its head up. "Go on now. Might as well get it over with."

The spotter tossed the pouch up again just as a loud *twit* cut through the air. He did not catch it this time, but the pouch hit the ground directly in front of Jayson's face. A moment later, the spotter's body landed face first in the dirt beside Jayson, an arrow stuck in his back. Another *twit* and the Gorelian screeched in pain, and then went silent.

Jayson wanted desperately to leap up and defend himself. This unknown assailant might very well kill him, too. But try as he might, the best he could do was to slowly bend the knuckles of his right hand into a weak fist.

He heard the culprit's feet scuffing the dirt as he approached, and then two boar-hide boots stopped directly in front of Jayson's face. The visitor squatted, prodding Jayson's shoulder with the end of his short bow. Jayson grunted angrily.

"So, you are alive after all," said Teak with an amused chuckle. "Well, I'm sure Ivy will be glad of that."

388

The feeling slowly returned to the rest of Jayson's right arm, and the left also. He tried to push himself up off the ground, but was still too weak. Teak lifted him by the shoulders and turned him onto his side. Jayson could see Teak clearly now, and as his lips and tongue began to function he managed a few words.

"What are you doing here?" he asked. "Where's Dianis?"

"At Naresh by now, I expect. Don't worry. Gerard went with her. When I saw that spotter and Gorelian trailing you out of the city, I thought it best I follow you, too. I wasn't going to interfere, but when that thing bit you…"

"Thank you," said Jayson, rubbing the feeling back into his legs. "I owe you my life."

Teak held out his hand. Jayson took it and pulled himself to his feet. His neck was sore, but other than that he felt nearly normal again. He headed immediately for his horse and untied him.

"Did you walk all this way?" asked Jayson.

"It wasn't hard to keep up, you were riding so slowly."

"I didn't want to lose the spotter."

"*Didn't* want to lose them? Why not?"

"I didn't want to take a chance of them turning back for Dianis, for one thing. The other is that I knew what they wanted, and if they didn't get it, they'd get word back to Emir. I couldn't let that happen."

"This is about Ivy, isn't it?" asked Teak.

Jayson patted his horse's neck, and then stroked the length of it. Her velvety coat was warm and soft beneath his palm.

"Emir is holding her hostage," he said finally. There would be no point in lying to Teak now. He would only press

Jayson for the truth anyway. "But he's promised to send her home once he gets what he wants."

He opened the pouch and removed the crystal, holding it up for Teak to see.

"This belongs to Ivanore. Emir wants it badly enough to kill for it. I think these two here," he added, pointing to the dead spotter and tracker, "they were supposed to get rid of me and take the crystal to Emir. That way Emir would not have to keep his end of the deal."

He dropped the crystal back into the pouch. "He's going to be surprised when he sees me, don't you think?"

"I'll go to Nauvet-Carum with you," Teak replied.

"No, you won't. You're not going back to the capitol."

"But I'm going with you—to rescue Ivy."

"You forget that Ivanore is *my* wife, Teak. Emir will keep his promise; I'll make sure of that."

"And what if he surprises you with another Gorelian or some other trick? He's not known for playing fair."

Jayson mounted his horse and gathered up the slackened reins. "You should go home, Teak. Go back to wherever it was that you came from. There's no need for two of us to kill ourselves over this. Ivy deserves to have one of us stay alive."

Teak opened his mouth to protest, but drew his dagger instead. Its blade was as long as Jayson's forearm with a handle of burnished silver. Teak held it out to Jayson.

"Take this, then," he said. "If you'd had one before, you could have killed that Gorelian yourself."

Jayson accepted the weapon, nodding his thanks. Then he dug his heels into his horse's flanks and snapped the reins. The horse shot forward past a stunned Teak and galloped off at full speed into the forest.

21

℮mir sat behind his desk stroking the neck of the little dragon in his lap. Pip made a contented sound, a soft guttural roll from deep in its belly. Emir did not even glance up as the young assistant showed Arik and Jayson through the door.

"I'd almost given up on you," Emir said.

"I gave my word," answered Jayson, his voice thick with contempt.

"You did. Forgive my doubt." Emir tapped the top of his desk with his finger. "Now, the crystal, if you please."

Jayson remained where he stood. "I want to see my wife."

Emir laid the now sleeping dragon carefully on the cushion beside his desk and clamped the lock shut around its neck. Then he stood up and finally let his eyes meet Jayson's.

"Of course," said Emir with beguiling sincerity. "I'll take you to her myself."

*   *   *

Jayson stood before the cell door, his eyes closed. Her scent reached him even here, and it made him ache inside.

Vengeance

How long had it been? Except for that brief, tortured reunion, he had not held her in a year and a half. That last embrace lingered with him still; the touch of her skin against his still warmed him. It was in a cell much like this one, in the Fortress at Dokur. He had been sentenced to exile for loving her and would soon be led away to the docks. Somehow Ivy had found a way to see him, whether through bribery or some other means he did not know, but she came to him draped in a dark cloak. He had gathered her into his arms and kissed her. They said little, for words were only echoes of their hearts. Later, as Fredric's soldiers led him away, she followed him from afar. They watched each other, he from the ship's deck and she from the cliffs, long after distance had obscured them from each other's view.

The door opened with a groan. Arik entered first, followed by Jayson and then Emir.

Ivy, who had been sitting on the side of the bed, rose to her feet. She wore traveling clothes: a clean gray smock and green woolen mantle fastened at the collar with a filigree buckle. Jayson was satisfied that at least she would be warm for her journey overseas.

Her hair, loosely braided, lay draped over one shoulder, the way she had worn it so often before. Strands of gold drifted near her face. Jayson reached for one of the strands and tucked it behind her ear. Ivy closed her eyes and pressed her cheek against his hand.

"We'd like a moment alone," Jayson said, glaring directly at Emir. "Surely what you desire is worth a spare minute with my wife?"

Emir nodded his consent and left the room. Arik reluctantly followed.

"We'll be waiting just outside," he told them, then exited, leaving the door slightly ajar.

Jayson did not hesitate. He enfolded his arms around Ivy's delicate frame and held her to him. Then he pressed his lips against hers. Ivy's fingers combed through his hair and then came to rest at the nape of his neck. Their mouths moved in unison, and their hearts beat so close to one another that they each could feel the other's rhythm. Jayson's lips moved to Ivy's cheek, then to her throat, and collarbone.

"Ivanore," he whispered against her skin, "how I've longed for you. My dreams are haunted by you. Life without you…" He pressed his eyelids shut, holding the tears at bay. "I can hardly bear it."

"Nor can I," Ivy whispered back.

Ivy took Jayson's face between her hands and raised it to hers. Jayson saw the tears that trailed down her face. He wiped them away with his fingers.

"Jayson, listen to me," she said, glancing toward the partly open door. "Arik and Emir are planning to usurp my father's throne. Everyone," she continued in earnest, "*everyone* who stands in his way is in danger."

She was warning him. He recalled what she had told him during their first brief reunion. Arik believed their son, the true heir to Dokur's throne, was dead. Should Arik discover that he lived, he would stop at nothing to destroy him.

"What threat can our son be to him now that he's dead?" said Jayson for the benefit of those who were certainly eavesdropping.

Ivy's eyes locked on his. "Where he is, he cannot be harmed. But he is not *alone*. There is—someone else. Do you understand?"

Tears streamed from Ivy's eyes now as she waited for Jayson's confirmation. Jayson studied her gaze. He had never before seen her so intense. She was trying to tell him something of great importance, something she dared not utter. He tried to decipher the message from her pleading eyes, but he could not. Still, he could not bear to witness more pain in her.

So he lied.

"I understand," he told her. Relief washed over her face. She blinked back some of the tears and released Jayson's face.

The door to the cell swung open, and Arik and Emir returned with two armed guards.

"I am sorry to interrupt," said Arik, "but time is short. While you were away we took the liberty of making arrangements for Ivanore's passage on The Silver Mist. I believe you know Captain Dawes?"

Ivy looked stunned. "Passage? Passage to where?" she asked.

Jayson spoke directly to Emir. "Yes, I know him."

Arik continued. "His ship wasn't scheduled to sail for another month, but he just happened to be in town. How convenient, eh? It didn't take much to coax him into our service once we explained the situation. In any case, the ship is being loaded with supplies as we speak."

Ivy gripped Jayson's arms. "Jayson, what is he talking about? Please tell me."

Emir held out his palm. Jayson reached into the pouch at his waist, wrapping his fingers around the half circle of crystal. He could no longer look at Ivanore. The confusion in her face cut through him like a hot dagger.

"I want your word," said Jayson.

"We've already given it," Arik said impatiently.

"I want to hear Emir say it."

"The Minister doesn't have time for this!" answered Arik. "Just hand it over, and let's get on—"

"I want to hear *him* say it!" Jayson shouted. "All this time, all I've heard is your voice, Arik. Your promises, your compromises, your everything! You claim to speak for him, but what guarantee do I have he hasn't threatened you? That you aren't his puppet?"

"I am no one's puppet!"

"Then let Emir, the great Minister of Hestoria, leader of the Vatéz, speak for himself!" Jayson pulled the crystal from his pouch and held it up. "You swear to me that you will let Ivanore go!"

Ivanore gasped when she saw what was in Jayson's hand. She grabbed his arm. "Jayson, no! You can't!"

Jayson used his free hand to pull Ivanore off of him. "I have no choice," he told her. "You must return to Imaness."

"But I want to be with *you*," Ivanore pleaded.

"You know that's impossible." Jayson struggled with the words. "We can never be together. I'm an outcast, a half-breed. You deserve better than the life I'd give you."

"That's not true! I need you!"

"You're going home, Ivy. You are needed there."

Ivy broke into sobs and tried to grab the crystal, but Arik held her back.

Jayson turned back to Emir. "Swear it," he growled, "or I'll smash the crystal into dust!"

Arik's eyes widened with fear. He glanced quickly from the crystal to Emir and back to the crystal. Jayson could not tell what frightened him more, his threat or Emir.

"Jayson, please," Arik said. "Just give Emir the crystal."

"No!" Ivanore was in tears now. "Don't give it to him, Jayson. You don't know what you're doing. Whatever he's promised you, it's too great a price to pay!"

Emir's expression did not change. It remained as composed as before as he gazed at Jayson. "Once the crystal is in my possession," he said calmly, "Ivanore *and Arik* will immediately board The Silver Mist. As I'll have no further need of you, you may go your own way as well. I swear it."

Jayson laid the crystal in Emir's outstretched palm. Emir curled his fingers protectively over it. Ivy's expression froze.

"Go now," Emir told Arik, motioning them out with a careless wave of his hand. "Take the Seer and get her to the ship. I always honor my promises."

Arik called to the guards in the hall. "Take her," he told them. Two of the guards stepped into the room and reached for her.

"That won't be necessary," Ivy answered, jerking her arm free. Without looking back at Jayson, she accompanied the guards out of the room. Arik stepped aside and motioned for Jayson to follow.

"I'd prefer you go ahead," said Jayson. "With you bringing up the rear, I'm liable to get a knife in my back."

The day had dawned bright and clear. The sea was a deep blue, the color of Ivy's eyes; the smell of it permeated Jayson's senses. For a moment, he thought of Dianis. Had she and Gerard reached the Guilde in time? Or had they met the same fate as Alay-Crevar? Once he was certain of Ivy's safety, he would go to Naresh. He hoped he would find it deserted.

The Silver Mist stood beside the dock. Seamen loaded the last of several crates onto her deck. As they approached, Captain Dawes greeted them with a wary nod of his head.

"Morning, gentlemen," he said, extending his hand. Jayson took it. "Is this the young lady I am to accompany back to Dokur?"

Arik stepped forward. "This is Lady Ivanore," he said. "And you know who I am. My guards and I will also be traveling with you."

"I don't much care for soldiers."

"They are our official escort, sent by Emir himself."

"The Minister, eh? Well, then I suppose there's not much point in protesting, is there?"

Dawes cast Jayson a questioning glance. Jayson knew what Dawes expected, but there was no escape plan. How could he take Ivanore and run when their son waited for her back home—their son and an entire kingdom that needed protecting? Though he longed for nothing more, to claim her would be the ultimate act of selfishness. He knew now that only one thing was more important to him than having her with him—to make certain she was reunited with their child.

Jayson met Dawes's gaze with a look of resignation. He saw the disappointment and pity in his friend's eyes before he looked away.

"All right then," continued Dawes, taking Ivy's arm in his, "I'll see you to your cabin. My boys will carry up whatever belongings you have."

"We haven't much," replied Arik. He strode up the gangplank and stood at the rail. When he noticed Jayson staring at him, he turned away.

Dawes waited until all but two of the guards had boarded, then turned back to Jayson.

"Are you sure about this?" he said in a hoarse whisper.

Jayson sighed.   "I'm not sure about anything, but Emir gave me his word—the crystal for Ivanore's safety. She'll be better off in Dokur."

"What about you?"

"I'm going back to the plantation. I have a contract to work off, remember?"

"And you remember what I told you, if I don't return, she belongs to you."

"You'll be back."

"If the gods will it. Come on then," Dawes told Ivanore, leading her gently toward the gangplank.

Ivanore had been silent until now, silent and still. But as she and Dawes approached the gangplank she suddenly broke free of Dawes's grasp and ran back to Jayson. With tears streaming from her eyes, she threw her arms around him and kissed him, hard and passionate. The heat rose inside of Jayson like a raging fire. He returned her passion, the fire in him burning out of control. He clung to her and she to him, the desperation welding them together. Just when Jayson thought he would break his vow and steal her away, she slid her lips to his ear and whispered fiercely, "I love you!"

Ivanore pried herself from Jayson's arms and hurried past Dawes, past the guards to the deck of the ship. She appeared at the rail, hands clasped over her mouth. Her entire body shook as she sobbed, but her eyes remained fixed on Jayson. Moments later, the ropes were set free and The Silver Mist pulled away from the dock.

They watched each other, their gazes unbroken until Dawes's ship had sailed out of the harbor and vanished behind the southern barrier. Even then Jayson remained fixed, his eyes on the horizon, too disconsolate to leave, too heartbroken to cry.

22

Where would Jayson go now? The obvious answer was the plantation, but having been separated from Ivanore again, the despair that had tortured him early in his exile overcame him again. It was as if his very soul had abandoned him, leaving only a dead, empty shell behind.

Jayson stood on the ship's dock staring out at the barren sea. What point was there in living now? How easy it would be to let the sea consume him. If not the sea, then he would surely turn again to the bottle. He thought again of Dawes's request that he manage the plantation in his absence. One day, Dawes had promised, it would be his. One day, Jayson would pass it to his son. And there it was. Something to live for, as insignificant as it might seem in the face of tragedy. It gave Jayson a point to fix his sights on. He would go back to the plantation and he would work the land. He would toil and sweat until there was no place left in him for sorrow. He would bury his broken heart in the soil.

Jayson turned away from the sea, perhaps the most difficult thing he had ever done. Daylight was ebbing, and the sky had turned a rich ginger. He would travel as far as Partha. Perhaps he'd visit with Magda for a while before continuing on. Jayson willed his legs to move and started forward, but he didn't get far before he smelled it—the rank stench of decaying flesh corrupted the air.

Mardok!

Jayson slipped into the shadows cast by the barrels and crates stacked high on the docks. He pressed his back against a bundle of sailcloth bound with rope and tried to steady his breathing.

The odor grew stronger, and with it Jayson smelled the distinct scent of incense and candle wax. There was no doubt Emir had sent the Mardok. He had no intention of letting Jayson go after all. He had sent this brute to kill him. And worst of all, Jayson realized, Ivanore would never know it.

The Mardok reached the dock, and Jayson listened to its heavy footsteps plodding along the wharf. There was a loud *thump* and a succession of crashes as several crates clattered to the ground. Another *thump*, and more crates fell. Barrels rolled away, dropping with heavy splashes into the sea.

Jayson clutched his dagger. He was all too familiar with the Mardok's strength and knew this blade alone would not be enough to subdue it. He could try to outrun it. He had done so before.

He waited for the next barrage of crates before making his move. He hoped the Mardok's attention would be diverted long enough to slip away. Then it came. The *crack* of wooden barrels exploding under the Mardok's hand sent tremors through the planks beneath Jayson's feet.

Jayson lunged forward, darting out of the shadows onto the open dock, but he had taken only two steps when the Mardok's massive hand fell on him like solid stone. A searing pain tore through Jayson's shoulder, and he stumbled forward crashing face first to the ground.

He managed to roll onto his back before the Mardok dropped another fist down onto his chest, thrusting the air from his lungs. A third direct hit would undoubtedly crush him, but he had no time to move. Jayson quickly held up his knife and let the Mardok's hand fall.

The blade pierced the heel of the beast's hand up to the hilt. The Mardok roared in pain and grasped its injured hand with the other. Jayson rolled to his side, quickly getting to his feet. He did not waste a moment looking back as he sprinted for the city gate.

Months earlier, when he had escaped the Mardok by leaping from Arik's window, he had never stopped to wonder why he was not pursued. Perhaps Arik hoped he would eventually come to his senses and hand over the crystal. Whatever the reason, Jayson was now certain he could not have outrun it had the Mardok pursued him, for that is what this one did now. The ground shook with its approach. Jayson could run faster than any human he had ever known, and yet this creature was gaining on him. He would never reach the gate, and even if he did, the Mardok would surely catch him just beyond it.

Jayson flexed his claws, thick and sharp as spikes, and then spun around to face his attacker. He slashed at the creature's already scarred face, leaving a deep gash in its skin, but the creature hardly flinched. The Mardok responded with a crushing blow to Jayson's shoulder. The pain burned through him like a rolling fire. As the Mardok readied for another blow, Jayson noticed that his dagger was still buried in its hand. The dull-witted beast had not even bothered to pull it out.

Vengeance

As the enormous fist flew toward him, Jayson snatched the dagger and jerked it free of the creature's flesh. Then Jayson leapt forward and plunged the blade deep into the Mardok's right eye. Blood and water squirted from the wounded orb like a piece of skewered fruit. The creature howled, but Jayson next stabbed the blade into its left eye.

Suddenly, the creature's thick fingers were around him, crushing him like a vise. Jayson cried out as he clawed at the Mardok's hand, but its grip only tightened. Deep inside of him, Jayson felt something pop, a rib snapping in two like a brittle twig. Another moment and he would be dead.

Jayson raised his blade once more and plunged it into the Mardok's already bloody eye socket. He buried it clear up to his elbow, thrashing it back and forth inside the creature's skull. Blood and pink scraps of tissue gushed from the gaping wound. Finally, the Mardok's grip relaxed, its hands fell limply to its side, and the creature collapsed lifeless to the ground.

23

The spray of sea mist was cool against Ivy's face, which was hot and flushed from crying. She was glad the dampness it left on her cheeks masked the tears that still fell at regular intervals. She wondered if she would ever stop crying. Before she'd come to Hestoria, before she escaped her father's relentless pursuit of her, she had done her share of crying, but the hope that she would one day find Jayson burned brightly within her. Now that hope was gone.

Ivy wandered forward along the deck until she reached the bow of the ship. She gazed at the vast expanse of blue. Somewhere out there was the Isle of Imaness. Jayson had given up the crystal so she could return there, had sacrificed everything that meant anything to him to ensure her safety. A fresh round of tears sprung up. She did nothing to hide them or stop them. Never before had she felt such despair.

A commotion drew her attention. She turned to see Arik's guards holding Captain Dawes at sword point while Arik gloated over him. She approached cautiously, listening to

403

the disagreement which seemed to have been underway for several minutes already.

"Turn this ship around," ordered Arik, his voice already pitched with anger.

Dawes's face was set with a defiant expression. "I'll do no such thing!" he shouted back. "This here's my ship, and I'll steer her as I see fit. I was paid to take her to Imaness, and I aim to fulfill my contract!"

Arik slapped Dawes across the face. Dawes hardly flinched at Arik's blow. Instead, he leered at him. "You're just a boy," he said, "trying to act like a man. Well, you're failing miserably at it."

Arik shook with indignation. "I act under the direction of Emir, Minister of Hestoria. He commands that you turn this ship around, not I."

"I was told he wanted the girl here to be taken to Dokur."

"She was never destined to return to Dokur," said Arik. "Emir would never let the Seer escape. He wanted the crystal. He wanted Jayson out of the way. So he promised Jayson he'd put her on a ship bound for Imaness. He never promised the ship would reach its destination. Now, turn this ship around."

Dawes made no move to take the wheel. Instead, his eyes searched for Ivy's. By now she had reached them and stood nearby. She met his gaze and held it.

"Arik?" she asked, this one word filled with more anguish and confusion than she had ever felt before.

Her brother turned to face her, and the expression Ivy saw there confirmed what she had most feared. Even now he betrayed her. How she longed for home, longed to hold in her arms those most precious to her. But it was clear now that this was never to be.

"Go back below deck, Ivanore," he ordered. Then he turned back to Dawes. "Command your crew to return to Hestoria. We're to sail past Nauvet-Carum to the northeast port of Bet-Amay."

In response, Dawes spat in Arik's face.

Arik clenched his teeth, wiping the spittle with the back of his hand. Without taking his eyes off the captain, he gave a curt nod toward one of the guards. The sword glinted in the sun as he pulled it from his scabbard, and Ivy understood what Arik had commanded the guard to do.

In response, Ivy flung out her hands, sending a ripple of energy through the air. The invisible wave struck the guard and knocked him onto his back.

The remaining guards grabbed Ivy's arms, twisting them behind her back. The old wound in her shoulder coupled with the injury Emir had caused sent daggers of pain through her body.

"What are you doing, Ivanore?" shouted Arik. "This is no place for you!"

Ivy gritted her teeth against the pain. "Exactly. My place is in Dokur, and so is yours. Let's go home, Arik. It's what Jayson wants—for both of us."

At the sound of Jayson's name, Arik grew enraged. He snatched up the sword from the fallen guard.

"Arik, no!" Ivy shouted, wrenching herself free from the guards, but it was too late. Arik ran the sword through Dawes's chest. The sea captain wavered a moment. Then he collapsed face first to the deck.

Ivy screamed. As Arik spun toward her, his hand still gripping the bloody sword, Ivy slapped him with such force that he lost his balance and fell back against the ship's rail. Immediately, he regained his footing, and in a violent surge,

405

swung the blade in a wide arc. The whistle of it slicing through the air ended abruptly as it found its mark on Ivy's arm.

Arik dropped the sword, and it clanked against the deck. Ivy clutched the gaping wound, blood oozing from between her fingers. Her brother stared at her, eyes wide with horror. But then he looked around and saw the crew of The Silver Mist and Emir's guards silently watching. Arik blinked, and the horror was replaced by stone-hard indifference. Seeing such an expression on her brother's face cut Ivy more deeply than any sword ever could.

"Take her!" he shouted. "Bind her wound, and keep her below. Restrain her if necessary."

A guard stepped forward and took hold of Ivy's elbow.

"You there!" continued Arik, pointing at one of the deckhands. "Take the wheel and turn this ship back toward Hestoria! Now!"

Ivy let herself be led to the cabin door at the opposite end of the deck. There were no more tears left in her to cry. Where there had been despair, she now felt contempt, for Emir, for Arik, but most of all for herself, for long ago she had allowed an Agoran to fall in love with her. She thought nothing of the consequences, of where her selfish desires would lead. She loved him and that was all she had cared about. The irony of it actually made her smile a little, that the Seer could not see the results of her own choices.

As she reached the door, Ivy glanced over her shoulder in time to see Arik set the sole of his boot against the captain's back. As Dawes's body rolled over the side of the ship and plunged into the sea, her stomach clenched. Arik wiped his bloody hands on his trousers. He looked up, and for a brief moment his eyes met Ivy's. How he had changed, she thought again. The boy she had called brother was gone and in his place was a stranger, someone she loathed, someone she hated.

Arik turned away and started barking orders at the ship's crew. The ship was turning. Ivy gazed over the rail of the ship toward the horizon. Somewhere out there was Imaness. As the ship reversed its course, Ivy stared back at the distance ever-growing between them, and she knew that she would never see home again.

24

The city was bathed in a blue haze, and the full moon shone white against the black sky. Jayson, smeared with the Mardok's blood, gazed up at the myriad stars. He thought of Ivanore and wondered how long it would take her to reach Dokur. As he stood staring at the moon, he thought of the crystal. Ivanore had trusted him to keep it safe, had begged him not to hand it over to Emir. True, to Jayson it was nothing more than a scrap, but he had protected it for Ivanore's sake. Why so many people valued a broken shard so highly was something he would never understand. Still, he had let them all down: Gerard, Dianis, and Ivanore. The only one who was pleased with the outcome was Emir.

Emir.

Jayson cursed the name. What if the crystal was still even partially functional? Could Emir use it to foresee the future as he claimed, to predict the outcome of his military campaigns, and then to carry out those strategies to victory? He had murdered Brielle and her child, had slaughtered an entire village, and had tried to kill Jayson despite having given his oath. With the crystal in his power, just how far would Emir go to satisfy his greed? How could Jayson live with more innocent blood on his conscience?

Jayson stood in the shadows and watched the door to the Ministry until the flow of people leaving for the night became a trickle, and then finally ceased altogether.

Swiftly, silently, Jayson slipped through the doors, through the shadows of the deserted main hall, and up the wooden staircase. Waiting in the abandoned closet as he had that night with Dianis, he listened until he was certain all was clear. Then he crept out and made his way toward the uppermost floor. He heard movement behind the third door directly across the hall from Emir's office. He approached cautiously. From behind the door, he heard the sound of a quill scratching against parchment, and then of it being rolled and slipped into some sort of container. He heard the hiss of candlewicks being pinched out and saw the light from beneath the door vanish. Finally, he heard the groan and creak of someone getting into bed.

Jayson waited.

Only once he'd heard the sound of deep, rhythmic breathing, the sound of sleep, did he open the door. Only a single lantern with a dim flame lit the otherwise dark room, but Jayson's eyes, accustomed to darkness, saw all.

In the first moment, Emir's eyes flew open to see the intruder hovering over him. In the next moment, Jayson's claws clamped tightly around Emir's throat.

"Where is it?" Jayson hissed.

Emir said nothing. Jayson squeezed harder.

"Wait! Wait," Emir gagged on the sounds. Small circles of blood appeared on his skin beneath each of Jayson's claws. Emir's hand, shaking with fear, darted beneath his pillow and emerged again as a fist. Jayson saw the pale green crystal between the Minister's fingers.

"Give it to me," demanded Jayson.

Emir's eyes narrowed as he rotated his right hand in the air. A surge of pain erupted inside of Jayson, burning him from the inside out. He grunted and clenched his teeth, but he did not release his grip. Agonizing pain coursed through his veins, and one by one his muscles began to seize. Jayson fixed his eyes on Emir's face, which had twisted into an expression of brutal pleasure. But Jayson looked deeper, past the pleasure, past the triumph, and saw what lay beneath— *fear.*

Emir was human after all. As a half-breed, Jayson had always considered himself less than human, something of an oddity. But now, feeling the fire scorching his insides that no human could endure, Jayson knew the truth. He was not less than human—he was more.

Jayson pressed his claws deeper into Emir's throat and squeezed.

25

The contingent of Ministry guards, fifty strong, halted just inside the forest's border. They had reached the foothills and could go no farther in this direction. They had followed the river as Emir had instructed, followed it all the way to its source. It had taken many days and the soldiers were worn out from marching. They had stopped several times along the way to loot villages for supplies. Emir had promised that at the end of their journey they would find the lair of the Guilde, but they had come to an end and found only a sheer rock cliff jutting high above them, impossible to climb, and a clear lake with gently sloping shores fed by a tall, roaring waterfall.

The soldiers grew impatient. The water gleamed in the sun. Their parched mouths yearned for it, but their commander raised his hand, ordering them to remain where they stood among the trees, and they obeyed.

Erland held his horse's reins tightly in his hands as he assessed the situation. Emir had told him to find a waterfall. Well, here it was. But where was the enemy, the Guilde who

411

threatened the very peace of Hestoria? If they had been living here at the lake, they were not here now. Erland felt a wave of anger sweep over him. He had been thwarted once again. He had missed them at Alay-Crevar and those who had helped the Guilde flee paid dearly for their treason. Had he missed them again?

He scanned the shoreline, glancing up to the top of the waterfall and following the water on its long journey down to where it exploded against the lake below. His horse shook its mane impatiently and struck a hoof against the ground. Erland let the horse circle. He gazed again through the cloud of mist that rose up from the lake where the waterfall collided with it.

No, he thought. It couldn't be.

Moments later, the shouts of fifty men exploded through the narrow rock tunnel. The high wall of stone amplified the din, making it sound as if a much larger army had arrived. The guards, drenched from coming through the waterfall so many at a time, held their swords at the ready, bloodlust driving them forward. None would be spared, not a child or animal. Emir had commanded it.

Erland led the way, hunched forward as his steed galloped through the low opening. When he burst through the other side, his men following full speed behind, the sunlight blinded him. For a moment, he feared that he and his men had fallen into a trap, that they would be ambushed by a hundred armed villagers. He plunged forward, shouting and brandishing his sword. His eyes quickly adjusted to the light. Behind him, the shouting died away. The pounding feet stopped, and the only sound was the sharp clinking of swords being thrown to the ground.

Erland dug his heels into his horse's flank and galloped around the perimeter of the little valley. "Not again," he shouted, his voice echoing against the rock walls. "Not again!" Finally, he stopped at the far side of the valley and turned to face his men. Between them stretched a vast, empty field.

To be Continued In . . .

Books 4 - 6
(Coming in 2016)

To receive notifications about THE CRYSTAL KEEPER and other Skyrocket Press titles, please subscribe to our email list at: http://www.SkyrocketPress.com

Jayson's story continues in…

THE CELESTINE CHRONICLES

Excerpt from
Book I, The Rock of Ivanore

The old enchanter rose from his cot, his joints creaking like rusty hinges. His sleep had been troubled, and thoughts of the days ahead worried him. Taking care not to wake his apprentice, Zyll went to the table in the center of the room, though his legs were so stiff that even traveling the width of his cottage required the use of a walking stick. With his free hand, he took a copper bowl down from a shelf and set it on the table. He grinned at the fresh bucket of water on the hearth, grateful that the boy had remembered to fill it this time.

Zyll ladled water into the bowl and peered at his reflection in it. How changed he looked, how unlike the man he used to be. His hair, once thick and dark, had thinned and grown white, and the skin around his mouth had creased. But his eyes still glowed with the vibrancy of youth. One thing, at least, had remained the same.

He laid his walking stick across the table, and then leaned closer to better view the image before him. The water darkened and another face replaced Zyll's reflection, a younger man not altogether human—a half-breed.

The image widened. Crouching in a dark corridor the half-breed crept from shadow to shadow. Slipping past two sentries, he entered a small chapel. He hurried to the altar and released a hidden latch that opened a small door near its base. Zyll watched as the half-breed removed a scroll concealed within and hid it beneath his cloak.

Just then, the chapel door flew open with a tremendous shudder. There, framed in torchlight, stood a man with red hair accompanied by seven man-like beasts with hairy faces pocked with repulsive scars.

The red-headed man charged angrily into the room, his sword slashing down in a wide, rapid arc. The half-breed hastily drew his sword just in time to deflect the blow, and then countered with his own. His blade tasted flesh, and the red-headed man collapsed to his knees, his hands grasping the side of his bloody face.

The half-breed spied a small object on the floor and managed to snatch it up before the beasts attacked. Though he fought them with inhuman strength, they soon drove him up against the wall.

Cornered and outnumbered, the half-breed turned to the window and gazed down. The image in the bowl shifted, and Zyll saw what the half-breed saw: angry ocean waves beating against the rocks far below. Suddenly the waves rushed up toward him, and Zyll realized that the half-breed had leapt from the window. Zyll watched him fall, and as he fell, the half-breed twisted his body to look up at the sky. For one fleeting moment, before he plunged into the sea, his inhuman cat eyes met Zyll's.

The enchanter's breath caught in his throat, and he stumbled back. When he looked in the bowl again, the image had vanished.

Zyll dropped into a chair resting his weary arms on the table. He glanced at the fair-haired boy who slept on, then choked out a whisper. "So it begins."

Thank you for reading

THE CRYSTAL KEEPER

We invite you to share your thoughts and reactions.

goodreads

amazon.com

Acknowledgements

I began writing *The Crystal Keeper* about six years ago while I was impatiently awaiting the publication of my debut novel, *The Rock of Ivanore* (Tanglewood Press). While writing that first book and its sequel, *The Last Enchanter*, I fell in love with the story of Jayson and Ivanore. It was as though they had taken on lives of their own apart from my imagination, and I felt compelled to bring their story to life.

I never intended to sell this. It began as a way to envision the history of the characters in my first books, but the story grew, as stories are wont to do, and what you hold in your hand is just the beginning.

I am deeply indebted to several people for inspiring me along this journey. Peggy Tierney for taking a chance on my first books. Alexandra Little, Dorine White, Teak Balena, Carissa Reyes, and Nate Vandermark for reading early drafts and providing invaluable feedback. My children for being my biggest fans. My husband for his encouragement and faith. My parents for their constant support. Emma Michaels for her astounding artistic talents. Katie Buniak for her amazing editing. Margaret Brown for introducing me to Katie. Susan Kaye Quinn for sharing her wealth of knowledge and experience. And my Heavenly Father for his abundant blessings and for endowing me with the drive to write.

About the Author

LAURISA WHITE REYES

After spending more than a decade as a newspaper editorialist, magazine staff writer, and book editor, Laurisa finally started living her dream of writing fiction. She is the author of three novels for younger readers, the editor-in-chief of *Middle Shelf Magazine*, and Senior Editor of Skyrocket Press. She lives in Southern California with her husband and five children.

Website: www.laurisawhitereyes.com

Blog: laurisareyes.blogspot.com

www.ingramcontent.com/pod-product-compliance
Lightning Source LLC
Chambersburg PA
CBHW061508020726
47502CB00006B/1986